CHASING FATE

Kat. T. Masen

Chasing Fate
An Enemies to Lovers Romance
The Dark Love Series Book 5

Kat. T. Masen

This book is a work of fiction. Any references to real events, real people, and real places are used fictitiously. Other names, characters, places and incidents are products of the Author's imagination and any resemblance to persons, living or dead, actual events, organisations or places is entirely coincidental.

All rights are reserved. This book is intended for the purchaser of this book ONLY. No part of this book may be reproduced or transmitted in any form or by any means, graphic, electronic, or mechanical, including photocopying, recording, taping, or by any information storage retrieval system, without the express written permission of the Author. All songs, song titles and lyrics contained in this book are the property of the respective songwriters and copyright holders.

ISBN: 979-8691793240

Editing and Proofing by Swish Design & Editing
Formatting by Swish Design & Editing
Cover design by Outlined with Love Designs
Cover image Copyright 2020

CHASING FATE

"Sometimes being a friend means mastering the art of timing. There is a time for silence. A time to let go and allow people to hurl themselves into their destiny. And a time to prepare to pick up the pieces when it's all over."

~ **Gloria Naylor**

CHAPTER
1

KATE

The name *Eric* flashes across the screen. I take a deep breath, then another. When it comes to Eric, patience is a virtue.

"What?"

The word stumbles out of my mouth too quickly, my mood suppressed and not caring for the idle chit-chat Eric is known for partaking in.

"Is that all I get?" he complains in his high-pitched tone. "You're on babysitting duty this week. I can't take that hostility on top of everything else."

Eric had recently broken up with Tristan over his own insecurities. Tristan went to Dubai to film a movie, and Eric was adamant Tristan would cheat on him. Despite Charlie and me trying to convince him he was in his own head, Eric acted on impulse and broke it off the day before Tristan left. It's been precisely thirty days since that happened, and Eric has been nothing but a sad and pathetic excuse of a human being. There's miserable, and then there's Eric Kennedy.

Between Charlie and myself, we are babysitting him emotionally. This week is my turn, and I already miss the peace from his over-dramatic retelling of how much comfort-eating he's been doing and how the scales refuse to lie to him.

"I'm sorry," I apologize, closing my eyes momentarily to get a grip on myself. "I've got a lot on my mind."

"You and me both. What's up your puss, or shall I ask *who* is up your puss?"

"Nothing," I respond, flatly. "I mean no one. Can I call you back? I'm just about to leave the office. It's been a hell of a day."

It is a lie but a much-needed one. I need to clear my head, and Eric is the last person I want to speak to.

"Fine, reject me, just like everyone else. *'I'm just a poor boy, nobody loves me'*..." he cries.

I groan into the speaker. Eric breaking out into song brings out the worst in him. His desperate need for my attention only accelerates my need to head home to a bottle of much-needed wine.

"Listen, drama queen. I'll call you back when I'm liquored up and immune to your melodramatic mood."

"Thanks, doll. Speak soon."

The line goes dead, the silence like pure bliss.

It's late, just after seven. The office is practically deserted with only the sounds of the cleaners hovering with their equipment while they work in silence. It's not unusual for me to stay back, seeking solace in work rather than go home to an empty apartment.

The sound of my phone pings, alerting me to a text

message. With frustration, I curse openly at Eric and his desperation during his so-called emotional breakdown only to see another name on the screen.

My chest begins to hitch, the heaviness of the text message impossible to ignore in front of me. Taking a deep breath, I allow the air to give me the confidence I need to shield me from the humiliation I'm almost sure to feel.

Dominic: *There's nothing left to say.*

My eyes dart over the words, half-expecting them to change into something less hurtful. Slowly, my shoulders curl over my chest, followed by an unsettling feeling in the pit of my stomach.

I spent a week waiting for any sort of response from him. Anything at all to show me he at least cared for me in any kind of way. I conjured up different scenarios in my head, like what he'd say as far as him busting into this office demanding to strip me down to nothing so he could devour me.

Yet everything my warped mind begins to envision is everything he's *not.*

I tried to play with fire, I got burned, and his text cements just that.

This moment is exactly how he said it would play out. Just somehow, over the last two months, I allowed myself to become someone I am not. I isolated myself more so than usual, detached my emotions from reality, almost as if I were walking in someone else's shoes.

Eric, being assertive even in his own mess,

questioned me multiple times, but I always found a lie worth telling to protect our friendship. At least that's the story I led myself to believe.

Every lie I spun became easier as if the truth no longer existed. I'd done things, out of character, out of my comfort zone, trying to latch onto someone who, from day one, made his intentions perfectly clear.

Yet, I craved something more, foolishly allowing my emotions to walk silently beside my tough exterior. I blamed society with all its ageist bullshit of ticking clocks and whatnot. I narrowed down my *ache* to experience intimacy with a man because of my circle, watching my friends and family on their journeys to find love and happiness.

Placing my phone down on the desk, I go through a few contracts in desperate need to steer my mind onto something else before I make a stupid decision like respond back.

There are a few emails that need answering, and one from Lex's assistant trying to sync dates of our travel schedule over the next few months. There's a summit in London Lex insists I attend since many of our stakeholders will be present. Going back home seems fitting. It's been over a year since I last set foot in London, and boy, do I miss my family.

But going back home will invite my family to ask questions about my personal life, which apparently, is their business. My mother, God love her, has always been a traditionalist. Marriage, babies, everything I *don't* have. I was never one to really want to settle down, nor does the idea of babies entice me. Sure, I love my

4

goddaughter, Amelia, and the other children I spend time with, yet I equally enjoy handing them back at the end of the day.

Around me, that's where everyone's journey has led them—happiness with a chosen person and extending their love by growing a family.

Lex and Charlie are happy, expecting baby number three and well-settled into their family life on the West Coast. Even Adriana found love with Julian. The universe works in mysterious ways with them, but nevertheless, they are in love and have just brought their daughter home from South America. The last I'd spoken to Adriana, she was the happiest I'd ever heard her, and despite my own opinions on Julian, he has made her happy, and it isn't my place to get involved in their relationship.

Back here on the East Coast, it's been a while since I caught up with Nikki and Rocky. The last I had heard, things were dicey between them. Again, not my place to get involved, especially since I have no wisdom to impart on the subject of infertility.

And perhaps my decision to remain single isn't without reason. Love appears wondrous and satisfying, yet with that comes heartache. Lex and Charlie have had their fair share of ups and downs, and unfortunately, I was caught in the crossfire without even knowing it at the time.

Adriana and Julian—I don't even know where to begin with how difficult that was.

As for Eric, his choice could've easily been avoided if he thought with his heart rather than his stupid head.

Then there's me, always the single one in the group who everyone feels sorry for, which results in not-so-subtle blind date setups on more than one occasion and the constant pressure to find the 'one.'

Yet, in their presence, I wear a façade. Everything was okay, and I was fine with not being in a relationship despite their concern over my non-existent love life.

The last four years changed everything about who I am and what I want in life.

My career and ambition have become an egotistical addiction. Ever since Lex promoted me so he could move to Los Angeles, I've made it my mission to show everyone exactly who is the new boss. I spent years shadowing Lex, watching him dominate the energy around him. He spent every waking hour becoming the mogul he had intended to be, and it paid off nicely. I'm not stupid, even though business associates thought it was a joke when Lex left the Manhattan office in my reigns. Nasty comments were said behind closed doors, the chauvinistic assholes didn't know I had the intelligence or capability of filling Lex's shoes.

And so, I was out to prove everyone wrong.

I busted my ass, worked myself into the ground all to prove a point. Somewhere, amid of all the chaos, my ego began to thrive on it. I almost enjoyed the fear I instilled inside the office, and as expected, people took notice and sharpened their work ethic around me. In order for me to succeed, I needed a team that would do their job plus go beyond what's expected of them.

I'd become Lex—ruthless, assertive, and zero fucks given because I held power.

Between us, Lex was never shy to tell me I had changed, praising me for my ability to push through the negativity and grow our business despite the challenges I faced being a woman amongst a boardroom of men.

Perhaps, it was his encouragement that drove me further. He was happy to slow down, focus on his family. I, on the other hand, refused to slow down because slowing down will land you exactly where I am now.

Humiliated.

Because I've got feelings for a man who has no interest in me.

Dominic Kennedy.

Eric's older brother.

The phone begins to ring again. Seriously, why can't everyone just leave me alone to process my thoughts? I let out an annoyed rasp glancing at the screen, questioning whether or not I should answer since *mother hen* has expressed her worry over my state of mind over the last few days.

"Hey," is all I manage to say.

"Okay, so not answering my texts will send me into early labor," Charlie rambles, equally annoyed in her tone with my uninterested greeting. "Is everything okay? The last time we spoke—"

"The last time we spoke, I was fine, and you made a big deal out of nothing."

"Kate," she forewarns. "You're not okay. Just admit it."

"I can't admit it." I lower my voice, aware of the hurt in my tone. "He told me, Charlie, he told me he wasn't the relationship type. Not only that, but he also explained

7

his lifestyle to me. There were never any secrets."

"It doesn't mean it doesn't hurt. You're human."

"Am I? I don't even know who I am anymore."

"Listen... I think you need to get away and spend some time here. You're all alone, and nothing good will come of that."

"I can't. Work, merger..."

"I'm sure Lex won't mind."

"No, Charlie, you know I won't mix business with pleasure," I remind her.

"Hey, every one of us has had a romantic meltdown and needed time off. Even Lex. Get your ass on a plane, and I'm not taking no for an answer."

I think about her suggestion. It's been a while since I've visited, and maybe I do need to get out of the city and breathe fresh air. Although, Los Angeles is hardly fresh air with that godawful blanket of smog that lingers and the sun which isn't compatible with my English skin.

I'd have to face Eric, yet on the bright side, he's known to drag friends into some unwanted shenanigan, which will ultimately take my mind off things. Lately, it has been all work and no play.

"But you're busy being knocked up, and didn't you say your cousin, Noah, is staying with you?"

Although I haven't met him, it's as if I know Noah inside and out. Ever since Eric caught wind of him moving to LA, he has been relentless in his pursuit to hook us up. Eric stalks his social media accounts, sending me picture after picture and disturbingly, found some website which morphed two faces to show you what your child would look like. Granted, the fake kid was cute, but Jesus Christ, Eric needs to get laid.

"He's not here yet. And don't worry about me. I'm worried about you."

"I know you are," I say quietly. "I'll speak to Lex and see if I can swing a week in LA. I'm not making promises, though."

"I think you're safe. He hasn't gotten laid in a week since he's been in Houston, so I'm sure I can convince him."

"Thanks for the update on your sex life." I laugh, followed by a long-winded sigh. "God, Charlie, when did I become so…"

"Fucked up?"

"I was going to say a dog's dinner."

"You know, I've known you four years, and your British slang still stumps me." Charlie laughs. "Meaning?"

"A mess."

"Ah," she says, catching on. "It happens to the best of us."

"I just…" I search for the words to relay the feelings I've buried deep inside. "I don't know who I am anymore. I miss the old me. So carefree, happy to date or not date. I enjoyed life and everything it had to offer, never afraid to take a risk on something amazing. And would it hurt to find a man who just wants to have fun without the melodramatic strings attached?"

"Are you saying Eric is *not* that?" Charlie asks in a sarcastic tone.

We both laugh, a simple sound which has been missing in my life of late. Eric is many things, call him high maintenance, and he will argue he isn't, only to storm out of the room cursing and making a scene.

"I just want to be me," I finally admit. "And be around someone who appreciates the real me. I'm not looking for a husband, just someone I can have fun with and enjoy life."

"It'll come, Kate," Charlie says encouragingly. "When you least expect it with the person you least expect it with."

Maybe she's right. When it came to relationships, Charlie was always spot-on with her advice.

The old Kate is still there, somewhere, and boy do I fucking miss her.

CHAPTER 2

NOAH
Three Months Ago

"I'll make you a deal," Tom, one of my best friends, says while bouncing the ball and then shooting it in the hoop. "Stay for cake and the speeches. Then you can go."

"I've got plans that night," Benny, another friend, complains as he fights Tom for the ball. He narrowly misses as Tom, once again, scores.

"Since when do you have plans?" I ask Benny, blocking Tom and pulling down a rebound.

The two of them hopelessly try to catch me to no avail.

Benny stops, leaning over with his hands resting on his knees to catch his breath. "Just something on."

"Is it that chick? What's her name..." I pause while thinking, "... Tina? The one with those big tits that bounce every time she laughs at your lame joke about the nun and the priest?"

Tom stops mid-step, laughing very loudly until he

breaks out in a nasty cough.

"That joke has gotten me laid more times than your mom has gone to church. And she goes every Sunday." Benny foolishly laughs at his own joke.

"Hey, hey." Tom walks over, raising his hands, then comfortably rests his elbow on my shoulder. "Cue the mom jokes, Benny."

"Speaking of which..." I add purposely, just to annoy Tom, "... this party you're dragging us to is for your mom's sixtieth. I'm all for a good time, Tommy, but cougars ain't my style."

Benny instantly curls his fist, covering his mouth while he hides his laugh, purposely goading Tom.

"Nice try, momma's boy. You're going. Mom has plenty of divorcée friends. Isn't that your style, anyway? Preying on the broken-hearted?" Tom carelessly points out.

He has a point. I'm known for my inability to hold down a relationship because I hate being tied down, and all the women I've spent time with carried enough baggage to fit into a cargo jet—cheating ex-husband, gay boyfriend, and worst of all, kids. No thanks.

"I'll compromise," I humor him. "I'll stay till the cake is cut. Give your mom one dance if she wears that low-cut purple dress with the rhinestones, and only if your hot cousin from Florida is there."

"Fuck you," he mouths in return. "I don't know what Mom's wearing, but it ain't that dress. Pass me the goddamn brain bleach. And my cousin is nineteen. We've been down that road, dude. Stay away."

I move closer to Benny and place my arm around his

shoulder. "If I'm going down, then you're going down with me."

"Fuck the both of you. I'll be there only till six. I'm not dancing with your mom. And you better keep your granny on the other side of the room," Benny warns Tom.

"What's wrong with Granny?" Tom cries, pretending to forget Granny has wandering hands with a fetish for pinching asses. "You know... fuck you both. You better be there. That's all. And Noah, make sure you bring your mom."

The two of them whistle, only riling me up more. See, here's the thing about my mom. She's young—forty-four to be exact. Got knocked up at sixteen to her then college boyfriend, who vanished into thin air when he found out. Unlike Benny and Tom's moms, mine is young, and according to them, has the body of a thirty-year-old. And just because they like to fuck with me, they also add she has the tits of an eighteen-year-old.

To them, the joke never gets old.

They've been my best friends since junior high, and yet still, to this very day, they crack jokes about my mom and her body like it doesn't bother me. It fucking bothers me, all right. No one—and I mean no one—talks smack about my mom.

"Screw you guys." I throw the ball back at Tom, challenging him to a half-court shot. "Your shot. You get it in, and I'll attend your mom's lame party and bring my mom."

"And your mom will wear her slutty black dress with the open back?"

Son of a bitch. "Just shoot, will you?"

Tom moves to the center, positioning himself in line with the ring. Raising his arm, he practices his shot before releasing the ball. We all watch, eyes wide, waiting in anticipation as the ball flies through the air, then touches the back of the ring before falling through.

Fuck.

"Woo!" Tom cheers, running up and down the court like a lunatic. "See you Saturday night, boys."

***

The party dragged on forever—divorcées drunk on cheap wine dancing the "Nutbush." Benny, being the dick he is, abandoned me well before the cake and dancing. One minute he was by my side trying to avoid being groped by Tom's granny, and the next minute, he disappeared.

I ended up pulling a Benny, slipping out, and leaving a drunken Tom to fend for himself. Plus, I think he was this close to hooking up with one of his mom's friends. He's always the first to admit he has a fetish for older women, specifically MILFs, so this comes as no surprise.

Then, I had to take care of me. I was itching to get laid. It felt like forever.

Okay, that's a lie.

I have a life most men fantasize about. A lifestyle filled with beautiful women begging to be fucked every which way possible, letting go of any inhibitions. Sometimes in the act of revenge, and other times, just to fill the empty hole in their life.

14

It's not like I purposely find these women. They seem to have a way of finding me. And I happen to be very intuitive. I've spent years studying women's body language, learning what each move means, when to strike, and when to walk away because their eyes begin to flash love hearts.

I have mastered the game.

And this game, the thrill of the chase, it's become too comfortable. Almost predictable.

I mean, I don't even have to try anymore. Where's the challenge? The back and forth flirtatious gestures leading to witty banter, the two-drink minimum, a promise to call, the exchange of phone numbers—goodbye. I'm not sure why, but of late, my followers on Instagram have grown, and women are sliding into my DMs. Unfortunately, some men as well.

I left the party and headed to our usual hangout—a local bar on the pier. I'm sitting beside a gorgeous woman I've just fucked.

Twice, if you want to count the insanely good blowjob.

She walked into this very bar an hour ago. Scanning the room with those puppy dog eyes, searching for something. A man, of course. It's the same look they all have—sad and depressed, tired, worn-out eyes, yet still dressed hoping for some miracle.

She looked broken-hearted.

I had it in the bag.

She's sexy. Short with lovely hips and long brown hair that flows down her back. The red fitted dress does extraordinary things for her curves,

15

and the strappy black pumps look amazing on her. They looked even better wrapped around my neck a few minutes ago.

She loved it. She begged me to finish her off, insisting it was exactly what she needed.

That's what they all say.

"Noah, I just need one night. Fuck me hard," they all plead.

"Noah, make me forget him. You're so hot with a big dick. Bigger than his dick," they all compliment.

Same old story.

But, hey, who's complaining? Definitely not my 'big dick.'

Women want to be placed on a pedestal, shown how the single life won't be so bad. Sex with another man gives them the satisfaction that, emotionally and physically, they have detached themselves from the one who broke their heart.

The woman beside me—Rose, I think—continues to sit in silence. Fuck, you can't remember her name even after you screamed it.

Lost in a daze, she traces the bottom of her glass, letting out a soft sigh every couple of minutes.

Usually, I don't entertain them afterward. We always agree that it's a one-time thing—they're rebounding, and I'm letting off steam from my stressful job. Okay, another lie I spin to make myself seem important. My job is breezy. But she asked me for a favor, a quick drink at the bar. And rarely do I do favors for people unless it's my mom or my best friends.

"I know you probably want to get rid of me now," she

suggests, half-jokingly. "Can I ask you something?"

I try my damn hardest not to look at my watch because, in reality, I don't have anywhere I need to be. With a forced smile, I nod encouragingly, hoping to end this encounter within the next few minutes. Unless, of course, she's up for round three.

Dammit. I'm getting hard again just thinking about it.

She takes a sip from her glass, and one sip soon becomes an entire mouthful until the glass sits empty on the coaster. She motions the bartender to replace her drink, turning to ask me the burning question, "Do you believe in karma, Noah?"

An odd question, especially coming from a woman you've just been inside of. I'm no saint. If there's such a thing as karma, it would've hunted me down by now, chopped me into fine liver, and fed me to the wolves.

"I haven't given it much thought. I guess so. Maybe. Why do you ask?"

She swivels the stool to face me, her eyes drunk and sleepy. The mascara that accentuates her long lashes has smudged under her eyes.

Jesus, was she fucking crying, and I had no idea?

"I'll be honest..." she admits, keeping her voice low, "... I really needed what happened
between us tonight."

They always do.

She picks up the toothpick that sits inside the glass, removing the olive between her fingers, and swirls the martini quickly. "It's just... I can't help but feel guilty."

Of course, she does.

I have the speech memorized. It's not the first time

17

I've heard this. See, first comes lust, then comes fucking, then straight after say hello to your good old friend, guilt.

"Rose, I'm not going to push you to open up to me," I tell her.

Please don't open up to me, I beg silently.

I need to ease her guilt and give her enough confidence to walk away with her head held high with no regrets.

"We all have our reasons for our actions, whatever they may be. You're young, beautiful, and whoever hurt you, he has what's coming to him." Reassuring her with a smile, I place my hand on top of hers.

Her lips curve upward, smiling innocently while taking some nuts from the bowl sitting on the countertop.

Oh no, not the urine nuts.

The number of hands that have touched that bowl— don't go there.

Just remember your mouth will no longer touch hers.

"I had a fight with the guy I'm seeing," she tells me. "I thought he'd spent the night trying to hook up with other women. We got into a fight, and then he tells me he loves me. I told him to back off, and the only reason he said that was because I told him it's over."

"Is it over?"

"I don't know. I think I love him. And now I've ruined everything. I came here looking for him, and I'm walking away sleeping with you." She painfully holds back her tears, shaking her head with guilt. "I practically bolted out of the room when he said he loved me. I was angry, hurt, and I couldn't get over my jealousy. Women are always texting him."

"That's understandable. Love can do that to you," I tell her.

Can you seriously hear yourself?

What the fuck do I know? I've never been in love, nor is it on my list of things to do. From my observations, emotions run high when you throw the word 'love' around. Nothing good can ever come out of laying your heart on the line only for it to get broken into a million pieces.

Maybe it could be compared to the time my mom washed my limited-edition Lakers jersey in the wash with her red shirt. I almost cried, and I didn't speak to her for days. Every night, I'd go to bed hugging the damn thing, remembering all the good times we had.

The memory's still painful.

"But here's the thing, we've seen each other on the down-low, and I didn't expect us to get this far, but we did. It's been... fast... you know?"

"So, aside from that, what's the problem? If you love him, then tell him," I respond casually, brushing off her overdramatic problem. "So, we slept together, he doesn't have to know."

She's clutching at the napkin, twisting it with a nervous jitter. I can see she's tormented by her decision to have sex with me tonight. She foolishly assumed she could emotionally detach herself from her ex-lover.

"I've ruined it between us. He's such a kind-hearted guy, and I ran looking for a rebound. You're Mr. Rebound. Karma won't let that one slide," she openly wails. "I've hurt him. When I ran, I think he took it personally. He's um... unique," she quickly adds. "But that doesn't change how I feel about him. I love his qualities, you know. He has such a big heart."

"Big heart, huh?"

That's usually code for a small dick. I laugh to myself.

"Unique like three-nipples unique?" I joke, thinking about Chandler in *Friends* and his 'nubbin.'

Rose manages to half-smile. "He has a prosthetic leg. I don't care, trust me, I love him for who he is inside and out."

My stomach flips, slowly churning as the gut-wrenching pain followed by the urge to vomit teeters on edge. I clutch at the beer in front of me, drinking it in one go to calm the nervous energy building up inside. The sweat on my forehead builds, increasing my anxiety.

Please, please, let this be a coincidence.

"That's... unusual." I gulp.

"He lost it in a boating accident when he was five." Bowing her head, she whispers in pain, "It's so sad, but he never lets it get to him. He told me it's because his best friends won't allow it. They're like brothers to him, and without them, he'd have probably killed himself."

No, this can't be happening.

Please, God, this can't be happening.

A gust of wind rushes past as the door to the bar swings open.

And there, behind me, I feel his presence.

The man she's running from.

The knot in my stomach tightens, on the verge of combusting. With the deepest of breaths, my body moves painfully slow until I'm met with his face.

Just like Rose believed, karma has a way of finding everyone.

It's found me.

And standing beside it is my best friend, Benny.

CHAPTER 3

NOAH
Present

My fingers trace the rim of the glass, slowly gliding against the smooth edge and eyeing the amber liquid with a desperate thirst. Around me, there's nothing but silence and darkness, which has fallen over my apartment.

Outside the large windows, the views of the Charles River are unsurpassed with the city lights surrounding it. Boston had been my home for most of my adult life, and after graduating from college, we boys made a pact never to leave.

The three of us grew up in a smaller town just outside the city—a place where we made memories and were equally glad to leave them behind. We earned a reputation, which, at the time, we somewhat reveled in. But our immaturity and careless behavior could only last so long before it landed us in serious trouble.

We were thrilled to get accepted at Boston University despite our parents worrying about the mischief, or shall I say, frat parties we'd find ourselves at. They had every right to worry—our college years were the best years of our lives.

But like everything in life, we evolve, and life moves forward. I became career-focused, saving every dollar I could to buy my first condo just out of college. From there, I grew my investment portfolio, making a comfortable nest egg for myself. If truth be told, I was the most driven of the three. Tom was happy with his studio bachelor pad because it had a view of some yoga studio, which according to him, free porn every morning at seven o'clock.

Benny lives just outside the city, working alongside his dad, managing a chain of sports stores across Massachusetts. He travels around, is the biggest sports fanatic, and never misses a game at Fenway Park.

Yet life hasn't been the same since that night with Rose. Benny knew straight away I'd fucked her. Running toward me at the bar, his fist connected with my jaw in a matter of seconds. I wanted so desperately to punch the fucker back, but I knew all too well it was my fault. I messed with the wrong girl. The girl my best friend is in love with.

How the fuck was I supposed to know that?

Only after it unraveled did it all make sense how he'd been distant from Tom and me, always making up excuses as to why he couldn't hang out with us. I just didn't understand why he went to those lengths to hide his relationship from us. Had he been honest from the start, then maybe, just maybe, this wouldn't have happened.

But deep down inside, I knew how much shit we both would've given him had he told us he was in love.

We don't do love. Not us boys.

In college, we made a pact—play hard, fuck hard. All around us, friends were dropping like flies, marrying their high school sweethearts and having babies. We were the last three standing and having the time of our lives backpacking through Europe and Asia after college, frequenting Cancun any weekend we had free. Next year, we were supposed to do Australia.

But now, neither one of them will talk to me.

Benny told me that fateful night he no longer considered me a brother, storming out of the bar without Rose by his side. He ignored my calls, and even Tom was quick to take his side. No matter what I tried, or the copious amounts of apologies I'd offer, neither one of them wanted anything to do with me. They had blocked me on all social media and even convinced the basketball team we played on during the weekends to drop me.

The unintentional drama which followed only made the entire situation worse.

Amongst our circle of friends, and in the community of our home town, news had spread like wildfire, much like the game 'telephone.' By the time it reached my mom, I had apparently fucked Benny's girlfriend, knocked her up, and was threatening to leave if she didn't get rid of it.

I had a lot to answer for. I don't deny that fact.

My mom and I always had a close relationship, being her only child and with no dad around. So, I was quick to tell her my side of the story. Nothing worse than your mom getting all up in your business.

I hated the fact I'd let her down. She treated Benny and Tom like sons, despite their inappropriate sexual references. She knew how tight of a bond we had and was quick to point out how easily I allowed my dick to act before my brain.

My hands wrap around the glass, raising it to my lips, and consuming the bourbon in one go. It no longer burns or clouds my vision. The only feeling ravaging me is *anger.* So, I fucked up. Yet Tom and Benny threw our friendship away like I wasn't fucking human.

With the fire of the bourbon running through my veins, the reality of my life became crystal clear. I was bored with my job, bored of this place, and tired of the same old Boston. The only thing which kept me here was my mom, but even she had her own life.

I need a fucking change.

Start new where I can reinvent and rid myself of this life I had relied on, the *people* I had relied on.

I pull my cell out of my pants pocket, scrolling through my phone until I come across my cousin Charlie's number. Pressing dial, I wait patiently for the call to connect.

"Um, excuse me, sir," Charlie greets, flatly. "Do you have the wrong number?"

A laugh escapes me. The sound of her voice is a welcoming change from my draining thoughts.

"I know, I know, I've neglected my cousin duties."

"Neglected would be an understatement," she informs me, her tone softening and more relaxed. "I'm surprised you're even alive. It's been like what... close to two years since I last spoke to you?"

"I comment on your posts."

"That doesn't count."

"I'm sorry, okay?" I offer my apology, sincerely. "Life has been..."

"Busy?" she answers, letting out a sigh. "For me, too. Okay, so before I grill you for not meeting your nieces yet, how have you been?"

I pause, trying to piece a reasonable answer together before she interrogates me even further. Charlie and I were close as kids whenever we spent our summers together. My mom and her dad shared the same biological father. According to my mom, she was the result of an affair my grandmother had with Charlie's grandfather while he was married. My own grandmother claimed it was a mid-life crisis affair on her behalf, but I've only met her a small handful of times since she remarried and moved to Washington state.

While Mom tried her best to stay in contact with her brother, Mark, it was actually Charlie's mother who became close to her, which is why we spent time with each other growing up.

I'd always thought of Charlie as a big sister rather than a cousin. We made so many great memories, but much like other families, time slipped away, and we both grew up so quickly.

"I'm thinking of coming out to LA," I mention, casually.

"Sounds great," she rushes with excitement. "When? You'll probably need at least a week to see everything—"

"No… I mean for good."

It has been on my mind nonstop for the last month. All I need to do to make it official is hand in my resignation. That, and lease out my condo.

"Is everything okay?"

"Yes." I pause again, letting out a sigh. "I just need a change of pace."

"But what about your job?"

"There are other jobs."

"Noah, c'mon, it's me," she reminds me. Although we don't speak as often as we probably should, when we do, it's as if time never passed. Charlie knows me too well. "This isn't like you. You love Boston, plus your mom is there and your best friends. I know those boys are like brothers to you."

"People change," I counter, dismissing the mention of Benny and Tom. "It's time to start somewhere new. So, any chance I can crash with you until I get myself sorted?"

I realized over time, I'd burrowed myself into a comfort zone here in Boston. Moving to California seems like a great idea, but I don't want to rent or buy a place just yet if I can't see myself staying for long.

"Listen, I'll have to clear it with Lex, but since he knocked me up again, I'll say yes for both of us," she grunts, seemingly unhappy with her predicament.

"Oh, shit." I laugh, curling my fist and bringing it to my mouth. "Congrats are in order, but hey, listen, two weeks at most. I just need to make sure it's right."

"Please don't congratulate me, I want to throw up," she complains with a groan. "So, when are you thinking of coming?"

"I need to give notice, settle things here so probably in a month or two?"

"We'll be waiting." I can hear the smile in her voice. "Built-in babysitter."

My laughter lingers. "I'm not great with kids. But happy to have Lex show me around town."

"You behave, okay?" she warns me. "Single men like you spell only one word."

"What are you talking about?" I tease, pouring myself more bourbon as we speak and walking toward my laptop. "Didn't you see my profile photo with the halo hovering over my head?"

Charlie snickers. "Listen, in terms of a job, a friend of ours runs a publishing house. Lex is a stakeholder, and I know they're looking to expand their marketing division. I'll get Lex to call you later, okay?"

"Sounds like a plan," I respond with a smile. "And Charlie... thank you."

"You're family, Noah. You don't ever need to thank me."

We say our goodbyes, and the moment the call ends, I think about Charlie's parting words. I'd always thought of Benny and Tom as family, but the last few months have proven how very wrong I was.

Moving to California is exactly the fresh start I need.

With my laptop switched on, I open a Word document and begin typing up my resignation letter. I'd been working steadily at this company for the last four years. Worked my way up from Marketing Analyst to Marketing Director. E-commerce is my strength, and I know leaving this comfortable position will be a risk.

But the biggest risk in life is not taking a risk.

Rereading my words and downing the remnants of my bourbon for extra encouragement, I attach the document to an email. Typing very few words, though with a heartful thanks for all the opportunities, my mouse hovers over the top of my inbox until I finally hit *send.*

It's time to move on.

CHAPTER
4

NOAH

I've never been fond of flying. Something about being crammed into a confined space along with two hundred impatient people all in a hurry to reach their destination seems unnatural. Add to that the cardboard food that's barely edible, coffee which tastes like water, and worst of all, the extremely claustrophobic restroom.

I avoid flying anywhere unless, of course, it's for leisure. Like Cancun last year. Leisure and pleasure all rolled into one. A boys' trip which turned into a weeklong fuck-fest with a newly divorced woman seeking revenge on her ex-husband by spending his money.

Life was so sweet back then.

It's a five-hour flight to Los Angeles, five hours of flying economy because business class is sold out, sitting next to a girl who bursts into tears every time she flips the page of her book. Cute girl, maybe early twenties, with a short brown bob tied back and reading glasses which make her look nerdy yet sexy at the same time. She's curled up, legs beneath her chin, resting against the window. The way she sits, along with the way she bites her nails nervously, warns me that Miss Goody-Two-Shoes should best be left alone.

But I'm bored and not in the mood to watch the crappy television shows or unpopular movies they show on the plane.

*Without trying to draw attention, I watch the way her lips tremble and her eyes glass over with every flick of a page. My stare immediately wanders to the title of the book—*Moving on After a Broken Heart.

Too. Fucking. Easy.

Then my mind halts, remembering the promise I made when I left home.

I promise not to prey on vulnerable women.

I promise to keep my dick in my pants.

I promise not to engage in sexual activity that may be construed as any form of revenge.

And so, this one-way ticket is supposed to be a fresh start—a way of reinventing myself in a place filled with superficial wannabe actors and actresses.

Hollywood.

I close my eyes with my earphones on, trying to drown out the aircraft noise.

Not long after, there's a gentle tap on my shoulder. "Sir, would you like a drink?"

I open my eyes to be met by a sexy red-haired stewardess waiting to serve me with a flirtatious smile. Fuck, those lips. Red lipstick—my weakness.

31

I'm not thirsty, but decide I need to leave a good impression on her and order a scotch. I've never fucked a stewardess.

It would be so damn hot if she left that uniform on while I fuck her from behind.

She pours the scotch into the glass, trying to disguise her smile. I know she's feeling it. Through her white blouse, her nipples are practically teasing me. Noticing my tray table isn't down, she leans forward, her tits so close to my face, and opens the table while accidentally brushing my cock in the process.

"Here you go, sir."

"Thank you, Ivana," I say, eyeing her nametag.

Only lingering for a moment, she turns her body in the opposite direction, purposely bending over to serve the gentleman across the aisle from me.

Fuck! What I would give to stick my fingers in her sweet pussy right now. I bet it's tight too. Barely touched from all the traveling she does.

Control yourself. Miss Goody-Two-Shoes next to you would have a heart attack if she knew what your dirty mind wants to do to Ivana right now.

What was that about controlling my dick?

Who fucking cares anymore?

New place, a new set of women.

Perfect.

The remainder of the flight is uneventful, and Ivana, much to my disappointment, hasn't come back for round two. With only an hour left until we descend, Miss Goody-Two-Shoes decides to strike up a conversation. Another reason I despise flying—small talk with random strangers beside you.

"Sorry about the blubbering mess," she apologizes while placing the book in the pocket behind the seat in front of her.

"Must be a good book," I respond politely, not interested in the slightest about making conversation.

"Good as in eye-opening. I feel much better now. I'm Amber, by the way."

I smile back. "Noah."

"Noah," she repeats. "Cute. Are you from LA?"

Cute? For fuck's sake, this is not going anywhere. Time to terminate the conversation. I'm not moving to LA to meet friends, especially ones who think my name is 'cute.'

"No, just moving there."

"I live not far from Santa Monica Beach with my two roomies," Amber informs me. "LA is a nice change if you're from the East."

"I like warmer."

"I miss the cold winters. When I stayed in Jersey with my girlfriend... I mean, my ex..." And there it is, the reason why she's been a train wreck this entire flight. I just never took her for a lesbian. It's kind of hot. Damn, she eats pussy. We have something in common.

"I loved being inside and watching the snow fall. Helps if you've got hot chocolate and are having wild sex in front of a fireplace," she reminisces.

The scotch swirling around in my mouth almost splatters onto the chair in front of me. She said what?

"Uh, yeah." I laugh nervously, unsure of where to go from here. "I wouldn't have pegged you for a wild-sex-

in-front-of-a-fireplace type of girl."

"Well, then, Noah, it's amazing how looks can be deceiving."

Her eyes dart back and forth, scanning the passengers around us. With most people asleep, she slides a little closer and rests her hand on my thigh, inching it closer until it's sitting on my cock. Stroking it softly above the material of my pants, I allow her to continue until she suggests we should take this out back.

"Back where?" I ask, wondering what she has in mind.

I turn my head, and I notice the back of the plane isn't full. I enjoy fucking in public, but this, this seems risky. Don't be a pussy, Noah. You've jerked off watching several pornos with girls getting off on airplanes.

I unclick my seat belt and stand, walking toward the back where the larger restroom is located, assuming that this is where Amber wants to fuck. Ivana is standing against the wall eyeing me as I walk down.

Oh shit.

With Amber following close behind, Ivana tilts her head and watches her.

"Well, this is a nice reunion." Ivana grins, eyeing us both from head to toe.

"Just using the restroom." I smile back.

"Let me open the door for both of you. If you need any assistance, please don't be afraid to ask." Ivana bites the corner of her lip, gazing at me with her sultry eyes.

"We could use some help," Amber whispers, latching onto Ivana's arm.

Ivana pulls a piece of paper from her pocket, taping it onto the restroom. The words Out of Order printed and stuck on the door.

"Ladies," I murmur, running my hand along Ivana's collarbone. "We need to get creative with this space."

Ivana places her juicy red lips on mine, rolling her tongue around while moaning in my mouth. There's a hand stroking my cock. I don't know who it belongs to nor do I care. Ivana continues to kiss me with deep penetrating moans almost biting my lip in the process. I pull away and see why.

Amber has shifted Ivana's dress up, past the top of her garters. She pushes Ivana's black lacey panties aside, exposing her beautifully shaved pussy. Fuck. I watch in awe, waiting for her to slide her tongue against her clit. I've been with two women before, but never in a restroom of a plane. This here is fucking heaven.

"If my ex could see me in here with the both of you, she'd die," Amber moans loudly.

Without any further delay, she shoves her head between Ivana's legs as Ivana curses at her, begging her to suck her pussy and stick her fingers deep inside. I'm at a slight loss for what to do, caught up in the excitement of it all. But time is of the essence because this plane isn't going to stay in the air forever.

My cock is throbbing, the blood pumping hard as I restrain myself from blowing too quickly. Knowing I don't have a condom on me, I settle for a blowjob while

Amber finishes Ivana off. It doesn't take me long—two women staring up at me with wild eyes, fighting to suck me off the hardest.

Fucking. Suck. Harder.

"Sir," a voice calls to me. "Sir, please fasten your seat belt. We're descending into LAX."

Startled and confused by my surroundings, it takes me a moment to realize it was only a dream. And Ivana, ironically, is the one who bursts my pornographic bubble. Still standing over me, she notices the hard-on and walks away with a satisfied smile.

Cock tease.

The girl beside me begins a conversation, introducing herself as Erika. Funny, I didn't peg her for an Erika. Much like my warped dream, she asks the same questions, buying time with mundane topics. When the wheels of the plane begin to drop, loudly echoing through the cabin, Erika drops the bombshell.

"I broke up with my boyfriend because he cheated on me with one of my friends. And you know what makes it worse? They're still together!" she cries loudly.

I want out of this plane.

Out of this conversation.

So, being the dick that I am, I don't say anything else and pretend to be enjoying the view through her window as the plane hits the ground and screeches to a halt.

"Ladies and gentlemen, welcome to Los Angeles," the pilot announces.

I give myself a moment to take it all in. The fact that

I'm here beginning something new, embarking on a new adventure, it would've been nice to have a moment of serenity as we taxied into the terminal, but Miss Chatty next to me takes the opportunity to go on about her ex-boyfriend.

She turns to face me, staring me down behind her glasses. "Give me your honest opinion. You're a guy, and I need a guy's perspective. If I hooked up with someone else, say, like a rebound, would that make him angry, you think?"

Oh, sweetheart. You're asking the wrong guy.

It's like dangling a bottle of scotch at an AA meeting. Here she is dangling her frigid little pussy in front of me. Clenching my fist, I try my hardest to answer her question without insinuating we should meet up so I can show her a real man wouldn't be cheating on her sweet, pretty ass.

"Erika," I say, standing up to open the overhead locker and remove my bag. "Do whatever it is you need to do to move on. Don't waste your time worrying about someone who doesn't feel the same."

Pat on the back for that mature response.

The chaos begins, passengers scrambling to grab their belongings to exit the plane. Erika thanks me for the advice, and I say goodbye, following the line that begins to move toward the exit.

Along with everyone else, I walk through the corridor, then turn the corner and see the crowds of people waiting at the gate.

Charlie's standing at the front with one of her daughters. I immediately recognize her even though I haven't seen her in years. Her normally brown hair is slightly darker, chopped into a shorter style that reaches her shoulders. Back when we were younger, she was a lot paler, but I'm assuming living in California is why her skin is so olive. She's always been a beautiful girl, a reason why every boy in town wanted to date her when we were young.

I wave hello, distracted by a tap on my shoulder. I turn around as Erika hands me a piece of paper. "My number. I'm taking your advice. Make sure you call me, okay?"

Wow! So even when I'm trying not to be sexy, I must come across that way. *Talk about an ego boost.* I wink back at Erika, following it up with a smile, shoving her number into the pocket of my pants.

"Uncle Noah!" The little girl runs toward me, wrapping her tiny arms around my leg. What the hell am I supposed to do? I don't even remember her name. She looks exactly like her dad—mousy brown hair with bright green eyes. I'd expect a little girl should be dressed in some sort of frilly dress, but not her. She's wearing a white T-shirt with #Superhero printed on it in bright green along with a cape. Okay, seriously, the kid already rocks.

"Well, well, well... look who finally made it to LA." Charlie grins.

"Hello, cuz." I smile back, placing my bag on the floor, then leaning in to hug her.

I may have left my mom behind, but Charlie is family. Something about her makes me feel at home. Perhaps it's the years of torture she inflicted on me when we were growing up—tea parties, wedgies—you name it, she made me do it every summer.

Pulling away, she holds onto my arms to look at me. Her eyes glass over, and she's on the verge of crying. I can see her small pregnancy bump and assume the raging hormones are on-setting the tears.

"You're a grown-up man now." She smiles proudly. "And I see you made a friend on the plane already." Raising her brow, she waits for me to respond.

"Californians are *very* welcoming."

The timing is impeccable. Ivana, the stewardess from the flight, walks past and stops just shy of where Charlie stands.

"I'm staying at this hotel. Call me." She slides the paper into the breast pocket of my shirt. Charlie frowns, shaking her head back and forth.

"Let's go, Noah. We have some rules we need to set in place if you're staying with us."

I let out a groan, a gesture that Charlie's daughter notices.

"Uncle Noah, you won't get bored at my house. We have a ton of things to do! Maybe your girlfriends can come visit, too?"

Leaning over to Charlie, I whisper, "What's the name of this daughter?"

"Amelia," she reprimands with an annoyed look. "She's the oldest."

"Right," I respond, smiling at Amelia. "Uncle Noah isn't used to being around kids, so you have to be patient. Do you know what that means?"

"Well, duh," she responds with a bored look on her

face. "I *am* almost five. Daddy says that men like you only have women friends, not boy friends. Unless, of course, you're like my Uncle Eric. He has boyfriends. He's gay."

I stop mid-step. "Uh... kid, should you know that?"

"Daddy also says I'm super smart and one day I'll run his company. He says if I'm the boss, I can make everyone wear capes to work."

"That's a pretty awesome idea," I tell her. "How about if you become the boss, I'll come work for you. I'd like to wear a cape to work every day, too."

"Deal." She smiles, happily skipping beside me.

Charlie directs us to the baggage claim area. Along with the hoard of people, I wait until my suitcases move toward us. The rest of my stuff is on a truck headed here. I didn't know what I'd need to survive living with Charlie and her family, a move in my life I never expected to make.

On the car ride to Charlie's house, Amelia falls asleep, giving us time to chat.

"Your mom told me about what happened back home."

"My mom has a big mouth," I tell her, staring out the window.

"You okay? It can't be easy to lose your friends like that, especially the ones who were like brothers to you."

Putting on a brave face, I follow with a smile. "I'm fine. I'm ready for new things, anyway."

"Good." She hesitates, turning her indicator on and driving up the ramp to another freeway. "You have Lex. He's going to enjoy having you around."

"Is he into sports, specifically basketball?"

"Uh... yes." She laughs. "He has courtside seats to all the Lakers games."

"Sweet. Maybe living out here ain't gonna be so bad," I mumble to myself.

And just for a moment, when things look bleak, the promise of courtside tickets perks me right up.

Then, I remember my golden tickets—the one sitting in the pocket of my pants and the one sitting in the pocket of my shirt.

To fresh starts.

To a new career.

To California babes.

Life is starting to look sweet—*again.*

CHAPTER
5

NOAH

There's nothing worse than being woken up to the sound of a crying child, a sound so irritating you wish you could grab one of those heavy-duty headphones to block the noise, similar to those used on an airport runway.

Comparing a crying baby to a plane should tell you how much I *dislike* children. Okay, maybe dislike is too strong of a word to use, considering it's my niece screaming down the house. Annoying? Yeah, that seems more fitting.

But who would've thought there's something more annoying than the sound of a crying child at five in the morning? There is—the constant movement of your bed from two kids jumping up and down relentlessly.

"Uncle Noah, wake up!"

I let out a frustrated moan, turning my back to them as the mattress moves underneath me. For fuck's sake, the girls have a trampoline outside. A massive one, at that. To think of how many times I annoyed my mom in the same way when I was a kid, karma is really late on delivering. She's found me, stuck with me, and, of course, I'm a sexist, assuming karma is a *she.*

Pulling the covers over my head to block out the noise, my niece, Amelia, pulls it back off immediately. "You're going to be late to work. Daddy says people who are late to work slow your business down and therefore create less productivity."

For her age, this kid has way too many brain cells. However, Daddy does have a point, probably why he runs one of the top empires in the United States.

"Girls, as much as I love your morning wake-up calls, how about you give me five more minutes?" I ask nicely.

"That's what you said yesterday, Uncle Noah," Amelia reminds me, placing her hands on her hips.

How can I resist their cute faces? It doesn't help that I'm massively hungover from a club I hit last night with Erika and Ivana. Yes, I fucked both of them. Yes, I do believe my dick is also hungover. I think I've only gotten two hours sleep if that. I've only been here three nights, and all of them resulted in not much sleep.

"I promise only five more minutes," I beg kindly.

"Okay," Ava, the youngest, says in her broken toddler speech. "I'm watching cock!"

"Clock, Ava," Amelia corrects her. "Cock is a rooster. Daddy always says to Mommy that she likes big roosters, remember?"

I snicker, realizing the girls are standing beside me watching me with confused expressions on their faces as I laugh. Amelia leans over, whispering into Ava's ear, then pulls away as both of them stare at me sternly.

"Five minutes, Uncle Noah. If you're not up, watch out," Amelia warns me.

They both jump off the bed and run out of the room, finally leaving me alone. I throw my head back into the pillow, drowning out a persistent headache.

Today, of all days, is the first day of my new job. Lex is a stakeholder in a publishing house in downtown LA. We spent most of yesterday discussing the role, what it entails, and how the business has grown over the last twelve months, not to mention several video calls with the CEO before I left Boston.

I haven't worked in publishing, most of my career has focused on marketing online stores, but he has an opening which seems like a good opportunity and should be a breeze once I understand how the industry operates. It's not like I'm strapped for cash, but idle hands are the devil's playthings. I like money, and not working makes me anxious. In ways, spending time with Lex and Charlie is refreshing. Intellectual and business-minded talk only drives me to want to work harder.

They're fucking *billionaires.*

According to an article I read, Lex is one of the youngest self-made billionaires in the United States. Only yesterday, Charlie took me on a tour of the property with acres of land, luscious gardens, and a massive garage holding all their 'babies.' My jaw literally drops to the ground when I see the cars sitting in there. One of which, Charlie has offered to let me drive during my stay until I get myself sorted.

This life she's living is a far cry from how she grew

up. All I know is that LA is looking more and more appealing. The fucking weather alone is perfect, and I could really get used to this lifestyle.

"Uncle Noah!" My name is yelled through the house, and before they get to me, I pull myself out of bed, using the bathroom quickly. I make my way toward the kitchen, still dressed in my sweats and tee.

The aroma of pancakes lingers in the air, drawing my attention as I enter the kitchen. Charlie's standing by the stove, pouring batter into the frying pan. Amelia and Ava are sitting at the table. Ava is sitting in her high chair, throwing cereal on the floor while Charlie cooks.

What a mess.

Charlie turns around, already dressed in a sharp black suit, and hands me a plate.

"Thanks, cuz." I smile at her.

"So, first day at the office. Shouldn't you be changed already?"

"It's only six-thirty. Relax, *Mom.*"

Charlie rolls her eyes, moving around the stove before turning it off. She takes a seat across the table handing a pancake to Ava.

"We didn't finish our conversation last night about the dinner party." She raises the mug to her mouth, carefully blowing the steam away. "So, Lex and I will be heading out that night. Are you sure you can handle *both* the girls?"

I brush it off like it's nothing, trying to disguise the mild panic. "It's only for one night, right? How hard can it be?"

Ava throws her cup across the table, smacking

45

Amelia in the face who, in turn, drops her iPad into her bowl of cereal. She begins to cry, and with Charlie telling Ava off for being naughty, the quiet kitchen suddenly becomes a zoo.

Shit! *What have I gotten myself into?*

"I'll be fine," I assure her, praying to God that their dinner is canceled. Maybe I can convince Mom to visit for the weekend. Stop panicking already! I change the subject to curb my growing anxiety. "So, tell me more about Haden Cooper, and what should I expect from him as a boss."

"Let's see…" she clears her throat, and begins, "… he's very passionate about publishing. To be honest, I don't know much about the business side of Haden. We usually get together only for social gatherings. His wife, Presley, and I have playdates."

"Publishing. It's an interesting change of career for me."

"Well, you're in marketing. Marketing books can't be that hard?"

"The fact that no one reads books anymore makes it difficult," I point out. "This generation is about binge-watching."

"Trust me," she says confidently. "Your generation may be all about gadgets and Netflix, but books are still very much alive."

"Yeah, for horny housewives."

"That's so sexist and so not true," she exaggerates, shaking her head in disagreement.

"Really?" I humor her. "Tell me what book you're currently reading on your Kindle." I motion toward it sitting on the countertop.

She narrows her brows, crossing her arms because she knows I'm right. She may be in her thirties, but she still has the same angry pout she had when she was ten years old.

"A book about a *strong,* independent woman."

"Uh-huh, and what *genre* is that book in?"

"Erotic romance." She coughs.

I laugh hysterically, continuing as Lex walks into the room and greets us. Like Charlie, he's dressed and ready for work wearing a navy suit and collared white business shirt. *Armani.* I know my brand names.

Lex is slightly taller than me. If you didn't know him or weren't related to him like I am, you could definitely see why he comes across as intimidating. It has something to do with his eyes—they're *very* green.

Back when I was a kid and Charlie was eighteen, there was a rumor going around that she was having an affair with Lex. He was a couple of years older than her and, at the time, married. Mom mentioned it here and there, but I have selective hearing when it comes to gossip, especially when it involves my cousin screwing a married man.

Lex places his laptop on the table along with his cell.

"What's so funny?" he asks, grabbing some coffee and sitting across from us.

"Proving your wife wrong that books are a dying breed, and the only people who read are horny housewives."

He laughs along with me, infuriating Charlie. "Funnily enough, women count for the majority of our book sales.

Specifically, in the erotica genre."

"Thanks for having my back." Charlie gritted her teeth.

Lex's smile remains fixed. "Hey, I'm not complaining. Kudos to the authors who write the smut that turns you on."

I'm grateful Lex and Charlie allow me to stay in their home, but the downside—they're awfully affectionate with each other. It's really quite sickening. Thank God the guest bedroom is located on a different floor than theirs. I'd hate to be next door. It explains why they have two kids with one on the way.

"Okay, guys. Awkward. I'm going to shower, and when I come back, I expect both of you to behave. Three kids are enough. Uncle Noah doesn't need any more madness in his life," I remind them.

I walk to my room and grab my clothes, hopping into the shower. After the shower and shaving, I change into my crisp, white shirt and charcoal gray pants. Charlie said the office isn't overly formal and suggested I keep the tie at home. I splash on some aftershave and make my way back to the kitchen, stopping just shy of the door. I hear an unfamiliar voice, a woman, and the accent is distinctively British. Eavesdropping on the conversation, I stand behind the entrance.

"Charlie, I'm fine," the unfamiliar voice says.

"Kate, you're not fine. He's a douchebag. I can't believe he ended things between you via a text message. He needs to grow some balls!"

"He had balls, Charlie. Nice, big, round ones," Kate jokes, chuckling.

I scowl at the image of another man's balls. *Gross.* Do women really like big juicy balls? This is unheard of. I've never had a woman say, 'Oh, let me touch your big balls.'

Normally, I'd have raised this topic with Benny and Tom. The reminder that they're not a part of my life anymore dampens my mood.

"Gross, Kate... now that image is going to be stuck in my head. Balls? Really?" Charlie complains. "Argh, let's stop saying 'balls.' Jokes aside, I hate that he did this to you."

There's a pause, followed by silence in the room. "I hate it, too, Charlie. But I'm not going to pine for him anymore. He's made himself perfectly clear, and so it's time for me to move on. I *can* move on," she says unconvincingly.

I promised myself no more. *Stop looking for women itching for a rebound.* It's a sick disease that I can't seem to shake.

I *can* resist.

Be strong.

Last night, for example, now that was just fun. Both women were looking for a good time. And just because Erika kept mentioning her ex, that doesn't mean anything, right?

Rebound. Rebound. Rebound. The voices scream as they slap my face repeatedly.

But this—I mean, the British accent is all types of sexy. It would be a waste to pass up this opportunity. All I need to do is see if her voice matches my imagination.

I enter the room, clearing my throat. The kids are gone, and so is Lex. Charlie looks up, her curious eyes watching me cautiously. Her friend, Kate, has already eye-fucked me, greeting me with a playful smile. She's a gorgeous one—dark blonde hair with cute little freckles scattered over the bridge of her nose. If she's wearing makeup, you wouldn't know, her bright blue eyes shimmering as she waits for an introduction.

"Oh, Kate, this is my cousin, Noah. The one I told you about," Charlie says carefully with a wary expression.

"The one you told her about. All good, I hope," I tease, smirking back at Kate.

"All good," she responds while biting her bottom lip. "I'm Kate." She stands quickly, almost knocking over the coffee pot.

"Noah." I shake her hand, holding on to it a bit longer than necessary.

She's going to be easy. See, it's all in a woman's mannerisms. The flirty smile and batting of eyelashes are simple to spot, but if you look closer, you'll see the way a woman's thighs clench together combined with the bites on the corner of her lip.

"So, Noah, I hear you'll be staying here a while," Kate says cautiously, waiting for Charlie to interrupt. I must be missing something here—some stupid woman code.

"Hmm... as long as Charlie and Lex will have me. I'll see how the new job goes."

"Oh, that's right, you'll be working for Haden." She laughs while Charlie hides her snicker behind a cup of coffee.

"And that's funny because?"

"He's a jerk," they say in unison.

"A jerk?"

"Yes, but since he's settled down, his jerkiness is wearing off." Kate laughs.

"We're kidding," Charlie says. "Listen, I have to go, or I'll be late for work. Do you need a ride?"

"I'll take him," Kate offers with a mischievous smile playing on her lips.

Too fucking easy.

"I don't know if that's a good idea." Charlie makes dagger eyes at Kate as if to warn her. There may have been some kicking under the table as Kate's expression becomes pained while mouthing, 'What the fuck?' and glaring back at Charlie.

"Sounds perfect." I grin.

"Fine, whatever," Charlie mutters, grabbing her bag and tossing me a spare set of keys. "Lock up when you're ready. I won't be home till late, but Lex will be here with the girls."

She walks toward the back door and stops. "You..." she points directly at Kate, "... I'll speak to *you* later." The door closes shut, and finally, she leaves us alone.

"I don't know what her problem is. It's not like I bite," I say half-jokingly.

"Oh, really? That's a shame," Kate notes with dark amusement.

I cock my head to the side, hiding the smirk on my face. "So... that ride?"

"Yeah, that ride. I guess we need my car keys, right?" She grabs them off the table and opens the back door.

I follow her lead, purposely watching her ass sway in a tight black skirt.

Charlie will kill me.

51

With her bare hands.
Unless, of course, we keep it a secret.
So much for making promises.

CHAPTER
6

NOAH

Charlie and Lex live in the Hollywood Hills in a property that sprawls across several acres with stunning views of the city. As beautiful as the house is, it's miles from where my new office is located. The roads are windy, and with Kate's erratic driving, I expect to end up dead in a ditch somewhere. When we finally hit the freeway, I bless the Lord above until we halt in traffic, sheer gridlock with no break in sight. It does, however, give us more time to chat.

The more we get to talking, the more I'm intrigued by the woman who sits beside me.

We have a lot in common, and her warped sense of humor makes it an entertaining car ride. She's smart, business-oriented with a strong head on her. I've slept with powerful executive women but only because they were looking for a quick fuck to get back at husband number two, who was trying to ride them for alimony.

Kate is different. Not sure why but it's somewhat refreshing.

She talks about her life in Manhattan, running the office on the East Coast, and how she used to be Lex's assistant BC—before Charlie.

"I'll set the record straight. I have no life aside from work. I don't really have time for anything else," she admits truthfully. "New York may be the city that never sleeps, but I'm sleeping alone every goddamn night."

"But you're here," I remind her, turning my head to glance at her profile. She's simplistic yet beautiful at the same time. "Is this not for pleasure?"

She smiles, loosening her grip on the steering wheel. "That depends. We've been chatting for nearly an hour, and you haven't asked me out."

Good point. Smart and sassy. I'm not the type of guy who asks a woman out. I don't date, I fuck. That's all I do. I'm not interested in relationships. After all, I'm only twenty-eight and still in my prime.

"I've been instructed to stay clear of any women associated with Charlie."

Kate laughs at my comment. "Charlie is a simple woman. She's relationship-oriented. She never grasped the concept of having fun. You know... letting loose."

"Please don't talk to me about my cousin letting loose." I shake my head while scowling. "She's still the girl who stayed at our house during summer vacation and made me watch *Clueless* on repeat."

"If it's any consolation, she's a happily married woman now. A mother."

"Unless she's a nun, can we please change the subject?"

A Porsche cuts us off, prompting Kate to mouth off at the driver. "I should flip him the bird, the arrogant asshole!" Letting out a frustrated breath of air, she continues to drive while calming herself down. "So tonight, what are you doing?"

I'm still processing her road rage. She's asking me out. A straightforward thinker. If only I hadn't overheard the conversation between Kate and Charlie or noticed that she glances at her cell every two seconds as she attempts to drive and battle the traffic.

"Nothing tonight. I've only been here for three days, so I haven't had a chance to do anything that doesn't involve tea parties or playing dress-up."

You're such a fucking liar. You were eating pussy hard last night. Did you forget that?

"All right, time to take you out to play with the grownups. We need to get around Lex and Charlie. Otherwise, they'll make a big deal out of nothing."

"I'll just meet you wherever you want to go," I suggest.

"Okay, there's this new bar out in Malibu. Let's meet around eight. Do you have a ride?"

"I'm sure Charlie will lend me her car. Otherwise, I'll find a way," I tell her. Of course, she will, and if she doesn't, I'll remind her that yesterday Ava got a red marker on my expensive shirt, which resulted in a last-minute dry cleaning so I could wear it today.

The traffic moves forward, and we continue talking about life in LA. Due to her time spent in New York, Kate is very anti-California. She dislikes the heat and the traffic. She often refers to Los Angeles as a fame-driven money pit. It occurs to me somewhere during a rant about the smoggy air that this British girl is extremely homesick.

"I can tell you miss home."

"I miss the cold weather, and my mummy's fish and chips with the mushy peas on the side."

"Excuse me? Mushy peas on the side of fish and chips?" I almost gag at the thought.

"Yes, it's my favorite dish. Don't you like peas?"

"Uh… I don't mind them, but together with fish? No, thanks."

"Such an arrogant Yank. You think that's gross, but you eat peanut butter and jelly."

Taken aback by her disrespect for one of the classics, I wonder how anyone could possibly knock a peanut butter and jelly sandwich.

"Are you comparing mushy peas to a PB & J?" I ask loudly with a confused face.

"Oh, please, it's weird, okay?" She cringes.

A horn honking breaks our argument, and in return, Kate slams her hand on her car's horn, cursing along with it. "Did you see that? He flipped me the damn bird!"

She looks hot when she's angry. *I wonder what would happen if I flipped her my bird?*

"We're here," she announces, parking the car at the front of the building.

There goes that idea.

I look outside the window and see a small brown building. It's not the high-rise I'd been expecting, nor does it even look like an office. It's nestled between two large modern buildings, prompting me to recheck the address.

"Are you sure this is the right place?" I question Kate while searching for the address on the email Lex sent me.

"It sure is. Just remember, don't judge a book by its cover," she says wisely. "I'd love to come out and introduce you to Haden, but I have a meeting to get to. Japanese businessmen *do not* like tardiness."

"It's okay. We can leave the hand-holding for later." I raise my eyebrow and follow it with a smirk.

"Sure." She turns her body to face mine, positioning her legs carefully so they don't expose what I'd love to have a look at. "Nothing like a good hand job. So, tonight?"

"Tonight." I grin, breaking out in a small chuckle as I open the door of her car.

She leans her head as close as possible to the passenger window, and with her lips cracking into a smile, she says, "You're a heartbreaker, Mr. Mason. And someone out there is definitely going to get their heart broken."

***

Kate's right. You don't judge a book by its cover. So you shouldn't judge a building in the same way. As soon as I step inside, I'm astonished to see such an architecturally well-presented office space.

The reception area has dark wooden floors and crisp

white walls. The back wall, where the receptionist sits, is old brickwork restored to its original condition. Hanging on the wall are various book covers sitting in large frames with an autograph at the bottom of each print. Moving closer to the reception desk, I notice that each book on that wall is a *New York Times* bestseller.

The sconces in the room are modern, illuminating the area and giving it a warm and inviting feel. And positioned in the corner is a vintage brown leather couch with a bookshelf beside it housing many books. There are more books positioned on the oval-shaped coffee table that sits on a huge, off-white shaggy rug.

The receptionist is wearing an earpiece and motions for me to wait a minute. The second she hangs up, she asks me who I am.

"Noah, Mason. Your new Marketing Director," I state, keeping my tone flat.

When it comes to work, I don't screw around. Perhaps, back in my younger years, I landed myself in someone's pussy which equated to hot water. Yet over the last few years, I focused on climbing the corporate ladder. Marketing often attracted younger girls looking to mix business with pleasure. Unfortunately, for them, I didn't tolerate such immaturity. When you're under my watch, you better deliver.

My personal life, however, is a completely different story.

There's work Noah and fun Noah.

The two never mix.

"Right. You'll want Mr. Cooper," she replies with a cute I-want-you-to-finger-me type of smile.

She stands and walks around the desk, careful to adjust her tight-fitting skirt. She requests I follow her, and I try my damn hardest not to look at the way her firm ass shakes from side to side as she leads me through the office.

I could do so many things with that firm little ass. *Clear your dirty thoughts.* She looks young. You like your women with a little more life experience, anyway.

We stop at the glass office at the end of the hallway. Opening the door, the man, who I assume is Haden Cooper, motions for us to come in.

"Mr. Cooper, this is Noah Mason."

He stands from his desk, extending his hand to shake mine. He appears noticeably young to be running a publishing house—he's almost my age. Tall with a muscular build, he's wearing thick-framed reading glasses. Irritated by his beard, which he seems to be repeatedly scratching, I can notice the wedding band on his finger—poor *fella.*

"Noah, pleased to meet you. Sit."

I take a seat in the plush chair as the receptionist leaves. His office is nothing special, scattered manuscripts all over his desk with barely room for anything else. There's a mug next to his desktop, which has a picture of Homer Simpson in his briefs with the caption 'The last perfect man.'

"So, Noah, Lex has only good things to say about you. But then again, that man could persuade anyone to do anything."

"He does have a way with words. Thank you for this opportunity, Mr. Cooper."

"Call me Haden. It's weird, you seriously look like you could pass as my twin brother." He chuckles.

I relax. "Perhaps. No ring on my finger, though."

"Ah…" he smiles, "… life works in mysterious ways. That, and my wife is a ballbreaker. I probably shouldn't say that out loud because she'll be lurking around here somewhere."

"She works here, too?"

"Senior editor. I'd show you a picture, but she doesn't allow me to put a photo on my desk of her and our son. She reckons people who do that in the office are lame and missing a pair of balls."

I like his wife already.

"So, I'm impressed with your marketing background. I think you'll fit right in here. We need a strong push on our upcoming releases, and the marketing interns we have need direction. Your position as director will help give our business an online presence, which is needed to stay competitive in our market. Let's have a meeting with them this afternoon," he suggests.

I nod, agreeing, only to be interrupted by a stunning woman wearing a fitted pantsuit and low-cut blue blouse. She has curly brown hair that's tied into a bun with a loose tendril falling over her face. This office is like a candy store, except instead of candy, it's filled with sweet, beautiful pussy.

But I have to remember the golden rule—*you don't shit where you eat.*

I need this job right now, and my raging libido has to sit himself in the naughty corner alone. California definitely showcases gorgeous women.

"Hello." She offers a friendly smile. "You must be Charlie's cousin, Noah."

She knows Charlie. Game over.

"That I am," I answer politely.

She introduces herself, "I'm Presley Malone."

Haden coughs while shooting her an annoyed, wary look.

"Sorry, Presley Malone-Cooper," she says, rolling her eyes at him.

I laugh softly. "Ahhh… the wife."

Definitely, game over.

"When the title fits," Haden quips, stroking his beard.

"Stop being a jerk, Haden," she fires back, trying her best to disguise her smirk. "Anyway, it's great to have you on board. I hope Haden was kind enough to invite you out for drinks tonight?"

"I hadn't gotten around to it yet. It's what happens when Mrs. Know-It-All interrupts," he complains. "So, Noah, are you free for drinks tonight?"

"I had plans, but I can change them to later tonight."

"I'm sure you men will have fun. Listen, I'm off. If you need me, I'll be trying to get through to an author about her manuscript having too much sex in it."

"And I told you, there's no such thing," Haden states with a playful smile on his lips.

I'd have the same smile if I were tapping her sweet ass every fucking night.

"Are we having this argument again? There needs to be a plot. A story to make the readers want more. A sex scene on every page is overkill."

Their argument continues on, and the more I observe, the more I see that Haden purposely riles Presley up to get a reaction from her. It's comical, to say the least. I see now why Charlie and Kate joke about him being a jerk.

After not agreeing on anything, Presley walks out, leaving Haden and me alone.

"My wife," he says with a small laugh. "Do you see what I have to deal with every day? Ballbuster. Too damn stubborn."

"Headstrong is a preferable word," I suggest with a grin. "Much like Charlie and her friend, Kate."

"You know Kate?" He follows with a whistle. "The three of them together are like Charlie's Angels... excuse the irony of the name, trying to battle with everyone while standing up for equality for women. Kate's a troublemaker," he finishes with a soft laugh.

"Interesting, I only met her today. A feisty Brit at that."

"She's fun. Not as uptight as Presley and Charlie. I think they have this need to protect her from the awful men lurking around Manhattan. They're forever on her back and don't seem to get that she's a free spirit. Doesn't care what people think, just does what makes her happy."

Interesting way to describe Kate. She comes across as fun-loving and relaxed, not one of those women desperate to get married and have babies. Maybe that's why I like her—I don't feel this unwarranted pressure around her.

"Look, I'm gathering that you're hooking up with

someone tonight, so don't worry about drinks. Seriously, I totally get it."

I don't want to tell him it's Kate. Having only just met Haden, I don't know if he'd encourage me to spend time with her or warn me against it. Despite what he's just said, people have a funny way of reacting to things, and it's best to keep it on the down-low for now.

"Someone invited me to some bar in Malibu, but it's no trouble."

"I'm not getting in the way of a man and a hook-up. Trust me..." He laughs. "We'll have drinks later this week. I'll try to convince Lex to come out, but knowing him, he'll be out of town as usual."

Haden turns his screen around to further explain how the business operates, including an organizational chart of how the company is structured. He then speaks about the top ten authors and upcoming releases. I recognize Julian Baker, having read his work, only remembering now Charlie mentioning him years ago. If I recall, and again, when it comes to other people's love life, I barely pay attention, Charlie was dating him when she and I were in Hawaii for a wedding.

I spend the remainder of the day being shown the ropes and meeting the team. By six o'clock, I'm done. Haden gives me a ride back home, giving us more of an opportunity to talk about the company. The traffic's awful, leaving me with not much time to shower and change into something more casual.

The next dilemma is finding my mode of transportation. I want to use Charlie's bike, and it takes a lot of convincing, especially because it's her baby. After a long lecture on road safety, she finally hands me the keys.

It's bumper-to-bumper traffic to Malibu. Some dick lost his load causing a major traffic jam. Thank God I'm riding her bike, swerving in and out of the traffic to avoid further delays. The last time I had ridden was back in college—a bike Tom's parents bought him for his twenty-first birthday. I push away the unwarranted memory, focusing back on the road.

By the time I arrive, I head for the bar, and couldn't be happier to have a drink in my hand. I know I have to consume less so I can ride back home.

Moving through the crowd, I notice Kate sitting out on the big deck staring across the ocean. She's wearing the same clothes as this morning, but her expression looks bleak. Nothing at all like the fun-loving Kate I saw earlier today or the one Haden described.

Same look.

Same story.

Someone has broken her.

That guy. The one with the big balls.

Ugh.

Charlie warned me—not once, but twice—to be on my best behavior. Focus on my career and not on women, especially ones in her circle of friends.

I try not to come across as a stalker, though I'm half covered by a large bush watching her from afar. *Not at all stalker-like, you idiot.*

I observe the way she quietly sits at the table with her cell in front of her. It appears to be a distraction. As if on autopilot, she picks it up, stares at the screen, places it down, then repeats minutes later. Her foot taps impatiently under the table causing her skirt to ride up. She doesn't appear bothered, allowing it to do so, then on second thought, she pulls it slightly down again.

I amble toward her until I'm by her side.

"Hello, stranger."

"'Bout time you got here, Mr. Mason," she greets with an upbeat cheer. "Time to have some fun."

"What do you have in mind?"

She grabs my hand and a large purse, pulling me through the not-so-crowded bar until we find ourselves on the footpath leading to the sand. As if in a mad rush, her heels click against the concrete until we reach the end of the path where the sand leads to the ocean. Bending down while holding onto my shoulder, she removes her shoes, her bare feet now touching the soft sand.

The sun has set, the sky darkening with a hint of pink. With her hand pulling me near the shore, she settles on a spot beside a metal lifeguard chair. My body jerks toward the ground as she pulls me down with her and removes a bottle of tequila from her purse.

Opening the lid, she takes a drink, letting out a roar as the tequila makes its way down her throat. "Goodbye," she shouts, holding the bottle up to the sky. "Too bad decisions and wankers who need to get a fucking life!" She takes another drink.

I warn her to slow down, attempting to pull the bottle from her hand.

"You know what your problem is?"

It didn't take long, the tequila already running

through her veins resulting in a drunken slur.

"What?"

"You're too uptight."

I let out a chuckle, followed by a triumphant smirk. "Oh, Kate, you honestly don't know me."

"Yes, I do." She stands up in a rush, swaying slightly. "You like to fuck women. Lots of women. You don't care about their feelings. You think with your dick, and your dick has all the fun."

"And what's wrong with that? I don't need to settle down… yet."

"Exactly," she points out. "I was just like you. I was doing my thing and having fun. I didn't want a relationship. Now look at me," she cries loudly. "I'm a goddamn mess."

"You're not a mess, Kate. Sit and slow down on the tequila."

She listens, plonking herself on the sand while letting out a huge sigh. "I need to let loose again. Have fun. Find a way to forget the last few months ever happened. I want to have sex. I want to fuck like I'm alive. You get me?"

I get her all too much. I let out a sigh myself. I'm not supposed to be back here. This *here* is everything that got me into trouble in the first place. There are plenty of people who'll have my face on a target if I touch her— Charlie, Lex, Haden. There could be more. We could just have fun. We could chat. I don't need to fuck her.

Be strong. She's messed up, big time. Don't succumb to your old ways.

"C'mon, Noah." She hands me the tequila, waiting for

me to take a drink.

I stare at the bottle, thinking about how this time six months ago, I was at the beach with Benny and Tom getting wasted while we played volleyball with a group of Brazilian women on vacation. We laughed until our stomachs hurt, drank until we puked our guts out, and fucked those three women like desperate cavemen.

And now, *I'm here.*

Without a friend.

Alone.

And living with my mistakes.

Unscrewing the cap, I bring the bottle to my lips and swallow the tequila until it burns my throat, and I can no longer stand it.

Kate cheers loudly, "That's my boy! Forget it all exists if only for tonight."

I repeat until we both fall into a fit of laughter, watching as the sky turns dark and the barely seen stars twinkle in the distance. We talk about Los Angeles, argue over politics, then agree we both dislike pineapple on pizza to end on a heated debate on alien conspiracy theories. Our voices get louder, our arguments become more of incessant rambling as we began slurring our words.

"Fancy getting wet?" Kate's eyes light up, waiting for me to respond, while the bottle of tequila touches her lips and makes its way down.

"Shouldn't I be asking you that?"

"Cocky bastard." She grins, inching her body closer to me. Her fingertip rests on my lip, then slowly drags along the bottom, stirring a reaction in my pants. "Trust me, I already am."

She shoves the bottle into my chest, and I finish the remaining tequila. Kate stands in front of me, removing her blouse then sliding her skirt down. In only her red lacey panties and bra, she holds my gaze with a devilish smile. "You only live once, right?"

That's what they all say.

And for tonight like every other night, I strongly agree.

CHAPTER
7

NOAH

I read somewhere that the West Coast beaches have frigid water compared to the East Coast due to the California current. Never in my life have I shivered as much as I am right now. It's spring, so granted, it isn't exactly beach weather, but this is fucking ridiculous. I won't allow my teeth to chatter, curbing the need by biting down and keeping my legs moving in the water. My skin is prickling, hurting so bad that I'm pretty sure I'm on the verge of experiencing hypothermia.

It's dark out. Only the lights from the horizon of houses sitting on mountains along with the oceanfront properties and restaurants illuminate the area. This stretch of beach is quiet, and the only sounds are the waves and Kate splashing around me.

"Cold?" she asks, giggling before dunking her head back in the water.

"Uh… you could say that." I try to remain unaffected, but I swear my balls have fallen off and swam to shore seeking refuge under a warm beach blanket.

"I'm from England, so this is tropically fantastic."

"Compared to the English Channel?" I tease, moving my arms in a circular motion to remain warm.

"I love my country, but our beaches suck."

"Interesting, you don't seem too fond of California."

"Not California, American men," she comments with an air of arrogance.

I swim closer to her, and with the feeling coming back to my frozen limbs, I place my hand on her hip, drawing her in and whisper, "I'm an American man, but trust me, baby, you'll have fun."

I move my mouth closer to hers and gently brush her bottom lip with the tip of my tongue.

She breaks away and circles me like a hungry shark, full of laughter and flirtatious gestures. She doesn't seem so sad now, but maybe the tequila has something to do with that.

"I need to confess something." She giggles with a hiccup. "This is the first time I've skinny-dipped."

"Well, technically, Kate, you're *not* skinny dipping unless you're completely naked."

She stops swimming and moves toward me. Stretching her arm around her back, she unclasps her bra, removing it in one go. Her tits float, making my dick slightly hard, her pink nipples teasing me through the moonlight.

"Happy now? Mr. American?" she teases softly.

I shake my head, prompting her to strip down completely. I've never had sex in the ocean—a first time for everything. Using a condom seems highly unlikely at this time, given that it's sitting in my wallet on the shore. And then I start to think about all the ocean life floating around us and try to ignore whatever the fuck just brushed against my leg.

Please let it be seaweed.

Kate leans forward, her arms moving around in the water until she raises one arm proudly holding a pair of panties. "How about now?"

This time, I move closer to her, and with our mouths barely apart, I move forward to kiss her lips while my hands shift freely around her ass. In my intoxicated state, every problem weighing on my mind begins to drift further away with the current. Her body against mine is the only thing I'm thinking about.

"I'll take that as a yes," she says, tracing the top of my boxers and pulling on them as best as she can. I shake my leg, motioning for them to fall off.

Goodbye boxers. *Fuck, they were my expensive ones too.*

"You should take this as a time to be quiet and let me have some fun."

My lips move to her ear, grazing the side of her lobe while my fingers trace her hips and move closer to the front, allowing me to slide my hand between her thighs. She lets out a small yelp while tilting her head back. A warm sensation runs through my body, relaxing my sore muscles from the nasty cold.

"You're gorgeous. You know that?" I whisper.

Arching her back, she wraps her arms around my neck for support, pushing herself against me. "I shouldn't fuck you…" she murmurs with a guilty plea.

"Give me one good reason why not," I demand, edging closer to her clit.

For once, she chooses not to talk and instead leads our bodies closer to the shoreline until we're standing on two feet. With her body naked in front of me, her erect nipples tease me relentlessly until I have no choice but to fuck her. *Right here. Right now.*

She's fucking sexy even in the darkness of night. Her body, not too skinny, tall in stature, has all the curves in the right places. I've been with plenty of gorgeous women, but perhaps Kate being somewhat off-limits makes her stand out even more.

"Not here," she says. "Let's get out of the water."

Pulling my hand along, I follow her to where our clothes lie as she grabs me and pushes me to the sand.

Okay. Fuck. It's cold.

She stands above me, giving me the perfect angle to admire her beautifully manicured pussy with a landing strip smack bam in the middle.

"Do you want to fuck me, Noah?"

"When your pussy is staring at me like a wild beast, how could I not want to fuck you?"

"Then, I ask one thing of you." Her tone, sharp and fierce, is unlike the giggly Kate, who was floating around the water only moments ago.

"What's that?"

Her chest is heaving, wild eyes staring at me, ready to pounce. "I'm going to fuck you. Do you understand? And I don't fuck quietly."

Is this happening?

Without drawing any attention, the corners of my

eyes scan the area around us, sure I'm being pranked on some reality television show. When I can see we're alone—aside from two people in the far distance—I nod my head, excited by the thought.

But as much as the thought turns me on, Big Dick refuses to follow. *Oh, for the love of God!* The more I think about it, the more it makes me paranoid, and he refuses to come to the party. Fuck! Surely, she can sense how limp it is lying beneath her. Maybe if I fondle her tits, I can make it happen. My hands move to her tits, groping them hard as she moans oddly. Perhaps this is her sex face. It's odd as she looks pale white then appears to cringe in pain. Good Lord, this isn't the face of a woman I want to fuck right now. She immediately jumps off me and stares down at me.

"Oh my God!" she yells at the top of her lungs.

Holy shit! Is it crab season, I think. Fuck I don't know. There's a crab on my dick, I just know it. Sealife, it's everywhere. I begin to panic, wincing as I wait for the crab to bite my dick off.

I'm going to have no dick.

I'm going to be dickless!

"Get it off me," I shout back at her.

"With what?" she answers in a surprisingly calm tone.

"I don't know!" I argue. "Your shoe or purse?"

"My purse cost a thousand dollars. You want me to wipe it off with *Michael Kors?*"

"Michael who?" I panic, not comprehending her ridiculous dilemma. "Just get it off me!"

"It's just blood," she says calmly, watching me with

judging eyes.

"I'm bleeding? The crab bit me?" My eyes dart down in a state of panic. "Is my dick still there?"

Kate's shoulders begin to move up and down, her laughter echoing against the sound of the waves crashing. Her continuous laugh begins to anger me. What kind of a sick joke is this?

"I got my period," she stumbles out in between her laughter. "The blood is from my vagina, not a crab. Your dick's fine."

It takes a moment for it to click. *Her period?* Oh my God. This is embarrassing.

"Holy shit." I fall back onto the sand, covering my face with my hands until I burst out laughing along with her. She drops beside me, both of us naked in a fit of hysterics, unable to catch a breath of air.

"I thought it was a crab." I laugh through my words.

"I thought I was *pregnant*," she admits, chuckling as if it's a joke.

I stop laughing, catching my breath as her words sink in. "You thought you were pregnant? Baby, I'm good, but not that good."

She punches my arm softly and picks up the empty bottle of tequila, throwing it behind us, only to remove another bottle of something from her bag.

"If you thought you were pregnant, why did you drink tequila?" I question her more seriously. I'm not one to judge, but alcohol and pregnancy don't exactly mix.

"Because I didn't want to be. Because I'm an idiot. Because of many things I just don't want to feel right now," she says in one breath.

I place my arm around her shoulder and bring her closer to me. "We're so fucked up. Look at us. We're naked and—" A tingling sensation runs up my thigh. "Was that you? There have to be crabs somewhere. Oh fuck, and scorpions."

Kate ignores my panic attack, staring back at the moon with doleful eyes, her lips trembling slightly.

"Who do you think is more fucked up?" she wonders out loud. "Me or you?"

"Me... no, wait. Maybe you."

We continue to lie there, quietly drinking the bottle of vodka which Kate pulled out of her bag, pretending the world around us doesn't exist. At some point during a rendition of "Lean on Me," I stop singing for a moment with a clearer head, despite the alcohol running through my veins.

"Then let's call this a successful night. You're not pregnant, and my dick is still intact."

"Intact, yes." She laughs, following with an obnoxious snort. "Just... afraid to *come* to the party."

It's impossible to hide my embarrassment. I'm not one to be red-faced, but I can feel my cheeks burning despite the cold air. All I can do at a time like this is laugh at myself. "Do you know how fucking freezing that water is?"

"So, that was just all to impress me? Mr. Tough Guy, who can handle the shriveling cold water?" She chuckles loudly.

"Shriveling is an understatement. I take it back... this night is awful. It couldn't get any worse."

And right when I say the words, a torch flashes over

our eyes.

"You're under arrest for indecent exposure in a public area."

Oh fuck.

CHAPTER
8

NOAH

When I turned thirteen, my mom gave me *the talk.* The one which involved girls, how my body would go through changes, and how sometimes I might want to act on my physical feelings by having sex with a girl. Given Mom's teenage turmoil, she wasn't leaving it up to some uninterested teacher to inform me about teen pregnancy.

Mom didn't hold back, teaching me everything from how easily a girl could get pregnant to how readily you could catch a disease. At the time, I was embarrassed and confused by the whole spiel. It only began to click around the age of sixteen when girls suddenly became interested in me.

Out of all the bad things I could do, Mom warned me that getting a girl pregnant shouldn't be one of them.

When I turned twenty-one and officially became a man of legal age able to go to clubs and drink, Mom gave me another talk. The one about how easily I could fall into the wrong crowd, how life can sometimes be overwhelming, and how, when that happens, we occasionally try our best to forget our worries by doing something stupid. Something illegal.

"Noah, I raised you well. Promise me, and I mean double promise me that I'll never see your face in a mugshot."

"C'mon." I brushed it off. "I would never do that to you, Mom. I promise."

Here I am at twenty-eight years old, staring into a camera and holding up a board with my name on it. *My mom is going to have a coronary.* Her only son, her flesh and blood, sitting in a jail cell arrested for indecent exposure. It wasn't like we were doing anything harmful, but according to the cops, we had broken the law.

An elderly couple on their nightly walk saw us and were disturbed by our behavior, quickly calling the police and reporting us.

Sitting in this cold, bleak cell while police fill out paperwork only makes the whole scenario even more depressing. Kate doesn't see the big deal, trying to flirt with one of the younger cops to help get us out of here. It fails, and she curses in her British slang—something about him being a wanker with a small John Thomas. I have no idea what that means, nor do I care to right now.

"My mom's going to kill me," I blurt out, resting my head in my hands to block out my surroundings.

"Your mom?" Kate laughs. "I didn't peg you for a momma's boy. Blimey, just when you were starting to earn cool points."

"That term is *so* overrated."

"Says the momma's boy," she points out. "I'm more worried about Charlie."

I run my hands through my hair, frustrated at the whole situation. "You didn't have to call her," I say, annoyed.

"Who else is going to post bail? Your mom?"

"Wait. Is that a mom joke?"

Kate moves across the bench and sits beside me. Poking her finger in my arm, just to annoy me, she says, "C'mon, this is kinda fun, right?"

The alcohol is still swirling around that crazy brain of hers. She's supposed to be sad, suffering from a broken heart. Kate, from what I've experienced, is nothing like I thought she'd be. That, or she's good at disguising her emotions with strange British humor.

"I'm all for a good time, but this isn't what I had in mind. Fuck! Do you realize how much trouble we're in? I came to LA to get a fresh start," I remind her. "Not get busted for nudity and sent to damn jail."

She remains quiet, keeping to herself. Maybe I was a little harsh. Kate has bigger worries and still must be processing that whole not-being-pregnant thing. Maybe she's not void of emotions after all. I definitely have enough emotions whirling inside of me for the both of us—anger, disappointment, and frustration—to name a few.

But even with my emotions running high, I can't

ignore the silence coming from the person next to me.

"You okay?" I ask, tilting my head to the side to check up on her.

Playing with the hemline of her skirt, she answers distractedly, "Yeah, why wouldn't I be?"

I grab her hand, not to be romantic, but with genuine concern. "The whole pregnancy thing, Kate."

"Oh, that," she plays it off. "Totally forgot about it."

Placing my arm over her shoulder, I pull her closer. I don't know why I feel the urge to protect her. Maybe because she's Charlie's best friend. I've never had friendships with women. There's always an agenda behind it. What makes this even more confusing is that I've only known her for less than twenty-four hours. Yet, something about her makes me feel like I've known her my whole life.

"You don't have to be okay," I tell her. "I don't know your story, but if you need an ear, I'm right here. They won't let us out for hours."

She buries the side of her head into my shoulder, absently staring at the brick wall. "I haven't told Charlie the whole story. So please, don't say anything," she begs softly.

"I promise I won't."

"Only Lex knows."

"Lex?"

"He was the one who warned me about the whole situation."

It makes sense. Charlie's the type of person to get all up in your business. She's passionate and fights for her friends and family. She's always been that way. So, I'm not surprised at all that Kate had only told her half the story.

"The guy. He's one of my best friend's brother. We kind of met accidentally, and I was instantly attracted to him. Not sure why."

"Wait, does your best friend know?"

She shakes her head. "Eric is too self-absorbed to really notice a change. That, and he recently broke up with his boyfriend. He's been doing his own thing of late and keeping busy with work." She continues on, "So this guy, Dominic, he warned me from day one that he didn't do relationships, not even sexual ones. So, immediately, I jumped to the conclusion he was gay. It turned out, he owns a sex club and, well... I'll just leave it at that."

"You can't just leave it at that," I berate her. "What kind of sex club?"

"The kind that makes me uncomfortable. I understand couples exploring their sexuality and desires, but I thought... never mind."

It makes sense, I guess. Again, this is unfamiliar territory for me. I've been with plenty of women, multiple at one time. I understand how people can love each other or want to commit themselves to one person, but I know that isn't a life I want. It's challenging to put myself in her shoes when I've never wanted nor would want a woman to look at only me because then I'd have to reciprocate the feeling.

"Can I tell you something, Noah?"

"Yes," I say, kissing the top of her head to ease her pain.

"I'm embarrassed and ashamed of the things I

allowed myself to do just to please him. For him to notice me..." She pauses briefly. "I told you he didn't do sexual relationships, but he enjoyed watching me fuck other men. That's how he got off. Having me in his sex club, sprawled out on some bed, fucking some guy I'd never met, let alone spoken a word to. Two guys, at one point."

My brain stutters for a moment, the alcohol still invading my system and blurring my normally rational thoughts. I'm all for a good time. I've done plenty of dirty things, but never gotten off on watching a girl I somewhat liked fuck someone else. I want to rip this guy's head off. This unwanted anger begins to swirl within me. Suddenly, the whole pregnancy comes to mind.

"Kate, who do you think you were pregnant by?"

Bowing her head, ashamed of her actions, she mumbles, "I don't know. A stranger."

I pull her in tighter, giving her the time she needs to let out her emotions while kissing her hair.

"I've always been proud of who I am, what I've achieved. But this..." she waves her hands around, "... I'm disgusted with myself. Charlie thinks I only slept with him, not other men. Lex knew of Dominic's past. Warned me about what I'd be getting into. I didn't listen. I thought I could change him because when he was alone with me toward the end, he gave me all the attention in the world."

I state the fact, "You loved him. You wanted a relationship."

"I wouldn't use the word love. I'm harboring strong feelings. But don't worry, I know you have a rep for screwing women looking for a rebound, so thanks for tonight." She chuckles softly, breaking the serious conversation.

"Hey! How did you know that?"

"Charlie," she says loosely. "Apparently, your mom knows your dirty secret, too."

"My mom?" I let out a groan. "It's not dirty. Well, sometimes it is. But for the most part, it's just two people having sex."

"Okay, so settle the rumor I heard. Cabo last year. Boys' trip?"

"Boys' trip turned into fucking a bored divorcée," I admit with a smirk.

"After the plane ride over here?"

How in the world did she know? Charlie!

"Uh... the stewardess and the chick beside me?"

"Noah!" She laughs loudly, smacking my bicep.

"Erika initiated it to get back at her boyfriend. Ivana was just... a nympho." When the words leave my mouth, I realize how bad it makes me sound. Those women I fucked. They all had their baggage and a story to tell. What if they were just like Kate with feelings and emotions, but carefully covering them up to prove a point to themselves that they could have sex with someone and push it all aside if only for that one time?

Argh, my head begins to pound as the alcohol wears off. Too much relationship talk.

"So basically, you prowl for women who've just broken up with someone?"

"I don't prowl..." I cough. "I merely happen to be there at the right time."

83

"Like some sort of sad pussy raider." She falls into a fit of hysterics, clutching onto her stomach. "I'm surprised you're not wearing a T-shirt underneath that dress shirt that reads 'Mr. Rebound.'"

"Ha-ha," I respond sarcastically. "It's not as bad as it sounds. I've been pretty good in LA."

What a big fat lie. The women here are gorgeous. Kate is no exception.

"Uh-huh, like this morning?"

"I live at Charlie's, and it's not my fault I overheard your dilemma."

Her shoulders slump, relaxing her body as she continues to lean on me for support. "What's wrong with us?" she asks. "We're sitting in a jail cell, wet and covered in sand, laughing about how I almost got pregnant to a voyeuristic nympho, and how you're a rebound hunter who's a momma's boy."

It's funny. I don't know why. The two of us laugh continuously until we hear someone clear their throat. Charlie's standing on the other side of the cell, along with the police officer. She's dressed in her yoga pants and a T-shirt that reads, 'This is my mom shirt,' and fittingly, it's covered in something orange. I look down and notice her hand is blue. *How odd.* With her arms folded, the creases in her forehead stare back at me, along with her eyes, which make her look ready to strangle my neck. She hands the police officer an envelope. He removes the keys from his waistband and opens the door, allowing us to leave.

"Hey, cuz," I tread carefully. "Thanks for bailing me out."

"Hey, bestie," Kate repeats in a sweet tone, attempting to kiss Charlie's ass. "Thanks for bailing me out, too."

There's growling, louder than the sound of wolves, coming from Charlie. Lex is standing in the foyer, trying to keep a straight face. I want to laugh, but both Kate and I know better than to anger the beast even further.

Charlie refuses to comment, turning around until we scurry behind her and follow them outside the building and into the parking lot.

The car ride home is quiet, soft tunes playing through the speakers as Lex speeds along the freeway.

I lean forward, resting my chin on Charlie's seat to catch her attention. "So, you're not going to talk to us?"

She remains quiet, purposely moving her head toward the window.

"You can't avoid me forever," I say nicely.

"I asked you to do *one* thing," she says, livid, seething through her teeth.

"It's not entirely his fault," Kate jumps in. "It was my idea. You can blame me."

"You don't need to defend him, Kate. He's a big boy," Charlie argues back.

I turn to look at Kate, who's shrugging her shoulders at me. Aside from my mom, who is a relatively laid-back woman, I've never had to answer to anybody.

As much as I love Charlie, I can tell we're going to butt heads very soon, like in minutes.

"It's just so..." Charlie bellows, "... irresponsible! I'm not even going to ask about the nudity part. You were both drunk, swimming in the ocean. God knows what could've happened to both of you! Haven't you ever watched *Baywatch?* There are no lifeguards at night to save you. David Hasselhoff needs his sleep, you know."

Baywatch? What the hell is she going on about?

"It's not like you can talk," I argue back. "When you were fifteen, you got busted doing the same thing with that boy you always hung around with."

Her head snaps my way, eyes like daggers.

Shit.

Lex interrupts our conversation. "What boy?"

Kate mumbles under her breath, "Here we go. I can't believe you mentioned another guy."

"I don't know. Some boy she always hung around with who everyone thought was her boyfriend," I say out loud.

"I wasn't naked," Charlie disagrees, keeping her tone pleasant.

"According to the town gossip, you were."

"The town gossip is *your* mother!" she responds, this time in a huff.

"Well, maybe so. But here you are, quick to scold us for our 'irresponsible' behavior, yet you did the same thing. And much younger, I might add. You weren't even of legal age."

Lex grips onto the steering wheel tight, turning his head to question Charlie, ignoring both Kate and me. "So, you skinny-dipped with *what's his face,* yet in Cabo when I asked you, you got all prudish on me?"

"Oh my God," she shouts in frustration, throwing her hands in the air like a child. "First, I didn't skinny dip. I was wearing a bra and panties. Second, sitting in a

Mexican jail isn't on my bucket list. And Noah, you better believe I'm calling your mom."

"What?" I yell back. "Mom doesn't need to know. Leave her out of this."

Kate shushes everyone in the car, attempting to create a Zen environment. "Look, let's forget this night happened. We're all grownups here. Let's thank the Lord that nothing more happened... it could've been worse."

"How?" Charlie shoots back. The steam is shooting out of her ears. "Tell me how it could be worse than getting a phone call that your cousin and best friend are arrested for public nudity? Do you know you'll have to go to court? And I bet you expect me to represent both of you since I'm a lawyer."

"I'm not pregnant," Kate blurts out.

Charlie falls into silence. I thought Kate would throw me under the bus, but instead, she saves me and buries herself under Charlie's overbearing ways. The car pulls into the driveway, and as soon as it stops, I quickly get out and follow Lex's lead. Charlie's not shy about lecturing Kate.

"Are you fucking kidding me? You fucked him bareback, and do you even know how many women he's been with?"

I stand beside Lex as he removes his keys from his pocket. Unlike Charlie, he keeps his opinion to himself.

"Sounds like you guys had fun tonight."

"Too bad Charlie doesn't see it that way."

"Don't worry, I'll take care of her," he tells me, followed by a disturbing smirk.

"Oh man, that sounds dirty." I cringe. "Any chance I can sleep in Amelia's room? Her loud snoring is exactly what I could use tonight."

"Trust me, Noah, your cousin is headstrong. Don't be surprised if you find me on the couch because she's on a men-and-their-stupid-dicks rant."

"The Lakers played tonight. I'll join you in watching the rerun." I laugh, trying to forget this night has even happened.

And in the short distance ahead, I see Kate rolling her eyes at Charlie. *The mouth on my cousin.* She's going on and on about how irresponsible Kate is, and what was she thinking taking me out tonight. No wonder Charlie's a lawyer. Her ability to argue is why she's so damn successful. Plus, a huge pain in the fucking ass.

We leave them out on the porch while Lex grabs us drinks and a bag of Doritos. The neighbor, who had kindly dropped by to watch the girls while Charlie and Lex left, leaves with a quick goodbye.

I tell him I'll be back and head for the shower. I make it quick, not wanting to miss a second of the game yet desperate to wash away the sand and itchy feeling all over my body. I know at some point I'm going to have to tell my mom, I know I can't hide this forever. But for now, I need to unwind. And a repeat of the Lakers game is just what I need.

Charlie enters the room and sees both of us sitting in the recliners. She seems to have aged tonight. Her face is withdrawn with dark circles starting to shadow her eyes. "I'm calling it a night," she says, defeated.

"Yeah, you look tired," I say, watching the screen as

Lex yells something about the game above the television.

"Well, let's see... I got puke on me when Amelia projectile vomited dinner. After getting her in the bath, I discovered that she took the blueberries out of the fridge and left them on the table where Ava decided they would be better squashed into the carpet." She sighs, continuing on, "Then I get a call that my cousin and best friend are naked and having sex on the beach. To top it off, my bike, which you begged to borrow, is sitting in Malibu waiting to be collected."

"I'll collect your bike, but we weren't having sex," I answer in my defense.

"You know what?" She points at me. "I don't care anymore. Do whatever the hell you want to do, Noah. Men and their dicks..."

And just like Lex said, the dick rant begins.

CHAPTER 9

KATE

The afternoon before meeting Noah for drinks...

Stupid, irresponsible, reckless, idiotic—and the list goes on of names I could call myself right now.

I'd succumb to my own insecurities, texting Dominic even though there *is* nothing left to say. Well, at least, he has nothing left to say. The second I hit send, I instantly regret it, falling into a heap on my bathroom floor consumed by the realization of my actions. Not only did I text him back, I questioned his ability to pretend like there was nothing between us.

I have royally fucked up, unsure of how I even got to this point. The memory of a stranger fucking me on all fours while Dominic watched haunts me every which way I turn. But like a double-edged sword, that moment is followed by our own intimate rendezvous inside his office.

"Everything you are is everything I'm not

supposed to feel," he whispered.

His stare was vicious like an animal ready to attack its prey. My heart began to beat erratically, a mixture of anticipation and adrenaline all rolled into one. Every kiss, and every touch, burned in my memory like a trail of destruction. I allowed my inhibitions to unleash if only for that night, and now I'm reveling in the mess I created for myself.

Waiting for a response and one week late on my *period.*

"Should I order the grapefruit arugula salad or the Caprese salad?" Eric asks out loud, tapping his finger against his lip as he scours the menu.

Letting out a breath, I distract myself once again by reading the menu and not checking my cell for the hundredth time today.

"Why are you even entertaining the salad option when we both know you want the pork marinade fillets with fries on the side?" I tell him, placing the menu down.

The waiter appears at our table, waiting impatiently to take our order.

"I'll have the grilled swordfish, and he..." I say, gesturing to Eric, "... will have the pork marinade fillets with a side of fries."

"Is that all?" the waiter asks, almost rudely.

"The chicken steamed dumplings," Eric adds.

I raise my eyebrows. A moment ago, Eric perusing the salad menu, and now he's ordering dumplings? I'm too mentally drained even to argue this

91

knowing all too well he'll complain later when he hops on the scale at the gym.

"Anything else?" the waiter repeats.

"A personality? For you," Eric mumbles under his breath.

I force a smile. "That's all. Thank you."

The second he leaves, I kick Eric under the table, causing him to yelp.

"What? He deserved it."

"Perhaps, but I don't want to find his spit on our food."

Eric lets out an annoyed huff only to parade a grin moments later. "Okay, so how long are you here for? I need all the scoop."

"What scoop?" I flatten the napkin on my lap, keeping my expression simple. "I'm here for two weeks at this stage, working, and thanks for letting me crash at your place."

"C'mon, you never have to ask. Besides, no one else is there," his tone softens, the rare yet vulnerable side of Eric emerging.

"Hey," I say, placing my hand on top of his. "Have you spoken to Tristan?"

He shakes his head. "No, only stalk him on Insta."

"That's not the way to stay in each other's lives."

"Speaking of Insta." Eric's face lights up. "Noah is here. Saw his picture in the pool with the girls. Arm porn at its finest. I'm heading over tomorrow with the hopes to turn him gay."

My lips curve upward into a knowing grin. I'd only met Noah this morning, and he's every bit as gorgeous as the photographs Eric had sent me over the last few weeks. Not only is he sexy with a great dress sense, but there is also something comforting about being in his company. We laughed, we flirted—and tonight is exactly what I need to take my mind off things.

"He's quite... attractive."

"How long until you tell me what *really* happened in the car this morning?"

My mouth falls open in shock. It's almost impossible to hide anything from Eric. Yet the biggest secret of all, I managed to keep between Charlie, Lex, and myself. Charlie knows better than to say anything to Eric, given that he loathes his brother and isn't shy in expressing just that.

"How did you... Charlie." I resign.

Eric rests his elbows on the edge of the table, clasping his hands with desperation etched all over his perfectly manscaped face.

"So? C'mon, Kate. My life is nothing but social media stalking and living vicariously through my other single friends who, as of this moment, are only you."

Well, that's a depressing thought.

"Nothing happened. We flirted. He's sexy. We're going to have drinks tonight."

"And you're hoping to get a little something... something to wipe out the cobwebs growing in your banana basket?"

I shake my head at Eric, barely able to laugh at this moment. If only he knew the truth, the life his brother led, the deep dark secrets he holds from his family. And how somewhere over the last month, I'd fallen for someone who didn't feel the same.

As I stare into Eric's eyes, trying to think of a response, I'm unable to see any similarity between him and Dominic. They both have Caucasian and Asian genes, though their features differ so much aside from a slight similarity in their eye color.

The day I met Dominic was at his mother's sixtieth birthday. Eric dragged me to the event to be his plus one but soon abandoned me for a shrimp cocktail waiter who was related to Celine Dion. It wasn't even of close relation, more like third cousins or something ridiculous like that.

Left alone, I had no choice but to strike up conversations with strangers not realizing Dominic was Eric's brother. He was gorgeous and undeniably sexy with a muscular build underneath the tuxedo he wore. A simple thing such as his black-rimmed reading glasses enamored me. The more we spoke and realized we had similar connections in the business world, the more fascinated I became and attracted to him.

And perhaps everything about Dominic should've come with a warning.

I began taking steps toward a trap I never expected to fall into at the age of thirty, an age when I'm supposed to be wiser and knowledgeable when it comes to men.

The sad reality—I'm none the wiser.

No doubt, the stress of everything is only adding to my late period, but I refuse to think about it, training my brain to focus on anything but this even if I have to entertain Eric and his over-imaginative vision of Noah and me.

"Just drinks. That's it."

Eric purses his lips. "When it comes to Noah Mason, something tells me you'll be unable to resist."

***

Meeting Noah for drinks...

From the moment Noah joined me, we'd instantly hit it off. Sure, I came prepared with bottles of liquor and a desperate need to forget my life back in Manhattan existed. And yes, my body began its signs of warning me of an impending period but still nothing.

We laughed so hard until my lungs struggled for air, teased each other with sexual innuendo while playfully splashing around in the water. Noah couldn't resist trying to make a move, which perhaps is exactly what my ego needed at that moment. Broody men are so yesterday.

I suggested we take it back onshore, carelessly making decisions drunk on tequila. There's not much I remember besides the cool air against my skin, the cold sand beneath my feet, and the torches illuminating the area around us.

Oh, and I finally got my period.

Tonight was surreal, sharing it with a complete stranger. The last few years have forced me to alienate myself from the social scene. If and when I did mingle, it was for business, and with that came a different persona. I can't recall the last time I had laughed so hard.

Noah was so easy to be around, which is why I admitted what was going on with my life back home. He didn't judge me, and I mean, how could he have given we were both sitting inside a jail cell for acting on impulse.

Everything about tonight is beyond crazy yet, at the same, time perfect. Whether it was the liquor or the careless decision to swim in the Pacific Ocean or the company of a sexy man beside me, tonight was the wake-up call I needed.

Life doesn't need to revolve around work. I just need to find a way to balance it all. If Charlie can run her business, take care of two kids while pregnant, and have time for her friends, I surely can do this without the added responsibilities.

Back at Charlie and Lex's place, Noah disappeared along with Lex. She suggested I stay the night, and luckily for me, I have some spare clothes which I left behind the last time I stayed here. After the longest, hottest, and most relaxing shower ever, I make my way back to the kitchen where Charlie is sitting with two mugs filled to the brim with hot tea and what appears to be homemade cookies.

"Have you turned English?" I question while taking a seat and eyeing the tea.

Charlie sits across from me. "I'm not allowed to drink coffee, remember? One of the many joys of being pregnant."

I nod my head in silence, grabbing the cookie and breaking it in half. Tonight, I drank copious amounts of tequila. I haven't quite sobered up even though I drank three glasses of water and strong black coffee the cop gave us while waiting to be bailed out.

"Can you please walk me through what happened

tonight? This isn't you… I know you like to have fun but not law-breaking fun."

"I don't know how to explain it," I admit, wrapping my hands around the mug. "At first, we were fooling around, but Noah isn't like other guys, he just… I don't know."

"He is *exactly* like other guys," Charlie tells me. "That's why he's here. His dick got him in trouble back home."

"You don't understand."

"Okay, so you guys wanted to fuck on the beach or whatever," she mutters, covering her mouth with her mug. "But you're both feeding into each other's bad habits. Noah prowls on vulnerable women like you, and you're trying to sleep with another guy to prove a point."

I'm hurt by her words, though sadly, she's right. This isn't me. I don't sleep around to prove a point to anyone, yet why did I so easily fall into this pattern? This woman I've become is cheap, cowardly, and running toward the wrong things instead of trying to fix the broken pieces inside of me.

My temple begins to throb, the hangover imminent if I don't control what I do over the next hour before I fall asleep. I can't recall the last time I drank so much, but holding liquor well is in my gene pool. I grew up with a dad who could chug a whole keg of beer and still run a marathon the next morning. His brothers, my uncles, were the exact same.

As if Charlie could read my mind, she leaves the table, returning moments later with a bottle of water and Advil.

"Take two of these, finish all the water plus your tea and cookies."

"You're right," I mumble, popping the Advil's into my mouth and swallowing them with a large amount of water. "I shouldn't have tried to screw Noah. I partially blame Eric for the pressure."

"There's nothing to stop you from being friends. It might do the two of you good to have each other since he's single, and so are you. Just lay off the hard liquor... and stay out of jail."

Charlie places her hand on top of mine, letting out a yawn. I suggest she go to bed, knowing it has been a long night for her, and she agrees.

Placing her dishes in the sink, she says goodnight but stops just shy of the door.

"Just so you know, if you were pregnant, I'd have been there for you, no judgment," she says in a neutral tone. "If anyone understands what it's like to make poor decisions, it's me. But sometimes, those poor decisions lead you down the right path."

I smile back at Charlie, knowing everything she just said is true. Charlie has always been supportive, and I consider her family, not just a friend or the wife of my boss. When it comes to our relationship, she knows me better than I know myself at times.

Following in her footsteps, I turn off the lights and head toward the guest bedroom. I know Noah is staying at the other end of the house but decide to send him a quick text once I settle myself into bed.

Me: *Thank you for tonight. You are exactly*

what I needed at this moment.

I didn't expect him to respond given how late it is. Still holding onto my phone, I stare into the ceiling. Charlie is right. I've made poor decisions, and now is the time to make sensible ones. I texted Dominic three days ago demanding he give me a better answer than 'there's nothing left to say.' I'm done trying to force him to be someone or say something he can't be or cannot say.

The mixture of tequila and vodka still swirling inside of me gives me the confidence to re-evaluate my life before I spiral out of control to the point of no return. Ironic, since it's supposed to have the reverse effect.

My mother always taught me to count my blessings, not my troubles.

I'm not pregnant.

Blessing.

How easily I could've fucked up my life for good. The walk of shame is something I don't take lightly, and for now, to steer myself away from it, I shut my eyes to welcome sleep until my phone buzzes.

> **Noah:** *Ditto, Bonnie. Next time we should try to rob a bank, make our criminal record worthy of the news. Sleep well, Kate.*

A smile escapes my lips, shaking my head with a gentle laugh at his suggestion to imitate Bonnie and Clyde with their notorious crime spree.

I place my phone on charge beside me, welcoming sleep once again. Tomorrow is a new day, and I'll be damned to live another day being someone I'm not.

Onward and upward, or follow Eric's mantra—bad vibes don't go with my outfit.

For once, Eric sounds perfectly sane.

CHAPTER 10

NOAH

Charlie is far from forgiving the next morning, purposely waking up the household early, banging on pots and pans plus running the vacuum just to annoy me.

The girls enter my room several times, and I vow that one day I'll wake up early enough to beat them to the chase. Since I've been here, I've stopped going to the gym and running each morning, something I did almost every day back home.

I barely slept. The entire night I had recurring nightmares that a cast of crabs had invaded my pants and had bitten off my dick. I kept waking up in a cold sweat, checking to make sure everything was intact, only then to fall asleep and have the same nightmare.

After showering and changing into my suit pants and collared dress shirt, I follow my usual routine by styling my hair and applying aftershave. I don't feel like shaving today, allowing my five-o'clock shadow to remain on my face.

Tired and irritable, I make my way to the kitchen, my stomach growling in the process. Even with the copious amounts of drinking last night, I crave something deliciously oily. *I wonder what the chances are of Charlie frying me up some bacon.*

Kate's already at the table, fiddling with her cell. She stayed the night instead of crashing at her other friend's place. Lifting her gaze away from the screen, she spots me entering the room and mouths something about Charlie, which I can't quite understand. Ignoring her for just a moment, I grab the pot of coffee and pour myself a mug along with a piece of toast that sits on a plate beside the coffee maker. I'm a coffee addict at the best of times, but this morning, it tastes like fucking heaven.

A second later, my cell vibrates in my pocket. I remove it and read the text Kate just sent me.

Kate: *Beware the wrath of a woman who didn't get laid by her husband last night.*

Oh, c'mon. I don't need to know this shit. I shoot her an annoyed look, responding to her text immediately.

Me: *Fuck you very much.*

"I don't know what it is you guys are talking about, but know this... I'm tired," Charlie tells us with her back toward the table while making a sandwich, which she slides into a brown paper bag.

"Good morning, my loving cousin, you look very nice this morning." I smile, trying my best to get back into the good books with her.

"Cut the bullshit, Noah. I look like death. This pregnancy feels like I've got my period every goddamn day, so death is an understatement."

"See this… this right here is the kind of information I'm *not* interested in. It would explain why both of you are crabby. I've heard about girls being in sync, although you're pregnant but still…" I say with a mouthful of toast, unaware of the minefield I've just stepped into.

"Did you also hear that period pain is like a thousand knives being stabbed into your vagina?" Charlie adds, taking a seat beside me. "And that it's extremely awkward when your tampon fills up, and you're running to the toilet with what feels like a grenade between your legs?"

Kate does nothing to save me. Instead, she bows her head, trying to hold in her laughter, almost choking on the banana she's eating. Serves her right, though on close inspection, she appears to have an excellent gag reflex. Always handy to have.

Lex walks into the kitchen, pulling a small suitcase behind him. He told me last night he has to be in Colorado for three days. Also, he told me that he's glad I'm here so someone can help Charlie, not that I've been much help. Ava soiled her diaper the other day, and I almost threw up in my mouth trying to find Charlie while carrying her at an arm's length so she could change her.

"Good morning, everyone," he announces. "Good morning, my beautiful wife."

Kissing her on the cheek, she mumbles something

before sliding the cup of coffee across the table to him where he takes a seat. The girls are watching television, something about a little girl with a whiney voice that speaks in Spanish.

"What did I miss?" Lex asks, taking his cell out of his pocket.

"Everyone is shitty and tired. Aside from that, you're off to Colorado to meet the Mackenzie Group, right?"

"Yes. Did Margaret email you the presentation?" Lex questions Kate.

Kate scrolls through her cell, shaking her head in response.

"Honestly, Kate. These older assistants HR is hiring aren't as switched on as the younger ones," he chastises.

"Oh, really?" Charlie questions with a raised eyebrow. "Maybe you should find someone younger like Montana, perhaps? Maybe give her a call, see what she's up to."

You could cut Charlie's sarcasm with a knife. Lex puts his phone down and looks at Charlie oddly. I don't know what's going on or who Montana is, but I really want to slide out of my chair and hide under the table, pretending I don't exist. Charlie's one hell of a moody bitch.

"No comment?" she asks, waiting for Lex. "I didn't think so. Now, since we're all here, and we have approximately two minutes before *Dora the Explorer* finishes, we need to set some rules in this house."

"Like not talking about menstrual cycles?" I tell her.

Lex nods in agreement.

"No, like your personal life ruining your chance at success," she answers back.

"How does that affect this household?"

"It affects Lex," Charlie points out.

"Explain?"

"Lex's business can't afford to have single men like you with a reputation for running naked around LA. Haden may run the company, but ultimately, Lex owns shares."

"What I do in my personal life does not affect my work," I quip, quick to defend myself. "I take pride in my professionalism, Charlie. I work hard, and yes, I play hard. But that doesn't mean I mix business with pleasure."

"He's right, Charlotte, and if you knew what my executives got up to, you'd…" Lex trails off as he watches Kate dragging her finger across her throat, motioning him to stop right there.

"What are you talking about? Of course, it affects your business. A nice, well-rounded man in a steady relationship shows commitment."

"God, Charlie, what do you want me to do? Become a priest?" I complain.

"No. I think you need to start getting serious. You're twenty-eight, Noah. When Lex was twenty-eight, he owned several companies and was set for life," Charlie says.

Kate interrupts the conversation, "Yes, he did. But Charlie, Lex was no saint. Granted, he was miserable and missing you, but nevertheless, he was far from being a nice guy. He only got that far because he threw himself into his work to forget how much he hated life."

I could kiss Kate right now for having my back.

"Thank you, Kate. I'm trying to block out his manwhoreness and prove a point to Noah," Charlie adds with sarcasm.

"Hey." Lex winces. "Can we stop talking about me being a manwhore? I'm offended."

"Oh, please..." Charlie rolls her eyes, "... you loved it."

I'm done with the nagging, ready to pull out some lame excuse about an early meeting just to be able to leave the house.

"Noah, you need to settle down. You don't have forever to get married and start a family." Charlie isn't afraid to speak her mind. "You've had enough time being Mr. Rebound or whatever they call you. Now is the time to find your lady. No more messing around."

"My lady?" I laugh.

Lex joins in, shaking his head.

"You know what?" Kate adds. "Charlie has a point. You've screwed more women than most guys. I once read that twenty-eight is the age to start planning for the future. You don't want to be forty looking for a wife. You're only one step away from a lifetime prescription to Viagra."

"Forty?" I scowl. "C'mon. That's the new thirty. I'm not interested in a relationship."

"So, there's no one at all you see yourself settling down with? If you could have any woman in the world, who would you settle in a relationship with?" Kate asks, teasing me because she can see this topic is testing my patience.

Charlie waits in anticipation as Lex scrolls through his phone with a look of amusement on his face.

On top of the kitchen table sits a trashy entertainment magazine. On the front cover is Scarlett Winters, an actress who's heavily in the tabloids due to her Oscar-winning roles and sometimes controversial love life. I won't argue that she's the most stunning woman on this planet. Platinum blonde hair with hazel eyes covered in long, luscious black lashes. Her body is amazing. Implants, perhaps, but amazing curves. And her ass—to fucking die for. I mean, that booty would look fantastic sitting on my cock.

"Scarlett Winters," I say in one breath.

"The actress?" the three of them say at the same time.

I nod, blissfully looking at her face on the front cover.

"So, if the universe delivered Scarlett Winters to your doorstep, you'd settle down with her?" Kate asks.

"Uh-huh." As if that would ever happen. An A-list Hollywood star wanting a relationship with a non-celebrity. I could possibly fuck her. I know that much. But a relationship? I fucking wish. I imagine waking up next to her every morning. I'd be in fucking heaven, tapping that ass every fucking chance I got. I have a better chance of winning the Lotto or even pigs flying and landing on the moon.

"I don't blame you," Lex grins. "She's quite something."

"Well…" Charlie says, annoyed, "… if it gets her off the market, so my husband has no chance, I'm in."

"You're in what?" I ask, confused.

"Kate and I will get you a date with Scarlett Winters. It only takes one date. Sprinkle that Mason charm on her, and before you know it, we'll be hearing wedding bells.

I have the perfect plan already." Charlie smiles with satisfaction.

"Um, we will?" Kate narrows her eyes while frowning. "How?"

"Because we're women... that's how. Girl power, baby."

"C'mon... Scarlett Winters?" I repeat, followed by a huff. "This is ludicrous."

These women have no clue how to even contact her, let alone get me a date. *Just agree, there's no way these two could pull this off.* Soon, they'll forget about this stupid dare and carry on with their sad, pathetic lives.

"You need to shake on this, promise us that you'll settle down once and for all if you start dating Scarlett," Charlie tells me.

I extend my hand. "Deal. And do you know why I'm agreeing?"

Both of them shake their heads in unison.

"Because it'll never happen. Do you know how hard it is to get in contact with a celebrity? She has an army of people you'll need to get through. It's comical, this whole settle-down-Noah plan." I laugh at my own words.

"I like to prove people wrong," Charlie responds confidently. "It's what I do for a living. So, wait and see."

***

I wait and wait some more. Nothing, of course, happens.

The week was hectic in the office. I finally met all the team who will be reporting directly to me—basically a bunch of young kids who just finished college. Eager

108

young men and women ready to get their hands dirty to climb the corporate ladder. Haden has given me a ton of projects which will involve a few interstate trips. The hours are long, but Haden ensures we enjoy ourselves, taking our team out for lunch and challenging us boys on the court.

It's late Friday afternoon when Haden calls an impromptu meeting, with even his wife, Presley, attending.

"Sorry about the late meeting. I'll be away this weekend and won't have access to work emails," he tells everyone.

He confided in me earlier in the day that his mother was in town, so he took the opportunity to use her as a babysitter and organize a quick trip to Vegas with Presley. A much-needed dirty weekend since they barely spend time alone without their son.

"I won't have access to emails either," Presley adds.

The group snickers, both Haden and Presley breaking out into smiles like their hands are caught in the cookie jar.

"Yeah, yeah... I know what you're all thinking." Presley laughs. "So, we got some exciting news today. We've been approved to increase our budget, so we can expand our publishing services."

"That's great news," I acknowledge.

"It really is. While we've got excellent results in the fiction department, given our geographical presence, why not take advantage of what we have around us," she reveals.

"I'm not following you," Pete, one of our editors, says

out loud.

Haden takes the lead. "Hollywood. There's such a huge demand for celebrity autobiographies. Now, granted, it's a different process for establishing a book with an author. We need to utilize ghostwriters, and there will be a major push on marketing given the fan base of each celebrity we choose." Haden tells us more about the plan but cuts the meeting short due to time.

As everyone leaves the room, he asks me to stay back for a moment. "So, I had an interesting conversation with Lex the other day," Haden says.

"Oh, yeah, about what?"

"About how the first celebrity we'll try to contract is Scarlett Winters." He follows with an underlying smirk

I almost choke on my own saliva. "Scarlett Winters?"

"Yes," he replies. "According to *Forbes* magazine, she's the most in-demand actress in the world right now. Anything with her name attached means big bucks. I've already teed up an interview with her on Monday."

"Are you fuc—" I pull myself up. "Are you serious?"

Haden breaks out laughing, then follows with, "I'm serious. Presley will attend the interview with you since she manages the team of writers, but you'll need to put together a marketing plan to entice her. What platforms will be leveraged, how we can stay in line with her branding. And, plus, I understand Charlie has a keen interest in you meeting Scarlett Winters."

"Look, I don't mix my personal life with business."

"I don't care what you do in your personal life, Noah. Between you and Presley, deliver me an autobiography of Scarlett Winters, and Head of the West Coast

110

Marketing Division is yours."

"You can't be serious? West Coast Marketing. That's a huge step up."

Lex owns three publishing houses on the West Coast, including here, San Francisco, and Seattle. I know the business is doing exceptionally well financially, given the number of *New York Times* bestsellers they published last year. This would be a dream position for me—a major step in my career as long as I don't fuck it up. If Haden can run this branch successfully, then I can take on that position with my eyes fucking closed.

"Noah, it's all yours. And if you fuck her, just make sure your name isn't slewed across the tabloids," he warns. "She's sexy, but she also has paparazzi following her every move."

"I promise to keep the tabloids clean."

I shake his hand and wish him fun on his dirty weekend, curbing my excitement momentarily.

On Monday, I'll meet Scarlett Winters.

I don't care about Charlie and Kate's stupid idea. I'll do whatever the hell I want to do. If that's falling in love with Scarlett, then so be it.

Let cupid target both of us.

Karma is finally on team Noah.

CHAPTER
11

NOAH

The beat of my new Italian, tan leather shoes echoes against the shiny marble tiles. I've tapped into my feminine side, shopping all weekend with Charlie and Kate for a new outfit—a suit and shoes to wear today. It was eight hours of my life I'll *never* get back. Who would've thought that women could be so indecisive? I had labels I stuck to and stores I knew by name, making it easier when I needed something new. That was back home. Here, it's all about status.

Rodeo Drive—friend or foe?

The sales assistants fussed all over me, handing Kate and Charlie champagne while they sat on fancy chairs making me try on several suits. I knew the first one I tried on was *the one*. It was a navy suit that fit me perfectly with no need for alterations. Yet, they still managed to convince me to try several others, despite my reluctance.

By the end of our shopping trip, I vowed never to go

out with them again. Charlie obsessed over every minor detail. And Kate? She's *that* annoying friend who constantly has her head buried in her cell.

Both of them rambled on about how I should act, what I should say, and things not to do around Scarlett. It was like I'd never been around women before.

And while I sit here, waiting impatiently, their silly voices ring in my head.

"Make sure you shake her hand. It shows professionalism. Plus, women like to touch men's hands. It gives them an indication of how big their pecker is," Kate said.

"Maintain eye contact. Women love eyes. And use her name often, nothing sexier than some pleasant-name calling," Charlie added.

"Unbutton your shirt a little. A nice, tanned torso is a real eye-catcher," Kate continued. "And do you have reading glasses? Nothing like a studious man with a dirty side to him."

Inside my head, I'm groaning and telling both of them to shut the fuck up.

The reception area is all white—leather sofa, desk, walls. It could easily be considered boring if not for the giant black-and-white portraits of Scarlett hanging on every wall. Her pose and sexy smile draw you in. Her signature sultry red lips are deliciously inviting. All of a sudden, my nerves consume me. I find my foot tapping louder, and this lush sofa, when I shuffle my body, it makes this squeaky sound similar to a fart. The room, large as it is, only echoes the noise giving the illusion that I just can't hold things in.

Presley is sitting beside me, twisting a loose curl around her finger while reading some notes in her file. She pauses for a brief moment, adjusting her jacket, before closing her folder.

"So, how was Vegas?" I ask, making small talk.

"Fun. We got drunk, and I mean blind drunk. Haden almost lost our life savings on the blackjack table, but aside from that, a nice break from a very energetic toddler." She smiles.

"I can imagine. Charlie's daughters are little firecrackers. Nonstop, on the go all the time. I don't know how Charlie does it, especially without a nanny all the time."

"She's a lot like me. Nannies are great, but I didn't bring my child into the world to be raised by someone else. It's all a balancing act, juggling work and being a mom. And some days, everything just falls apart, and a nanny would be like a walking angel." She sighs, continuing, "We got home last night, and Masen, our son, wouldn't let go of Haden. We were so tired and desperate to crash, but he wanted our attention. Life doesn't stop just because we're exhausted."

She swipes through her cell and shows me a picture of her son crashed out in the middle of their bed. "This happens almost every night now. I try taking him to his own bed, but he wanders back in, and Haden just lets him sleep with us."

I don't want to say it but talk about killing the romance in the bedroom. If I ever have children, they

114

will never, ever, be allowed to sleep in our bed. I'd want my wife to myself every night. Yes, I'm that selfish.

Stop. *Now you are talking kids?* You're being brainwashed.

She continues to talk more about her son, how her sister and partner live not far away and help out whenever they can. She also talks fondly about Haden, despite their petty arguments in the office.

"Haden's great at running that office. He knows people, and he knows business," I compliment, impressed with his management skills.

"He's extremely intelligent, but trust me, first impressions aren't his strongest point. I couldn't stand him at first. In fact, he was such a jerk that I couldn't be in the same room as him."

I laugh. "But look at you now. Some things have a way of working out."

"They do," she happily agrees.

The receptionist, an older lady, is dressed very professionally in a white pantsuit as she busily types away at the keyboard, her fake acrylic nails tap at a fast pace.

"Mr. Mason, Mrs. Malone-Cooper?"

Standing at one of the doors is a woman, it's not Scarlett, although she bears some similarity. *The eyes, perhaps?* Or maybe, you've jerked off to the image of Scarlett's face way too often.

She waits patiently as we both stand and make our way toward her. She extends her hand, introducing herself as Ms. Bentley, and motions for us to enter the office.

115

The office is large with the back wall all glass looking out toward the hills. Unlike the rest of the office, this room has a splash of color, and funnily enough, there's no portrait of Scarlett on the walls.

"Thank you for seeing us, Ms. Bentley," Presley begins. "Not to be rude, I thought this meeting was with Miss Winters?"

"Unfortunately, Miss Winters had to reshoot a scene for her upcoming movie. Besides, all press and business go through me first. I'm her assistant."

How disappointing. I'd worked myself up for no reason.

Oh well, at least I can relax somewhat now. My body sinks into the chair, making it very comfortable. I'm quick to notice how really bland the office is. Although there's color, it's incredibly neat and tidy with not a single speck of dust on the glass table.

Ms. Bentley looks at her notebook, giving me a chance to gaze at her. Her jet-black hair is tied up in a tight bun, accentuating her cheekbones. She wears some makeup, making her face slightly flushed but in a smoldering way. She finishes reading the contract, her eyes focusing between Presley and me as she adjusts her red glasses so she can see us. The glasses are kind of quirky, something you rarely see.

There's something unique about her, and when I scan her face again, my attention focuses on her eyes. They're crystal blue—I mean, so blue you can't help but stare at them. I brush it off as contacts. We're in Hollywood, after all. On closer inspection, her tits look too perky. *Probably fake too.*

"When Mr. Cooper contacted me, he was very

insistent about how this autobiography would be a bestseller for Miss Winters," she tells us, switching her attention between Presley and me.

"Yes." I clear my throat. Pulling my laptop out, I click on the presentation, talking my way through what we project along with Presley's input. Presley has a way with words, talking Ms. Bentley through how best we can capture Scarlett's story in a positive manner. I, on the other hand, focus on the marketing side, tapping into Scarlett's already huge fan base and how we can double that.

"Thank you for this presentation. Miss Winters has expressed an interest in a project like this. However, she's a very busy woman. Most of the work and information you need will be collaborated by myself."

Huh, that's an odd situation. An autobiography on Scarlett Winters from the perspective of her assistant? I don't think it can work, and my dick is arguing, swearing profanities like a drunken sailor. This wasn't supposed to happen. I should be spending time with Scarlett, spreading my so-called charm, then getting her into bed.

"Not to be rude, but this autobiography is on Miss Winters. I'm not understanding how it'll work if you're giving us the information?" I question her with slight arrogance.

"Perhaps I'm not making myself clear." She pushes her glasses above the bridge of her nose, her deep blue eyes watching me with a harsh stare. It's rude to stare, so I break away, pretending to be interested in the view behind her.

"I've been Miss Winters's PA and publicist since she

first entered the business as an adult. You'll have contact with Miss Winters to ask her some personal questions, all with her prior consent. However, any general facts will go through me," she states.

She doesn't break a sweat, and just when I begin to talk, Presley's cell rings, distracting us both.

"I'm so sorry, I have to take this call." Presley leaves the room, closing the door behind her.

"We're keen to start this project. Mr. Cooper would like to see a first draft by the end of next month. It's a quick turnaround time, but he thinks this will make a great Christmas release," I add, trying to ensure she understands what kind of deadline we're working with.

"Of course," she responds, tapping her pen against the table, watching me with a curious gaze. She's making me uncomfortable, and I *never* get uncomfortable.

"Regarding Miss Winters, we need to meet with her. After all, this project is about *her*."

Ms. Bentley keeps her expression to no more than a faint, slight smile, continuing to watch me with a persistent gaze. "And what, may I ask, is *your* intention with Miss Winters?" she asks, her voice rigid.

God, this fucking woman is unbelievable! I understand her duty as an employee, but this is taking it too far.

"My intentions, Ms. Bentley, are purely professional." I bite hard, trying to control my need to give her my opinion on her rigid ass.

"I see, Mr. Mason." She breaks my gaze long enough to look at the computer screen and clicks her mouse before looking back my way. "Miss Winters will be in the desert shooting a movie over the next two weeks. There may be a few nights when she'll fly home. I could possibly organize something then. That is if you don't have any commitments after hours?" she asks with a stern and righteous tone.

I am committed to fucking Scarlett. Any which way possible.

"I'm all open," I say, not breaking her gaze, wanting to make her uncomfortable.

She tilts her head, and although I may have said that with a slightly seductive tone, Ms. Bentley seems to brush it off. *Argh, she looks like a prude, anyway.*

Presley is taking longer than expected, making the small talk between Ms. Bentley and me extremely awkward.

"Nice office you have here. Do you go on set with Miss Winters much?"

"No," she responds flatly.

"I see. It must be exciting, though, and a rewarding job. Miss Winters is deemed one of the most talented actresses of her generation," I try again.

"It is. And yes, she is."

Okay, this is like pulling teeth. Her shirt is buttoned up, no exposure of her ample tits which look nice and fake underneath the fabric. Her skirt is long, almost reaching her knees, not giving me any glimpse of her panties. The only thing that's turning me on are the very tall pumps she's wearing—a camel color that looks nice against her California tan. I have no idea how she walks in them, and when I lean my head to peer through the glass table, she's purposely pushed them as far back

119

under her chair as possible so I can see nothing.

Jesus, I might as well have walked into a nunnery.

Frigid, prude, probably still lives at home, possibly with several cats—such a waste. Stunning woman. She needs a real man to show her a good time unless she's batting for the same team.

My God, *yes! She likes pussy.* Such a waste, but it wouldn't stop me from jerking off to an image of her and some woman eating each other out.

The door opens, and Presley bustles through, apologizing for taking longer than anticipated. With Presley in the room, Ms. Bentley talks more animatedly about the project, even laughing on occasion.

Huh, I wonder why she was so stiff with me? Probably because she can sense how desperate your dick is to find her boss. Plus, she's not into dick, so she's awkward around attractive men like myself.

"Well, then, it was really nice to meet you, Ms. Bentley," Presley says, standing up.

"And you," she replies with a genuine smile.

Presley shakes her hand and moves around the chair. I follow her lead and extend my hand, making sharp eye contact with her.

"Thank you, Ms. Bentley, I look forward to working with both you and Miss Winters."

Ms. Bentley hesitates, unlike with Presley, and reluctantly extends her hand. I move in closer and shake it, holding on for a bit longer and never breaking her gaze. Just in case she does like men, and Kate's theory is true, I give her a good handshake so she knows what I'm sporting below.

She looks at me for a brief moment, breaking my stare and pulling away. "Likewise," she responds coldly.

Presley has left the room, and just when I'm about to walk out, Ms. Bentley calls my name. "Mr. Mason?"

I turn around, surprised to see her leaning against her table in a suggestive pose. That or my brain is desperate to conjure up that image.

"Please, call me Noah," I say.

"I'll be in touch, Noah." This time, she smiles softly, cocking her head to the side before walking around her table.

"Looking forward to it, Ms. Bentley."

I step out of the room to Presley who's waiting for me. That was odd, whatever that was. Talk about multiple personalities. Or, she's afraid of me.

It doesn't matter, anyway.

I'm *this* close to finally meeting Scarlett Winters.

CHAPTER
12

NOAH

"What was she like? Did she have the red lips on? Is she as tiny as the magazines depict her?"

Kate and Charlie are throwing a thousand questions at me, interrupting my meal. Charlie's an excellent cook. Tonight—chicken parmesan. It looks so delicious, the cheese melts to perfection on top of the breaded chicken. I take a bite, ignoring them for a moment, hoping Lex will save me from the interrogation.

"What about her face? Does it look like she's had a nose job? Because those before-they-were-famous pics floating around look nothing like what she is today," Eric says in one breath. "Word on the street is that she was sleeping with Beverly Hill's top plastic surgeons."

I lift my gaze to meet Eric's waiting stare. We met last week during one of his so-called impromptu visits, and after several warnings from both Charlie and Kate, he's exactly who they described him to be.

Lex shakes his head while enjoying his dinner. Throw

me a lifejacket, I beg him with pleading eyes. I attempt to sway the topic to something else, but every time I try, we wind up right back where we started.

Finally, after much deliberation, I tell them, "I haven't met her yet."

The girls look at each other confused, then focus their attention back on me. Eric is tapping his fingers on the tabletop with an annoying beat.

"What do you mean, you haven't met her? I thought that was today," Charlie expresses with disappointment.

"She was tied up with some movie shoot. We met her assistant instead."

"Argh, movie stars. So unpredictable," Eric complains.

"This is so exciting," Charlie squeals, changing her tune. "Can you imagine if you marry her? You'll be Mr. Winters. And imagine the guestlist at the wedding? It'll be like an episode of *Dynasty*."

"What the hell is *Dynasty*?" Both Eric and I say out loud.

"Never mind. Not a TV show from your generation. Something my mom used to watch," Charlie rambles on. "I could be related to Scarlett Winters. She could end up being my BFF, which would bring me closer to Leonardo DiCaprio because they star in that new movie together. It's like six degrees of separation."

"What exactly do you think will happen if you meet Leonardo DiCaprio?" Lex questions her, jealous, and clearly not impressed by her enthusiasm.

Charlie grins. "Two words for you, baby… Hall. Pass."

"So, what happens to me, your original BFF?" Eric

asks with a slight hurt expression.

"One problem at a time," Charlie huffs. "You're the OG. You'll never be replaced, so chill the hell out, drama queen."

Lex mumbles something which prompts a mini argument, and to stop the pettiness, I throw in my two cents.

"Listen, can you guys seriously lay off the marriage talk?" I warn them. "You're jumping the gun a little, don't you think? Plus, do we even know if she's single?"

"According to her *Glamorous Stars* interview, she's single. She just broke up with that guy, the one who was photographed naked in Cabo and hung like a horse," Charlie informs us, spreading her hands to measure the length. Thank God, the girls are busy playing in their toy room.

"Oh," Eric mouths, followed by a cheer. "Hung, like hung?"

"Hung," Charlie drags out with her eyes wide open.

Lex stops the conversation. "Will the two of you stop saying hung? I've completely lost my appetite."

I nod, agreeing with Lex. The image alone is disturbing. Is this what women really talk about? Again, the only woman I spend a lot of time with is my mom. If she spoke about hung horses, I think I'd send myself to a mental institution.

"Interesting," I voice curiously. "So, Scarlett just broke up with a hung horse, which means the next guy she's with will be somewhat of a rebound. I thought I was supposed to stop prowling for the broken-hearted?"

"This doesn't count. It's Scarlett Winters," Charlie

repeats. "This is where your experience will come in handy. Sure, she may be looking for a rebound, but why not turn that rebound into something more?"

How convenient for Charlie. It wasn't long ago she was all up in my business about my past, but now, she's encouraging me to fall back into my bad habits for the sake of finding true love. I feel like a pawn in their sick and twisted game.

"Uh, are you forgetting the deal?" Kate interrupts, lifting her head from her cell.

"No," I groan. "The deal is to find someone to settle down with. It doesn't have to involve marriage. De facto relationships are up fifteen percent in the last year."

Both Charlie and Kate stare back at me with confused faces.

"It's true," Lex intervenes, his eyes diverting from his cell.

Thanks. The lifejacket—five minutes too late.

"I don't even know where to begin with that." Charlie shakes her head. "Of all the facts you can retain in your head, it's the percentage increase in de facto relationships? Yet, when it comes to the car keys, you have no idea where you've placed them."

"That's because car keys have these tiny legs like a robot and move when you put them somewhere," Lex states seriously, shortly after breaking out into a silly smile.

"Do you see who I married?" Charlie says, laughing, grabbing his chin and bringing his face close to hers.

Ugh, honestly, these two are so in love it's sickening.

"Yes. A guy with a logical answer," I respond,

distracted by the beep of my cell. Opening the message, I see an unknown number sitting on the screen.

> **Unknown:** *I've got an opening tomorrow afternoon if you'd like to begin working on the marketing plan for Miss Winters. Regards, Morgan Bentley*

Morgan. Cute name. It's a very formal message, and with Charlie and Lex talking in the background, and Kate on her cell, as usual, I think of an appropriate way to respond. Eric is watching me like a hawk. It's quite bothersome, so I shift my glance back to the screen.

> **Me:** *I'll take your opening. Just name the place and time. Sincerely, Noah Mason*

After hitting send, I regret it and worry that it came off as unprofessional. I'm glad she finally has an opening. I just wonder if she can read between the lines. I'd love to see her opening. Fuck, you need to let this one go.

Jokes aside, I want to text her back and see if she has an affirmative date for when I'll meet Scarlett. I decide against it and check my emails instead. There's an email from Presley. She says that Ms. Bentley has contacted her for a meeting. The same meeting she just invited me to.

I scroll through the email, wondering why she chose to message me rather than include me in the email—odd behavior from the frigid lesbian. Morgan texts back moments later with a place and time. Bored with the uneventful text, I respond with a 'see you then' and tuck my cell back into my pocket.

"Okay, this is why it sucks having two males in the house," Charlie goes on.

I have no idea what they're talking about, having been engrossed in the boring exchange of conversation with Morgan Bentley.

"So, I was thinking of apartment hunting this week," I say casually when their conversation dies down to silence.

"Really? Are you sure?" Charlie asks, her expression concerned. "Don't you think it's too soon? Plus, there are so many bad neighborhoods in LA. I really think you should hold off."

"I have a spare room," Eric offers with a wide-spreading grin. "And a nudity clause. As in free feel to make yourself at home, clothes off."

Kate snickers, shaking her head while throwing a napkin at Eric.

"C'mon, guys. You know I think you're awesome, but I don't want to impose any longer."

"Impose is far from it," Lex reassures. "But if you need a pad to let off steam, I feel your pain, brother."

Charlie pinches Lex's arm, scolding him once again for encouraging my behavior. "Just hold off for a while. And if you really need a "letting-off-steam" pad..." she air quotes, "... I'm sure Lex can hook you up with a suite downtown."

"Okay, guys, I'll hold off for a bit. More time to have tea parties, right?" I joke.

She smiles, putting down the sippy cup in her hand,

and wraps her arms around my waist to hug me. "Except the next time we play tea parties, I promise it won't be air but tequila instead."

"Now you're talking," I laugh. "Desperate for a drink, much?"

Charlie nods her head, rubbing her stomach, which looks like it has gotten bigger overnight.

"You have no idea." She lets out a huge breath before composing herself. "So, what are you two up to tonight? Or should I brace myself again?"

"Hey!" Eric pouts. "Why wasn't I invited?"

"You're a cockblocker," I tell him with a smirk.

Kate covers her mouth while trying to hold in her laughter, knowing all too well that in the short time I've known Eric, it's way too easy to rile him up for amusement.

"I'm so offended." Eric places his hand on his chest, glancing toward his left to ignore us. "Plus, annoyed you're stealing my BFF."

"You said I was your BFF?" Charlie berates him.

"One drama queen at a time!" Eric yells before leaving the table and exiting the room.

I turn to face Kate, shrugging my shoulders. It's her last night on the West Coast before she takes the red-eye back to New York.

"I have something planned." Kate winks, yet I'm wary of her so-called 'plan' after our last incident.

"Does it involve nudity?"

Kate shakes her head. "No… we'll keep all clothes on."

"Does it involve drinking?"

This time, she nods her head. "Sure, something old-

128

fashioned, perhaps?"

"You're an impossible woman with your cryptic clues," I tell her, grabbing my wallet and phone. "Can I at least drive?"

Kate lets out an annoyed huff. "What's wrong with my driving?"

"I don't have a death wish..." I mutter beneath my breath. "Let's go."

Charlie calls our names as we both walk away. "Behave, or you're both grounded."

A laugh escapes Kate as she leans into me, "Did you hear what mommy said? Behave, naughty boy."

I knock her shoulder, making our way toward the garage where our argument continues on who will drive.

This time, I win.

CHAPTER
13

KATE

"How did you seriously not know John Cryer was in *Pretty in Pink?*"

Noah walks alongside me, ice cream cone in hand as he shrugs his shoulders. I question his choice of flavor— mint chocolate. He might as well have been eating toothpaste.

"The *Two and a Half Men* guy?"

"Yes, the *Two and a Half Men* guy," I repeat, walking beside him while indulging in my own delicious choice of butter pecan. If Americans do anything well, it's their ice cream. "He played Ducky."

"Is this like some rom-com movie?"

I stop mid-step, yanking him back to me, which almost causes his ice cream to topple over. Annoyed, he performs a balancing act before expressing an annoyed look.

"Just to be clear," I state, passionate about the subject we're discussing, "You're telling me you've *never* heard of the movie *Pretty in Pink*?"

Again, he shrugs his shoulders, oblivious to the serious nature our conversation had just turned. I'm mind blown while observing him. Watching him carry on like this isn't a big deal.

Sure, he's a guy, but *Pretty in Pink* is like a rite of passage into adulthood.

"The movie has the word 'pink' in it," he complains, furrowing his brows together. "*Die Hard* doesn't have the word 'pink' in it. Now, that's a great movie."

"Oh, Noah." I sigh, continuing to walk with my head shaking. "There's so much I need to teach you, young grasshopper."

We stroll along the boardwalk, welcoming the sea breeze. I'd only ever been to Santa Monica Pier once, and the experience was extremely enjoyable. It reminds me of a lot of Brighton Pier, a seaside amusement venue in East Sussex. My parents took us there as children, and along with that came great memories.

As we stroll along the pier, the sun begins to set, sinking into the Pacific Ocean, which surrounds us. The view is amazing, cathartic, and easing the stress building within me as the time ticks closer to going back to Manhattan.

Various shops line the pier, snack shacks to shops selling trinkets as well as souvenirs. We've already hit the old-fashioned soda shop, but nevertheless, I still enjoy looking at each store and seeing what they offer for sale.

A few local fishermen are hovering by the edge, toying with their yarn in hopes of scoring the catch of the day. They don't appear annoyed by the noise of the children running around or the screams echoing from the thrilling rides surrounding us.

We head toward the large Ferris wheel called the Pacific Wheel. Noah buys us two tickets, and then we stand in line behind two other patrons. It's been years since I last rode a Ferris wheel, the novelty of it all somewhat amusing in my head.

"Are you looking forward to going back home?" Noah asks before the attendant opens the carriage door to let us on.

We sit side by side as I lace my arm into his to block myself from the sea breeze knocking the carriage about. Holding onto him feels comfortable, and unlike other men I've been around, he never makes me feel uncomfortable when our bodies touch. Perhaps our misadventures that first night broke all tension between us. Though funnily enough, Noah and I never feel any tension—the two of us just gel.

I purse my lips, staring into the ocean and admiring the panoramic views as we begin to rise. "If that's what you want to call it."

"You don't like New York City?"

Letting out a sigh, I think about his question. Noah has this odd way of reading my mind before I've even said a word. In ways, he's much like Charlie. The two of them are very intuitive, or perhaps I'm just too comfortable around them, and my body language is readable.

"Home isn't Manhattan..."

"Then what?" he questions. "England?"

I shrug my shoulders, the void in my answer only raising more questions within my racing mind. What's wrong with being a nomad? Perhaps I don't need a home. My purpose in life can be to wander the earth alone. *Gee, can I sound any more pathetic and morbid?*

"Does it have to be a place?" I pose the question back to him. "What if you don't know where home is because it's not a physical destination?"

Noah nods with his distant stare. Like me, the ocean view becomes magnetic, almost as if with every crash of the waves onto the shoreline, a piece of us washes away.

"So, this guy, Dominic," Noah mentions the name with slight animosity. "If that's what you want to call him."

I laugh, knocking his shoulder trying to lighten my mood. "Do you think I faked a name? That's his real name."

"You're in love with him."

"I'm not..." I stammer, hating the words 'love' and 'Dominic' in the same sentence. "It's not love, okay? Yes, I feel something, but I'm not "in love" with him." I use air quotes to accentuate it.

Rather than speak, Noah nods his head knowingly, a habit of his when he either tries to think of something inappropriate to say or has nothing to say at all. I watch his profile, admiring his sharp jawline. He has the kind of face that stops you in your tracks—handsome and striking like an iconic movie star.

"So, help me out here. Connect the dots... you're not *in love* with him?" Noah asks, raising his brow while watching me. "But you've still got no response, and you're pining for him?"

"Pining for him?" I laugh again, his choice of word humorous. "Who are you? Danielle Steel?"

His eyes gleam as his chuckles softly, making him even more handsome.

"Look, I spent this week with a bunch of romance authors, so cut me some slack. I'm trying to understand this whole love thing."

Our carriage stops at the top of the Ferris wheel. The view is breathtaking, the California coastline stretching for miles in the distance. Beneath us, a ray of bright lights illuminates the pier as crowds of people stroll around. It's nothing like Manhattan. The open space allows me to breathe for just a moment to take it all in.

"This is beautiful," I murmur. "I feel so..."

"Content," Noah says, while I squeeze into his side tighter. "It's like a whole other world up here."

"It really is," I whisper, breathing in the fresh air. "So, are you telling me Noah Mason has never been *in love* before?"

With a slow and steady gait, his usual long pause is accompanied by him loosening his shoulders. "I'm not cut out to fall in love. I just want to have a good time."

Noah's honesty is very forthcoming, and what makes our friendship unique. In his presence, I feel my complete self without the lies I often tell to please everyone. Eric is great, but his immaturity at times, becomes too much for me. I crave a real man by my side, and not necessarily someone I need to fuck or marry.

Despite our closer relationship now, Lex will always be my mentor. I rely on him to educate me, teach me how to succeed. We have a professional relationship as well as a personal friendship that took years in the making. Even if Charlie wasn't in the picture, he isn't the type of guy I'd sit around the couch with and watch movies with an oversized tub of popcorn. However, in the boardroom, there's no one else I would rather be with.

Yet with Noah, there's this feeling of completeness between us. Like I've known him my whole life when, in fact, it's been two weeks.

"How do you know you're not cut out to fall in love if you've never been?"

"I guess you have a point," he agrees, his expression indifferent. "I can't say it's something I think about. As I said, I just live life on my terms."

I nod, agreeing with everything. Before Dominic, I lived life on my terms, and now I'm here in a cul-de-sac of regret.

"So question..." I pose, shuffling onto my side, so I'm facing him. "Why did you agree to the bet on settling down?"

Noah raises his eyebrows, the smug expression radiating superiority while he rests his arm on the back of the carriage.

"I don't like to lose."

I roll my eyes, smacking him on the chest lightly causing him to scowl.

"Charlie is so determined. She's like cupid reincarnated," I tell him, hoping he understands Charlie's passion to spread love in this world. "If she thinks she can get you to settle down, have babies so she'll have nieces or nephews, she'll make it happen."

"Cue the baby talk," Noah groans. "I'll keep the charade up, so she thinks I'm serious. But don't you dare tell her otherwise. Whose team are you on, anyway?"

I let out a long-winded sigh. "You're preaching to someone who thinks love is a giant fucked-up ball, and relationships are—"

"Unnecessary?"

"Trouble."

The Ferris wheel begins to move again until finally, our carriage is at ground level, and it's time for us to hop off.

We hit up the arcade, passing the time with some old favorites while we laugh over our competitive streaks. Noah doesn't treat me differently because I'm a woman, and his competitive streak only wants me to prove him wrong for once. We argue while lost in the world of Pac-Man, battled each other at pinball, and then, I challenged him to dance revolution. At first, he argued and said not a chance in hell, but with a much-needed push of calling him a loser, he relented and won the goddamn competition. The guy *can* dance.

"So, you can move. Big deal," I complain.

"You're such a sore loser," he gloats, jabbing my ribs with his finger. "Just when I thought you were unbreakable, I broke you."

Catching my breath, we leave the arcade and step back outside. I quickly check my phone, noting the time. With an early morning flight, it's almost time for me to leave if I want to catch any sleep.

"I should probably go," I tell Noah.

"Wow, I knew you were competitive, but now you're bailing on me because you lost?"

With a wide grin, unable to hide my true feelings, I push him toward the edge of the pier trying to spook him.

"Don't get so cocky. I'll be back, and your arse is my target."

"You think you're so fancy with your British *arse* talk," he mocks, throwing an accent to imitate me. "I expect you back here. I'll challenge you, but I'm pretty certain those legs of yours can't keep up with me."

"Hey," I shout, oblivious to the people surrounding us. "I'll have you know I work out a fair bit. Maybe it's your big mouth that distracts me with all your *smack* talk."

Noah snickers. "Oh yeah, that's it."

I lace my arm into his as we walk toward the end of the pier for one last look at the view. Even though I haven't spent a lot of time around beaches having lived on the mainland for most of my childhood and young adult life, something about the view of an ocean always conjures comforting ideas into my head. It's renewing my soul, my values, and standing here with Noah makes it all the more evident.

The past two weeks have been exactly what I needed. Charlie is right. Being surrounded by family and friends eliminates the loneliness which surrounds me in Manhattan. I've slowly found a piece of myself, learned not to take things so seriously, and somehow being with Noah restores my confidence.

I left New York City with uncertainty of who I was

anymore, but I'll be damned if I'll return the same woman.

Noah places his hands on my shoulders, relaxing me with the grin spread wide across his face. It's incredibly easy to see how women fall at his feet. The arrogant bastard is so damn good-looking. Yet deep inside, the comfort he gives me is more than I could've asked from someone who, to begin with, was supposed to be a hook-up.

"Why are you smiling like that?" I question, running my tongue along my teeth. "Do I have food stuck in my teeth? A bird shat on me? I knew those damn seagulls would get to me."

He shakes his head, pursing his lips. "You're going to be okay."

"Huh?"

"You're going to be okay," he repeats, keeping his gaze fixated on me. "You're going to go back, be the fierce boss you were born to be. And then, you're going to be okay. You don't need him, and you'll be just fine."

I stare into his eyes, searching for any sort of reasoning to his words. "How do you know?"

"Because I know."

Noah inches closer. Leaning down, he places a kiss on my forehead, lingering while reality begins to sink in. A simple gesture, one filled with nothing but pure belief, gives me the confidence I need to realign my head and heart once again. There's every reason why I should be okay and only one reason why I shouldn't.

The good outweighs the bad.

Pulling away, my shoulders finally relax as a wave of

calm steadies my anxious heart. With a weightless gaze, I reach up to graze my finger along his cheek in a friendly gesture.

"I better go. I'll text you tomorrow to complain about my flight and remind me to ask you how exactly do you hook up with a stewardess."

Noah dips his head, a smile creeping across before his eyes lift to meet mine once again. "A gentleman never tells."

I touch his hand one more time before turning around to head back toward the car. He mentions he will Uber home, so I can return the rental to the airport first thing tomorrow morning.

As my steps away from him begin creating distance, he calls my name one more time. I turn around, and still, where he stands leaning with his back against the ocean, he folds his arms with his signature smirk.

"Don't go falling in love on me. Remember the bro code? We don't do love."

I bow my head, unable to hide the smile gracing my face. "I'm kind of new to this bro code thing, but I promise not to fall head over heels for a guy."

Noah shakes his head, letting out a laugh. "Bye, Kate... you crazy bird."

"See," I nod, grinning back. "You're becoming a Brit already."

CHAPTER
14

NOAH

I think of a million ways to get out of meeting Morgan, none of which seem plausible.

I texted Kate a dozen times, each response back from her was to grow some man balls. The conversation then led to an uncomfortable discussion on man balls in which I warned her of my need to block her number if the conversation persists.

"You know, if you lived here, I wouldn't have this problem," I tell Kate after calling her, frustrated with her text responses.

"How on earth would that make a difference?"

"Well, for starters, Charlie wouldn't push the whole relationship bullshit if she thought I'd stay out of trouble. If you were here, I'd be busy with you."

Kate laughs through the receiver. "Gorgeous, if I were there, we'd get into *too* much trouble. We're good that way. Listen, I have to go. Now be a man and show her who has the balls." She hangs up the call abruptly, leaving me in a no better position than I was earlier.

Presley wants to get started with this project and has worked on some basic questions she wants to ask Morgan. Nothing too personal, just run-of-the-mill questions which will educate the reader on how Scarlett grew up to how she found herself in Hollywood. Presley makes mention of some of the more challenging questions she wants to ask Scarlett herself. Some of which are not public knowledge and will definitely be the focal point with the press. I'm not sure how she dug up the information, and I decide to let her handle the scandalous side.

The marketing interns are a great team. Haden is a strong recruiter and knows talent when he sees it. I spent the morning running through some less critical projects to clear the way for this more significant one, making sure everyone knows what their performance targets are and the deadlines for which they need to adhere.

A little after lunch, Haden walks into my office.

"Hey," he says casually.

I look up from my laptop. "What's up?"

"Bad news. Presley's come down with a stomach bug."

"Is she okay?" I ask with concern.

"She pretends to be." He laughs sincerely. "Our son caught it off some kid he was playing with, so now it's her turn. I'm probably next. Nothing worse than having to hold your wife's hair back while she projectile vomits in the car."

I cover my mouth in disgust. And the poor fella has a

sweet ride too.

"So, listen, I know you have that meeting this afternoon with Morgan. Presley is adamant we still move forward despite her not being there." He removes his cell from his pocket and taps away. A few seconds later, my email pings.

"These are the questions she wants to ask Morgan today. If you could ask them instead, that would ensure we don't fall behind."

My whole career has been in marketing and only that. This seems to be a little in left field and entirely out of my element. How should I ask the questions, and what type of answers am I looking for? Do I counter questions if I'm unsatisfied with a response? Jesus, I don't want to fuck up this important project.

"I know what you're thinking," Haden mentions before I speak. "You're not sure how to ask the questions in a way we can capture and translate it into words."

"You read my mind, boss."

"All you need to do is inform her you're recording the conversation. Simply ask the questions Presley has mapped out. I think you'll do great."

With the slight boost in my confidence, he leaves my office, and I quickly read Presley's notes before departing and driving to the meeting.

I arrive at the coffee shop early, not wanting to come across as unprofessional. And so, with plenty of time to spare, I open my laptop and answer some work emails. Right on time, I see Morgan walk through the door. Her stride is elegant with an air of confidence in her white dress which is shorter this time, and more noticeably, the plunging neckline shows off some very sexy cleavage. Her hair is loose but tied halfway up, and she's still wearing her signature red glasses.

She scans the table, looking around me. "Good afternoon, Noah."

"Morgan," I greet, standing up and courteously pulling her chair out.

"Thank you," she responds with a forced smile.

That smile irritates me. So unnatural and cold. Do I really bother her that much that she can't stand being in the same room as me? She appears almost repelled.

"I apologize for Presley's absence. She's quite unwell. However, I do have her notes, which I'd like to go through with you."

Morgan's expression changes to panic, her eyes looking everywhere but at mine. "She's not here?"

I shake my head, pursing my lips. "Just you and me. Is that a problem?" Posing the question and goading some sort of reaction from her, I wait patiently, tapping my fingers on the stark-white linen tablecloth.

Her eyes unwillingly watch the tap of each finger, and slowly, with a deep breath, she parts her lips and raises her eyes to meet mine. "Certainly not, Noah," she says with a reassuring smile. "Shall we begin?"

The waitress stands at our table, young and blonde with a playful smile that screams 'fuck me tonight.' Her uniform is a white tank and a short black skirt. Extremely short. I'm thinking of ways to get her number on the sly because I need to feel a woman's body against mine.

It's been forever since I've seen a pair of tits, let alone

hold them in my hands.

Except for Kate's, but we all know how that night ended.

"Can I please have an espresso and a glass of water?" Morgan orders, her head buried in the menu.

The waitress takes her order, then waits for me to answer, moving a little closer as she jiggles her small titties in front of her notepad. They're cute, but lack that mature bounce I've grown fond of over the years.

"I'll have the same."

"Nice order," the waitress says, striking up a conversation. "You don't sound like you're from around here?"

"I'm not, actually," I answer politely. "I moved here a few weeks ago."

"I hope you like California. I've been here my whole life. A true California girl." She giggles, creating more bouncy tits.

Fuck. Keep going, beautiful.

"I can tell." My smirk fades as Morgan clears her throat, prompting the waitress to leave.

She scurries away, and in the corner of my eye, I try to get a glimpse of her ass in that short skirt. It's perky but nothing special.

"Should I leave you alone with the waitress, or are we here to conduct business?" Morgan voices with a touch of malice.

"Just a friendly conversation," I insist. "Rule number one in marketing... opportunities can present themselves anywhere."

"Like between her breasts?" Morgan mutters,

keeping her lips tight and arms folded.

The evil witch has risen. I decide not to comment and begin asking the questions Presley gave me until Bouncy Tits comes back with our beverages. This time, not to rile the beast even further, I simply smile at the waitress and focus my attention again on the meeting.

The first stage of the book will focus on Scarlett's childhood and how that evolved into acting. It's public knowledge on the internet, but I was hoping to get some hidden facts that will interest the readers, an added bonus for the die-hard fans who think they know everything about her. I tell her, "I'll be recording the conversation."

But she's quick to shut down, stating, "I'd prefer this conversation not to be recorded."

Haden needs the information, and my memory isn't the greatest. Could this bitch be any more of a pain in the ass?

"Look, Morgan. These are Presley's questions. I'm just doing her job for the day. I'm really not understanding why it's such a problem."

"Because this is Hollywood. Anything you say can be held against you."

Her stare is fierce, penetrating with an ice-cold expression. The glass of water sits beside her espresso. She carefully has a drink, then returns her attention to me. "Fine, if you must. Perhaps you're not as multi-skilled as I pegged you to be."

Did she just put me down? I'm moments away from walking out.

Taking a deep breath and remembering how much I

need this job right now, I bite my tongue so damn hard I can taste the blood.

Breathe... one... two... three.

"So, let's start with childhood. Hard and fast facts to clear up any misinformation in the media." I press the record button. "Scarlett, real name Sarah Jo Winters, born the fifth of August 1990 in Littlerock, California."

"Correct," she states.

"Her father, Max Winters, was a farmer and mother, Marjorie Winters, formerly a housewife, passed away. Siblings... Violet Winters. Two years older."

"Uh-huh."

God. Did she suddenly climb back into that shell? I read the next lot of questions, hoping to gain more of an extended answer from her.

"Okay, so growing up, Scarlett has always aspired to be a star."

Her body gestures indicate she's bored with the questions. Granted, they're not about her, but her boss instead. I finish my water in one go, counting down the time until this is over.

"From the age of three, she entered beauty contests in every county. Her mother would save every penny, sometimes doing odd jobs for locals so she could spend it on her outfits."

"The American Dream, right?" I joke.

"To some."

"Sorry, go on."

"At the age of ten, a Hollywood producer happened to be driving through town and saw her at a local diner. She was singing and dancing for the patrons, and so he dubbed her the next Shirley Temple."

"Quite an image to live up to, don't you think?"

With a long pause, she puts the glass to her mouth and drinks some water, continuing her silence. How long do I have to fucking wait for an answer?

"She dreamed of being that. So, no, to answer your question, she aspired to something, and she followed her dream. Not many people get that chance, Noah."

Watching her closely, Morgan fidgets with the napkin sitting on the table. The way she says those words seems odd, but perhaps I'm reading too much into it. The espresso is running through my veins, making me extremely alert.

"She's determined," I say.

With a darker tone, she responds, "That, and luck. She happened to be there at the right time."

"Good karma." I laugh inside. How ironic, me believing in karma.

"Karma?" she repeats with a sinister laugh. "C'mon, Noah, you can't possibly believe in karma?"

She's waiting for me to respond, but I'm taken aback by her odd question. When Rose asked me this question, I laughed it off. Then ten minutes later, my world completely falls apart. I don't want to take that chance—Karma's watching me with a magnifying glass.

"A wise person once asked me if I believe in karma. I don't, but five minutes later, it bit me in the ass," I say honestly.

She arches her brows. "What do you mean?"

"We all have a past, don't we? Mine just collided with my future."

147

"I see," she says quietly. "So, shall we continue?"

I go back to my notes. Distracted by our change in subject, I move my cursor over the next point, trying to grasp some professionalism. Why the fuck does she make me feel so uncomfortable in my own skin?

"Her first three movies were blockbuster hits. What insight can you give me into that?"

"She loves acting. It distracted her from her mother passing away. Her sister gave up college to take over her career and made sure she stayed with the right people."

"I guess you hear these horror stories that come from being in Hollywood. How does she manage to stay grounded?"

"The right support networks."

Morgan talks about the team Scarlett works with, from her makeup artist to wardrobe assistant to her PR team and her newly created social media team. She has sixteen people working for her, not including her housekeeping staff and multiple chefs. I can't believe one person can have so many people surrounding them. It shows how in-demand she is, and why directors are throwing scripts at her left, right, and center.

"Is there anything you can share that perhaps isn't public knowledge?" I ask openly.

Keeping my gaze, she answers, "That's a question best directed at Miss Winters."

"Right, and that would be when?"

She shakes her head, keeping her smile at bay. "You're very keen to meet her, aren't you?"

"Well, it is the point, isn't it?" I question her back, annoyed by her uninteresting question.

She doesn't respond and avoids my persistent stare. I wait patiently, wondering what comeback she'll have to that.

"I'm going to make something clear, in case it isn't already. Can you please stop recording?" she demands.

I press stop, unsure why I'm following her request.

"Scarlett's relationships are well monitored by the tabloids. Despite some of the trash you may read, Scarlett's team tries extremely hard to protect her personal life," she informs me. "Now, given your display of... what's the word I'm looking for... *interest* in the waitress, I'd hate to think that your fascination in meeting Scarlett is anything but on a professional level."

My jaw is clenching, biting down to stop me from saying the words I want to say. The nerve of this woman! How dare she question my integrity based on some harmless flirting with a waitress. I can feel my blood boiling and the vein on my forehead ready to burst at any moment, creating an ugly display of the hostility between us.

"I'm many things, Ms. Bentley, but unprofessional isn't one of them. I work hard, and yes, I play hard," I insist with a bitter tone. With my anger contained, barely, I veer in the opposite direction. She's made me uncomfortable this entire meeting, and so now, I'll turn the fucking tables on her. I've done this over and over again. I'm good at reading women, and this bitch just needs a reality check.

"Tell me, Morgan, do you get much of a social life given the hectic schedule you have?"

Her body stiffens, taken aback by my forthcoming

question. "That's a personal question, don't you think?"

"Perhaps, it depends on your answer."

Without saying a word, she starts packing up, answering loosely, "Not much. I'm busy. I don't need a social life."

"Everyone needs a social life," I tell her, leaning slightly closer. "You'd be surprised how much fun you can have."

I watch her sit in awe of my comment, and the way her legs twitch as she crosses them under the table.

Wow, way to go. You got through to the prude's legs. Now what?

"I have fun, but perhaps my idea of fun is slightly different than yours."

"Really, you think?"

"I bet you," she says, leaning in closer to challenge me.

"I don't take bets lightly."

"Neither do I, Noah."

And there it happens again, that electric current that runs through my body every time she says my name. I don't know why, I don't know how, and every part of me knows I can't fuck her if I want to keep my job, and, of course, get to Scarlett.

Charlie will win.

Kate will call me a *wanker.*

But I have difficulty letting this one go. She ruffles my feathers in the most annoying way. I don't know what I've done for her to be so resentful.

"So, tomorrow night. Why don't we work over dinner and then have your type of fun afterward? I'm new to Cali, so I'm sure a local like yourself knows where all the fun places are," I suggest, calling her bluff.

The prude won't last two seconds with me in a social environment. She'll probably break out in hives and have to go straight home. I can see it now. She's not that tough.

"Tomorrow? Night?" She stops long and hard, thinking about my proposition. "There's a restaurant just off Sunset that's nice. Perhaps we can go for a walk afterward."

A walk is her idea of fun?

Already bored with the idea, I put on a fake smile. "Sounds great."

"I have to be somewhere at eight. Can we make it early, say five?"

"Of course. So tomorrow."

"Tomorrow," she repeats.

Her body, across the table, sits only an arm's length away. My hand itches to run my finger across her lips, and imagine what they would feel like wrapped around my cock. Fuck. Stop thinking about this! You just want what you can't have, and she's the most frustrating woman you've ever met. If her mouth was all over your cock, you'd shove it further down her throat just to see her eyes water. Maybe then, she'd loosen the grip on the giant pole she has that's stuck up her ass.

She looks at her watch, telling me she needs to leave. Argh, honestly. This whole meeting's a bust.

I can only imagine how boring her life must be.

All work, no play.

Then home to her litter of cats.

"The cats need feeding," I mumble beneath a breath.

151

With her purse and laptop in hand, she throws some bills on the table, moving her stare back to me. "I gather you have all the information you need for today?"

"Yes, Ms. Bentley," I respond in a formal tone.

Pushing her chair under the table, she leans forward close to me. The scent of her perfume lingers in the air, igniting my senses—her expression changes. And just when I think she'll say goodbye, her eyes become hard and hostile—a hint of fire raging inside them.

Leaning her right hand on the table, giving me the perfect glimpse of her cleavage, she watches my lips as they part with curiosity.

"Not cats, Noah, just one pussy. And yes, it does need feeding."

CHAPTER
15

NOAH

Morgan Bentley's words eat away at me. I don't know if it's her words, the insinuation, or the way she said them with such hatred. And then she goes and talks about her *pussy*. Given her unpredictable mood swings and personality shifts, I have no clue what it means. I think about asking Charlie, but mentioning the word pussy feels exceptionally awkward. Kate's busy with some merger deadline and isn't responding to my desperate texts to decode woman talk.

It's massively fucking with my head.

I'm not the type of man to dwell on things too much. And although I've spent the day in Morgan hell, I manage to get over it by distracting myself with a Lakers game.

Lex kindly offers to take me, and with his courtside seats, how can I say no. Throughout the game, I think about Benny and Tom. How much I miss being around them, and even though Lex is great to hang out with, the boys know exactly how to have fun. The perks of not being in a relationship—we did whatever, whenever.

As I lay in bed, my conscience gets the better of me. I send Benny a text again apologizing for what I'd done and that I had moved to LA. The stupid fella still has his read receipts on—something Tom would continuously nag him to switch off because then the women he was trying to avoid would know he read their messages.

He obviously reads mine, doesn't respond, and that's the end of that.

Every time I shut my eyes, my mind does this crazy thing, racing through different memories and different people, reminding me that life has become complicated, and somehow, I feel out of place in this world and in my own skin. I don't think in my entire life have I ever reflected back on my actions as much as I'm doing now.

And why? Because Benny and Tom never allowed it.

We didn't wallow in pity when things turned sour. Instead, we got drunk and flew to another country to party away our troubles. It worked every time. Unfortunately, now, I don't have that luxury. Not only are the guys not talking to me, but I also can't let Lex and Haden down. They work themselves to the bone, and I'm not a slacker.

Opening my eyes, I stare at the walls of the guest bedroom. Although it's dark, the white and navy striped wallpaper creates a shadow, capturing my attention for a moment. I miss my own apartment. I miss having the freedom to bring women back to my place. And mostly, I miss being five minutes away from my mom.

My cell lights up, reflecting off the dark wall, and sitting on my home screen is a text from a chick I slept with last year. I sit up in bed with a smile on my face. Zoey's a great gal, gorgeous, and extremely giving in the bedroom.

Zoey: *Hi. What have you been up to?*

I respond with a slight eagerness.

Me: *Hey there, stranger. Long time, no speak. I'm in LA now. About a five-hour drive from you if I'm not mistaken. So what's been happening in the world of Zoey Richards since we last left off? And BTW, where we last left off, would be a great place to pick right back up.*

Great line. I'm mentally patting myself on the back for that one. Like most of the women I wind up in bed with, Zoey had just broken up with her ex. She was going through a rough period, and our worlds happened to collide. The second time around was pure coincidence. I ran into her at this bar while visiting a friend, and she happened to be there. It was just what I needed. In fact, I wanted to hook up again, but her dumbass roommate seemed to always be in the way.

Zoey: *Nothing much. I moved closer to the beach. So you're in LA? With a girlfriend?*

I chuckle quietly at her comment.

Me: *C'mon Zoey, I don't settle down. Free if you are, gorgeous.*

I begin typing a dirty message, reminiscing about the time we fucked in her room and how, when she came, her body did this delightful shudder. Nothing like a walk down memory lane. But somewhere in the middle of my text, another one appears, and it's from Morgan. I quickly abandon my text to Zoey, opening the one from Morgan.

Morgan: *I can see a flaw in your marketing plan. Perhaps Noah Mason is not so perfect after all?*

The blood in my veins begins to boil. This woman has some sort of radar on me. She knows how to beat me down when I'm already feeling low. Quickly, I type back.

Me: *Not everyone can be perfect like you, Ms. Bentley.*

The bubble appears as I twitch my legs underneath the sheets impatiently, crossing my arms while I prepare myself for the wrath of her words.

Morgan: *Never said I was perfect, and trust me, I'm far from it. Send me another draft with your dates correct for my perusal tomorrow. Good night, Noah.*

Are you fucking kidding me? I'm meticulous with my work. And rarely do I get my dates wrong. I scramble out of bed to grab my laptop, powering it up as I wait for it to load and check my spreadsheet. In the meantime, Zoey sent me a long, drawn-out text about her being engaged or some shit. I skim through it quickly and respond with 'Good luck. Your roomie's a lucky guy,' leaving that conversation immediately.

When I scan through my spreadsheet, I can see that one date has a slight error in the calculation, but nothing that affects the project. Miss Stuck-Up-Multiple-Personalities-Bitch obviously has nothing else to do but torment me.

> **Me:** *Thank you for picking up that MINOR detail. Corrected, resentful, and I apologize for being the center of your attention tonight.*

I hit send, tapping my cell hard. That should shut her the fuck up. A few seconds later, she responds.

> **Morgan:** *What can I say, Noah, attention to detail is why I'm great at my job. And as for being the center of my attention tonight, you can only wish you were.*

What the fuck does that mean? I think about a witty response, but through my anger, nothing comes to mind. Instead, I toss and turn the whole night, barely getting any sleep.

***

The next morning, I wake at the crack of dawn, eager to get the day started. I begin by going for a run through the neighborhood, then follow with some weights in Lex's gym. It's nice to get back to a routine that feels natural. That, and I don't want to lose my muscle. One great thing about staying here—Charlie's cooking. She knows how to cook, and with every meal she serves, she makes sure I have seconds, worried that I'll starve to death.

I've never in my life been concerned about my weight, but the amount of pasta I ate last night will be a reason to avoid scales at all costs. And so, keeping up my fitness is paramount.

My need to burn off the excess energy is also from Morgan's text. God, she riles me up even when she isn't around. I'm this close to telling her where to shove her prissy attitude but focusing on the silver lining—she's my golden ticket to Scarlett Winters. Once Scarlett's mine, I'll demand she get rid of her and find someone with less attitude.

Geez, cocky bastard. Listen to yourself, *once Scarlett's mine.* It's comical to say the least.

Showered and changed, I head downstairs to be met with dead silence. It's a heavenly sound, one I've yet to experience in this household.

"Wait," I say as I walk into the kitchen, pausing, raising my hand to my ear. "Is that what I think it is?"

"What?" Charlie's scanning the room in confusion.

"Silence."

She laughs, switching on the pot of coffee, still dressed in her pajamas. "This happens only twice a day. Before six and after eight," she says with a peaceful expression. "You're up early and dressed. Quite fancy, actually. Someone special you're seeing today?"

"No one special," I tell her. "Just another meeting with Scarlett's assistant."

"That'll be your third meeting, right?"

I shrug my shoulders. "I guess so."

Charlie's inquiring mind continues to watch me quietly. I really want to tell her to stop because I know at any moment, she's going to put on her lawyer hat and ask a million questions. She has the inability to let something go.

"It's odd, don't you think, that you haven't met Scarlett yet?"

I delay my response, purposely bringing the cup of coffee to my mouth. "She's out of town. She's supposed to be back next week."

"But her *assistant* hasn't scheduled anything in?" she says the word 'assistant' like it's a false title.

"Her name's Morgan," I correct her. "And no, not yet. Like I said, she's out of town."

"Morgan, eh?" she repeats with a twisted smirk. "First-name basis?"

I roll my eyes at Charlie and let out a childish groan. Here we go again, Mrs. Meddler. Mrs. All-Up-In-Your-Business Charlie. Now would be the perfect time to air my frustrations with Morgan's behavior. But I know Charlie will read *way* more into this than what it is. And what is it? Nothing more than a prissy, stuck-up,

159

wannabe actress with a pole shoved so far up her ass, she can barely walk.

"I don't know what you're getting at," I respond in an extremely neutral tone. "I'm not attracted to her. Okay?"

"Okay." She grins, dropping the subject altogether. "So, next month Lex and I have this thing. What are the chances of you still babysitting the girls?"

"Chances are slim." I cringe, then immediately follow with a genuine smile. "Fine, why? I thought that the work thing was canceled."

"They switched the dates. It would be nice to get out for a few hours, have some adult time," she says innocently. "I love my girls. I really do. But sometimes, I think I'm going to go insane. They aren't the type of girls to sit in the corner and color. Actually, yes, but the walls not in the books. I'm a terrible mom, aren't I?"

I steal the bagel from her plate, and with a mouthful of cream cheese, I tell her, "I don't think it's supposed to be easy, Charlie. I think you're doing a great job. They're alive, aren't they?"

"Yes... I guess so." Her tone becomes serious. "It's because I work. Well, at least part-time. Maybe if I were a stay-at-home mom, it would be different."

"I don't think so," I disagree. "My mom worked two jobs since I was born. I turned out fine."

A laugh escapes her mouth, followed by another one until she's giggling uncontrollably. "Way to cheer me up. You did turn out fine."

I throw the rest of my bagel at her face, the cream cheese smacking her in the forehead. "You're a pain in my ass."

"That's what family's for. Like hemorrhoids, just lingering around your anus annoying the fuck out of you."

My throat closes in. The comparison turns me off the blueberry muffin, which a couple of minutes ago was teasing me relentlessly next to the bagel.

"Please don't ever say that again," I growl in disgust.

She smiles happily, standing up from the table. "I'm off to get ready for work. Behave yourself. I don't want a call that you're locked up again. And speaking of which, you owe me *big time* for that."

"Uh-huh." I motion for her to scurry on, and the second she leaves the kitchen, I let out a bothersome huff then yell back at her, "And don't you dare give the girls sugar that night."

***

All day, I can't stop thinking about tonight.

Part of me wants to make up some excuse because I just can't be bothered with her. And the other part of me—sadistic Noah—wants to meet with her, so I can push her buttons and irritate her just like she does me.

I bury myself in work for most of the day, and when there's an hour left, I get a text from her.

> **Morgan:** *I'm sorry, Mr. Mason, I won't be able to meet tonight. I will organize another time to complete this. Regards, Morgan Bentley*

What the fuck? I reread the message, making sure my eyes aren't playing tricks on me. *She bailed on me.* I've been reading the wrong signs, and why I care, I still have no idea. Fuck! Just as I'm about to send a text back when Karina, one of the girls in finance, taps on my door.

"Hey, Noah." She smiles.

Karina has been tailing me since day one. Cute, but young. Younger than I usually would entertain. Fresh out of college, young.

"Oh, hey, Karina," I respond with a forced smile.

"You look annoyed," she points out, motioning for the cell that sits in my hand.

"Just an unprofessional client."

"I know what you mean. Today, I spent an hour on the phone arguing about an invoice. The person on the other line had the audacity to tell me to go back to high school."

Ouch. Like I said, she's young.

"Is there something I can help you with?" I ask, tired and desperate to get out of here. Maybe Lex will be up for a drink tonight. I need male bonding time more than anything.

"Oh yeah, duh." She laughs, walking further into my office. "A bunch of us are heading to Melrose for a drink. Just wanted to see if you're free to come hang with us?"

I could fuck her. I mean, she's easy. Wearing that low-cut top and her tits jiggling and bouncing around everywhere. But much like my almost-dirty text to Zoey, this would be a way to vent my frustrations with Morgan. Buried in some other woman's pussy.

"How about I meet you guys down there?" I suggest.

"Sounds like a plan," she cheers. "Okay, so see you there, Noah."

She stumbles awkwardly out of the room, leaving me alone. I'm still annoyed as to why Morgan would flake on our meeting, and the more I think about it, the more riled I become. I take out my cell and dial Kate's number.

"Hey, what's up, my California bro?" she answers, way too cheerful.

"Would it be wrong to go to drinks and screw a twenty-two-year-old?"

"That depends. How did you meet her?"

"At work," I reply.

"Uh... hell to the no. Remember what Charlie said... don't shit where you eat."

"You're no fun," I complain. "And when Charlie said that, she was referring to you."

"Why the sudden urge to get your pants off?" she questions intuitively. "Besides, what's happening with Scarlett?"

"Absolutely nothing. I still haven't met her," I respond, defeated.

"Why? I've already bought a dress to wear to your wedding. It's low-cut with just the right amount of cleavage to attract the single men, but not so much that I outdo the bride and get called a slut."

I laugh through the receiver. "She's out of town, but her assistant—"

"Uh-oh," Kate interrupts. "Why do I sense something brewing on the horizon?"

"Nothing's brewing," I shut her down immediately. "It's so far from brewing that the seeds haven't even

163

been planted yet to be considered brewing material."

"Then, what's the problem?"

"The problem is that her assistant is weird. Plus, she keeps flaking on me, making my job difficult to do."

Kate laughs at some inside joke that I'm yet to be included in on. "Oh, why didn't I see this earlier? You want to shag her assistant."

"Shag?"

"Shag, get her panties off, tap that ass. As you American folk so kindly say."

"It's not like that, Kate. I just—"

"Can't stop thinking about her?" She fills my mouth with words. "It's a trap."

"A trap?"

"Yeah. That whole playing-hard-to-get thing. It does something to our brains, which makes us think we should chase them. It's just like in school. When someone likes you, they do all these nasty things to make you think they hate you when, in reality, they're just crushing on you."

Is Kate right? Have I been looking at this the wrong way? Can it be as simple as *she's crushing on me?* The idea—as lame as it sounds—isn't as farfetched as one may think. Having a female perspective is much more beneficial than what the boys would've told me. Their advice would have been to 'ditch the bitch, you don't need no ball breaker.'

But Kate is smart, and she knows women.

"What's happening with you?" I ask, switching subjects. "You being a good girl?"

"By a good girl, do you mean working long hours and

not getting laid *at all*?" she drags, seemingly frustrated by her predicament. "Then, yes, I'm a good girl."

"Well, offer stands if you need any help in the laid department." I snicker.

Kate chuckles through the receiver. "The last time we tried, you kind of let me down. Excuse the pun."

"One time," I almost yell. "It was freezing."

"Hey... the first-time impression is everything to a woman." There's a noise in the background as Kate covers her phone before raising her voice. "Do you think it's that hard for people to do their fucking job correctly?"

"You sound like Lex." I smile.

"I have to go. But listen, stay away from screwing any colleagues. Don't go breaking your own rule. And as for Morgan... be careful."

"Be careful? Of what?"

"Of falling in love," she finishes.

Kate receives some email about a deal falling through, so she panics and practically hangs up on me. Whatever I try to do, it just doesn't sit right with me. Kate just wants to spook me, talking about 'love' and shit. Love is *not* hating on a woman who's so far up her ass and wanting to avoid her at all costs.

But you also want to see her, dickhead. And you can't stop thinking about her.

I pack up my stuff and walk to the car. All I can manage to do is sit for a while, staring out of the window.

I've been with many women in my lifetime. And as infuriating as this is, I don't know what irritates me more—her canceling our meeting or the fact she's wasting my time, and I haven't even met Scarlett yet.

And there's Kate's theory.

In a rash move, I slam my hands on the steering wheel, letting out a frustrated roar. Overwhelmed by the complexity of her constant mood shifts, I decide I have to do what's best for me in this situation.

Confrontation.

I need to find her right now.

CHAPTER
16

NOAH

I turn on my GPS and drive myself to Scarlett's office. I have no idea what I'm going to say. Battling the traffic only elevates my already irritated mood. There's an endless sight of brake lights and equally frustrated commuters getting nowhere.

Inside my head, I'm talking like a madman, airing my frustrations with no conclusion. I almost miss the off-ramp, swerving the car last minute with a bunch of drivers releasing their horn at my reckless driving. Finally, I reach the office at the exact time we're supposed to meet at the restaurant.

Driving the car close to the building, I park behind another sedan and place my sunglasses on, disguising my face and lowering my body incognito.

In my entire life, I've never been on a stakeout, except for every Christmas up until I was ten where I'd wait for Santa to arrive who obviously turned out to be my mom.

For ten minutes, I wait until I see Morgan carrying a

bag and her laptop toward a white Mercedes. She doesn't see me and dawdles as if she has nowhere to be. She's dressed fancy today, wearing an ivory pencil dress that stops just below her knees. Around her waist is a skinny black belt, accentuating her attractive curves.

You're not thinking clearly. Stop looking at her damn clothes and focus on HER!

I open the door to my car, marching toward hers at a fast pace. "Morgan," I call out stupidly.

She turns around abruptly, shocked at the sight of me. Pursing her lips, and relaxing her worried frown only minutely, she stumbles out, "Wh... what are you doing here?"

"Why did you cancel our meeting?" My voice is filled with malice and judgment.

"I have another commitment that came up..." she says, uncertain, adjusting her posture and straightening her back. "You can't just turn up here. It's very unprofessional, Mr. Mason."

"Why are you calling me, Mr. Mason? I don't understand." I raise my voice above my normal level, unable to control the anger that's built up on the drive over here. I run my hands through my hair—something I do when I'm frustrated and want to shout at someone.

"I need to go." She opens the car door, and I grip her arm, perhaps a bit too tight. She stills, unwillingly making eye contact with me. Her chest rises and falls, and somewhere beneath this tough exterior of hers, I know my presence is doing something to her. I just need to find out what.

"Noah," she speaks, in a calmer, more pleasant tone. "I really need to be somewhere."

I let go and stand close, obstructing her way. A wave of insecurity almost knocks me down, the emotion crushing my ability to think straight.

"Is that somewhere another man?" I blurt out of nowhere.

What the fuck, Noah? Is that what this is? Jealousy?

Pausing and turning my way, her eyes plead with me to back off. "No, but please... I need to go. I'll text you tonight with somewhere we can meet up tomorrow. Scarlett's back, so maybe we can meet at her place," she says, defeated.

Scarlett. How easily I forgot about the real reason behind all of this.

And as if her personality has different buttons, her face contorts into a bitter stare. "Isn't that who you're after? Scarlett Winters... the movie star?"

My grip on her arm is tight.

Like she's my possession.

The wicked *bitch* from the West.

I release my grip, instantly pleasing her. With my hand free, I raise it to her chin and pull it closer to me, slowly twisting as I caress her face with merely one stroke. Behind all the animosity, her eyes reflect defeat. And with the gentle rise and fall of her chest beating against mine, my chest tightens, restricting my breathing. Yet, even without releasing a breath, the excitement streams through my veins and settles in the pit of my stomach.

This mad, sexual, tormented feeling pushes me to

inch my mouth closer to hers until I feel her warm breath against my lips. "I want a lot of things, Morgan. I'm selfish that way."

I could take her right now. Spread her legs and push her against the car. My mind is conjuring up a million different ways I can fuck her, yet I'm brutally interrupted when she shoves my chest in the opposite direction creating distance between us.

Clearing her throat while opening her car door, she blatantly says, "I'm not a giver, Noah. I like to receive. I'm selfish that way. Remember that for future reference."

Leaving me standing like a fool as the engine revs, I stare in disbelief as her words echo in my ear, watching her car drive away while I stand in the middle of the parking lot in sheer and utter confusion.

***

I'm not up for drinks with the work crew and instead settle for a tea party with the girls. The complete opposite of what I'd typically do back home. I'm beginning to grow fond of my nieces, despite my initial distaste for children.

Amelia decides we need to bring out the fancier china since I'm the honored guest.

"Uncle Noah," she says in a weird, overdone British accent. "Would you like some more tea?"

"Yes, please," I say, drinking the air with my pinkie raised.

"I'd prefer to be addressed as Your Highness."

Lex is sitting across from me, covering his mouth

with the little cup. Charlie hides her smile as well. At the same time, Ava announces the food is served.

"So, what are we eating today?" I ask, staring at the blank plate.

"We're eating a delicious sponge cake and caviar."

"Together?" I cringe.

"Yes, Sir Mason. We here at the Edwards' mansion enjoying only fine dining," Amelia states confidently.

We all pretend to eat our sponge cake and caviar until Ava loses interest and walks to the other side of the playroom to amuse herself with some puzzles.

"Miss Ava is a *horrid* guest," Amelia raises her voice.

"I've eaten all my food," I announce, at the same time Charlie and Lex follow.

"I can see," Amelia announces. "Oh, would you look at the time?" She looks at her wrist, vacant with no watch. "I believe Miss Ava and I have an appointment to attend."

"Would that appointment happen to be Alvin and the Chipmunks on TV?" Charlie questions them.

They both nod before disappearing into the living room. The three of us relax, finally indulging in adult conversation.

"So, tell me what happened. Did you get the info you needed?" Charlie is quick to jump to the subject of Morgan again.

"Not really. She's supposed to text me with details on meeting Scarlett tomorrow."

"Noah, what's going on? She's Scarlett's assistant, right? There's a contractual agreement in place to complete this book. I don't understand why she's delaying this."

Neither do I. I hate this uncertainty, and not only does it drive me insane, it questions my professionalism. I don't want Lex and Haden thinking I can't complete this project within the timeline given. But I hate to admit that emotions are running high—unfamiliar *emotions.*

"Charlie, I honestly don't know. I can't explain it. Morgan is... there's something, and I don't know. I'm trying to get to the bottom of this."

Lex shakes his head and comments, "Here it is in black and white. She's obviously attracted to you but is holding back because she's either in a relationship or she values her career too much. It has nothing to do with your professionalism. You're great at your job. Haden only has positive things to say about you. Don't let this cloud your vision and aspirations."

"Since when did you become Dr. Phil?" Charlie chuckles.

"Since I'm forced to listen to you and Kate ramble on and on about relationships. That, and you force me to watch *Sex and the City* in bed almost every night, and because this happens to me all the time," he says plainly.

Charlie reacts, "I hate to admit it, but it's true. The problem with you, my dear husband, is that you're extremely handsome and carry that dominant CEO persona. You're like the ultimate book boyfriend."

"Oh no, here we go with the book boyfriends," Lex complains.

"What's a book boyfriend?" I ask.

Lex humors me, cutting Charlie off before she answers. "It's a man, usually a male lead in a book. Quite often, he's handsome, tall with a muscular build, light eyes with a sharp jawline. He has a tattoo inked somewhere on his body. Most often, he's rich, CEO... oh, and who could forget... extremely hung."

I burst out laughing. Charlie shakes her head as she chuckles along with us.

"Oh, he's described it just right." She laughs. "Basically, your dream man but on paper."

I turn to Lex. "Should I even ask how you know this?"

"Both Charlotte and Presley enlightened me one evening. From a marketing and sales perspective, it makes sense. The books we published that had these strong male characters of that description are our bestsellers. Don't underestimate the power of a horny reader."

"Book boyfriends, huh? Interesting. So, you think she's attracted to me? I'm a book boyfriend?"

"Oh, c'mon, Noah. Don't play coy. The women fall at your goddamn feet, which is why you're in LA in the first place. I'm your cousin, so to me, you're gross on so many levels, but you do have that charm women seem to fall for."

"Gee, thanks for the confidence boost," I drag out.

"All right, not to come across wrong. You're young, handsome, and have a successful career. Women love that. The thing, though, is whether or not you're attracting the right woman," she informs me. "This Morgan doesn't seem to be the right one. You need to meet Scarlett. She's more your type. I even googled some facts." Pulling out her phone, she continues, "She's a Lakers fan, and so are you. She dates only guys who have brownish hair, that's you. So, see... match made in heaven."

I look at Charlie with a bleak face. Really? *How on earth is that a match made in heaven?* "I'm not a relationship guy. I like to fuck women, that's it. I don't crave anything else."

"We had a deal," Charlie reminds me.

"Yeah... yeah. I haven't forgotten. I can't guarantee you that Scarlett and I are the perfect match."

"Don't listen to Charlie," Lex interrupts. "If you want to fuck women, then go for it. Most men would love to be in your shoes."

Charlie turns to face Lex, and he's quick to shut her down. "Not me, so don't give me those devil eyes. I fought long and hard for you. You're stuck with me for life."

That seems to lift Charlie's mood. She leans her head against Lex, then plants a soft kiss on his lips.

"Hey," I warn. "No PDA at the tea party."

Up until this moment, I had no interest in anything but fucking women. But as I look around me and see the love in this house, the two beautiful daughters plus another on the way, and the bond that Lex and Charlie have, I question whether or not I want a life like this. Isn't this the end goal in life, to find someone to grow old with? I know I have plenty of time. My so-called *marriage clock* isn't ticking. Anyway, isn't it all about finding the right person?

I made a mental note to ask Kate these questions later during our midnight sessions via text.

And then her face pops into my head, Morgan

Bentley, the bane of my existence. The woman who left me alone with *that* thought planted in my head. *She loves to receive.*

My mind wanders to places like her sweet—albeit uptight—pussy. This woman clearly has a degree in being a *cock tease.*

Seconds later, I'm distracted by a vibration in my pocket. Pulling out my cell, I see a text from her.

Morgan: *Meeting tomorrow with Scarlett Winters. Address to follow.*

That's all the text says. Is this seriously all I get? It's so cold and impersonal coming from someone who's shared intimate details with me. *She's got a hungry pussy that loves to receive.* Her words, not mine.

My hand grips my cell tight, the urge to throw it across the room curbed only moments later. I don't even respond. Screw giving her the satisfaction of knowing she's on my fucking mind.

Focus on this—*you'll finally get to meet Scarlett.*

I should be breathing a sigh of relief.

I should be bouncing off the walls.

Tomorrow will finally be the day.

But what if after all this time, this isn't what I want?

CHAPTER
17

NOAH

It's just as I imagined—a modern, almost all-glass home sitting on top of the hill overlooking the Hollywood sign. It's your typical movie star palatial mansion. There's a large gate at the bottom of the hill with a security guard sitting beside it. After he does his check, he allows me to drive through up the steep driveway until I reach the main entrance. I park my car, admiring the huge fountain that sits proudly in front of the property.

The door is tall and made of frosted glass. I ring the doorbell to be greeted by the housekeeper. She ushers me into the sitting room, which opens onto a back patio that overlooks the pool. The infinity pool sparkles in the backyard, and everything about this home screams Scarlett Winters—movie star.

Morgan is nowhere in sight, and throughout her text messages, she made no reference as to whether or not she'd be here today. I didn't want to push her. This meeting is about Scarlett. I wait patiently in the sitting room, staring at the glass cabinets showcasing her awards. Rows and rows of statues and plaques rewarding her for her acting. Oscars, Golden Globes, the list goes on.

"Talented, isn't she?"

I turn around, and Morgan's standing at the entrance of the room. Her face appears distant—her eyes look worn out like she's been up all night. Wearing a sleek black dress, she places her keys on the glass table.

"It appears so," I acknowledge, moving my attention to Morgan.

"She should be here any minute," she says plainly, void of any emotion.

"About yesterday…" I trail off.

"I get it." Staring straight at me, without blinking, she says firmly, "You were frustrated. You want to meet Scarlett and move forward with the project."

"Yes… I mean, no. Morgan…" I move closer to her, her body now only an arm's length away, "… you never answered me about yesterday. Why did you cancel our meeting?"

"I said I had—"

There's chaos at the door, followed by the sharp click of heels on the marble floor tiles. Scarlett walks into the room, followed by three other women behind her, rushing around like nervous servants.

"Oh," she exclaims, following with a playful smile. "So, this is Mr. Mason." She walks to me, extending her hand as I shake it politely. She's everything in real life that she is in the movies—beautiful with flawless skin and perfectly styled platinum-blonde hair. Her signature lipstick has been applied to perfection, not a single smudge or mark out of place. With a body like hers, she manages to pull off a white jumpsuit with gold strappy heels, which make her look exactly like what she is—a movie star.

This should be a jaw-dropping moment for me, yet something isn't right. My jaw is perfectly holding up without any desire to move. My dick stirs slightly, but I wouldn't consider the stir anything of value to talk about.

"Very nice," she says without breaking eye contact. Her eyes are blue, however, washed out, almost gray looking. "Has Morgan been kind enough to show you around, offered you a drink?"

"Actually, she just arrived, but I'm fine, thank you." I smile politely.

"Well, then, please, let me give you the grand tour." She motions for the housekeeper. "Esmerelda, please bring drinks out to the back patio."

I follow her lead as she shows me around the house, giving me a tour of each room, what they represent in her life, along with the artwork. The house is even grander than it appears on the outside. Each room is large and filled with plenty of furniture and art pieces. She conveniently shows me her master suite, something I usually would've welcomed, especially when she eye-fucks me, describing how her bed was made by some new designer and has all these fancy things it can do.

I keep quiet and pretend not to notice the silver pole at the entrance of her closet. Okay, maybe there's been a pick up in the pace of the stirring. She must detect my curiosity too, and she's quick to mention she installed it after playing a stripper in a movie. I'm well aware of that movie. What fucking guy isn't? I have to admit, she's charming, and you can't help but fall in love with her, figuratively.

She ushers us to the patio where Morgan takes a seat beside her. She's awfully quiet, not saying much as Scarlett talks on and on about the movie she's shooting.

"You're very busy, Miss Winters. Hard to get a hold of," I tell her.

"Please, call me Scarlett," she responds with a twinkle in her eye. "Sadly, I'm not home as much as I'd like to be. Aside from the hectic filming schedule, there are constant photoshoots and endorsements. Now this book. I don't know where I'd be without Morgan in my life."

There's a sense of admiration in her voice for Morgan. Surprisingly to me, I had expected a diva-like movie star who bossed her assistant around and demanded unreasonable things.

"I'm sure you'll manage fine, Scarlett," Morgan adds with a thankful smile.

"Please, half the time I have no idea what day it is," she says with a slight chuckle. "I just roll with the punches. One minute you're hot, and the next minute you're not. That's the business we call show."

I laugh. "Something tells me you're always hot, Scarlett. At least, that's what the media seems to portray."

"I'd say don't believe everything you read. But sometimes, more often so, they're spot on. However, my love life seems to be their weakness. Any man I'm seen with is apparently in my bed as well," she tells me. "Did you hear the latest? I'm apparently carrying George Clooney's baby. It's the price I pay for eating that burrito during a work lunch. Bloated stomach and work colleague equal pregnant homewrecker."

"Scarlett, you know it's rubbish, and they will do anything to sell those magazines," Morgan scolds her.

I'm surprised at the tone Morgan takes with Scarlett, almost berating her, but equally surprised that Scarlett brushes it off like nothing.

"Please excuse, Vee. She's always at the press for spinning lies. Ever since I can remember, she's fought hard for me."

"That's a good friend you have by your side," I mention, then pause, confused. "You called her Vee? Is that some sort of nickname?"

Morgan stiffens, and Scarlett doesn't change her carefree sing-song attitude. "It's just a nickname. Her name is really Violet. Beautiful, isn't it? I don't know why you want people to call you by your middle name."

Violet. I've heard that name before—*Violet Winters.*

The wine I'd just swallowed lodges in my throat, creating a gurgling sound. "Your sister?"

Scarlett looks from me to Morgan, surprised by my forward comment. "You didn't tell him?"

"It wasn't something he needed to know," Morgan answers in a stiff tone.

What the fuck? Of course, I should've known that. All this time, she was hiding the fact she's Scarlett's sister? What else is she hiding? God, here I am pining for

Scarlett, looking like a goddamn fool. No wonder Morgan's defensive around me. She was—and still is—protecting her sister.

One of the ladies who had followed Scarlett in interrupts our conversation and requests Scarlett take a call, leaving Morgan and me alone. The second the patio door closes, my body turns like a possessed man, demanding answers.

"Why would you keep that a secret from me?" I grit, clenching my jaw to curb the growing anger inside me.

She brushes a speck of dust from her black dress, answering in an artic tone, "You didn't ask."

"I didn't ask because it never occurred to me," I almost yell.

"Well, it's not a big deal. So, I'm her sister."

I stand, frustrated. Again, running my hands through my hair like a crazed lunatic. "I don't get you, Morgan."

"Noah, you don't need to get me. You don't need to even think about me, okay?"

I move back to the table. "What's that supposed to mean?"

"I'm not stupid, Noah. You have a personal interest in Scarlett. When you're hot, you're hot, right?"

Our eyes battle as if we're playing some sick, twisted game, neither one of us backing down. Scarlett walks back in, apologizing for her absence. With lunch being served, our conversation is forced to the backburner. Yet, the whole time Scarlett speaks, my head is elsewhere trying to make sense of the argument that just occurred. Morgan seems unaffected, quietly listening to Scarlett speak, but maybe she isn't. The food

181

on her plate is barely touched, yet the glass of champagne is completely empty.

Throwing myself into work, I discuss with Scarlett how we expect to roll out the book launch and leverage her online platforms, a little bit about the party, and a few in-store signings which have been scheduled to precede the launch. She appears to be keen on what's presented, throwing in a few of her own ideas.

"What do you think?" she asks Morgan. "Will my schedule allow for it?"

"We can rearrange a few things," she says simply.

Esmerelda, the housekeeper, cleans up the table, which prompts Morgan to finish the meeting, citing she needs to be elsewhere. Scarlett stands. Giving her a quick hug and avoiding my eyes, Morgan says goodbye to me then leaves the area in a rush.

"I probably should be going, too," I suggest with the hope of catching Morgan outside. "I've got a ton of work to do back at the office."

"Here's my direct number." Scarlett hands me a piece of paper, placing it in my hand longingly. "Don't be afraid to call. I may be busy, but I've always got time for a handsome man like yourself."

I smile politely, shocked that I don't stick around to see how much time she really has. With my goodbyes said, I bolt outside to where Morgan's parked toward the side of the property. With the sun hiding behind the clouds, the side entrance is dark, covered in massive bushes that protect the property from the paparazzi.

I've learned my lesson, and this time, I don't call her name. Instead, I reach for her arm, willing her to stop so we can talk.

"Noah, don't," she begs, trying to wriggle her arm away from my grip.

I turn her around to face me, both hands latching onto her arms. Refusing to make eye contact, her gaze fixates on the ground.

"What's this, Morgan? All this lying. All these games," I demand answers, furious and momentarily I'm beyond words. "I don't do well with women treating me this way."

"What way, Noah? Should I just take my clothes off and beg for you to fuck me? Is that what you're used to?" She forces a laugh and waits for my reaction by tightening her lips.

I didn't expect that. She makes me sound like some goddamn pimp.

I let go of her arms angrily. "You don't know me. And you're awfully quick to judge me based on what? Huh?"

"Based on many things," she blurts out. "Noah, I don't know what it is about you, but I know your type. You like women. Many women. Not one woman. Or perhaps, my sister could sway you."

"I don't care about your sister," I half-lie.

"C'mon, Noah. I wasn't born yesterday. You've met her. You have her personal number, right? I need to leave." She presses the remote, unlocking the car.

"Morgan, stop." I slam the door shut, resting my hand on the glass to block her from entering. My body is almost touching the back of hers, so close, I can inhale her sweet scent. I close my eyes for only a moment, trying to get a grip on my body's reaction to hers, and just when I think I can control my desire to touch her, I lean in and whisper in her ear, "I think you want me. In fact, I can bet my life on it."

"Noah, you don't know what you're talking about..." she trails off.

"When you're hot, you're hot." And with the words escaping my mouth, I turn her around until our faces are an inch apart and slam my lips onto hers, kissing her deeply, pressing her body against the car. She tastes beautiful, and when my tongue finds hers and glides with ease, I hear her moan into my mouth, arousing my cock as I press hard against her.

She struggles out of my grip, pulling her head away as she takes a breath. "I can't do this. I want to... but I can't," she begs through a moan.

"You have no choice," I whisper back to her. "I want you. And when I want something, I'll do everything in my power till it's mine."

"Noah..."

"Don't fight me, no more games. Tomorrow, I get to meet the real Morgan Bentley," I demand, my hands still clutching her arms.

"Okay," she murmurs, her posture rising slightly as if the weight of the world has lifted off her shoulders.

I release my grip and run my finger along her bottom lip. Her innocent stare into my eyes does something unimaginable. Something I can't quite figure out. Something that makes my heart thump really loud, almost beating out of my chest.

I know this isn't a good sign.

Chasing Fate

My heart's in the game.
Fuck! It definitely isn't a good sign.

CHAPTER
18

NOAH

I let go of Morgan, allowing her to drive off and think about my words and even surprising myself. That kiss. Fuck. It left me craving more of her. It's times like this I need my own place, my own room, where I can jerk off for hours, or better yet, bring her back and fuck that beautiful body of hers.

The longer the drive back home, the longer it allows my thoughts to linger on her. What the fuck is it about her that does this to me? Confused by my feelings, I hit dial on my cell and call on Dr. Kate.

"Wazzup!" she barrels through the phone.

"Is every conversation going to start this way? You're like fifteen years too late," I complain.

"I'm slightly buzzed." Kate hiccups, followed by a small giggle. "We had this after-work function, and someone brought out the fancy champagne. That, and I got dragged into karaoke with Japanese businessmen."

"Choice of song?" I ask, amused.

""Livin' on a Prayer,"" she answers quickly. "You got to stick to the classics."

"So, I met Scarlett tonight—"

"Are you serious? What's she like? Is she as beautiful as she is in the movies? Are her tits real or fake?"

"Yeah, she is, and quite nice."

"Nice? Are you talking about Scarlett Winters or my nanna?"

"I kissed Morgan," I blurt out, unsure as to why.

"Oh..." Kate goes quiet for a long while. I assume her intoxicated state is delaying her thought process. "French kiss or Aussie kiss?"

"Excuse me? Aussie kiss? What the hell is that?"

"A few of the Australian guys that I bunked with when I was younger used to say it a lot. You know, a kiss down under," she hints playfully.

I let out a laugh about how I'd desperately love to give her an Aussie kiss. In fact, now it's all I can think about. Damn Kate.

"Thanks for the visual. I'm pretty much going to go home and jerk off to the thought of an Aussie kiss. Oh, wait..." I exaggerate, "... I can't because I'm staying in a zoo."

"Charlie would sooo kill you for saying that."

"Nope, she calls it a zoo, and she's the zoo master," I joke.

With a huge sigh, I release my frustrations. "I really need my own place."

"Sorry. Maybe you should surprise Morgan. Knock on her door with a bottle of champagne and a trench coat with nothing on underneath."

"Firstly, I don't know where she lives. Secondly, men don't do that. Free-balling isn't cool. At least free-balling under a trench coat." I turn the conversation to a more serious tone. "Kate, what does this mean? I've never wanted to *kiss* a woman, but she pissed me off. I was so angry at her for one… flaking on me, and two… the fact that she lied about being Scarlett's sister."

"She's Scarlett's sister," Kate exclaims. I nod, even though she can't see me. "Okay, so here it is. You won't like what I have to say. You only want her because she doesn't want you. You're always used to clicking your fingers and getting a woman in bed. She obviously has something going on, and you're not that person. Let it go, and if she wants you, she'll make it happen."

"I don't like that answer."

"Of course, you don't," she roars. "Because it means you won't get laid like right now. What about Scarlett?"

"She's a movie star, Kate."

"Uh-huh… just not Morgan, right?"

I let out a frustrated breath as Kate yells out loud, "You fucking wanker. Stop honking your horn, you goddamn knob."

Pulling back to save my eardrum, I wait until her rant is over. It goes on for another minute or so, her profanities never cease to amaze me.

"Anyway, how are you doing?" I ask in an effort to be a good friend. "Lex mentioned how busy you've been."

"Yes, apparently too busy to have any sort of life."

"Look on the bright side?"

"Uh-huh, what is it?"

"I'm not sure," I admit. "But isn't it better to be single

188

than in a fucked-up relationship?"

Kate laughs. "Bro, I need to get laid. This date I went on last night—"

"Wait," I stop mid-step. "You didn't tell me you were going on a date?"

I'm slightly annoyed she hadn't mentioned anything to me, especially since it had to do with another man, and she practically tells me everything else. We speak almost every night. Sometimes via phone, and other times just text. The past few nights have been on and off with Kate being tied up at work.

"Yes, I did, the Irishman."

"Um, no, you didn't."

"Are you sure?" she questions. "Well, I went on this date, and that's the end of that story."

"He couldn't have been that bad."

"His John belonged to a leprechaun."

"You fucked him?" I blurt out with an angered tone.

The shift in my mood catches me by surprise. I'm tired, frustrated—that's all. I should be happy Kate is enjoying her single life and not being dictated by careless emotions.

"No," she drags. "He kind of whipped it out, and well, I left."

I breathe a sigh of relief, unsure why this bothers me.

"I'm not even going to ask how a man kind of whips it out. I feel attacked as a man. But listen, you don't need anyone. Stop letting Charlie and the girls get to your head."

"You're right. I don't need a man. I've got you, my bitch boy."

I laugh through the receiver. "Call me that again, and you'll pay the price."

"Oh, I'm so afraid. You coming at me with your big muscles?" Kate chuckles. "Listen, I need to hop into an elevator. Be a good boy. Don't do anything I wouldn't do."

"Sound advice," I smile. "Bye, sexy."

"Yeah, yeah… bye, bitch boy."

***

I was having one of those dreams where you're falling, and just when you're about to hit the ground—certain you'll plummet to your death—you wake up, drenched in sweat. My lungs move up and down while I'm trying to catch my breath. I turn to my cell to view the time— it's three o'clock. Ugh. I toss and turn, willing my mind to go to sleep when all I can see is Morgan's face.

The way she almost melted into me when we kissed.

Fuck! Curb the damn hard-on.

I continue to lie wide awake until the sun rises with a huge boner which can't be tamed. Correction, I do nothing to tame it. My surroundings, given that it's Charlie and Lex's home, make me feel like I have Mom staying next door. Awkward and uncomfortable. I need to find some other way to release the enormous amount of tension building up inside of me.

The usual run and quick workout in the gym relieves it somewhat, that is until I hit the shower. Running the soap down my arm, back up onto my chest, then moving down, I have to think of something else to get my mind off it. And so, I start thinking about life back home. What the guys are up to, especially if Benny's continued his relationship with Rose. I haven't heard back from Mom after texting her a couple of times. Having her own small business as an interior decorator, she works strange and long hours.

"Uncle Noah!" There's a bang on the bathroom door, and then more banging. It continues like the beat of a drum.

I turn the water off and grab a towel, wrapping it around me. The longer I leave it, the more banging. I swear to God these damn kids.

"What is it, Amelia?" I ask with a groan.

"It's Ava, Uncle Noah!" More banging.

I finally give in, opening the door. "Yes, Ava."

"Good morning." Her smile, cute and cheeky, spreads across her face. She's still wearing her pink Minnie Mouse pajamas and matching slippers.

"Good morning, Ava." I smile softly.

She raises my cell toward my chest and says, "You got a text from your girlfriend."

I immediately take it from her. "Ava, we talked about this. You're not supposed to be playing with my phone."

Her lips quiver, but she manages to hold it in. "Sorry, Uncle Noah. I was playing your game. Lookie!" She points to the game. "I did all this extra stuff," she says excitedly.

"Did you use all my coins?" I ask in a mild panic.

"Uh-huh."

Don't freak out. It only took you like a year to save those coins and gems. This is clearly not a first-world

191

problem. People are dying in Africa. You can handle this. This stupid game is an unnecessary addiction.

I want to man cry massive ugly tears about the hours upon hours of wasted time collecting these coins, around the clock, on the hour.

"Let it go…" I chant.

"Uncle Noah, why are you singing the *Frozen* song?"

"Ava," I say as calmly as possible. "I need to get dressed."

She smiles and skips happily out of the room. Meanwhile, I'm having a nervous breakdown. Unable to shower without interruption, my phone continually being touched. Argh, I need some privacy! I can't prolong the apartment hunting. As soon as I have a spare moment this week, I'll find myself a realtor.

The text is from some woman I hooked up with last year. In the space of a year, she's managed to get married again and divorced. I ignore the text, not interested in conversing with someone who has that much emotional baggage.

Before getting changed, I sit on my bed and decide to text Morgan to see if she's free to meet up today. That, and to make sure she doesn't back out of our agreement.

> **Me:** *Good morning. Are you free today? I could do lunch at midday. Please say you're free. This morning has kicked my butt already.*

Great. Like that didn't come across as desperate and needy. She instantly responds, immediately lifting my mood.

Morgan: *Good morning to you too. How is it possible that your butt has been kicked before six am? An early riser, huh? Sure, I can do lunch. I'll text you the details when I'm in the office.*

It's just too easy like shooting fish in a barrel.

Me: *An early riser, yes. But, baby, trust me, it's worth waiting for.*

The bubble appears on the screen, and I rip off my towel while I wait for her message and put on my boxers.

Morgan: *I walked right into that one, didn't I? Okay, okay... Noah 1, Morgan 0. I'll see you at lunch, and make sure you behave. After all, we will be in public.*

I laugh out loud, surprised by her sense of humor. There's something refreshing about our confrontation yesterday. Finally, all secrets have been let out, and now I can get to know who she really is. My fingers type quickly, eager for her to respond.

Me: *A lot can go on under a table. But hey, I'll behave if that's what you want.*

I put the rest of my clothes on and head back to the bathroom to quickly finish styling my hair. When I make my way to the bed, my cell that sits on the duvet has a message from her.

Morgan: *I want a lot of things, Noah. But life doesn't always work out that way.*

She isn't saying anything untrue. Look at where life has taken me. If I had my way, the boys would have forgiven me, and life would've continued on back home. But here I am trying to figure out how easily our conversation has become so severe.

Midday can't have come quick enough. I meet her at the restaurant she suggests, early as usual. When it's well past noon, I think only one thing—she flaked on me again. Just when I'm about to text her, she bustles through the door in a state of panic.

"I'm so sorry!" She rushes. "My cell died as in decided to do this random update and won't turn on. Then this moron got a flat tire, causing this massive traffic jam. I'd have texted you but—"

I touch her arm. Her breathing slows down. Then her face relaxes as the two of us take a seat.

"It's okay," I say with a reassuring smile. "Just means we need wine."

"I can't drink. I've got a meeting in an hour with the execs at the studios," she tells me, but I can tell she's disappointed.

"Wait," I say in a serious tone. "You mean I can't get you drunk? How else will you go to bed with me, then?"

With her deep blue eyes dancing flirtatiously while watching me, she struggles to hide the grin behind the menu, which sits tall on the table. It's so cute and beautiful. And I just want to see her smile a million times over and kiss every inch of her soft pink lips until that

194

smile is replaced with a seductive moan.

"Not shy to say what it is you want, huh?" she answers with a smirk.

"I'm an early riser, remember?"

She openly laughs, shaking her head at me. The waitress working today walks over, requesting our order. The restaurant serves quality cuisine, and Morgan's not shy in ordering a decent-size meal.

I tell the waitress I'll have the same, uninterested in the food and more interested in Morgan. Noticeably, the waitress lingers long enough for me to glance up and see what she's waiting for. After a moment's awkwardness, she walks away.

Morgan takes a sip of water from her glass, placing it down and focusing her attention back to me. Unlike every other time, she maintains eye contact, staring at me with curiosity.

"So everywhere you go, is this what happens? Women just wanting some Noah love?"

"No," I tell her, leaning forward, resting my elbows on the edge of the table. "There's this one woman. Pain in the ass, really. She's all against the Noah love. Probably heads home to her litter of cats and sticks pins into a voodoo Noah doll."

She remains speechless, lifting the glass of water to her lips again, hiding a playful smile. "So, tell me…" she begins. "You're new to LA. Why here?"

This would be a perfect time to be honest about why I came here, but something warns me about being too forward at this very moment may not be such a good idea. And so, I hold back the information, keeping the topic to a bare minimum. "Let's see. Things back home got complicated. My cousin lives out here. I wanted a new start, and luckily her husband owns a very well-known publishing house and needs someone to run their marketing department here in LA."

She purses her lips, shaking her head. "Complicated? As in relationship complicated?"

Should I tell her now that I don't do relationships? No point giving false hope. And if I don't do relationships, what exactly am I trying to achieve here?

You want her in bed with you.

You want to boost your confidence because lately, you've been questioning everything in your life.

I switch to a darker tone, inviting her to drop the subject. "It involved a woman but no, not a relationship."

She seems to pick up on my tone, dropping her eyes to the table following with a chagrined expression. I immediately regret not being honest, apologizing by resting my hand on top of hers to rebuild the connection between us.

Lifting her eyes to meet mine, she gently slides her hand back and forces a smile. "So, you're staying with your cousin and her husband?" she asks, switching subjects.

"And two daughters. Hence... my early morning woes. Did you know that kids have the ability to invade your personal life in ways you can't imagine?"

"Yes." She follows with a chuckle. "It's crazy how the littlest things you take for granted are somewhat misplaced when you have kids."

"Have you spent much time around them?" I ask cautiously.

"Yes, just close family," she says plainly. "Scarlett can't stand them. But don't ever tell her I told you that."

I nod my head slowly, watching the way her eyes examine my face with pure intensity.

"I need my own place. Noah needs plenty of private time," I hint.

"I can only imagine," she says, eyes wide, her lips parting softly.

Those lips. I need to do something with them. The restaurant is busy, people seated all around us. Surely, stealing just one kiss wouldn't be inappropriate?

The waitress returns with our food, distracting me if only for a moment.

We talk a little bit about work.

She tells me how she got into the business and why she doesn't allow her relationship with Scarlett to go public. "I'm not interested in being in the spotlight. That's why I go by my middle name. The tabloids would be following me if they knew I was her sister."

"And Bentley?"

"Just a random name I chose." Taking a bite of her fish, she chews gently, swallowing then wiping her mouth daintily with the napkin. "How good is this fish?"

I agree, quick to remain on topic. "Why did Scarlett tell me you guys were sisters?"

"I don't know. She's quite fond of you..." she trails off.

"But I'm quite fond of you," I tell her.

She holds my gaze, eyes fixed and narrowing slightly as she tilts her head, exposing her neck. The skin, soft and edible, drives me insane. I want to taste every inch of her. With her hair out, she purposely flicks it to one side, giving me a full view of her heaving chest.

"Are you, Noah?" she murmurs, just above a whisper.

Leaning in, taking her hand in mine, I kiss the top of her knuckles before whispering, "Yes, Morgan. Ever since you informed me your pussy needs feeding."

There's silence, only the noise of the patrons around us filling our ears with sounds. I don't know how she'll take my forward behavior because, with her, I have no clue how to hold back.

She leans in further, her face close to mine, our lips inches apart. "You have no idea, Noah."

Morgan stirs something inside me like a tornado beginning its collision course. I grab my wallet quickly, taking out some bills and throwing them at the table, leaving our meals unfinished. I tell her to hold her stuff, practically pulling her out of the door. With her heels dragging across the concrete, she repeatedly asks where we're going. My car is conveniently parked at the back, in the corner. When we reach it, I pin her against the door and slam my lips onto hers, giving my hands free rein to explore her body.

I don't care who sees us. The adrenaline is pumping hard in my chest, unleashing some sort of wild beast desperate to escape. My hands move of their own accord, sliding up her thigh and cupping her ass. It's so firm and sits perfectly in my hands.

Fuck, the things I could do to this ass. Spread her cheeks nice and wide, slide my cock slowly into her asshole, feeling her tighten around me. See the pain mixed with pleasure etched on her face. Hear her call my name, desperate and out of control.

She wraps her arms around my neck, tight, holding onto me as if her life depends on it. Her scent is intoxicating and drives me to the brink of insanity.

Between her moans, I graze my lip against her lobe. "Let's go. Now."

"Where?" she manages between breaths.

"Anywhere," I plea with desperation. "Your place, your office, my car."

Pressing her lips with such force, her tongue flicks against mine, gently sucking while I push my body harder into hers. I can't control myself, and I know she's equally affected, purposely pressing her pussy against the tip of my cock.

"C'mon, please," I beg again. "I'll settle for you to suck me off."

She smiles into my mouth, reaching down and stroking my shaft on the outside of my pants. "I like to receive," she reminds me. "But for you… I could suck you off till you're screaming my name and blowing in my mouth."

The rush of blood runs straight to where she's stroking, causing me to buckle in agony, desperate to blow in her mouth right now. I latch onto her tighter. Then suddenly, without warning, the air rushes cold against my skin as she pulls away abruptly.

"I can't, not now," she pants.

I slide my hand back up her thigh, purposely grazing against her panties. They're drenched.

Holy fuck. Someone kill me, right now.

"Noah, please stop. I can't... I have to go," she pleads with desperation, forcing me off her body.

Pulling back, the loss of contact hits me like a wrecking ball. My breathing, uneven and shallow, slowly regulates, and with her beautiful body against my car, I take one more look at her.

I can see it in her eyes, the desire and reluctance to stop right now, but I also see something else, almost sadness. And then, it occurs to me, because I've seen this look before—it's the look of guilt. It explains her unusual behavior, her initial distaste toward men, and her hesitation with opening up to me.

Some fucker out there has broken her.

Every part of me knows I should walk away, but I want her in ways I've never imagined.

"I'll let you go," I tell her. "But only for now. Not forever."

She places her hands on my cheeks, bringing my face to hers as she places a soft kiss on my lips. "I'll make it up to you. In more ways than you can imagine." She turns around and begins to walk toward her car.

I concentrate on the way her hips sway from side to side, teasing me relentlessly. And just when I think I've controlled my breathing, she turns around, sending back a flirtatious wink while blowing a kiss.

She's fucking beautiful.

I may have calmed my cock, but my heart's equally racing beside it, desperate for first place.

CHAPTER
19

NOAH

So, this is what it feels like to be *crushing*.

Thinking about her all day and night.

When some song comes on the radio, it reminds me of her. And I don't enjoy romantic songs. Yet, for some twisted reason, I switch to radio stations with ballads on repeat. Somewhere in this universe, my balls have gone missing.

Every moment she has spare, I beg her to meet me. It's mainly lunches or a quick coffee, and at night, she's always tied down with Scarlett. Both our schedules are hectic, mine occupied with back-to-back meetings. And being that we're still in public, my hands have to remain to myself, much to my disappointment.

She made it clear during our second lunch that due to the tabloids, we need to appear civilized because the last thing Scarlett needs is her assistant caught having sex in a parking lot.

And so, since that day, I haven't touched her, not even a kiss.

Karma, delightfully, has pulled its reins and started a vendetta against me.

To point out and make myself sound completely undesirable, it's been four days since I mauled her in the parking lot.

On Thursday, she flew to San Francisco to meet with magazine officials who are doing a four-page spread on Scarlett. With the meeting running late, she missed her flight home and is forced to stay an extra night at the hotel.

It's late when she calls, her name appearing on my screen as I climb into bed.

"Are you calling me for phone sex? Because if you are, I charge a dollar a minute," I answer, grinning.

"Sounds cheap," she teases. "A man like yourself could surely fetch more."

"Maybe," I say, unable to hide my smile. "You're alone in a hotel, can't help yourself?"

"I already did that. Now I'm flicking through the movie channel trying to find something to watch."

I cough, a tickle caught in my throat as I almost choke on her words. How does she manage to do this to me all the time? A buzz distracts me. Pulling my cell away from my ear, I see a text from Kate.

> **Kate:** *My doorman asked me out on a date. I said I was seeing someone and now it's awkward every time I walk past him. HELP ME.*

Shaking my head with a smile, I bring my phone back to my ear to focus back on Morgan.

"You okay there, soldier? You seem to be at a loss for words." I can hear the smile in her voice—the little tease knows how to rile me up.

"You're one of two things right now... a terrible liar or the biggest cock tease ever to walk this earth."

"I guess you'll never know..."

I shake my head, laughing. "Then I suggest settling for the porn channel. If you're lying, that should get you started."

"R-rated porn is not my style," she says simply.

"R-rated porn is not your style?" I repeat. "What porn is your style, may I ask?"

"A lady never tells," she taunts. "But you, you're easy to peg. I'd say you're into anal. Fisting is probably too much for you."

This time, I'm rendered speechless. There's only one guy I know who isn't into anal—Tom. He tried it once, freaked out, which, in turn, made the girl freak out, and he never tried it again. As for the fisting, she's right. Something about having an arm up someone's pussy seems a bit too much. Keep it tight—that's my motto.

"It appears the cat got your tongue, Noah?"

My fucking dick is raging like fire, stiff as a board underneath my boxers. *What's this woman doing to me?* She's killing you, little by little.

"Your pussy needs my tongue," I harden my tone. "God, what are you doing to me?"

"The same thing you're doing to me, Noah Mason." It

follows with silence, shallow breaths echoing through the speaker.

"We need to change subjects. Any minute now, Ava will sleepwalk into my room," I tell her, reluctant to walk away from this subject.

Morgan laughs. "Is that your niece?"

"Uh-huh, and she's the behaved one."

I tell her about Charlie, what it was like growing up with her and how much of a great mother she is to the girls. It compels her to open up about her mom, and how, when she died, she felt the need to protect Scarlett from the nasty people in Hollywood. "Scarlett has a huge heart, and quite often, she'll only see the good in people. I just don't want anyone taking advantage of her. There are some horror stories about young women being taken advantage of. I can't have that happen to my sister."

"But what about you?" I ask her with good intentions. "Is this what you want to do?"

"I want the best for her. But no, I always wanted to be a Disney princess."

I burst out laughing—it's cute, and something Ava would say. "Don't most little girls?"

"Oh no," she says. "I wasn't young. I remember one year when I was eighteen, I think, Dad, Scarlett, and I went to Disneyland. I'd just been accepted into college, and Scarlett's career was starting to take off. Dad wasn't coping well with both of us almost leaving home, so he decided to take us there. We were watching the parade, and there was this kid sitting in a wheelchair. She'd have been maybe five. Her head was completely shaved, and her skin was ashen. She was awfully sick," she says sadly, then continues, "The princesses, all of them, stopped the float and climbed off, so they could all shake her hand. You should've seen her face. It's just stuck in my memory, you know. How happy they made her doing something so simple."

"Do you know what happened to the little girl?" I ask, hopeful.

"No," she mumbles. "I'd like to hope that wherever she is, she's in peace."

"So, you wanted to make people happy."

"Yes, I did. I wanted to spend every day smiling and making people happy."

"Then what happened?"

"I went to college. Got caught up with the wrong crowd, the wrong guys. I ended up in places I never knew how I got there... random beds. I was a mess. And so, one morning, I decided I didn't want to be a poor example for Scarlett. She looked up to me."

"And so, you went on to help her," I fill in the blanks.

"Yes." I can hear her smile through the phone.

"So, a princess, eh?"

She giggles softly. "Yeah, but a badass one who has tattoos hidden underneath my gown and a shotgun tucked into my garter for all the villains wanting to mess with me."

It's easy to picture it. She's so damn beautiful, she can make any costume look sexy.

We talk for hours about everything—both of us laughing at each other's stories. I love hearing her speak. She's led an interesting life, a little on the dangerous side when she was younger, but thankfully, she outgrew that rebellious attitude.

After our yawns become consistent, we both decide to end the call and catch up if possible tomorrow. She has an early flight to LA, and I'll be in meetings with clients for most of the day.

It never seems like time is on our side.

***

I'm tired the next day.

Our phone call ended somewhere around three o'clock when Ava decided to wake up and scream the house down. Charlie said she had a nightmare. Great. I still have to function as a human being.

I'm on my third coffee when Haden strolls into my office.

"Got a minute?" he asks.

"Sure," I tell him, prying my eyes away from my laptop. "What's up?"

"Presley's called an impromptu meeting. That woman will be the death of me."

I follow Haden's lead to the meeting room while he complains the whole way there about her overbearing ways. The editing team is already seated, and so I take a seat, leaving an empty spot beside me.

Karina, the young girl from finance walks into the room, immediately she spots the seat beside me. She walks over, sits down, which forces me to say hello.

"Hey, Karina."

"Hey, Noah." She grins, keeping her voice low. "It's a

shame you weren't able to make it out to drinks. You missed Larry, the editor, doing a round of shots, then proceeding to do his rendition of *Magic Mike*."

I contain my laughter, looking across the table at Larry, a scrawny geek with glasses who rivals *Harry Potter*. He knows he's embarrassed himself, retreating behind his notebook, pretending none of us know about his stripping abilities.

The boardroom begins to fill when Presley enters, carrying a large folder.

Karina leans in and whispers, "This book is costing us a fortune. John, head of finance, said we need a lot of sales to profit, and if—"

She doesn't finish her sentence as Presley calls for attention. I click on my screen, unlocking my program when I hear, "Miss Winters and Ms. Bentley will be attending this meeting."

My eyes dart to Presley.

Morgan's standing beside her.

Despite our late night, she looks gorgeous. Her shiny black hair is pulled into a sleek ponytail, accentuating her cheekbones. She's wearing a suit, navy with a very low button-up blouse. I can't peel my eyes away from her until the people in the room gasp when Scarlett walks in.

Scarlett introduces herself, leaving the entire room— aside from myself—star-struck. Like I said, she knows how to charm anyone. And between her dazzling smile and entertaining monologue, she's left the room speechless.

She's quick to notice me, grinning with her winning

smile. I can't for the life of me argue she's not stunning. But I don't know her. And my mind is preoccupied with the beautiful creature sitting alongside her.

"And so, let's begin with any concerns," Presley begins.

Morgan's gaze lingers on mine, a mischievous grin closely following.

John fires questions about budget restrictions, all of which Morgan takes in stride, answering on Scarlett's behalf. Haden, being a level-headed businessman, puts the kibosh on John's tirade.

I never understand how finance people can get their pants in such a twist.

Karina raises her hand, just like in school. "Miss Winters?" she asks nervously.

"Please, call me Scarlett," she corrects her gracefully.

"Scarlett," she repeats. "Given the worldwide success of your latest movies, plus the fact that you have the largest fan base on social media, I personally follow you everywhere. How do you think your fans will react to this book?"

Scarlett coyly brushes her curls to the side, her diamond ring almost blinding us. "I think they'll enjoy it. Understand that life isn't always what you see splashed all over the tabloids. That, and the fact I'm really just another human being like them."

Haden joins the conversation. "I have no doubt in my mind that it'll be a number one bestseller. We expect pre-orders to go up in a month. The cover shoot is happening at the end of this week, and we have the printers ready to go the end of next month for the first print run."

"That's a fast plan of action, Mr. Cooper," Presley questions, her eyes disagreeing with his projected timeline.

"Yes. I believe we discussed this last night," he seethes, trying his best to remain calm.

"Excuse my husband, everyone. His version of discussion is him talking and me biting my tongue," she says half-jokingly.

Everyone in the room laughs, and across the table, my eyes meet Morgan's, playfully flirting until Karina's hand touches my arm, and she leans in to whisper, "Do you think I can get Scarlett to follow me on social media?"

Jesus.

I whisper back in her ear, "If it's important to you, just ask."

My focus moves back to Morgan. Her smile has disappeared, and she's no longer eye-fucking me. Instead, she's looking at the opposite end of the table with a stern glare. With all the questions flying around the room, one is directed at me by Morgan herself. "The success of this project lies heavily with the marketing strategy. Since Mr. Mason is in charge of this project, perhaps we should direct any concerns to him." Her tone is condescending, drawing everyone's attention to me.

Did she seriously just do that?

I want to pull her over this desk, bend her over, and fuck the living daylights out of her to prove I can take charge. But, of course, I answer a million questions that have been thrown my way instead. When the firing line is almost over, I pick up my cell and type a quick text to her.

Me: *You are so going to pay for that.*

She picks up her cell, and thankfully, no one seems to notice as John begins to talk about profit margins. The corners of her lips rise, hiding the smile wanting to escape. She taps on the cell, then places it down and turns her attention to John, blatantly ignoring me. I give it a few moments, not wanting to draw attention to myself.

Morgan: *All talk, no action.*

This woman is driving me insane. I'm the one begging her to the bedroom, yet here she's saying I don't act quickly enough? That's it. I've had enough.

Me: *Keep sitting there with your pretty little smile. When I'm done with you, you'll be speechless. And for the record, I do enjoy anal.*

I wait patiently. She takes a sip from the glass of water sitting on the coaster in front of her. While opening her text, I watch on as she gulps, almost choking. Scarlett turns to face her, asking her if she's okay. She nods, her nostrils flaring like a raging bull.

The voices in my head are laughing, celebrating with a victory party.

Checkmate.

I focus my attention on Haden and talk about the deal we had agreed on with a major book retailer who wants Scarlett to do in-store signings. I also mention the contract with the largest eBook provider in the world, which will showcase the book on their featured page. The advertisement itself is costing us a fortune, but the return will be far greater. Haden, myself, and John discussed this yesterday, agreeing that we need to invest the money to see a return.

"If your time is dedicated entirely to this project, then perhaps, the deadline is achievable," Morgan implies.

"Ms. Bentley, I can assure you that Noah's focus is only on Scarlett Winters. We have a great marketing team which he now manages. The team has taken on the smaller projects to free up his time," Haden adds in my defense.

Great. That made me come off like a pussy. I want to add more to his point but decide to bite my tongue instead.

"I'm glad his focus is only on Miss Winters." Her smile fades, her eyes bitterly staring back at me.

"I'm a firm believer in multitasking. And no task will be left undone, Ms. Bentley."

The chatter between Scarlett and the editors continues on, and unwillingly, I zone out for a few moments, trying to understand why Morgan's mood has suddenly shifted to bitch.

Scarlett tells everyone she needs to leave because of a red-carpet event tonight, which she has to start preparing for. It seems to create a buzz amongst the ladies in the office and Larry, for some reason.

211

With the meeting wrapping up, Morgan picks up her cell and taps away, ignoring Scarlett as she says her goodbyes. Moments later, my cell vibrates.

Morgan: *Let's see how focused you really are.*

And following that text appears a picture. My cell almost tumbles out of my hands like hot coals. She's wearing only a white tank in the picture with her legs spread wide open on the bed, and her hand is conveniently positioned right where her pussy is.

I just got selfie-porned.

Fuck me.

I've received pictures from women before, but never one that left me drooling like a St. Bernard staring at a bowl of dog food. I have to control myself. The entire room will notice if I stand up with a boner.

Think of something disgusting.

Naked men in the steam room.

Naked men in the steam room, giving each other backrubs.

Okay, that does it.

Stop, now, for the love of God, thinking about naked men.

With everyone filing out of the meeting room, I stand up quickly, moving around the large meeting table until I'm by her side.

"I need to see you in my office… now," I demand quietly.

With her head bowed down, she hides the smirk planted on her face and then lifts her head back, ignoring my presence. "Haden, it's nice to finally meet you." She shakes his hand politely. "Presley, are you still free to meet with Scarlett tomorrow afternoon? It'll have to be on set. She has about two hours to spare before they head out to the desert to do the night shoot."

"I've got it scheduled in. Thanks so much for your help, Morgan." Presley smiles in return.

My presence, along with Morgan's sudden shyness, creates an awkward tension in the room. Haden and Presley watch both of us curiously.

"Well, I must head off. I've got a meeting across town this afternoon. Mr. Mason, did you need to discuss something?"

I force a smile, nodding my head as I walk toward my office, and she follows me. Closing the door behind her, I curse the glass walls that give everyone a view directly into my office. Sitting at my desk, I ask her to take a seat. She sits in front of me, purposely adjusting her collar giving me a bird's eye view of her tits. Fuck me dead. Just act professional, remember the glass windows and the fact that everyone can see into the office.

I quietly observe her, my pen dangling off my lip as she gazes at me with such innocence as if she never sent me any picture at all.

"I meant what I said. You're going to pay for what you did to me in there."

She leans forward, sliding her cell in front of me. "Such a shame about the glass walls," she says, looking back. "I was going to apologize in person, but we can't have everyone knowing, now can we?"

My eyes are entirely fixated on her tits, the lace

barely covering her nipple. I tighten my thighs, trying to control my dick exploding in my pants.

"So, maybe this will help ease the situation." She presses play on her cell, and my eyes are glued to the screen. Her hands are sliding down her thigh, across her black panties. Her back arches, and without any delay, she slides them inside her panties, rubbing her clit.

I have officially died and gone to heaven.

My pen has teeth marks where I've unknowingly bitten down, controlling my thirst to have her right here on my desk. She pulls the pen away from my mouth, leaning back against the chair and placing it in hers, biting down exactly where my mouth was.

"How hard is it for you to get out of that meeting this afternoon?" I say roughly. "I could pretty much fuck you all afternoon and night."

"Apparently, you can multitask," she reminds me with a sly grin. "I have to go."

I stand quickly. "You can't go," I complain like a spoiled child. "It's fierce to leave a man this hard, not to mention unprofessional."

"Oh," she drags out with a pout. "Poor baby. I'm sure we can sort something out later."

"I'm serious, Morgan. You can't keep doing this to me. It's unfair."

Her expression changes, sympathizing with my predicament, and just when she's about to talk, my office phone rings. "Excuse me for just one minute," I ask, pressing the speaker.

"Noah Mason," I answer.

"Oh my God! You're alive!" Kate barrels down the

phone. "You didn't text me back last night, and it was even worse this morning. Hello, I need you!"

I pick up the receiver. "Yes, I'm alive, but kind of busy right now."

"Workaholic," Kate says, annoyed. "So, listen, I'm flying to LA for work in a couple of days. There's a work event, and you're going to be my plus one. I can't be a loner. How else will I pick up?"

"Sure, just text me the details. Listen, I have to go. I'll see you then."

"Oh, you're a boring old sod," she complains, then hangs up the phone.

Morgan is standing, watching me. "Who was that?"

"Just a friend."

"A friend? It sounded like a woman."

Her tone catches me off guard. "What's wrong with having a woman for a friend?"

"Because Noah Mason doesn't come across as a guy who has women friends. Not unless, of course, there's a hidden agenda."

"You don't know me. How could you assume that Kate is anything but a friend?"

"You're right. I don't know you, Noah. I guess I'm the ass for assuming. Or, I could be the intelligent one for figuring it out before I make a mistake." She turns around and opens the door.

"Morgan," I call her name.

Her heels tap against the wooden floor, avoiding my plea for her to stop. She repeatedly taps on the elevator button, and with a slight delay, it allows me to catch up to her.

215

I enter the elevator along with her. "What the hell was that?"

She avoids me, staring at the doors. Pretending I don't exist.

"Morgan." I pull her arm toward me. "I don't get you."

"Like I said, you don't need to get me."

I'm fucking frustrated that we're back to square one, despite me thinking we were moving forward. "Are we back here again? You acting like a goddamn bitch on some power trip?"

Quick, and with a vengeful stare, she tightens her lips as her cheeks flush with anger. "I need to go," is all she says.

"You always need to go. You always need to be somewhere else. Why won't you make time for me? The man standing here, right in front of you."

Something changes. Her eyes are pleading with me to understand. But understand what? I don't know how to fucking read her. She places her hands on my chest—the electricity between us is undeniable.

I pull back, surprising myself. "No, Morgan. I'm not going to touch you anymore. I fucking want you. In my bed. Now," I tell her with complete and brutal honesty. "No more games. I'm laying my cards on the table. You can see them. Until you show me yours, I'm not going to touch you."

She releases a disturbing laugh, increasing my anger. "That's not possible."

"Sounds like you're the one panicking?"

The doors to the elevator open, and inside the lobby, a few of the staff are casually standing around having a conversation. They notice us, say hello, then continue to converse amongst themselves.

"You know what, Noah? I can't do this, whatever it is."

"Excuse me?"

"You're a player. Women want you. In the restaurants, at the workplace, calling you on your desk phone," she says in a frustrated tone, then continues quickly, "I want you. But I don't have the time for this. Goodbye." And with her harsh words, she exits the building, leaving me alone.

This is *not* goodbye.

I'll make damn sure it isn't.

CHAPTER 20

NOAH

Three days have passed, and I haven't heard a word from her.

Presley mentioned, in passing, that they had met for lunch. But that was all. She could tell I was fishing for more information, but I can't let my pride interfere with work.

Both of us need time to cool off after our heated argument. I just can't understand how a woman—so frustratingly beautiful and stubborn—can affect me so much. I struggle to sleep, and my appetite is minimal, even adopting Kate's terrible habit of checking my cell a thousand times a day.

I've kept Kate out of this problem, not wanting to highlight Morgan's dislike for our friendship. Charlie's been busy with a critical court case, so I barely see her at home. It's only Lex around. He's taken a couple of days off to work from home.

"What's she done now?" he questions, watching me

on the couch, absently channel surfing.

I find myself stuck on some show about renovating a house in England. Sending Kate text after text, I question the weird things they keep saying. Her visit to LA has been canceled due to some last-minute business she needs to take care of in Chicago. It soured my mood even more, missing her overbearing ways.

I let out a grunt. It's barely a response.

"Let me guess? She won't fuck you. Doing that annoying thing that women do... the cat and mouse chase."

I laugh. He's on point. "Yep."

"Let her go. C'mon, you're in LA, there are plenty of women out here."

"You're right. It's not like we're in a relationship."

But I can't let it go.

It eats away at me how she can so quickly walk away.

The next day, I take matters into my own hands, turning up at her office. The receptionist informs me she's out and won't tell me where. I slip her a twenty, and she stares at me with an insulting frown.

"C'mon, please," I beg for a solid ten minutes.

"I'll tell you, but I can lose my job. So, don't you dare tell her I told you."

I drive over to the address she gives me. Leaning my head forward, I look at the surroundings. *It's a park.* My eyes graze over the piece of paper again—this is definitely the right address.

Parking the car in a tight spot, I step out and walk through the gates. It's not too busy, a few kids playing at a playground and some ladies walking their dogs. None of these people are her, though. I'm wondering if the receptionist has sent me on a wild goose chase.

Toward the back of the park, there's a basketball court, and I can see someone shooting hoops. I move closer until I'm at the fence.

It's her.

She's wearing tight shorts, Nike sneakers, and a black tank as she nails a three-pointer.

I clap loudly, watching her turn to face me.

"Noah, what are you doing here?" she says out of breath.

"It's been three days," I merely say. "I didn't know you played ball."

She smiles. "This is what I do for fun."

"I don't know whether to be happy or disappointed."

"Why would you be disappointed?"

"Because I was hoping your idea of fun was whips and chains. You know, some light bondage."

This time she laughs, throwing me the ball. "Mind out of the gutter, Mason. I actually coach a kids' team."

"Really?" I pass her the ball. "Then show me what you got, Bentley."

Unpinning my cuffs, I roll up my sleeves and move in closer. She backs up into me, and when I reach to steal the ball, she beats me with a spin move and nails the layup.

"Damn, girl, you got skill."

Standing only a few steps away from me, she catches her breath. In a severe and apologetic tone, she says, "I'm sorry."

I pull her arm toward me. Placing my hands on her

face, I kiss her lips. *I fucking missed her.* And it feels like forever. I don't want to be apart.

"What other hidden talents do you have?" I question her playfully, my hands wrapped around her waist.

"I can drink a gallon of milk in less than a minute." Her eyes light up proudly.

"You cannot." I smile.

She nods her head. "Sadly, true."

I laugh, kissing her again. "So, tell me, Morgan, where do we go from here?"

"I don't know, Noah," she speaks quietly. "I have a meeting I need to get to, but I promise to call you afterward. I'd try to reschedule, but these businessmen have flown in from France, offering Scarlett a big endorsement. I need to be at the Four Seasons in less than an hour."

Why am I not surprised she has to be somewhere else? I can feel the anger and frustration slowly building inside of me, my fists clenching to control the unnecessary outburst. Factoring in someone else's behavior, especially someone I'm growing fond of, is new territory for me.

God, why the fuck is she making this so damn hard? Patience is a fucking virtue.

"You live close to here?" I ask to distract myself. I look around. There are many houses but nothing like Scarlett's home. Smaller town homes are all bundled together with communal yards.

"Uh… not far from here."

"Do you need a ride home?" I raise my eyebrows, hopeful.

She's quick to shoot down the idea. Disappointing me instantly. "My roommate's home."

"You have a roommate?"

"Uh… yeah, I do," she answers, uneasily.

"So, I'm sure she won't mind?"

She bounces the ball then looks at the time on her watch. "He doesn't like visitors, so I'm not home much."

Her roommate is a guy!

The excitement of being here with her is overshadowed with the jealousy which rears its ugly head. I don't like this one bit. *Why would she choose to live with a guy?* Indeed, given the car she drives, she has money to be able to live alone. Or better yet, move in with Scarlett. She isn't strapped for cash.

"You never said it was a he?" I ask bitterly.

"Noah, don't look at me that way," she pleads.

I'm unable to control my tone. "You give me the third degree about Kate, and yet *you* live with a male?"

"It's different," she's quick to defend herself. "I really need to go. Call me tonight. We'll talk more then, I promise, okay?"

"Morgan," I call out, frustrated at her abandoning this conversation.

She continues walking to her car, ignoring that I'm standing here, in the middle of a basketball court, having a mental breakdown.

I head straight home, making a mental note to call her tonight. There's no way that I'll allow her to avoid my questions.

Charlie's back and cooking something so delicious, I'm practically drooling on the floor. The second she sees me, she knows something's wrong.

"What's up? You have that look on your face, the same one you had when I accidentally flushed your toy car down the toilet."

"That wasn't an accident. You did that because I cut all your Barbie's hair off."

She throws her hands in the air. "It was a Barbie-and-the-Rockers doll. Without the crimped do, she wasn't a rocker!"

"She needed a haircut." I snicker, grabbing a chocolate chip cookie from the jar that sits on the countertop.

"You're so annoying," she complains. "So, what's up your annoying ass today? Wait, let me guess, someone rejected you."

"Uncle Noah," Amelia says, walking into the room with wide eyes. "Are you in love with Morgan?"

My head turns fast. "How do you know Morgan?"

"It's on your phone."

"Amelia," Charlie and I say at the same time. "I've told you not to read my phone."

"I'm sorry, Uncle Noah." She almost cries. "I needed to use your phone for the torch."

"What did you need the torch for?" Charlie asks skeptically.

"I accidentally dropped Uncle Noah's toothbrush in the toilet, and I couldn't reach the light, so I tried to use his phone when he was outside with Daddy."

I bury my head in my hands. "My toothbrush?"

I begin to dry-retch while Charlie lectures Amelia again on personal property. Amelia leans her head on my arm. "Sorry, Uncle Noah. I didn't mean to do it."

What a way to end the night. Despite being grossed out about my toothbrush, I ruffle the top of her head, kissing her before she pulls away and walks down the hallway.

Amelia halts at her door. "Uncle Noah, I think you love Morgan. That's why you're sad. Daddy says when a man loves a woman, they're sad if they aren't together."

Can a five-year-old have the answer to my problem? No. I can't be in love. The thought alone is ludicrous.

"Morgan?" Charlie questions. "So, what about Scarlett?"

"Charlie—"

"Okay, I won't butt in," she says. "But I'm here if you need me, okay?"

"I know..." I trail off. "What would you do if you were me? If you weren't getting the answers you so desperately need."

"Me?" Charlie asks. "I'd sit back and allow life to lead the way."

"And you?" I turn to Lex who has been sitting quietly at the table.

"I'd go find her now, demand she gives you answers, and not leave until she does," he states firmly.

"She's busy, some meeting at the Four Seasons."

Lex pulls his cell out and dials a number. "Karl, it's Lex Edwards. I need a room."

There's silence followed by Lex saying, "Thank you," and hanging up the phone.

"It's all yours." Lex smiles.

Charlie watches my reaction, surprisingly keeping

quiet. I sit on it for moments, then realize that life's too short.

I grab my keys, making the decision before nerves have me backing out.

"I'm going after her."

CHAPTER
21

NOAH

Lex has gone all out.

The Four Seasons has a grand entrance, marble floors with a gold table sitting in the center of the lobby. The expansive flower display on the table is an eyesore adding to the scattered plants decorating the entrance.

There are a few guests waiting in the reception area, luggage beside them as they check in to the hotel. I stay behind them, then make my way to the guy checking me in. It's a quick and straightforward process, and with adrenaline running through my veins, I find the restaurant in the lobby level—an Italian place called *Culina.*

There's no one manning the entrance, and upon scanning the crowded room, I spot her sitting near the window with a group of men. They're younger than I expected. Possibly in their late twenties if not early thirties. The three of them are gazing at Morgan with lust in their eyes, unprofessional and downright rude.

Are you fucking kidding me? No one looks at *my* woman that way.

The taller one with the dark brown hair tied back into a girly ponytail, puts his arm around her chair. A gesture that she seems to notice and brushes off. The wave of jealousy almost knocks me over, and without any sense of reason, I walk toward her, avoiding the maître d' chasing me down.

"So, you'll see that Scarlett has—" She stops mid-sentence, her eyes widening while she observes me standing beside her at the table.

"Noah, what are you doing here?" she questions, shocked yet trying to compose herself.

The men seated at the table stare me up and down with their arrogant smirks. The one in the ponytail not retracting his arm that so carelessly rests behind Morgan. My hands are prepped, ready to strangle him at this very moment. As much as I hate him for his foolish behavior, I straighten my posture and act confidently trying to irk him.

"I apologize, but we have some unfinished business that needs sorting out." I turn toward the men with a fierce look. "I need to borrow Ms. Bentley for… say…" I look at my watch, "… ten minutes."

"Noah, can this possibly wait?" she asks, annoyed, plastering a fake smile for her guests.

"Not anymore."

She excuses herself and follows me closely out of the restaurant. When we're out of sight, I grab her hand and lead her toward the elevator.

"Noah, are you out of your mind? That was an

important deal, and they're only here for the night," she sputters, momentarily beyond words.

The elevator is on level five, and impatiently, I grab her hand and open the door to the stairwell.

"What are you doing? I'm in heels, and you want me to climb... how many steps?"

This woman needs to shut up.

I grab her waist, lifting her and throwing her over my shoulder. She kicks and screams, begging me to put her down. When we hit the second floor, the room is right beside the elevator. I swipe the card and enter, finally putting her down.

She stumbles for just a moment, her eyes wild and fueled with anger. "This is insane, and I don't think you understand—"

I press her up against the door, fast and hard, smashing my lips against hers. Her tits are soft and round, pushing hard against my chest. *I want to bury myself in them. Get lost for hours upon hours, if not a lifetime.* Wait, what did you just think?

"Noah," she pants, gripping onto the lapels of my suit jacket.

I place my index finger on her lips, motioning for her to be quiet. "I'm not waiting anymore, Morgan," I say just above a whisper. "I've waited long enough. I don't care what happens tomorrow. Right now, I need you."

I know I have only ten minutes. I'm a selfish bastard, but I don't want to jeopardize her career. My hands run up her dress, lifting her ass into my hands. She laces her arms around my neck, drawing me in and proving to me she feels the same way.

Waiting is overrated, anyway.

Her long, lean legs wrap around my waist, giving me the perfect angle to take her against the door.

In one swift move, I unbuckle my pants, dropping them around my ankles. I bury my head into the crook of her neck, inhaling her skin. She smells like her, a scent so pure and sensual mixed with a bit of coconut. My senses are heightened, and the smell of her skin sends my body into the meltdown phase, and I haven't even entered her yet.

Her panties feel expensive, lacy with tiny crystals scattered along the top. I can always replace them later. That's what money is for. And so, I scrunch them in my hands and tear them away, making sure I don't hurt her. The sound of her gasp sends delightful shivers throughout my body. Her body arches back, and the vein, visible on her neck, invites me to kiss every inch of it, wanting to taste the blood pumping through her veins like a goddamn vampire.

She's ready.

I reach down and latch onto my shaft, taming the persistent throb and teasing her entrance with the tip of my cock. She's delightfully wet, soft, and warm. *So very warm.* This moment should be savored, but I'm a selfish prick. I slide myself in as her stomach shrinks, sucking in the air as she takes a deep breath and moans splendidly all around me. She chants my name, softly sounding the syllables in tune with our bodies moving.

I push deeper, feeling her walls tighten around me. She's almost there. *I know she's almost there.* She releases her grip on me, leaning back against the door while her eyes meet mine.

And something in the way she gazes longingly at me draws me in.

The desire.

The lust.

The greed.

With the mightiest of thrusts, I slam into her hard, feeling her pussy contracting around my cock followed by her loud cry.

I'm done.

I pull out quickly, releasing all over her thigh while my body jerks forward in utter delight. Breathing heavily into her neck, my vision is blindsided seeing only stars, moons, and fucking fireworks.

What did she just do to me?

Grazing my thumb across her thigh, I take what's mine because I'm greedy and want her to taste me. She lifts her head and studies the way I move my thumb upward and gently slide it across her bottom lip. Her lips remain parted, tiny breaths barely escaping as her eyes, wide and full of desperation, begging me to give her more.

"Just a taste of what's to come," I murmur, my mouth hovering over hers.

She smiles wickedly, running her tongue across her bottom lip. "I've got quite an appetite."

"You need to go," I tell her with discontent. "But don't for one second think this is over. I'll be here, waiting, as soon as you're done."

She runs her hands down my arms, gripping onto my biceps as she frees her legs. Even now, after all is done, her simple touch is melting away at me. Her legs shake while she tries to maintain her balance, latching onto me again for support.

I reach down and pull my pants up, leaving my belt unbuckled. After all, I expect her back here as soon as her meeting is over. Then, the real fun will begin.

She makes a dash to the bathroom to grab some tissues. After cleaning herself up, she straightens her dress and fixes her hair. I walk to where she's standing and position myself behind her back. Our images reflect in the mirror, and as if my heart has completely fallen out of my chest, I know only one thing.

This feels right.

She breaks my gaze and latches onto the door handle. I reach out for her arm, pulling her into me one more time.

"Are we okay?"

The silence falls between us, worrying me that something's wrong. As the panic begins to build, she traces the bottom of my jaw. Her lips, swollen and pouty, curve upward into a dreamy smile.

"Noah," she asserts, rolling her tongue, seducing me with only the call of my name. "We're more than okay."

CHAPTER
22

MORGAN

He has no clue what he's done to me.

And I *hate* myself.

For wanting him.

For desiring every part of him.

The moment he stepped into my office, I saw my former self. The person I used to be before I allowed myself to be burdened with the weight that rests on other people's shoulders. I tried to resist him, but his cocky attitude got the best of me. His presence alone, sitting across the desk the first time we met, stirred this buried emotion—*desire.*

A muscular build hid behind this perfectly fitted navy suit. Tall, with hair styled modern and slicked to the side, accentuating his strong jawline. And although my body instantly craved to touch him, it was his deep blue eyes that had me drowning and begging for a life jacket.

But I have a terrible habit of screwing guys and walking away. *Or at least, I used to.*

Noah Mason is a wrecking ball. He's taking me along with him, even though every part of me tries to push him away.

And then, without any warning, he fucked me. Against the door, challenging and full of grunt. In less than ten minutes, he'd done things to me that I've never experienced in this lifetime. He's opened the doors and freed Violet Winters—a woman caged and living in the shadows of her famous sister.

I manage to wrap up the meeting without too much trouble. Jacque offered me a nightcap in his room, which I kindly refused.

I know Noah has difficulty expressing his emotions, but he plays the part of a jealous man to a T.

The question remains—*Do I go back up to Noah's room or not?*

For minutes, I sit at the bar, contemplating my next move, wondering how I find myself here, why life chooses to throw this giant curveball at me as if I don't have enough on my plate.

And then there are no more questions.

I quickly find myself outside his door, knocking, and the moment he opens it wearing only a towel, which he conveniently drops when he sees me, I know I can't turn back.

He retakes me, against the wall, this time turning me around and fucking me from behind. He has the stamina of a stallion, and although I'm utterly exhausted, he finishes by laying me on the bed and giving me everything I need at that moment—slow, dirty, erotic sex.

My body has exerted itself—something I haven't experienced sexually before. I've done many things, and many men, but he's like some sex god attentive to all my needs. Previously, I had joked that I was a receiver. Selfish would be the appropriate word. Yeah, I've blown guys, but almost always, I want all the attention.

Yet with Noah, I want to give back.

Running my nails along his muscular, lean torso and grating his abs, his cock teases me relentlessly, standing tall and begging for attention. I don't hold back, nor do I tease, running my mouth down his body like a marathon race until I take him all in. My lips envelop around his shaft and relaxing my back muscles, I push down as far as my throat will allow. His groan follows, deep and husky, hands messing my hair as he pushes me onto him deeper.

My body reacts again. Although sore and sensitive from where he's been on me, my nipples become erect, the hardening, a mixture of pleasure and pain. He begs me to stop, but I'm cruel that way, carrying on because I need all of him in my mouth.

But his strength outweighs mine. And in just one move, he has me on all fours. My knees begin to wobble, tired and exhausted. He knows what he's doing to me, but the selfish bastard doesn't care. He tells me what he wants.

All of me.

Now.

Here.

Tonight.

And I want all of those things too. I want him to take

me everywhere in this room and show me what he's got. Lay all the cards on the table. Take me in every way he's imagined in his dirty mind until my legs are no longer wobbling but paralyzed.

But reality has a way of knocking the fantasy straight out of you. I know I can't stay, and I have learned relatively quickly that Noah isn't a patient man. He demands things and doesn't take well to his needs not being met.

Although the hotel sits in a busy part of Los Angeles, the noise outside can't be heard inside the four walls of this room. Dead silence, just the beats of our hearts crazily in sync with each other, the most terrifying sound you can hear. Each beat, loud and peculiar, sends chills throughout me.

Noah runs his hands along my arm, slowly warming my skin. He doesn't realize nor understand the complexity of the situation. And now isn't the moment, so I do the only thing I've learned to do around him— run away.

"I need to go, Noah, I have things I have to do in the morning."

"Why can't you stay?" Anger and desperation filters through his tone.

Questions. *More damn questions.*

Every time I try to be civil, we end up arguing and getting into a fight like we're an old married couple. And sometimes, I purposely pick a struggle because I have no idea how else to push him away. I don't want to hurt him, and every part of me knows that every second that goes past, I'm weaving a bigger web for myself.

"Because I've stayed as long as I can tonight. Please, don't fight with me. Don't ruin what just happened between us," I say, keeping the sadness away from my face and replacing it with the smallest of smiles.

He brushes his finger along my lip, hooded eyes watching me suspiciously. "Tomorrow."

"Tomorrow," I repeat, above a whisper.

His cell buzzes on the table beside him. He glances over but is quick to place his cell down. I can see his expression has shifted, a look of concern as worry reflects in his eyes.

"Is everything okay?"

He nods, "Yeah, just a text."

I wanted to ask him if it was Kate. For some reason, she gets the better of me. They have this bond, this so-called friendship that doesn't sit right with me. Noah doesn't appear to be the type to hold friendships with women unless, of course, it has benefits.

I'm not an emotional person, always finding some way to block the pain. And even at my mother's funeral, I didn't shed a tear for fear of coming across weak in front of our family and friends. It was three days later when I finally broke down driving to campus for an important exam. I never told Dad or Scarlett how my car stopped at the red light, and by the time it turned green, I couldn't move, paralyzed with pain. The hurt hit me with such force that my catatonic state alarmed the drivers around me. When I managed to snap out of it, I drove myself to the nearest frat house and lost myself to alcohol, drugs, and sex with random guys. It was my darkest hour. An hour that lasted four days until my friend found me and physically dragged me out of the house.

But something about Noah has struck a nerve. One that I'm struggling to hold back.

I dress and leave him there, hurrying to my car, where I drive home in a confused state of mind.

It's late, just before midnight when I step inside the house and quietly place my keys on the hall table.

"You're late," he says from within the living room.

The room is dimly lit, only the small lamp illuminating a corner of the large room. I stop and keep my back to him, afraid he can see it etched on my face.

"I had stuff that needed to be taken care of."

He remains silent, breathing quietly as I wait nervously for him to speak. "He asked for you."

And then, the guilt and shame override any happiness I felt for the past few hours. My heart almost falls to the floor, heavy and saddened by the hurt I've inflicted on him. Unintentionally, yet still, I should've known better.

Dragging my feet, riddled with guilt, I make my way toward the back of the house and quietly open the door to his room. His nightlight is on, sitting just above his pillow. With gentle snores, I tiptoe to his bed and see him curled in a ball, holding onto his favorite train, *Gordon*. The oldest and wisest train that lives on the island of Sodor. I don't dare take it out of his hands, instead pulling the blanket over and stopping just below his chin.

Leaning in, I kiss his forehead and pull away, watching him for a few moments. He doesn't realize how special he is. Despite the challenges he faces daily, he belongs in the hearts of so many people. Mine, utterly full of love for him, and all I want to do is protect him.

I close the door, leaving it slightly ajar in case he calls out through the night. I walk back to my room, where he's lying on our bed, keeping to his own side.

"He didn't settle well."

I apologize again, displaying my guilt. "I'm sorry I wasn't here."

"You're busy," he says with his iPad in his lap. "I'll be out of town this weekend. Will you be okay?"

His eyes linger on mine, and I can read him perfectly. Like me, he carries his own guilt. I know he isn't comfortable admitting it, and I'm not comfortable asking about it. I know this—her name is Jessica, and she has a knack for messaging him when he's in the shower.

I remove my bracelet and place it on the dresser. "Uh... yeah, I think Dad's coming into town, anyway."

He nods, shifting his focus back to his iPad. I make my way to the bathroom and peel off my clothes. My skin is red, marked, and tainted by Noah. I close my eyes for a brief moment, running my hands along my breasts, tracing his steps. I shouldn't want more, but my body craves it more than I could have imagined. I shower long enough to ease my sore muscles, and when I'm dressed for bed, I turn the light off in the bathroom and stand beside our bed.

He keeps to his side, again, and I climb in—the click of the lamp echoes through the room. Then darkness falls between us.

"It'll work out, Morgan," he says quietly in the dark.

My cell beeps inside my hand. I lift it to read the text.

Noah: *Something urgent has come up. Raincheck?*

Me: *Of course. Is everything okay?*

Noah: *It will be.*

I didn't have the heart to ask if that something is a someone. I have no way of controlling how I feel anymore, and no way of pulling my heart out of this game. I'm afraid the feelings, which have consumed me since the moment Noah stepped in my office, have led to one thing.

I am *in love* with him.

CHAPTER
23

KATE

I stare at the equations on the screen, computing numbers in my head as Richard, our director of finance, is talking a mile a minute.

"I'm not pleased with these numbers," Richard declares, removing his glasses as he wipes them with some old handkerchief. "Our numbers are unachievable."

We've been inside this boardroom for over four hours. Aside from the sandwiches brought in an hour ago, I drank several coffees, and my nervous system is on the verge of combusting.

"Richard," I begin, swiveling my chair to meet his direction. "We're bleeding money with these small enterprises. The funding needed to boost their capital will be better off spent on our more profitable sectors."

"Kate," Richard says with a condescending smile. "My numbers don't lie."

"They're not accurate, Richard," I tell him, frustrated

for having the same conversation over and over again. Pinching my lips together, I piece my thoughts like a puzzle clicking in place before criticizing him for being incompetent. "Jonathan, in our London office, has tripled profits in our European market. How? Because he projects accurate numbers to begin with. I don't understand why we aren't able to replicate this here."

"Agreed," Lex interjects, his face tightening while he crosses his arms. I've worked with Lex long enough to know he's frustrated with Richard's excuses. When it comes to business, Lex does not tolerate incompetent employees. "Why are we not seeing the correct numbers here? Frankly, Richard, I'm not impressed and want to meet tomorrow. Show me a better result, or we're going to make some significant cuts."

Richard's face turns beet red. The asshole better step up his game rather than throw the blame onto everyone else and pretend like it's not his fault. On more than one occasion, he's gone straight to Lex to complain about my directives. He's a chauvinistic caveman who hates reporting to a woman. His complaints hold no merit, and Lex doesn't even question me knowing all too well I've done my job correctly.

I end our meeting, dismissing the team but not before a harsh warning on what I expect from them over the next week. As the final person closes the door, I let out the breath I've been holding in, rolling my neck from side to side to alleviate the knots forming.

It's been an incredibly stressful week, and the weekend can't come fast enough.

With just myself and Lex in the room, it gives us a

chance to discuss more private matters without the remaining executive team present.

"I'm not happy with Richard's performance," Lex says, placing his cell down for a brief moment. "This isn't what I want to see."

"I warned you, Lex. Month after month he's focusing on the wrong numbers. This is costing us."

"You're right," he agrees. "Let's get HR in here. I want Richard out. In the interim, we offer Jonathan more money, and he can take over. We'll overhaul our finance department and strengthen the team."

I wasn't new to this process, having fired many employees for performance. Richard is no exception. It's been a long time coming, and I'm just glad Lex can finally see his true colors.

"So, I have something to discuss with you. Actually, two things."

Beneath the table, I cross my legs. With a nervous tap of my foot against the floor, my gaze fixates on Lex's expression. Most of the time, the man is unreadable with the exception of when he's angry. Whenever Lex has something to discuss with me, it ends up with me working countless hours.

"I met with Anton Laurent last night."

Anton Laurent is one of Europe's wealthiest entrepreneurs. He's the chairman of Western Europe's largest media corporation. I've read about him, his business model, and the recent success of merging with a well-known production company based in Italy.

"Oh," I mouth. "I can see your mind ticking already."

The corners of Lex's lips fight a smile, his eyebrows

slightly raised.

"You know me well," he admits, a sly grin following. "So, we've been in discussion for a while about expanding in Europe. There are several opportunities I'd love Lexed to pursue, but, of course, with Charlotte due in the next few months, I have no choice but to stay close to her."

"Uh-huh." I nod, folding my arms beneath my chest as I wait for the giant ball to drop. "I'm waiting for the big surprise."

"I want you to run this project from the ground up. You've done so well with our Manhattan office, managed to keep London running smoothly, and frankly, I don't trust anyone besides you."

I pull in a deep breath, listening to him as he continues to talk about his plans to expand and precisely what he needs me to do. A sense of pride engulfs me. Lex wouldn't ask if he didn't think I was competent. He's business-focused, making professional decisions, and never shows favoritism toward me because of our personal ties.

Though slowly, the more he speaks, my concerns grow, and doubt begins to creep in. There's so much I need to learn, and although I've been accredited having completed my Masters in Business, my practical experience falls short. It's been only four years versus Lex's massive experience in the field.

"Europe is... wow," I confess, my voice in disbelief. "I'm honored, but I don't think I can—"

He raises his hand to stop me talking. "Don't even finish that sentence. You know you can. If I've taught you anything, it should be self-confidence. Don't plant failure in your mind without even trying."

"Yes, I understand, but Europe?" I try to gather my thoughts. There are so many questions. Logistics, timing, and the list goes on. "So how? Where?"

"France. Paris, to be exact." His stare fixates on me, a mixed looked of intimidation and compassion. He knows me well knowing I will doubt myself before even trying. Yet he also knows I perform well under pressure. "You'll need to be there for at least three years."

"Three years in Paris?" I question, tilting my head with confusion. "But what about this office?"

"I think George can manage it. He's proven his worth, and honestly, Kate, you're ready for that next step."

"But... Paris," I repeat, lowering my gaze toward the table. "I'd have to leave everyone behind."

I think about Charlie, not seeing the girls grow up, and the new baby joining their family. Then there's Eric. Despite his dramatic ways, his presence balances the corporate chaos in my head. There's nothing quite like Eric bringing you back down to earth with a conversation revolving around circumcision. The words 'meat jacket' will forever be etched in my memory.

And *Noah.*

It's silly for me to miss someone who has only been in my life for such a short time. Sure, our friendship has deepened since the fateful incident on the beach. We speak almost every day, and with him, life is *bearable.* Yet of late, there's been a shift, and I know it has to do with Morgan. I'm reluctant to probe him, knowing all too well Noah will deny his feelings by trying to stroke his ego and maintain his single-guy persona.

Lex clears his throat, resting his hand on the desk and tapping it with his fingertips.

"Is there someone specific you don't want to leave behind?" he asks, watching me furtively.

"N-No," I stumble. "There's Charlie, for starters, and of course Amelia and Ava. Eric is getting on my nerves, anyway."

He nods his head. "And Noah?"

"Noah is a friend," I reiterate. "Wait! Is this you asking or Charlie?"

"I'm not answering that for fear of retribution." Lex lowers his gaze, unable to hide the smirk on his face. "So, back to Paris. Will you consider my proposal? You'll be compensated very well and staying in a penthouse apartment owned by Anton's son."

At times, I wish money drove me. Lex already pays me an executive salary, and I've invested my savings into a small flat in London, which is currently being rented out. Aside from that, I have nice clothes and a few fancy purses. But of late, none of that brings me joy.

"It's an amazing opportunity," I tell him.

"But?"

"No buts. Just processing."

With a crisp nod, Lex understands my needs and ends the conversation of Paris for now.

"So, about my second thing. The Charter Group has a black-tie event tomorrow. It's not something I had planned to attend, but Winston Charter, chairman of the Charter Group, will be attending." He shuts down his laptop, distracting me momentarily. "I've managed to grab two last-minute tickets hoping you don't have plans. I'd really like for you to meet him."

"I'm single, and it's a Friday night," I remind him with a small laugh. "What other plans would I have?"

"There's just one thing..." Lex trails off, looking somewhat uncomfortable. "Before I mention it, I want to clarify that Charlotte insisted I tell you, so you could make an informed decision about attending."

"What is it?"

"Your so-called friend, Dominic, will be at the event."

The name has been absent from my mind with work taking priority. But just like a giant wrecking ball, everything attached to it comes crashing back with force. Lex is waiting for me to respond, and not to come across too feminine with a fragile emotional state, I straighten my posture with a poised smile.

"It'll be fine," I say with a forced expression. "Let me know where and when."

Lex gives me all the details, and the second he leaves, I begin to pace the room in a mild panic. First, I have nothing to wear. Specifically, I have nothing worthy of being seen in by a man who destroyed my confidence and left me to hang out to dry.

Second, I'm panicking—unable to breathe, heart racing, sweat-forming type of panic.

Shit.

I grab my cell, scrolling through my contacts to call Noah. Just as I'm about to tap his name, I abruptly stop. Something holds me back. Whenever the topic of Dominic has come up of late, Noah berates me for even contemplating trying to communicate with him. And when it comes to lectures, Noah does *not* hold back.

This would be the exact same lecture, and so, I decide to call Charlie.

"I was waiting for this call."

"You could have given me a warning, so I could've saved face in front of Lex," I complain.

"Save face," she ridicules, followed by a small huff. "Lex doesn't care. Well, actually, he does care. He wants you to meet Winston. That's all."

"I understand that, but—"

"I, on the other hand, think it's a bad idea."

"Of course, you do," I say, panicked by the whole dilemma. "All those years ago, when you ran into Lex at that charity ball, do you think you would've gone if you knew he'd be there?"

"No, I wouldn't have gone knowing that."

"I've heard many things come out of your mouth, missy, but that right there is a crock of shit."

"Fine," she shouts over the receiver. "I possibly would've still gone, but that's completely different."

"Yeah, I'm not engaged or tied down to anyone. What's to stop me from doing anything?"

"Um, for starters, your pride should care?" Charlie says while I pinch the bridge of the nose to curb the frustration of our conversation. "And your self-respect. The bottom line here is no good will come from you seeing him."

"I beg to differ," I blurt out. "I'm a big girl, Charlie. I can handle the heartbreak."

***

The street is crowded, lined with limousines and luxury vehicles all vying for a spot in front of the museum where the event is being held. Flashes are going off right, left, and center. The paparazzi are scurrying around like rats up a drainpipe snapping away at those who pose on the red carpet.

As we walk through the large doors, I'm blown away by the sight of it all. The room is enormous. Its size big enough to hold all of the elite in New York City and then some. Each guest is dressed in the black-tie dress code. Exquisite gowns and dashing tuxedos are everywhere I turn.

Thanks to Adriana, she contacted a designer friend of hers who fitted me early this morning. The dress is stunning, a long black gown made of lace with a plunging neckline. My hair has been styled into a tight bun, allowing the gorgeous white gold necklace to be showcased around my neck. It's been a while since I've worn something so extravagant, welcoming the confidence boost I desperately need for tonight.

Deep breaths.

You haven't seen him yet.

Inside the room, the tall ceilings are covered in rows of draped, sheer-white organza fabric, creating a medieval feel with a modern twist. A large chandelier hangs from the middle, its crystals reflecting the light shimmering on the dance floor. Scattered across the room are artificial trees with the branches draped in fairy lights.

There's a band wearing black and white tuxedos, perfectly positioned on the stage playing soft swing music, their hums and beats drowning in the noise of the growing crowd.

Lex finds our table, and after admitting to me he dropped a lot of money to secure our tickets, I tilt my head back with a confident pose and greet everyone who Lex introduces me to.

Our table is occupied by only wealthy entrepreneurs and their trophy wives. It reminds me of when Charlie told me that some woman called her that, and, of course, in true Charlie style, she argued the demeaning title and set that woman straight.

Throughout the course of the evening, we only speak business. It takes my mind off the nerves hiding in the shadows. Scanning the room briefly, he's still nowhere in sight. Perhaps he bailed. Dominic isn't a social person unless, of course, it involves people fucking in his club.

I control my consumption of wine and champagne so I'm able to converse without sounding like a drunken idiot. And somewhere during a conversation with Winston Charter, Lex mentions Paris.

"Paris?" Winston nods with a warm smile. "To quote Ernest Hemingway, there are only two places in the world where we can live happy... at home or in Paris."

"I guess I'll have to see." I grin, eyeing Lex.

Lex and Winston continue the Paris talk, all of which I'm still processing. But I don't let either one of them think any different, offering some suggestions on how and where to start, upward trends in the market, and other ideas which come to my mind.

By the end of the conversation, Lex looks pleased with our discussion.

"Is it a yes?" he asks, waiting patiently.

"It's a... more processing," I tell him while grabbing champagne from the waiter.

"Well, while you're processing, I'm going to have a chat with some old business colleagues, then call it a night," he mentions, keeping his smile fixed. "I have a late video call I must attend."

"You tell your video companion that I'm just fine, please."

Lex leans in to kiss me goodbye, thanking me again for coming tonight on such short notice. I know he has an early flight in the morning, never wanting to be too absent from his family.

I decide to use my time wisely, introducing myself to a few CEOs also based here in Manhattan. As the night wears on, my champagne wears off, and home sounds so good.

Ignoring my disappointment at not seeing Dominic, I say goodbye to a few guests I have been chatting with and make my way through the crowded room toward the exit. As I excuse myself, trying my best to be polite, though fucked off people have to be so rude and not listen, I tap on a shoulder with a loud, "Excuse me."

The man turns around, and just like that, my heart tumbles toward the floor. Unable to beat, unable to feel anything besides numb.

Dominic.

His eyes bore into mine, the same they have always done when we were in each other's company. Behind that weighted stare, my imagination runs wild. Conjuring up a world where the two of us, alone, succumbed to our desires and let go of our inhibitions. It's more than a sexual thirst, and more than a physical connection.

I wanted it all.

And the more I stare back into his eyes, the deeper I fall apart.

"I'm s-sorry," I stutter, shifting my gaze toward my feet. "I was just trying to get through and didn't realize it was you."

"How have you been?" he asks, a hidden smirk lingering behind the persistent gaze. "I'm sorry I didn't respond to your text."

He is sorry he didn't respond to my text?

I cross my arms, my beaded clutch nestled beneath my arm securely. With my lips pressed tight, I think of a response that doesn't relay my anger toward his pathetic excuse. "Look, it is what it is? Besides I—"

A woman dressed in a white strapless gown laces her arm into his. With a gleam in her eyes, she lowers her gaze, tracing my dress from the bottom up until she forces a smile. "Honey, I was looking for you." She diverts her attention to Dominic. "The Kleinmans would love to talk about our wedding being held at their Hamptons property."

Wedding.

Did I hear right?

Tilting my head to the side, I purse my lips while narrowing my eyes.

Wedding.

The word repeats in my head until the woman extends her hand. My eyes dart toward her finger where an expensive diamond ring sits.

"I'm Allegra, Dominic's fiancée," she introduces with an air of arrogance. "And you are?"

I clear my throat, unable to even think of my name or even a title to claim.

Fiancée.

Wedding.

The words taunt me to no avail.

"Kate," is all I manage to say.

With her hand still waiting for a friendly shake, I quickly reciprocate before retracting.

"It's nice to meet you," she says, flashing her fake smile once again. "Dominic, honey. Please join me as soon as you can."

She pulls away from him, disappearing in the crowd.

I'm blindsided by my humiliation, bowing my head and unable to look him in the eye, let alone question his ability to lie to me. Everything we did, everything we experienced was just one giant fucked-up lie.

"Kate, please," he silently begs. "This isn't what it seems."

My head snaps to meet his stare. "You're engaged to be married, is that correct?"

"Yes, but—"

"You're engaged to be married," I repeat, raising my voice. "You told me you don't settle down? You don't even date. As you can imagine, I'm rather confused."

"It's complicated," he mutters.

"Complicated?" I say, followed by a disturbing laugh. "You know what? It's fine. I get it. Goodbye, Dominic."

As I pull away, Dominic latches onto my arm, his

commanding touch killing every inch of me still fighting to breathe for air. I begged for things to be different, but nothing can erase the cold, harsh reality of what I am to him.

Absolutely *nothing.*

"What we had, K-Kate," he stammers, searching for words. "It scared me."

Once again, my gaze drifts back to his eyes. Searching for the truth, an impossible mission when lies taint the path in which we walk upon. Inside me, a raging battle to control my angered emotions becomes overbearing.

"If you're scared, you run and hide. Or in your case, you fuck some stranger in front of a crowd," I tell him, my words laced with malice. "You don't, however, commit to someone else for life. And, I'm sorry, when did this even happen?"

"We should talk more," he suggests with slight desperation in his tone. "But to answer your question, it happened three weeks ago."

I shake my head, releasing my arm from his grip.

"It's all about timing, Dominic." I take a deep breath, clutching onto any pride I still carry. "You had your chance. And now, you go live your life, and I'll go live mine. Just like it's always been between us. Nothing more and nothing less."

I don't give him a chance to respond, taking large steps to distance myself from him. This time, I'm rude, pushing people without warning and desperate to escape. Outside, in the cold night's air, I hail the first cab driving past, hopping in, requesting the driver to haul ass.

253

It's only a ten-minute drive home, but ten minutes to a broken heart is almost a lifetime.

Racing past my doorman, Jack, I bow my head, not wanting to welcome his flirtatious banter and head straight for the elevator.

I fumble for keys, unable to open the door. The more I turn them in the keyhole, the more desperate I become for the door to open. When the lock finally turns, I push the door open, then enter, slamming the door quickly behind me.

Leaning against the door, a pain inside my chest restricts my breathing, and with that, my limbs begin to tremble.

I fall to my knees, the same time, a loud sob escapes me. Unable to control the swirl of emotions, my hands rest on the ground for support begging for this to all go away.

"I will never be the man you want me to be," Dominic admitted with a cold stare. *"If I touch you, you'll get hurt."*

And just like he said, just like he predicted, he hurt me.

In the worse possible way.

CHAPTER
24

NOAH

It has been the day from hell.

The sheer number of idiots wasting my goddamn time make me incredibly short-fused.

I'd barely stopped for anything to eat, nor had my usual caffeine fix. A headache lingers, threatening behind my eyes, making it difficult to concentrate.

Realtors.

Would it be so hard for them to do their fucking job?

I told them my budget and exactly what I was looking for. Not too hard since there are plenty of vacant properties on the market. Yet, their incompetency left me without a place to call home. Five fucking condos I looked at, and all of them utter trash.

All that combined with a long day at work left me absolutely drained.

Now, I have to go home to a house of kids demanding my attention when all I want to do is be inside *Morgan.* I already have to postpone meeting her tonight after the realtor called me yesterday with their only open homes scheduled for this afternoon. It's just one disaster after another.

I walk through the back door and see Charlie sitting at the table. She's still dressed in her work attire from the day, and much like me, she appears exhausted. Fiddling with her cell and typing a quick text message, she lifts her head for a moment to connect with me before focusing her attention back on the screen.

On the table, there's homemade lasagna. Charlie knows how to cook, so leaving this place will be hard. Back in Boston, I rarely ate at home, opting for eating out or chilling at Tom's because that man also knows how to cook a feast.

"Hungry?" she simply asks.

"Famished," I respond, placing my laptop down. "The girls asleep already?"

"Yes, it was a long day for them."

Charlie places a plate in front of me, working silently with what appears to be an occupied mind. Something is of concern, her smile strained as she places a spoon in front of me only to realize it should've been a fork.

"Is something wrong?"

Her gaze lifts to meet mine. Behind her eyes, I see a sign of distress and know something isn't right.

"Um... it's nothing."

"Okay..."

I dig my fork into my lasagna, and as I raise it toward my mouth, Charlie accidentally drops her cell on the ground. "Shit," she cusses in frustration.

"Right," I state, placing my fork back on the plate. "Sit

down and talk."

Letting out a sigh, Charlie sits at the table directly opposite me. Her stomach has grown, making it difficult for her to sit too close to the table. I pray to the Lord above it has nothing to do with the baby she's carrying.

"Noah, have you spoken to Kate?"

I shake my head. "Not since... I can't remember our conversation. Why?"

"There was a black-tie event last tonight. And, um... Kate and Lex attended."

"That's nice," I say, waiting for something newsworthy. "And you're worried because?"

"Dominic was there."

The name hits me like a thousand knives. I loathe the guy, and with that, anger begins to swirl inside of me. The thought of him being there, and most likely brainwashing Kate with his anti-commitment talk, will make her question her worth. And fuck him for even doing that to her.

"I fucking hate that guy," I mutter, crossing my arms.

"You're not alone," Charlie agrees, rubbing her face. "We got into a small argument. I didn't think she should go. And now I haven't heard from her since yesterday."

"So, you had a disagreement. Don't you women have them a fair bit?"

"Yes, no." Charlie purses her lips. "Kate and I don't. I just have this gut feeling, Noah. Something isn't right, and I'm worried she's not okay."

"I'm sure she's fine." I pull my cell out of my pocket. "She's probably busy."

I dial her number. It rings out straight to voicemail.

Her pompous British accent relays the message making me smile. I try again, but nothing. Her phone never rings out. It's practically glued to her hand. Quickly typing, I send a text telling her to call me.

"That's what I'm worried about," Charlie admits. "She's busy… with him… in his club. And this is exactly why I didn't want her around him, especially after the pregnancy scare. No good will come of this. Some people are just assholes, and he fits the bill to a T."

Charlie mentioning the whole 'sex club' thing only makes my blood boil. The looming headache comes crashing in full force, causing me to wince as I try to ignore it to no avail. Rubbing my temples, I do my best to alleviate the pressure.

"I'm sure she's just processing," I lower my voice, not even convinced myself. "You know her and her processing phase."

Charlie nods, her tired eyes lingering in thought. "You're right. I need to sleep."

"I'll clean up," I offer. "Go rest, Charlie, I'm sure by morning, she will have texted one of us back."

With a good night, Charlie leaves the kitchen. It's only just after eight, but Charlie rarely stays awake past this time, knowing the girls wake up early. That and her pregnancy wears her out. I worry about her being so tired, but Lex assures me this is normal for pregnancy, hence why he does his best to help out as much as he can and be in town, except for the last two days, of course.

Moving toward the cupboard, I grab some Advil to rid myself of this headache once and for all, then gulp plenty water along with it. My appetite has disappeared, and so

I clean up the kitchen and put the remains away.

My mind is unable to think about anything else besides Kate. I recheck my cell, and still, nothing. Heading to my room, I hop in the shower to wash today's stress off, but the more I linger beneath the hot water, the tenser I become. What if Kate did fall into this trap again? Who the hell is going to pull her out and save her from the misery?

I turn the water off, hopping out quickly and grabbing a pair of jeans and a tee. With my hair not even styled and still dripping wet, I grab my cell and check the screen. Nothing. Opening my search engine, my fingers type profusely with a sudden urgency.

American Airlines—leaving ten forty-five.

I book the ticket without hesitation and grab my wallet, Charlie's car keys, and head toward her bedroom. Gently knocking on her door, she tells me to come in.

"I'm going to New York."

Laying inside her bed, I watch relief wash over her face, her shoulders relaxing instantly.

"Thank you, Noah," she says with an exhausted smile. "Please make sure our girl is okay."

"I promise she'll be fine."

***

I bang on her apartment door, calling her name. After the fourth attempt and no answer, I yank the key Charlie gave me out of my pocket. I only managed to get to this level after Charlie called security to inform them I was coming. Since she owns the apartment Kate stays in, they don't question her request and let me up.

It's just after seven in the morning, and with the change in time zones, my body is out of whack, having not slept on the plane. Some old dude kept snoring, plus I couldn't shut down my thoughts, desperate to land and get here.

Placing my key inside the keyhole, I turn the lock and open the door to be met by silence. The sun is shining through the drapes, lighting up what appears to be the living room. There's no sign of her here, but I'm quick to notice a black clutch purse sitting on the coffee table. Taking small footsteps, careful not to startle her, I find the bedroom door. It's wide open, and there, on the left side of the bed, is Kate curled up still in her evening gown.

She's asleep, tiny snores escaping her perfect lips. Even in her sad state, she looks beautiful. I let out a breath, relieved she's okay until I notice a bottle of Valium sitting beside her nightstand along with a bottle of tequila.

Fuck.

Okay, stop panicking.

She's fucking snoring, so she's alive.

I sit on the edge of the bed, the mattress moving slightly with my weight. With a small moan, she slowly opens her eyes and notices me sitting beside her. She doesn't appear shocked to see me, but behind her tired expression, only sorrow surrounds the dark circles shadowing her normally vibrant eyes.

"Noah," she barely breathes.

"Kate..." I stroke her hair away from her face, running

my thumb down her cheek.

"Why didn't he choose me?" she whispers with a tremble in her voice. "He's getting married."

I move in closer, removing my shoes and climbing into bed. Wrapping my arms around her, I hold on tight, allowing her to sob into my chest. It dawns on me she just said he's getting married. This can't be the same man who supposedly didn't date, let alone engage in a relationship.

Her sobs come hard and fast, a stream of pain she needs to release to move on. There's nothing to do but hold onto her, reassure her in our embrace that she'll be just fine.

"He was there last night with his fiancée," she mumbles, swallowing her tears. "He told me he got scared... I scared him."

The nerve of this fucking dickhead.

"He's a fucking idiot, okay?" I almost growl, holding her close. "You get scared, you fuck someone else. You don't get hitched."

"That's what I thought," she gulps, clutching onto my chest.

"Why didn't you tell me you were going and would see him?" I ask, slightly hurt she held this information back from me.

"Because you're busy... I know Morgan has—"

"Hey," I interrupt her, pulling back slightly to look her in the eyes. "I'm never too busy for you. You got me?"

Kate nods, a small smile pulls on her lips. Just seeing her smile makes this all worth the trip. That, and I want to hunt him down and slam my fist into his smug face.

How dare he think he can do this to her.

A thought comes to mind. "You know what would make you happy?"

"Valium?"

I shake my head, quick to scold her. "What were you thinking taking Valium and tequila? You could've killed yourself."

"Yes, I took some Valium," she admits. "But the tequila was a gift, and it's been sitting there for weeks."

"If anything was to happen to you..." I trail off.

"I'm stupid but not *that* stupid," she answers, defending her actions. "Look, Noah. It just hurts, okay?"

Silence falls between us. As I think about my history with women, I can't say I've ever felt hurt or heartbreak. I've dated, a few women lasted a couple of months, but never a relationship with any sort of commitment. Sure, my ego has been bruised, but even then, it didn't measure up to what Kate is experiencing.

Perhaps, it's a woman thing.

"So, what will make me happy?" she asks, tired and suddenly withdrawn again.

"Me... watching *Pretty in Pink*."

Her eyes swim with tears, but they fall with the laughter escaping her mouth. Wiping them with the back of her hand, she nods her head in agreement.

Before we put the movie on, Kate takes a shower, desperate to remove her gown and wash away what she now says is the worse night of her life. Several times during her shower, I knock on the door to see if she is okay since she's taking forever.

She emerges what feels like hours later, dressed in a

262

pair of bed shorts and a tee that reads, 'My Spirit Animal is Vodka.'

"Can you give a gal a moment to herself? What did you think I was doing in there? Dying?"

"Frankly, yes," I admit, channel surfing while waiting. "Who takes showers that long?"

"Someone who has a broken heart, that's who."

I roll my eyes to curb her dramatic woes. She's just as bad as Eric. As much as both she and Charlie complain about him, the three of them combined are no different.

Climbing in beside me, we turn the movie on with the drapes drawn to darken the room. The movie begins, but not before Kate warns me of several things to take note of.

"Will you just shut up and let me watch the movie?"

"Yes, but one more thing," she adds, pulling the sheet up to her chest. "No talking throughout the movie."

The movie begins, and after a short while, I ask, "Who the hell has a name Ducky?"

Kate pauses the movie. "I said no questions. Just watch."

Ten minutes later, I glance to my side noticing Kate staring at me with a goofy smile. She's making me self-conscious, and it's rather annoying.

"Why the creepy stalker look?" I ask, my gaze back fixating on the screen.

"I like watching you watch the movie. I live vicariously through you watching it for the first time."

I let out an annoyed huff. "Just watch the goddamn movie and stop creeping me out."

The movie continues, and I'll admit, the jerk pissed

me right off. Ducky was the poor loser on the side. His comedic relief made the movie worth watching.

When the movie ends, she's quick to hound me, turning to face me until I notice her tits bounce with excitement. *Okay, get a fucking grip, Noah.*

"So... what do you think?"

"It's a good movie, but not exactly memorable or worthy of repeating."

Kate throws her hands up in the air, then pushes my arm, irritated by my response. "I don't even know how to process that. You know what? The problem with men is their lack of emotions. Why can't you guys just say how you feel in real time? Why do you have to act all butch and in the process, hurt the woman you love?"

The rant is uncalled for, and I feel somewhat attacked as she waits for a response, her face turning beet red from anger. I think the Valium has worn off.

"Okay, first... why are you looking at me that way? I've done nothing wrong here," I remind her, trying to keep my cool not to anger the beast further. "Second... you need to eat."

Her shoulders slump, defeated from the whole mess of trying to decode men's behavior.

"Yes, father. But I don't cook. You know, the whole living in a city of fine restaurants."

"Takeout, baby."

I order food, which arrives rather quickly. We continue to lay in bed eating and laughing. I notice the time, having not booked a return ticket but needing to get back home. If I can catch a flight out tomorrow, I will still make it back in time for work on Monday morning.

"Noah, you came all the way here," Kate murmurs, digging her chopstick into the small takeout box but pausing while staring at the food. "No man has ever had my back like you."

"Well, no one in my life has been a hot mess like you." I smirk, lightening her mood to ease her guilt.

She slaps me softly before her face falls, and the realization kicks in. This whole thing with Dominic has affected her more than I realized. I've never been around a woman so vulnerable and exposed. Usually, I fuck them, then abandon the ship before it sinks around me.

"Hey, no more sad faces."

I motion for her to come closer, wrapping my arms back around her. The smell of her strawberry scented hair reminding me of this soap my mom used to have in our bathroom. Reassuring her once again, I take a moment to just hold her without any words to ruin the moment.

"Why can't it be easy?" she whispers. "You know, like what we have."

"Because we're special. A human experiment on how people *should* interact."

I can feel her mouth widen against my chest, her smile unable to hide with my sarcastic response. We are easy, too easy. And slowly, the guilt of ignoring Kate the past week consumes me. *Why do I have to choose?*

"Noah, you should probably get back. I'm sure you want to spend time with Morgan."

Morgan. I completely forgot. Fuck!

"Shit," I mouth.

Kate pulls away, watching me dubiously. "You didn't

tell her you were coming?"

"I told her something came up."

"Oh, bro," she shakes her head with disappointment, "... such a rookie relationship mistake."

"I'm not in a relationship," I correct her. "We just fuc—"

"You fucked her?" Kate blurts out, shuffling away.

There's a change in her expression.

Almost of hurt.

Why would she be hurt?

She's the one pushing me toward her.

"Of course, you did."

The two of us remain silent. I'm not sure what to say. In a split moment, things have become awkward, and to make matters worse, we're lying in the same bed. It's not exactly like I can go on continuing to ignore her.

"Are you upset?" I question, trying to understand.

"No," Kate admits quickly. "Maybe jealous because you're having all the great sex, and I'm not."

My lips curve upward, grinning at her response. "We can have all the great sex if you want. Promise I'll get it up this time. It's warm in this bed, and truth be told, your tits have been teasing me all night, so yeah..."

Kate's laughter breaks the tension between us. "Explains why you've knocked into me with your pecker a number of times."

"Can you use a more appropriate word besides pecker? It makes it sound small and that, my gorgeous lady, is far from the truth."

"Schlong," she chuckles.

"Perfect."

266

Kate begins to tell me a story about a time she went to a gay club with Eric. Somewhere through it, we both yawn, and my eyes begin to droop. Unable to hold back any longer, I drift off to sleep.

***

My eyes open cautiously, darkness still surrounding me. As I strain to open them wide, I see a small gap in the drapes where the sun barely peeks through. Kate is nestled into my arm, and careful not to wake her, I notice the time on her clock. It's just after six in the evening.

Beside me, she begins to stir. "Hey, you're still here."

"I'd never just leave you," I tell her.

Opening her eyes, she struggles, much like me. Letting out a yawn, she shuffles to sit up, rubbing her eyes.

"You should go, though," she suggests, touching my hair so effortlessly. "I'll be okay, Noah."

Allowing her to touch me, there's something which lingers in her stare. I don't want to leave her, wanting desperately to stay and just be like this. Yet back home, I have responsibilities, and, of course, Morgan.

I run my finger down her cheek, stopping at her chin. "You'll be okay."

"Just admit it, you only came here to get into bed with me," she jokes.

"To quote Ducky... *'This is an incredibly romantic moment, and you're ruining it for me!'*"

Kate tilts her head back, laughter consuming her until she gets into a coughing fit, forcing her to slow down.

When she's got a handle on herself, she fixates on me once again. The gaze, the same as the one only moments ago, sends this unknown feeling throughout me.

"You and I don't do romance," she reminds me.

She's right, we do many things, but romance isn't one of them.

"I'm here, Kate. Always."

"I know, Noah." She lowers her head, a shift in her expression as her eyes distance themselves from me. "Go back home. I'll be just fine."

I move forward, planting my lips on her forehead. As I slowly pull away, inches away from her, the beat of her chest knocks into mine. Something makes me linger, craving her in a way which blurs the lines between us.

We've been down this road that night at the beach. And we both agreed we were perfect as friends.

One wrong move, and I could ruin everything between us.

Pulling back, I graze my thumb against her lip, offering a smile and pushing aside the confusion within me.

"Noah," she whispers. My name suddenly sounds so different. "Take care, okay?"

There's a ray of finality in her words. Almost as if this will be the last time she sees me. Nothing will change between us. I have always promised her that.

And I refuse to break my promise, especially when it comes to Kate.

CHAPTER
25

NOAH

Leaving Kate has been difficult but for the best.

In just a few days, my life has shifted from depressing to exhilarating. Something in Morgan has changed—her fun and carefree attitude is a breath of fresh air and takes my mind off Kate.

Although I haven't told Morgan my whereabouts the past weekend, it doesn't really matter because she's everything I need in my life right now. It's almost as if subconsciously, she knows I don't need any more stress in my life and shifts her focus to being more open to exploring where we could go, *sexually*.

Work is hectic and pulls both of us in opposing directions, yet we still manage to find time for each other whenever we have a moment to spare. If it weren't for our day-to-day responsibilities, I'd demand more of Morgan's time. However, I know how dedicated she is to her job and her sister, putting my selfish needs on hold until we're alone.

269

And I never hold back.

I'm obsessed with her body and find myself worshiping every inch of it. She's so fucking beautiful that even when I'm not with her, my mind and cock are in sync, desperate to smell her skin and taste it with my tongue.

We have pushed the boundaries, fucking anywhere we can—from the car to the restaurant restrooms. The thrill of almost getting caught only heightens the experience, but neither of us really care. She's insatiable, and I can't get enough. My mind is unable to concentrate on anything else besides her.

Something switched—she's started to open up to me about her life. It comes as a surprise, but one overdue. And one thing I learned about her is that she lives her life on the edge, and so many of her stories replicate myself back home.

Charlie, which comes as no surprise, is overly happy with my newfound obsession. Although, she's never one to want to lose a bet, she accepts defeat for the greater good. According to her, I have a bounce in my step. Lex is quick to point out that I've been getting more action than he's seen in years. A joke Charlie so passionately weighs in on.

"If my vagina's closed for business like you claim it is, then perhaps you wouldn't have two daughters screaming this house down," she responds sarcastically, then rubs her stomach. "And the bun in the oven which, might I add, is breach and very uncomfortable."

"Perhaps you need to stop talking about your vagina," I tell Charlie, almost gagging on my toast.

As much as I love Charlie, Lex, and the girls, it's definitely time to find my own place.

I have another meeting with a realtor on Monday, hoping to find an affordable place close to work. The LA traffic is still a thorn in my side, the annoying commute doing nothing to calm my growing road rage.

Life almost seems too good to be true. Morgan is happy, and together, we are enjoying our time when we are able. Work gets busier, but I thrive on pressure. The long hours don't faze me, passing the time while LA soon becomes a part of me.

As the weekend begins to roll in, Charlie decides to have an impromptu barbecue lunch.

"Lex doesn't get much time off, so when he's here for the entire weekend, he likes to fire up the grill," she informs us. "Oh, and Kate will be staying here because she and Lex have a business meeting in Napa on Monday."

My movements slow down as the coffee machine continues to spout the much-needed beverage my body has been craving.

I nod my head in silence. The guilt of ignoring Kate the past two weeks consumes me. The nagging voice inside my head reminds me that we're just friends. Kate has a demanding job, more so than me, and with that it means she has no time to stay in contact.

And being the mature man that I am, I choose not to contact her for the integrity of our friendship. She doesn't need details of how often, or where, I have been fucking Morgan.

"Is everything okay between you two?" Charlie

questions, beside me.

"Why wouldn't it be?"

Charlie rubs her stomach, something she often does when I assume the baby is kicking her.

"I sensed Kate's resistance when I mentioned her staying her. I mean, it took some persuading," she admits, still gazing at me. "Eric has some couch surfers staying with him, and before you say anything, I'm still unsure of exactly what that entails."

I don't want to discuss Kate with Charlie, nor mention Morgan. Frankly, I don't understand women, but I know this—Kate being here this weekend will be a problem for Morgan. I can't exactly tell Charlie to uninvite Kate, so the next best thing would be not to attend. Find some excuse.

"If you can help out Lex on the grill, that would be great," Charlie adds.

There goes that idea.

Saturday morning rolls around fairly quickly. The last few days have been a blur with back-to-back meetings and a quick trip to San Francisco. I shower and pull my chino shorts, black tee, and sneakers on. White seems like a bad idea with all the meat splatter off the grill.

I leave my room, heading toward the kitchen when I hear Kate's voice.

"I'm fine, Charlie," Kate asserts, her tone warm yet not her usual perky self. "Work has been busy. That's all."

"I know you have a lot going on. I hope you're practicing self-care?"

What the hell is it with women and self-care? They

thrive on it. Men, however, do not.

"Yes, mother," Kate responds more sarcastically. "I'm taking care of all my needs. Sometimes, even twice a night."

I chuckle quietly. It's a typical Kate response, and I realize how much I miss the sound of her voice.

"I love you," Charlie assures her. "But trust me, no vibrator can replace a real man."

"But mine tells me he loves me, and sometimes, if you play nice, he'll even snuggle by your side and whisper sweet nothings in your ear."

Charlie's laugh breaks the tension. "Mine used to do that, too. Then Lex got jealous and threw it out."

The two of them laugh as I inch my way closer to the room. I clear my throat, not wanting to ambush her.

Charlie is quick to say good morning, eyeing the two of us as Kate's eyes glance toward me. Something odd washes over me, a sense of guilt and pang at the same time. It's unusual, and I'm not sure what the hell the feelings are.

"Hey." I smile, keeping my distance.

"Hey."

Quickly, she diverts her eyes back to her plate. The move surprises me, and while I'd typically call her out on it, Charlie is still watching us.

"I need to grab something in the..." Charlie stares at the ceiling, "... basement."

"I'll get it for you," I offer.

"No, no... it's small, and I can use the exercise."

She disappears in a flash, leaving us behind in this awkward position.

Silence falls over the kitchen. I'm unsure of what to say, not wanting to bring up Morgan, so I try to find another excuse for my distant behavior.

"I'm glad you're visiting. Charlie can use some female companionship. A bit too much testosterone in the house."

"I'm only here for work," she claims, standing and still avoiding me.

I reach out, grabbing her arm with my hand. The second I do, every part of me misses her, and I realize I've been acting like an idiot. "I'm sorry, Kate."

"I'm not sure what you're sorry for," she recites, still unable to look at me.

"Can you look at me, please?"

She lets out a sigh, her blue eyes meeting mine. I miss her crazy ass. The way she pokes fun at me, the endless rants on men and their fucked-up emotions.

"Noah, it is what it is."

"It is what it is?" I repeat, slightly confused.

"You've got another life. I mean, you're committed now. It's fine. Listen, I've got some emails that need answering."

She tries to shrug out of my grip, I let go but quickly add, "Kate, please don't. I need you. Life isn't the same, and you're important to me. This is all a learning curve for me. I'm sorry I haven't checked in."

"You don't need to apologize. You're in love."

"I'm not in love," I concede, thrown back by the brutality of her words. "Bros don't fall in love, remember?"

She nods her head, but the silence lingers until I pull her back to me and embrace her tightly. Her hair still smells like strawberries, and I can't help but smile at the familiarity once again. Against my chest, I feel her sigh and her body relax. We just need to find a new normal between us, that's all.

"So, I heard you're getting serious with your vibrator," I joke, kissing her hair. "You know he'll ruin you for all men?"

Kate smacks my chest, pulling back but remaining in my embrace. "What makes you think it's a he?"

"Because it's shaped like a dick."

"Oh, good point…"

"So, are we good?" I ask, resting my hand on her shoulder.

She nods with a grin. "We're good."

Charlie walks back in with a fancy plate. "Okay, so let's get this show on the road. Lex is marinating chicken outback. I tell you what, he never tells me what's in the marinade since, according to him, it takes hours to prepare, but it tastes amazing. He could be a chef."

"Is there anything that man can't do?"

"Do you want the clean or dirty answer?" Charlie asks seriously, keeping her grin to a bare minimum.

"Clean," Kate and I almost yell in unison.

"Let's see…" She taps the spoon over her mouth. "He can't do a French braid."

My face remains placid. "Can he do a regular braid?"

"Yes," she responds with a smile. "If you've got girls, you've gotta learn."

"Okay, this conversation is over," I tell them. "So,

275

listen, can I bring Morgan to the barbecue? I think it would be good for her to meet you guys."

"I finally get to meet the girl who tamed the beast," Kate snickers.

"Beast? Give me some credit, Kate."

"Oh, fine. I finally get to meet the girl who stole your heart."

I almost choke on my coffee. "No, there's no stealing of hearts. In fact, there are no hearts involved whatsoever." I laugh nervously.

Charlie puts down her mug and watches me sternly along with Kate. These two women could bring a whole army down with their patronizing stares.

"Shall I tell him?" Charlie looks at Kate, goading a response.

Kate nods her head, agreeing.

"Tell me what?"

"You're falling for her. Hard," Charlie asserts.

"I am not," I lie. "I really enjoy being with her."

"Denial will only get you so far, Noah," Kate adds her two cents' worth. "So, I guess Scarlett's out of the picture, then?"

"Never say never."

When the words leave my mouth, I instantly regret them. Scarlett is beautiful. She can charm the universe with just one smile. But I have to admit to myself, as much as it troubles me to do so, that my defense mechanism went up because I'm scared that I am falling for Morgan. I don't even know how that feels or what it truly means. But whatever it is, I haven't thought it before, and it's terrifying me. I'm confusing great sex with love.

"You can't pursue Scarlett if you're seeing Morgan." Charlie's quick to judge.

I grit through my words. "I'm not seeing her."

"Then, what are you doing?"

"Having fun. It doesn't need a label."

"Okay." Charlie coughs. "Commitment phobe."

Kate's annoying laughter bounces off the walls at the same time the doorbell chimes.

I offer to get it since these two women are driving me insane. I walk to the door, open it, and find my mom standing with a suitcase.

"Mom?"

She steps forward, touching my face before giving me a great big hug. I wrap my arms around her, not realizing how much I've missed having her around. She holds onto me for a while, and although I tower over her, her presence alone reminds me of being back home.

"What are you doing here?" I ask, lifting her bag inside.

"An SOS call. Plus, I kinda missed ya, kid." She smiles.

Closing the door behind her, she follows me to the kitchen. The second Charlie lays eyes on her, she jumps out of her chair and runs to Mom, holding onto her tight. Both of them look sad, almost in tears.

Really? Did someone die here? *Women.*

Kate introduces herself. Mom watches me with curious eyes. I shake my head and circle my finger around my ear, motioning that Kate is cuckoo.

"I can see that," Kate bellows. "I'm the crazy one? I'm not the one falling in love with a movie star's sister."

Silence falls over the room. I could strangle Kate right now with my bare hands. Mom hides the smile on her face, Charlie turning around and pretending to make coffee.

"I think you forgot to take your crazy pills." I laugh it off. "Hurry along, Kate, the bus to the mental facility will be here at any moment."

"Ha-ha." She smirks. "Should I hand you a collar now or later?"

The girls enter the room, distracting us all while Mom fusses over them. Charlie knew she was coming but kept it quiet to surprise me. Mom's flown in for a few days for a potential job offer in LA. I have mixed feelings about her being here, mainly because I know it means she'll have to meet Morgan.

When the kitchen becomes quiet, Mom asks to speak to me outside, alone. We sit on the porch watching the girls play in the backyard.

"I like Kate," she begins. "The two of you have some uncanny connection."

"No connection, Mom." I'm quick to shut down the concept. "Kate is Kate."

"And what's that?"

"I don't know," I say, unsure. "Someone who I can be myself around without any judgment. She just gets me."

"And this Morgan?"

I know why Charlie's not outside watching the girls. She's hiding because her big fat mouth can't keep shut.

"Mom, I don't want to talk about it."

She appears offended. It's not that I don't trust Mom. It just seems like the more I talk about it, the more of a big deal everyone makes it out to be.

"Sorry, Mom," I quickly say. "It's complicated, and I'm not sure what to say."

Pursing her lips together, she remains quiet, not pushing me further. "I ran into Tom last week. He asked how you were."

My ears perk up immediately. "And Benny?"

"Not sure, kid. I haven't seen him around much. One of the ladies at the hairdresser's said he was moving up north somewhere."

"The ladies at your hairdresser also thought I had knocked up his girlfriend."

She laughs and rests her hand on my arm. "I'm sure they both miss you. The three of you were inseparable."

I don't want to discuss them anymore, either. They have moved on, and so have I. I have a new life out here and new friends. What happened between us is a thing of the past. It's time to forget about them and go on with life out here.

I excuse myself when Ava asks to play Barbies and hands me a boy Barbie, ducking to my room to call Morgan.

"Hey, I've only got five minutes because I've got lawyers coming in. Some moron took pictures of Scarlett in an exclusive spa and wants to sell them to the press," she answers all in one breath.

"Uh-oh. If it's any consolation, she's got a great body. If you've got it, flaunt it."

She keeps quiet over the speaker, and perhaps my words weren't the right choice. I don't know how to save myself from here. "So, Lex and Charlie are having a barbecue. Are you free? I'd really love for you to meet them."

"My dad is here," she replies.

"That's okay. I'm sure Charlie won't mind."

She remains quiet, then responds in a worried tone, "Uh… okay. So, I guess you'll meet my dad."

"Okay, and so for my next piece of news… my mom's here," I say slowly.

"Okay." She follows with, "Is that good or bad?"

"Good, I guess, because I miss her. Bad, maybe, because she, uh—"

"She'll whip out a baby photo of you in the nude wearing a handbag?"

I laugh. "Ironically, I do have a photo like that. I've never brought a girl home…"

More silence.

I hate silence.

"Are you saying you've never been in a relationship?" she asks, somewhat shocked at my admission.

"Yes," I admit, not ashamed of my playboy nature.

"Wow," she exclaims over the receiver. "After all these years, how do you get out of staying with a woman?"

"Easy," I answer. "I just wasn't interested. I didn't exactly mingle with women wanting a relationship."

There's noise in the background. Morgan apologizes, saying goodbye and hanging up the call. A few minutes later, I get a text.

Morgan: *Don't for one minute think you're getting out of that conversation.*

It was bound to come up, and if life has taught me anything so far, I need to start being honest with everyone including myself. Sure, I have a past. Don't we all? But I've left it all behind. My baggage didn't carry itself here to Los Angeles, and I'm certainly glad that Morgan is equally baggage free.

***

The food smells delicious and true to Charlie's word, Lex is excellent at the barbecue. There are many guests who Charlie introduces me to, from her neighbors across the street to Lex's parents and sister. I politely say hello, making small talk like the well-mannered son my mom raised me to be.

Eric brought his couch surfers. Basically, it's a bunch of Swedish men crashing in his apartment. I ask no further questions on that matter.

And, of course, Kate, who has conveniently positioned herself next to the table with the punch wearing a big sun hat.

"Are you wearing that to shield the earth from all the galactic forces?" I mock her.

"I'll have you know that skin cancer is a deadly disease."

"It is..." I agree. "You'll turn into a lobster, won't you?"

"An English lobster at that, but hey, I got the magic juice." She holds up a solo cup, cheering herself on.

I leave her alone to get drunk and sunburned to see Morgan enter the yard with her dad by her side. He's the spitting image of Scarlett—same eyes, and even the eyebrows are shaped the same. Given that he's from Little Rock, I expected some hick-town old man and am surprised he looks young and fit for his age.

She waves at me, and I walk toward her, unsure whether or not I should kiss her. So, I lean in and kiss her cheek as she pulls back and introduces me, "Noah, this is my dad, Max."

I shake his hand as a sign of respect and then offer him a beer. Lex and Charlie have joined us, introducing themselves. Charlie seems to take to Morgan, pulling her aside and introducing her to the girls. This is all new to me. I don't know why I feel incredibly uncomfortable. It's like all my worlds colliding in one backyard.

"I'm Ava, Uncle Noah's favorite," Ava says confidently.

Morgan leans across to me. "The sleepwalker and toothbrush bandit?"

I ruffle Ava's hair. "Yep. She also enjoys using my cell and buying apps because Uncle Noah has never had to lock his account before."

Ava has a way with her words, talking endlessly about anything and everything. Morgan has the patience of a saint, weighing in heavily on which *Wiggle* she likes best. I don't even know what the hell a *Wiggle* is.

We sit down at one of the picnic tables when Kate and Mom walk outside with bowls of chips and some salad. I turn my head as Kate sees us at the table, her usual mischievous grin playing on her lips. She leans over to whisper into Mom's ear before they both turn around and walk our way.

Here we go.

This is it.

Why the fuck are you sweating bullets?

I turn around, pretending not to notice when Kate purposely wraps her arms around me, giving me a big hug. "Hey, momma's boy."

I pull her arms off me, noticing her eyes are glazed over caused by too much punch. "You know my mom is standing right here?"

"Yes." She grins. "She gave me the go-ahead to call you that. In fact, she insisted."

In the space of a few hours, Mom and Kate seem inseparable. I don't understand why. Kate is great, but I made it clear that nothing would happen between us. At least, nothing *else* would happen between us.

Mom clears her throat, raising her eyebrows at me. I shake my head, forgetting that Morgan and her dad are standing beside me.

"Morgan, Max, please meet my friend, Kate, and, of course, my mom," I say, toning down the enthusiasm.

"Mom, Kate... this is Morgan, my uh... girlfriend." I gulp.

Morgan's eyes widen.

Damn! I don't know what compelled me to call her that.

What the fuck is wrong with me?

Kate extends her hand, shaking Max's first, then reaching out to Morgan. I notice that Morgan's withdrawn and appears quieter than usual. She has that same expression on her face from when I first had that meeting in her office.

"I'm so happy to finally meet you. Noah's told me so

283

much about you," Kate mentions happily.

"Interesting," she says, monotone. "He never talks about you."

There's an awkward silence.

Of course, I don't talk about her.

What's there to say? We're friends, that's it.

I don't understand Morgan's abrupt change of attitude.

Beside me, Mom has struck up a conversation with Max, leaving the three of us alone as they walk toward where Lex is cooking.

Kate looks at me, raising her eyebrows. "It's really nice to meet you. I'm going to grab a drink. The good stuff is inside. Aunty Kate needs some grownup drink to get through the game of hide and seek that's just about to start."

She offers for Morgan to join her, but she refuses. She's coming off rude and snobbish. With her dad walking back toward us, it allows me to excuse myself for a moment to head to the house. Both Mom and Charlie are in the kitchen preparing some snacks for the kids. Kate is nowhere to be seen.

"Mom," I call. "I need your help."

"What have you done now?" she's quick to question.

"Nothing... at least, I don't know. Morgan's acting weird all of a sudden, and I want to ask her why but she's with her dad. Can you distract him again, so I can pull her aside?"

"I noticed she seems introverted."

"She's normally not like that," I say in her defense. "She just met Kate and then got all weird."

Charlie and Mom look at each other, both of them with smiles on their faces like I'm missing out on their private joke.

"Noah," Charlie says. "She's probably jealous. I know you and Kate are really close, as in friends, but for those who don't know that, you guys look like a couple."

"But we're not."

"I know that. Kate knows that. Women can be finicky. I can try to talk to her if you want?" Charlie suggests.

"No, I should probably try to fix this." I sigh.

This, here, is why I don't do relationships. Factoring in someone else's emotions is draining. I walk outside and find them again. This time, Mom comes to my rescue, following with a plate of snacks, offering them to Morgan and her dad. Max continues to make more small talk with Mom, some joke about cheese which gives me a moment to pull Morgan aside.

"Thank you for coming today and meeting my family and friends." I wrap my hand around her waist, pulling her close to me. *I want her now.*

"Your family is really nice, Noah."

"And my friends?" I laugh.

"I've only met Kate. She seems nice." And there's that odd tone again.

"She is nice. But she's only a friend, Morgan, nothing more."

"I know."

"Do you?"

"Yes." She sighs, leaning into me.

I kiss the top of her hair. "You're cute when you're jealous."

"Argh. Is that what this is?"

I laugh again. "Apparently so. Anyway, I'd like you to spend some time with Kate. She's really awesome."

"Okay," is all she manages to say.

The party continues, and much to our surprise, Mom and Max get into a heated conversation about politics, which strikes me as odd since Mom never talks about anything political.

With Morgan chatting to Lex's sister, I chase the girls around, making growling sounds as their screams echo around us. Between the running around and multiple times in the bouncy castle, I'm beat.

"Uncle Noah," Ava calls again. "One more time in the bouncy castle."

I groan, setting down my drink and following Ava into the castle. We play this game where I pretty much throw her against the inflatable wall, and she giggles, asking me to do it again. On my fourth attempt, her cousin Andy stares back at me with a pale face.

"Are you okay, bud?"

He shakes his head, then tilts forward, projectile vomiting all over my shirt. My throat closes in, my stomach contracting as I attempt to control the dry heaving. The kids scream, frantically jumping out of the castle as Andy cries. I'm barely able to contain my own need to projectile vomit, but extend my hand out to him just as his dad comes in.

"It's okay." His dad, Julian, soothes him. Picking him up into his arms, not caring at all that he's now gotten vomit all over his shirt.

"Sorry, man," Julian apologizes. "His mom warned

him not to have too much Jell-O, and, well... this is what happens when you have too much Jell-O."

It explains the array of colors splashed all over my black shirt. I tell him it's fine, and then follow them out as Charlie enters with a bucketload of cleaning products which Lex's sister, Adriana, takes off her.

"Do you need help?" I ask, still reeling from the godawful stench.

"No, it's okay. You clean yourself up, but thanks for offering. I think Lex ran off and vomited in the bush."

Morgan looks back at me with a sympathetic expression while I walk toward the house cringing. I don't know what to do with my shirt, wanting to throw it in the trash but remembering the hefty price tag on it. I leave it in the bathroom sink and hop into the shower, quickly scrubbing myself clean. When I hop out, I dry myself and change into my jeans before heading into my room. There's a knock on the door, and Morgan enters, closing the door quietly behind her.

She can't peel her eyes away from my torso, her lips clenching as she stands in utter silence.

"Geez, I have a face, you know," I tease.

She shakes her head, breaking her gaze. "Cocky bastard."

I move closer to her, wrapping my arms around her waist. "Cocky, yes."

I grab her hand and place it on the bulge of my jeans. She squeezes for just a moment, then tries to pull away. "Noah, there are kids here."

"Downstairs. Outside. Not in this room. It's just you and me."

287

I kiss the side of her neck, desperate to taste her. Running my nose along her collarbone, the smell of her skin draws me in. *I need to fuck her so bad.*

"Let's go to your place tonight. Fuck your roommate." I bury my head in her hair, desperately hoping she'll agree.

"I have this thing tonight. For Scarlett."

"C'mon. Scarlett will understand. Just say you need the night off. After all, you're my girlfriend."

That word is foreign and sounds odd every time I say it.

This is why I hate labels.

"About that..." she begins, then stalls. "That was out of the blue. You could've warned me. My dad was right there."

I let go of her, annoyed and walk to the dresser where I grab another shirt and put it on.

"C'mon, Noah, we haven't even talked about any of this."

"Is that my fault? I'm forever trying to reach out to you, yet you pull away. Isn't that what I should be doing? I'm the guy here. I should be the one constantly unavailable," I yell out of frustration.

"That's sexist and unfair, Noah. I get it, you've been with several women. That's all you do, fuck around. Possibly with Kate, too, right?"

"Don't even start..."

"She had her arms around you, I can see your connection with her."

"We're. Just. Friends," I shout, sick of defending our relationship.

"This is too complicated," she mumbles to herself. "I just really needed you. I can't explain it."

I can't help but release a sinister laugh. "Yep, that's what they all say."

Her face contorts to a shocked yet angry stare. "Excuse me? I'm not like your other girls, Noah."

"No," I say, looking her directly in the eye. "That's the problem here. You're not at all like them."

Standing apart, silence falls over the room.

"I can't do this anymore. This fighting—"

I interrupt her. "And running away?"

"I'm not running away."

"So why can't you cancel tonight? Or even invite me? God," I tell her, embittered. "Are you embarrassed to be in a relationship with me?" It kills me to say it, but I can't deal with her fucking secrecy anymore.

"Of course, n-not," she stutters. "Tonight is just..."

I grab my cell that's sitting on top of the dresser. "I'll call Scarlett."

"Why?" she asks, panicked.

I scroll through my contacts and dial her number. When Scarlett answers, I place her on speaker.

"Hi, Scarlett," I say in a much sweeter tone. "I had a meeting with Morgan, and she mentioned she had something to attend tonight with you."

"Hi, Noah," she responds cheerfully. "Yes. There's a red-carpet party on Sunset. You should come. And bring some friends."

I stare at Morgan, satisfied.

She turns her head away, looking toward the window as she folds her arms.

"You know what, I'll take you up on that. We ran out of time, and I was hoping to catch her there."

"Sounds great. I'll have her text you all the details. I'm really looking forward to seeing you, Noah."

I say goodbye and hang up the phone. "So, I guess you better forward me those details," I remind her, sarcastically.

"You're a fucking stubborn ass, you know that?" she huffs.

"It's like looking in the mirror, isn't it?"

"Fuck you," she mouths, before storming off and slamming the door behind her.

CHAPTER
26

NOAH

I should've known better than to invite Charlie and Kate to the red-carpet event. Lex warned me it would create this bizarre frenzy within them. I laughed it off, being the naïve dickhead who underestimated the power of a woman possessed by Hollywood.

With Mom in town and willing to babysit the girls, Charlie jumped at the chance to go out for the evening. Both Charlie and Kate went into 'wardrobe meltdown' as they called it, spending a good hour in Charlie's closet trying to figure out what to wear.

Morgan left with her dad, apologizing to everyone that she had to be at an event. Max was kind enough to say goodbye. Morgan chose to ignore me, without a goodbye, taking her stubborn and childish ass along with her.

We arrive at the party in separate cars, Charlie taking it upon herself to invite Haden and Presley. I don't mind so much. It just put Kate and me in an awkward position being surrounded by married couples.

The room's large, an ample event space that's decked out like a nightclub, dimly lit with a stream of neon lights. The bar area takes the whole back wall, each barstool occupied with guests. The music is playing loudly in the background, making it difficult to hear each other.

"I think I just saw Zac Efron," Kate squeals into my ear, squeezing my arm tight.

I roll my eyes, then lean in. "Isn't he young enough to be your son?"

She slaps my chest instantly, knocking me back slightly. "You had no problem with my age before our beach incident."

"That's before I knew you were a grandma," I joke lightly.

Kate's only a year older than me but has a youthful glow, quickly mistaking her for being younger. I just like to poke fun to rile her up.

"By the way..." I add, eyeing her up and down, admiring her sexy body in front of me. I'll admit it again, she has great tits having already seen her completely naked. "You look hot tonight."

She's wearing one of Charlie's dresses, a sheer black dress that sits short with tall black pumps, making the top of her head sit just below my eyes.

"Why, thank you." Kate grins happily. "You scrub up surprisingly good yourself. Nine out of ten."

"Nine out of ten? Where did I lose the point?"

"I'm not sure," she says playfully. "But if I rated you ten, then I'd have to take you home and shag ya. So, you can see the bind I'm in."

I keep my opinion to myself, distracted by chaos at the door. Scarlett has walked in, wearing a long silver gown that sparkles, almost blinding me. With her signature red lips, she's tied her hair into a sleek ponytail, posing with guests who are taking selfies.

She's gorgeous, no doubt, but my entire body comes to a complete still the moment my eyes land on Morgan. She's standing a few steps behind Scarlett, carefully camouflaging herself. The second Scarlett steps away, she's in full view.

Everything in the room slows down, and the music sounds distant. My eyes are fixated on her, and only her. She looks angelic, the white dress only accentuating her natural beauty. She's wearing her hair out, pushed to one side, flowing down the side of her body and stopping just above her hips.

My body gravitates toward her, long steps in sync with the loud thump banging in my chest. With just the tilt of her beautiful face, her eyes meet mine.

"Noah," she mouths, smiling.

"I'm glad you're happy to see me. After this afternoon's little tantrum, I thought you might banish me to the corner of this room."

She moves closer, careful to keep a reasonable distance between us. "I couldn't banish someone so hot to the corner. Unless, of course, I'm there riding you."

I can only respond with a wide smirk, keeping my head down as I try to compose myself. God, I fucking *love* her. The way she makes me laugh even when we're in the middle of a petty argument.

"Noah!" Scarlett calls, leaning in and kissing me hello. The cameras flash everywhere around us, and I'm not sure what to do. I follow her lead, posing along with her while scanning the area looking for Morgan.

"So, who did you come here with?" she asks, pulling me aside.

"My cousin, her husband, and a friend. Oh, and Haden and Presley."

"Great," she says with enthusiasm. "I'd love to say hello."

"Kate's here?" Morgan's mood shifts, watching her from across the room. "Why did you come with her?"

"I didn't come with her." I smile through my teeth as Scarlett watches us. "She tagged along with Charlie and Lex."

"I need to go... a work thing has come up." Morgan storms off before I have the chance to question her behavior.

Scarlett takes the opportunity to introduce me to some friends. They are actors, and I recognize them from some action films.

I look around again and can't find Morgan, so I begin to move through the crowd to where everyone's sitting. Charlie's the first to react, her eyes spinning with stars. Kate's no different, squealing like an overly hormonal teenager. Lex is more reserved, keeping his expression to nothing more than a polite smile. I know him well enough to know he wouldn't react with enthusiasm in front of Charlie, or she'll drag him by the balls back home.

Scarlett says hello to everyone, keeping her

conversation friendly and laid back. Haden and Presley can't help themselves, talking about work and the progress of the book. I haven't found Morgan again, pulling Scarlett to the side.

"Where's Morgan?"

"Probably doing business somewhere," she brushes me off.

She continues to chat with Charlie and Kate for a few more minutes before she has to leave to do some press interviews.

"Can you believe that," Kate exclaims with such awe. "She's so beautiful. Flawless even."

"I know," Charlie follows. "I wouldn't kick her out of bed."

Lex hides his smirk behind his drink.

Haden's quick to comment, "I believe you've just been invited to a threesome."

Both Lex and I laugh, annoying the girls.

"You know what, Haden?" Presley says, annoyed. "You're such a jerk."

"Perhaps," he says through a satisfied grin. "A jealous jerk."

"Oh, sure," she teases sarcastically. "You guys are all talk. I'd love to have a threesome… blah, blah, blah… but I bet if it came down to it, you'd freak out."

I don't involve myself in this conversation. I've had threesomes and never freaked out. Quite the opposite, actually. Lex remains tight-lipped, but Haden has to weigh in, of course, because the two of them continuously argue.

"Really? You think I'd freak out?" he challenges Presley.

She nods her head. "Uh-huh."

"Well, then... bring it on."

"So, you don't mind another guy being in bed with us?" she asks with a sarcastic smirk lingering on her face.

Haden doesn't take the joke lightly, his nostrils flaring like a wild beast. "You're such a pain in the ass."

We laugh as they continue to goad each other, and I only break away when Morgan's by my side. She appears worried but quickly puts on a smile, saying hello to everyone, including Kate. I ask her for a moment in private, taking her outside and around the corner, ready to question the goddamn mood swings giving me whiplash.

There's no one here except for a few passing by. The urge—unable to withhold—consumes me while I pull her into me and kiss her soft lips. She parts them evenly, allowing my tongue to meet with hers while they battle in a frenzy. My hands move of their own accord, sliding around to her back, which is exposed. Her skin is warm with tiny goosebumps forming the deeper I kiss her.

Out of breath and panting heavily, she whispers, "Noah, I think we need to talk."

I place my lips on hers again, not wanting to talk but instead taste her.

She pulls back, this time with a slight force. "Noah, please listen to me."

"I'm listening," I half say, buried in the crook of her neck. "You're so beautiful."

296

She places her hands firmly on my chest. Her expression remains fixed, then pleads with me to stop.

I don't know why I listen. Maybe because that's what you're supposed to do in a relationship. Or at least that's what I think you should do. I know I'm not thinking straight. I've missed her, yet I'm angry about the way she stormed out earlier this afternoon.

"Can we talk tonight? After the party?"

I run my finger along her cheek, watching her eyes close for a brief moment only to flicker wide open seconds later.

"Noah, please stop touching me and listen to what I'm saying," she demands, distancing herself from me.

My bruised ego has had enough.

This is fucking bullshit.

"I'm listening, Morgan, because it's the only thing I can do," I bellow in frustration. "I can't fucking see you whenever I want. You won't let me see your place. You don't want Scarlett to know about us. For some reason, you can't get it through your head that Kate is a good friend. What else are you going to request? That I place a fucking paper bag over my head while I'm in the same room as you?"

The hurt and pain mixed with anger reflect back at me. Perhaps I've gone too far, but I never claimed to be a saint or a patient one at that.

"You see, this here is why you'll never understand," she says with a sick laugh.

I don't even comment. Walking away, I leave her behind. This whole thing has become drama after drama, and I don't do *drama.*

297

Back inside, the party's only just starting. A famous band is playing on stage. Everywhere you look, celebrities are surrounding us—some with their significant others, and the rest mingling in the crowd.

Charlie and Lex are on the dance floor along with Haden and Presley. Kate is standing at the bar, conversing with some old dude. She looks over to me, pleading with her eyes to rescue her from the situation she's found herself in. I casually walk over and rest my arm over her shoulder in desperate need of a drink.

"Oh, would you look at who's arrived?" she says with a fake smile. "It's my boyfriend. Going on five years tonight. Definitely going to be celebrating all night long if you know what I mean?"

Winking at the old man, he seems to back off, excusing himself rather quickly. "He knew what you meant," I tell her. "The whole room knew what you meant."

"Why the foul mood, Mason? You're such a Debbie Downer tonight."

I'm about to open my mouth when I notice Morgan standing behind me. Kate is quick to say hello, and in typical Morgan style she acts like a fucking bitch, returning a forced smile.

"I should probably go," Kate says cautiously. "Over there." She points randomly into the crowd, but Morgan stops her.

"Why don't you stay for this? Apparently, Noah has all the time in the world for you but doesn't have a few minutes to listen to me," she notes with dark amusement.

Kate purses her lips, unsure of what to say or do.

I don't understand what the fuck Morgan's problem is, quick to defend Kate's and my relationship again. "Ignore her, Kate. Wicked bitch from the West is back," I say out loud, never breaking her gaze.

Morgan looks stunned, her mouth slightly open with her eyes narrowing. If the music quieted down, I am sure you'd be able to hear her teeth grinding. She looks livid. And I know I'm in for the biggest fight of my life. The storm is looming, and it's about to strike.

"We're so done, Noah."

I no longer care, fed up with the ridiculous games she plays.

"Great girlfriend material," I mention sarcastically. "At least I can say I tried a relationship. Definitely not for me."

Folding her arms with her chest rising and falling rapidly, she says, "You assumed I'm your girlfriend. As you assumed we're in a relationship."

That fucking hurt.

Bitch.

She moves toward me, closing the distance between us. I stare into her eyes, hoping that for just a moment, this is a petty fight. But her eyes are cold, so cold that the woman behind them isn't the Morgan I've grown to love. Her lips brush against my ear, and in the sweetest of voices, she whispers, "I was only looking for a rebound, Noah."

Like ice hitting my skin, I freeze. Paralyzed by the malicious intent of her words, she pulls away from me and begins walking in the opposite direction. I stare into the crowd, vacant and without any emotion. The fire inside my belly is stirring, building into a fit of rage as her words sink in.

The fucking bitch!

Kate warns me to calm down, witnessing the whole encounter. I push her out of the way, scanning the room in an attempt to hunt down Morgan. *She's gone.*

The crowd has grown, and willingly, I turn around and motion for the bartender to serve me.

"Noah," Kate warns me again.

I don't listen.

I'm done with women.

Slamming the shot down, I demand another. After four in a row, my nerves seem calmer. I head back to our table. Charlie and Lex are too touchy-feely for my liking.

"Fucking get a room already," I yell at them, mid-shot.

Haden's no better. For someone I work with, he has no problem practically groping Presley under the table. I've been with enough women to know that he's either brushing his fingers against her clit or fingering her under the table. Either way, I need to leave.

My only problem—I shouldn't have drunk so much because I'm too intoxicated to drive.

When Kate strolls over, I wrap my arms around her and tell her how beautiful she is. I can always rely on Kate. I should never have allowed Morgan to make me believe otherwise.

"Okay," she says plainly. "What do you want?"

"I need a ride," I tell her, kissing the top of her hand.

She pulls it away. "Do I have 'Uber' written on my forehead?"

"No. You have 'horny woman who needs to get laid by Zac Efron' written on your forehead."

She nods her head, agreeing. I manage to convince her. She's also eager to leave the couples to get on with their business.

"Take me to Scarlett's place," I demand, slurring.

"Why?"

"I need to talk to her."

Lies. I want to fuck her to forget. That would be the final nail in this fucked-up coffin called our relationship. Morgan would be hurt, and payback would sure be sweet right about now.

"But you're drunk, Noah, and upset," she reminds me, starting the engine. "What do you need to talk about?"

"Just do it. Okay?"

Kate lets out an annoyed huff before taking off.

It's late, and the traffic is moving nicely down the freeway. Kate turns up the radio, playing some Katy Perry song. She hums along, distracted by her own thoughts until I startle her.

"Fuck!" I shout.

"What?" she responds, panicked, trying to look over.

"My cell died."

She rolls her eyes, ignoring my first-world problem and driving up the windy street until we reach Scarlett's home. For most of the ride, she tries to convince me not to go, but also knows me well enough to drop the subject after I basically tell her to fuck off.

The security guard calls through and opens the gates, allowing me in. When we reach the top of the drive, Scarlett comes out with a concerned look on her face, eyeing our surroundings.

"Hey," I smirk, stumbling out of the car.

"Didn't you get my text? I also tried to call you," she says in a high-pitched voice.

"My phone died at..."

In the corner of my eye, behind the large tree, I see Morgan's Mercedes. "Morgan's here?"

I walk toward the house, ignoring Scarlett's plea to stop. *I don't want Scarlett.* And maybe this is a blessing in disguise. I have to apologize in person to Morgan and tell her I fucking love her.

Because I do.

She's nowhere to be seen, so I move toward the patio where I see an outdoor fire pit and guests sitting on chairs. Scarlett calls my name in a panic, demanding to know what I'm doing. Then, I see her. She's sitting on a chair, laughing with a glass of wine in her hand.

I step outside, and the second she sees me, her face drops. Pained and pleading for me to understand, she remains silent, not saying my name. I'm confused, and I look behind me where Kate stands and Scarlett's biting her nails.

"Noah," Scarlett says, pulling my arm back.

There's a man, roughly my height, wearing a knitted sweater and dark blue jeans. He has a bottle of beer in his hand, and next to him sits a boy about Amelia's age with Max.

He stands, extending his hand. "You must be Noah. Scarlett and Morgan have spoken quite fondly of your work."

I should be flattered, but my confusion only stems

further. "Thank you. And you are?"

"I'm Wyatt, Morgan's husband, and this is our son, Michael."

The core of my insides stiffens, and the echo I hear is only that of my heart being torn into shreds. The muscles inside my neck strain to remain composed, my posture demanding I fall over at any moment. But throughout the pain that's currently crippling my every move, I twist my head to meet Morgan's eyes.

"Noah," she pleads.

I rip my arm away from Scarlett's grip, trying not to lash out in front of the kid, but my tongue is tied, no words or sounds can be spoken. *I want to die.* Throw me into the pool and let me sink to the bottom. And then I remember her words. The ones that tore me apart more than I could ever have possibly imagined.

I was her *rebound.*

And standing in front of me is the person she was running from—her husband.

I latch onto Kate's arm and pull her through the house, ignoring my name being called. Pushing through the glass door, I stomp toward the car, getting in the driver's seat and roaring the engine to life.

"Noah, calm down," Kate begs, motioning for me to get out of the driver's seat. "You can't drive. The last thing you need is a DUI on record."

I tell her to get in and shut the fuck up, my anger fueling me to leave this place and everyone behind. There's banging on the window, Morgan desperate for me to open, but I refuse. Placing the car into gear and slamming my foot on the accelerator, I kick up stones as

303

I drive down the hill, almost taking out a few statues.

"Where are you going?" Kate cries, holding onto the handle while I skid out of the property.

"Anywhere but here."

CHAPTER
27

KATE

"Noah, you need to stop."

We've only driven out the gate and a few houses down before I manage to get him to stop, so I can take the wheel.

A whirlwind of emotions blurs my rational thoughts, still reeling at the sight of Morgan with her family—her husband and son.

His eyes are the first to react, stunned with a hurt glaze while he momentarily pieces the puzzle inside his head. My eyes are immediately drawn to his fists curled up against his side, and almost like I throw myself into battle mode, I do my best to prepare myself for a physical altercation.

The tension of his muscles is evident, and his inability to think clearly soon follows.

He's in a world of pain.

And I have no choice but to comfort him as he has done for me.

His anger becomes an explosion of rage, but I don't have a death wish. Drunk Noah behind the wheel isn't how I want our lives to end.

With my hands firmly on the wheel, at least controlling our lives for just this moment, I ask him where he wants to go. He refuses to go home, needing to let off steam and not wanting Charlie all up in his business. So, we settle for a bar not too far from the strip. Maybe, with more alcohol in him, he will pass out rather than go on some sort of angered spree.

But like the idiot I am, I began to drink—subconsciously trying to do the same. Forget certain feelings because they aren't worthy of holding my attention anymore. After my second drink, I decide to stop. One of us needs to be responsible, and it sure isn't going to be Noah.

"I don't need to do anything..." he slurs, dipping his hand into the peanut bowl and eating the urine infested nuts. "Oh, these taste crunchy with a slight tang."

I motion for the bartender to stop serving us, and he happily obliges, warning me several times to calm Noah down or my ass will be on the pavement. *Fucking wanker.*

"She's fucking married, Kate... and with a kid," he shouts for the millionth time.

"I know, Noah. I was there."

"*Married* with a *kid*," he repeats, running his hands through his hair as he closes his eyes. "It makes sense, all of it. I'm so dumb. I was too caught up to see what was really going on. I'm just some secret affair to her."

"I don't think it's just that, Noah. Maybe there's more—"

"Wait, you're defending her?" He turns his head swiftly, eyes blazing at me.

"No," I say, raising my hands in frustration. "I'm not defending her, but maybe there's something missing here. She doesn't strike me as someone who would have an affair and jeopardize her family."

"Yeah, and you don't strike me as someone who enjoys lesbian anal fisting," he says, monotone.

My mouth gapes open, and I quickly try to cover it up. "What makes you think that?"

"I accidentally saw it on your phone when my battery died yesterday. I needed to check the Lakers score."

I cough, beet red, unable to speak clearly. "It was for research purposes."

"That's what they all say. I'm not judging you. If you want to get fisted in your ass by another girl, then so be it. And, hey..." he says with a devilish smile, "... I'm free now, so I'll book courtside tickets."

"Ha-ha," I respond sarcastically. "Stop saying 'fisted.' It's weird. Besides, it stemmed from a conversation with Eric."

"Let's go home," I say, defeated, wondering how I can drag him to the car.

"Only if you'll fuck me."

From the moment Noah and I met, we had this connection. We grooved so effortlessly, making it comfortable for us to be ourselves. We gave it just as hard as we received it. But somewhere over the last two weeks, something has shifted between us.

There was a moment, beside me in my bed, when this line we both agreed needed to stay between us, suddenly obscured.

I saw him differently.

And craved him immensely.

I blame my insecurities and a broken heart for latching onto what I thought was *more.* So, I pulled away in the best interests for both of us. It's obvious to see Noah has developed strong feelings for Morgan, scared by his own journey into uncharted territory.

As for me, I have a lot of emotional baggage to work through and started the recovery process once again to piece myself back together.

But, Noah's actions and words question everything between us.

We drive silently to Charlie's house. I expect him to pass out on the ride, but the alcohol almost works in reverse. His eyes are wide, too alert for someone who drank so much.

When I pull into the driveway, I turn off the engine. It's way past midnight, on the brink of dawn. I have to be on a plane to Napa in a few hours and freshly attired to meet some business associates.

Noah shuffles beside me. "I meant what I said."

I shut him down, refusing to do this. "No."

"C'mon, I just need… you know—"

"You want a rebound. Someone, to take your mind off her?"

"Promise I'll get hard this time. Look…" he place's my hand on his cock, and true to his word, he's rock hard. "See?"

I remove my hand, exiting the car, and walking to the passenger side to open his door. Instead of getting out, he twists his body, sliding his hand up the side of my ribcage, whispering, "Please, Kate, let me fuck you. I promise you'll forget about him, too."

The weight of his touch is sending mixed messages throughout my body. I crave the touch of a man, a man who will give me what I need. Yet Noah will only *half* satisfy me. The physical connection will be amazing, but his mind will be elsewhere.

Certainly, not on me.

Definitely on Morgan.

With a delayed response, giving him false hope, I bow my head, trying to control the anger swelling within me.

"Noah, I don't care if you're drunk, okay? You and I are not each other's rebounds," I tell him as if I splashed cold water all over his face.

"Kate, I—"

"What Noah? You love her," I blurt out even though it hurts somewhat. "You're hurting because you love her."

"I'm not hurting because I love her, okay?" he shouts, removing his hands from me. "I'm hurting because she lied. I'm hurting because I've been following this feeling, but maybe it's wrong? Maybe the person has been there all along…"

I shake my head, distancing myself from him. How dare he throw something like that at me, staring at me as if we are anything else.

"Kate, please."

"Please, what, Noah?" I lift my gaze to meet his. He has gotten out of the car, his tall stature standing in front of me. "We don't do this, you and me. We do not use each other whenever it's convenient."

"I'm not using you, Kate," he preaches, an odd tone escaping him. "I'm just saying—"

"No, Noah. There's nothing left to say," I plead, desperate to end this right here. "You need to sober up."

"You and I..." he continues, "... we are—"

"Friends," I finish, ignoring the hurt festering inside. "We'll always be friends. Nothing more, nothing less."

And just like that, I've shut down anything between us.

He loves her.

Not me.

Noah may not have realized it just yet, but I was never supposed to the woman he fell for. He's confused, plain and simple. My job is to be his friend, help him heal from the pain of a broken heart.

Nothing more, and of course, nothing *less*.

CHAPTER
28

NOAH

I roll over to my side, my head pounding to the beat of a drum. No, wait, it's actually drums. *Argh, that damn drum set.* I throw my pillow over my head until there's a knock on my door. Amelia walks in carrying a bottle of water and two white pills. She turns around to look at Charlie, who encourages her to hand them to me.

"Uncle Noah, Mommy says take this medicine to make you feel better."

I take it from her, swallowing it in one go. Amelia runs out of the room, leaving Charlie behind. She sits on the edge of my bed with a worried expression.

"I heard what happened."

I throw my head back onto the pillow. "From Kate?"

She nods her head. "It's okay to be angry. I know I would be."

I close my eyes, wishing this nightmare away. "Am I *that* stupid I didn't see the signs? I pride myself on knowing how to read women. God, that's how I managed

311

to get through these years without being tied down in a relationship."

"You're not stupid," she tells me. "When you're infatuated with someone, you can barely think straight. It's like a whirlwind of emotions where nothing makes sense, and you're being taken on this wild ride that consumes every part of you."

Her theory makes sense. I saw the signs, but I chose to ignore them, thinking it was nothing more than my wild imagination. And I didn't press on for fear of losing her. Stupid as it may seem, it was never my intention.

"Charlie," I say softly, afraid to admit the truth. "Am I in love with her?"

"I don't know, Noah. Only you can answer that."

"But I don't even know what that feels like. And I've only known her for three weeks. How can you fall in love with someone after three weeks? Isn't that too soon?"

She smiles, toying with the wedding band on her finger. "I don't think there's a set time. Sometimes it's love at first sight, and other times, it is with someone who has been there all along. Like a friend, for example," she trails off, watching me with curious eyes.

"I know where you're going with this."

Charlie purses her lips, remaining quiet. Of late, she's been vocal about my friendship with Kate despite both of us telling her there's nothing going on.

"Just go with your gut."

"My gut doesn't fall in love," I inform her. "It preys on broken women looking for a rebound. Just like Kate." I bury my head in my hands, pieces of last night flashing before my eyes. "Did I... you know... with her... last night?"

Charlie stands. "I don't know, Noah. Kate is upset. I'm not sure what happened, but if you don't want to lose a friend, you better fix it."

Great. Now I'm stuck in some sort of problematic triangle all because I followed my gut. The last I can recall, we argued, and I started yelling at her. As to what we argued specifically about, I have no recollection.

"How do I fix it? With Kate, I mean."

"Give her space right now, okay?" Charlie warns. "Even friendships need the storm to pass to see the rainbow."

"How do I fix it if you're telling me to give her space? Why do women have to be so complicated?" I question, though knowing no answer will fix my ninety-nine problems. "Aside from Kate and her obviously being angry with me, I don't even know where to begin with Morgan."

"Noah," she continues, keeping her voice low. "I don't know what's going on with Morgan. I like her, I really do. But you need to remember she has a family. A husband and a son."

"I know, Charlie," I respond with a bitter taste in my mouth. "My morals tell me to walk away, you've been played, and karma is a goddamn bitch."

She leans in and kisses my forehead, staring back at me with her big brown eyes. "Karma may be a bitch, but sometimes, she's your best friend."

"So, you think karma is a woman, too?" I chuckle.

"Hell, yeah," she laughs along. "Only women would

have mood swings like that."

Charlie leaves me be but not without reminding me to shower and change as we are taking Mom out to Malibu for lunch.

I spend all of Sunday being present for Mom. It's refreshing to be around her. Mom's jokes are the highlight of my day along with a delicious meal at Nobu. Charlie joined us with the girls, who Mom absolutely adores.

We reminisce about our childhood, and thankfully, both of them steer clear of my toxic love life. After a nice dinner Mom offers to cook, I call it an early night, trying to catch up on sleep.

***

Monday is a new day. At least that's the pep talk I give myself while working out this morning at the gym. I've only been in the office for an hour, and my mind won't shut down.

It's bugging me that I don't recall what happened with Kate, and she hasn't bothered to call me. She left for Napa yesterday morning, due to return tonight. I decide to call her and ease my troubled mind.

"Hey," she answers oddly.

"I knew it," I say, angry at myself.

"Knew what?"

"We fucked. That's why you didn't answer the phone in your annoying '*wazzup.*'"

She chuckles softly, releasing a long sigh. "Uh no, I didn't answer that way... it's just things are tense."

"I'm sorry, Kate," I apologize for my behavior I can't even recall. Only pieces of last night linger. "I don't know what I was thinking."

"Noah," she interrupts. "We didn't have sex."

I breathe a sigh of relief. "Are you sure?"

"Yes. You talked on and on about anal fisting, completely killing my buzz."

I place my cell on my forehead—this shit just gets worse and worse. "Jesus. I'm sorry. For everything."

"You were upset. I get it. I was upset for you and for myself. It was just a bad night all around. I want to forget everything as much as you."

I lean my chair back, tilting my head up until I'm staring at the ceiling. It's nothing but all white, a blank canvas that calms me if only a moment. The creak of my door alarms me, and I pull myself forward and see Morgan standing at the entrance.

"Kate, I have to go."

"Sure... but Noah?"

"Yeah?"

"We need to talk, soon. Okay?"

I say goodbye, hanging up the phone and placing it on my desk.

Morgan closes the door behind her and continues to stand in the same spot. She looks terrible, dark circles behind her glasses. Even her hair doesn't look as neat as it usually does.

Although she looks like death has found her, she's still a beautiful woman.

And I hate that fact.

I should be looking at her with complete contempt

and disgust right now.

"I guess I deserve that, and am not surprised Kate is the one you run to."

I keep silent.

"I came here to talk to you... to explain what happened." She tries to control her tone, remaining still.

"You can't just ambush me at work," I tell her in an artic voice.

"It's the only place where I know you'll have a civil conversation."

"There's nothing civil about you being married with a kid, Morgan."

She continues to stand at the door, barely moving yet still remaining composed. "We need to talk, Noah. Please?"

Staring at the floor, I avoid meeting her eyes. The pain is etched all over her face, but who says she even feels pain? Maybe it's guilt for treating me like shit. Just your run-of-the-mill guilty conscience when you know you screwed someone over but only have yourself to blame.

Just like you did with Benny.

"What's there to talk about? I was a fool. You lied. I got played. End of story."

She moves a few feet closer. "No, Noah. You didn't even give me a chance to explain myself... the situation."

"The situation? The fact that you're married?"

"Separated."

I laugh at the ridiculous technicality. "Such a loose word. That's what they all say, 'I'm separated.' Because it gives you the right to fuck around."

"But it gives you the right to prey on women even

though you know they're not over their ex?" she argues back.

And right there, she made it all clear. *Not over an ex.*

"I think, Morgan, you made yourself perfectly clear. So, tell me, why should I even bother with you now? That would be a hasty decision because you're not over your ex... husband."

"Noah, please. This is hard... don't do this to me," she pleads, keeping her tears at bay.

"Do this to you?" I raise my voice. "This wasn't in my plan. *You* weren't in my plan! This is supposed to be a new life for me. I wasn't supposed to fall for you."

"No. Just Scarlett, right?"

"Fuck you," I tell her and fumble for the keys to my car while ignoring the fact that she's standing there about to cry. Every part of me wants to run to her and beg her to choose me. Not him. But my pride won't allow it. I refuse to be second best.

I stand, pretending to ignore her as I walk past while she calls my name. She's only a few feet away, but her scent has invaded my office, making it nearly impossible to walk away at this moment.

"Noah, please, let me explain to you."

I hold back, uncertain as to why. I hate she has something over me, and that my pride and ego are willing to stand still for just a moment to listen to her.

"Michael is technically not my son. He's my stepson."

I hate to admit that upon hearing those words, it makes me feel slightly better, though I'll never admit it to her. I continue to stand in silence, unsure why I feel the need to listen to her explanation when the damage has already been done.

"Michael has special needs. I don't know if you know much about it, but he has autism," she continues, the crack in her voice filtering through. "Wyatt and I have joint custody of him, and every second week he spends time with his mother."

She moves her gaze to the floor, shuffling her feet anxiously. "Last year, Wyatt and I decided to go our own ways. We thought it would be easy, but Michael took it hard. We'd worked so hard to create a stable home environment for him. He reacted poorly, and his behavior changed, sleeping became difficult for him. The school was concerned for him. He doesn't adapt well to change of any kind. There are ways around it, ways we need to adapt. But it's a prolonged process that takes a lot of dedication from both of us, his mother, teachers, and our therapists. We saw a behavioral specialist last year, and Wyatt and I agreed that for now, we'd continue to live in the same house and transition the move slowly."

She takes a breath, waiting for me to respond. I don't have words, or at least my words make no sense in my head. I don't know a thing about autism. The kid didn't look any different at Scarlett's house, so I don't understand at all what she's going on about.

"You lied, Morgan."

"I had no choice, Noah. I didn't expect any of this. I didn't expect you to walk into my life... you just pissed me off so much I couldn't think straight. I wanted to tell you, but I knew when I did, you'd act exactly the way you are now."

"What the fuck do you expect?" I yell.

"I'm sorry. I just wanted you to know the truth." She straightens her posture and stares directly at me. "So where to now?"

"You're asking me that?" I ridicule her, shaking my head, almost laughing at her ridiculous question. "You're the one carrying the baggage."

She appears offended, her wolfish expression quickly following. "And you're not? Tell me now, why did life get so complicated back home?"

I stand in silence, not answering her question.

"Yeah, exactly. We all have our baggage. We all have our lies. The question is, are you ready to lay all yours on the table for me to see?"

More silence.

What the fuck does she expect me to do? Turn around and forgive her, then play happy houses with her and her husband.

"I didn't think so. So, before you go judging me, take a look at yourself. None of us are perfect," she fires back hastily. Morgan turns around, attempting to leave the room before I do.

Just before she steps out into the hall, I fire one more question at her—the one question eating away at me. "Answer me one thing," I snarl. "Do you still sleep with him?"

Her complete body swivels to face where I'm standing. Wearing an emerald-green dress which flares out toward the bottom, it showcases her long, lean legs, which my eyes try their hardest to ignore. Even when I'm looking at the floor, I see her gold pumps strapped around her ankle, and all I want to do is rest them on my shoulder and kiss every inch of her skin.

"Yes, Noah. I sleep with him. I don't fuck him, but we do share the same bed. For the sake of our son."

And the thought that threatened to eat away at me just took its first bite.

I laugh, covering up the hurt and anger swirling throughout my twisted mind. "Right, Morgan, you answered my question perfectly."

CHAPTER 29

NOAH

It would've been easy to drown my sorrows in a big bottle of Jack Daniels, but I was sick of feeling hungover and out of control. Not to mention, I have terrible judgment when I'm intoxicated.

Mom has an afternoon flight back home, so she's spending most of the day out with some friends. I left work early, picking her up to take her to the airport. When it comes time to say goodbye, I can't help but miss her already.

"You'll get through this, kid," she tells me with a reassuring smile. "You can get through anything. Just don't end up in jail... again."

I wish I could believe her, but I question everything in my life with no conclusion reached. It's way too much for me, so I just block it out. *For now.*

We say our goodbyes, hugging it out until she disappears through the terminal.

Charlie calls to inform me that the girls are staying

over at Lex's sister's house so we can have a decent night to adult. Now, I'm assuming a bottle of tequila will be present, but I'm misinformed. It's Monday, and I still have a long week of work ahead of me. That, and Charlie can't drink.

When I arrive home from the airport, Charlie is dressed in her pajamas and with what she calls a messy bun. Kate is beside her, dressed casually in a tank top and sweats. I know she arrived back around noon with a flight back to the East Coast tomorrow.

Even in her casual attire, Kate looks even more gorgeous, flawless without the ridiculous makeup women often cake themselves in.

"Do you guys realize it's only five o'clock?" I remind them.

"Yes." Charlie smiles. "Go put your PJs on."

"Uh... why?"

"Because when girls have their hearts broken, this is how we recover. Now go get changed and be back here in ten minutes."

I laugh loudly, watching the two of them stare at me like a pack of angry wolves. I shake my head repeatedly while making my way upstairs. I decide to wear my gray sweats and a white tank since it's almost identical to Kate. I don't own pajamas with fluffy bunnies on them like Charlie, thank fucking God.

As I step closer down the stairs, the aroma of pizza lingers in the air. I didn't have much of an appetite today, stopping only for coffee and a pack of mints. But I sure feel hungry now.

"We're eating pizza. Is that it?" I ask both of them.

"No, silly," Kate scolds playfully. "That's just the first course."

Charlie stands in front of the television. "Okay... do we watch *The Notebook* or *Titanic?*"

Should I mention that both movies sound awful? Why on earth would they want to watch such depressing shit?

"Go... *The Notebook,*" Kate suggests. "And remember the rule... no talking."

Charlie smiles, clicking the remote and locate the movie on the hard drive. She dims the lights in the theater as I plonk myself next to Kate. She's holding a box of tissues, then grabs a slice of pizza as the movie begins.

"Hey," I whisper, leaning over to Kate. "You wanted to talk?"

"It's not important, Noah." There's an uncertainty to her voice, but she's quick to smile. "Not anymore."

Thirty minutes into the movie, I've lost interest.

"So, why is this helping us right now?" I complain.

"Because it's one of the greatest love stories. It'll make you smile, laugh, and cry all at the same time," Charlie responds with a waver in her voice.

I've devoured a whole pizza when the movie becomes interesting. Okay, the female lead is fucking gorgeous, and the story becomes somewhat sad. Somewhere during the middle, it all begins to make sense, and the girls beside me have their tissues scrunched up in their hands with tears streaming down their faces. I'm not sure why. Sure, it's sad, but nothing that depressing.

And then, the old lady screams at her husband, and

the realness of the situation leaves an empty pit in my stomach. Charlie and Kate are a mess. I swallow the lump in my throat—it's actually quite sad.

Charlie pauses the movie and tells us she'll be back in a few minutes. She returns with three tubs of ice cream. I pick the strawberry, and she presses play again as we all eat out of the cartons.

The end of the movie is almost near, and I seriously can't take it anymore. It's so sad and depressing, I finish the carton of ice cream, and I'm not any closer to feeling better about myself.

Kate's leaning on my shoulder for support.

"If you and I fall in love, will you visit me every day and tell me stories?" Kate asks between sobs.

"Sure," I humor her. "Do we need to fall in love? What if this Rachel McAdams is single? You know I'm not one to settle."

Kate pulls back. "Three words for you... Lesbian. Anal. Fisting."

I shake my head while grinning, pulling Kate into me as I kiss her cheek to annoy her. She wipes her face, complaining I left ice-cream on her skin.

Charlie scowls, not getting the joke. "Honestly, the two of you are terrible... two peas in a pod. Maybe it's not such a bad idea that you guys fall in love. Then I'd stop hearing about your tragic love lives..." She pauses, then continues with a mouthful of ice cream. "And I don't want to know why you're talking about lesbian anal fisting. Is that even a thing? My ass wants to die thinking about that."

Lex walks into the room wearing a suit. He's just

come home from a work dinner celebrating someone's retirement.

"Oh no, they got to you, didn't they?"

Charlie runs up to Lex and gives him a great big hug, crying into his shoulder and telling him that if she ever lost her memory, she'd want him to read to her every day about their lives and the girls. He indulges the hug but rolls his eyes at the same time. Lex sits down, and Charlie curls on top of him, trying to get comfortable with her protruding stomach.

"Thanks, you guys. You know what's more depressing than this movie? Seeing you guys all lovey-dovey," Kate says, slumped in the chair.

"Aw, come here." I grin, pulling her onto my lap, goading her because I can. "I'll make you a deal, if we're single when we're thirty, we'll officially hook up."

"I'm already thirty, you nob." She punches my arm, sliding herself off me. "And I know you too well. You try to charm me that way, and the next minute, you're gabbing on about anal fisting again."

Lex watches us, amused. "Should we leave you two alone?"

"No," Kate jokes. "Please don't. Noah just likes to push my buttons because he knows he can."

"It's very true," I voice with a sinister smirk.

Lex grins at us, followed by a small chuckle. "I'm all for a good time, but please, for the love of God, please stop talking about anal fisting."

The four of us laugh until we're out of breath, just when Lex gets a call from his London office. Kate joins him in his office, leaving Charlie and me alone. She suggests we go outside to get some fresh air while the other two discuss work.

"Noah," Charlie says my name softly, sitting beside me on the chair on the patio. I don't want to talk to anyone, wallowing in self-pity seems much more fitting. And I know she wants to talk about Morgan, *again.*

"Charlie, I don't want to talk about it."

"Okay, we can talk about something else," she suggests. "Do you remember your last summer back home before you moved to the East Coast?"

"Uh... I think so."

"You were thirteen and had just gone through this massive growth spurt."

"Oh yeah, a year of awkward growing." I chuckle lightly.

"So that summer, all the girls in your year were talking about you. How Noah Mason was *the* hottest thing to happen that summer and they were fighting about dating you. There was this one girl, Georgia, I think."

"Head of the cheer squad, Georgia?"

"Yes... I think. She was two years older than you. She was at the local store one day, and I overheard her telling her posse that she wanted to date you because you were the hottest thing ever," she exaggerates. "I knew she was a skank, and I was furious when I heard that. I actually went up to her and told her that if she went near you or hurt you, I'd punch her in the vagina."

"Charlie." I laugh. "You didn't? She was the hottest chick back then."

"You're my family, the brother I never had. I didn't

want anyone hurting you. And now is no different."

"Now we're adults, I should be able to take care of myself," I remind her.

"I'm struggling here, Noah. I know you have feelings for her, but she's married. It's a big deal... the whole marriage thing. I'm not going to pretend to understand how she feels because every situation is different. I just know this... I hate the fact that she hurt you."

"She's separated, supposedly." Even when I'm trying to defend Morgan, it comes out wrong.

"But don't you think she owes it to her marriage to make it work before running off with someone else? Marriage is hard work."

"I don't know, Charlie. I'm so angry. She told me she has issues with the kid. Apparently, it's her stepson, and he's special or something. I just don't know. I was so angry and not really comprehending or listening to what she was telling me."

A gust of wind sweeps through the patio, warm and calming my anxious nerves. The view from the back of the house is stunning, stretching into the darkness of the mountains. It's quite serene, and I understand now why Charlie and Lex love this property even though it's a fair distance into town.

"Kids can be finicky," she informs me. "If her stepson has special needs, then I can understand that a marriage breakdown could be difficult for her family. Again, I don't know her circumstances. Why don't you try to sit down with her and discuss it more openly?"

"Because I'm too angry, Charlie. I don't understand why she can't just walk away. It's not even her son."

"Well, Lex and Haden think that your problem would be better solved by some girl-on-girl mud wrestling."

I laugh again. The boys know me well, though I play coy. "I'm not sure it's exactly what I want to see right now."

"That's what I said, but what do I know?" she voices with frustration.

I rest my head on her shoulder, thankful that at times like this, I have family around. Even though Charlie and I have drifted apart over the years, she was and always will be my older cousin, the girl who can take anyone down.

The back door opens, and Lex is dressed in his jeans and a black polo shirt followed by Kate behind him. "So, boys' night out?" he asks, hopeful.

"I think you need to take him out," Charlie agrees with a smile.

"Wait, is my wife actually agreeing with me?"

"Show him some tits and ass. He needs to get his mind off things."

Lex looks stunned, and Charlie brushes it off like it's nothing. But she's a woman, and I know her feminist side is rocking itself in the corner, demanding him not to go.

"I think I have the best wife in the world," he says, gushing, wrapping his arms around her waist and planting a kiss on her neck.

Charlie smiles happily as if nothing else in the world matters. "Just take care of him like he's my brother," she tells Lex before winking back at me and walking inside the house.

Kate is still standing on the porch, watching me with

a mixed expression.

"What do you think?" I ask, waiting for her incessant rant on women being objects to men. "You think I'll survive a boys' night out?"

"I think you're going to be just fine, Noah," she reassures me with her easing smile. *"Just fine."*

***

"Fuck, look at her *ass*," Haden comments. He has a tub of popcorn and a beer, watching the wrestling like a crazed fan.

The two ladies are wrestling it out, drenched in mud, wearing the smallest of bikinis. The one with the big ass—Haden's favorite—has fallen to her knees, exposing a very muddy crack.

"Damn!" he yells out, much to Lex's and my amusement.

"I've never really decided whether I'm an ass or tits man. It's been confirmed, I'm an ass man," I yell over the noise.

"I've always been an ass man," Lex follows, drinking his beer.

"Nope, you're not allowed to talk about anything ass-related because somewhere in your brain, it leads to Charlie, and my brain senses those vibes, and everything about that image is very wrong."

"Is it wrong that I desire your cousin?" he asks, taking a dig at me.

"Desire sounds dirty and old-man like."

Lex hides his growing smirk. "I don't dare say what

my brain thinks."

"Enough you two. You're killing my buzz," Haden complains, his eyes never leaving the arena.

"Speaking of which, how on earth did you get Presley to agree to you coming here?"

Haden takes a sip of his beer with a dirty grin on his face. "I pretty much had to screw her brains out to the point where there's no more sperm left in me. Her words... not mine."

Lex breaks into laughter. "Me, too."

"What? How is that even possible? It only took me ten minutes to get dressed until you said you had to help Charlie move some boxes in the attic to get to the special waffle iron because she wanted to make waffles."

He shakes his head along with Haden, who's laughing with his eyes still watching the wrestling.

"The waffle iron is in the pantry. But hey, thanks, cousin-in-law, for waiting around."

Mental note—*Contact realtor again and make sure they haul ass to find me a place.*

That's no different than the time I accidentally found 'battery-operated goods' in Mom's closet while searching for some cash.

"Ten minutes, Lex? Really?" Haden queries with judgment.

"Twice. I had time restrictions."

"Well, screw the both of you. I haven't gotten laid since Kate's and my second failed attempt. Can we change the subject now, please?" I beg of them.

"All right, Kate's like a sister to me and also an employee of mine. Please, don't talk about her in that way, let alone indulge me in any conversations that mention lesbian anal fisting again," Lex states, disapprovingly.

"Ouch," Haden adds, squinting his face on par. "Really? Anal fisting. She's into that?"

"No... yes... I don't know," I say, not wanting to elaborate.

The girls move closer to us, and in one swift move, Miss Big Ass has pinned the other girl to the floor and has removed her bikini top. Her nipples are covered in mud. Wet and erect. Damn.

This beats watching *The Notebook*.

Ginger, one of the waitresses, serves my drink and lingers around. "So, boys' night out?"

On cue, Lex and Haden lift their hands, revealing their rings. *What a bunch of pussy-whipped fuckers.* I down the drink in one go and grab Lex's. Ginger is starting to look really lovely—blurry, but fuckable.

"And what about you?" she asks, lifting my hand to see it empty.

"Free as a bird." I wink.

She whispers in my ear, leaning forward, "I get off in twenty minutes, and I'd like to get off with you."

Fuck.

And as if that moment isn't what I need, the guilt rushes over me so fast it almost knocks me over. She walks away, turning back to wink at me.

"Go for it, you need to fucking let those blue balls loose," Haden tells me.

"Nice mouth on her," Lex adds. "At least get blown if the guilt is too much to fuck her."

I don't want to continue feeling like this, and so somewhere during the final round of wrestling, I say goodbye to Lex and Haden and make my way over to the bar. Ginger is hanging up her apron and talking to another waitress. I blink my eyes repeatedly, the alcohol making it hard to concentrate, and pull out my cell, typing a message.

Me: *I fucking hate you.*

"You ready?" Ginger asks with her purse in hand.

I follow her lead outside the venue and cross the street with her hand in mine. There's a cab stand in front of the restaurant, another couple waiting for one to pull up. It takes me a few moments to realize that my pocket buzzed, and inside sits my cell. I pull it out, my fingers stumbling as I tap the screen. I squint my eyes and can barely make out the message.

Morgan: *Probably why it hurts so much.*

I stand still as Ginger repeatedly calls my name. It hurts all right, it hurts like fucking hell. In fact, hell would probably be a vacation compared to the place I'm in right now.

There's a loud 'hurrah' coming from the entrance of the restaurant, and with my eyes dashing toward the sound, I watch as the door opens.

It's her.

And standing right beside her is her husband, his hand resting comfortably on the small of her back.

Morgan sees me, and instantly, her face falls. The dark circles covering her eyes become darker when her eyes land on Ginger, kissing the side of my ear.

"C'mon, Noah, time to have fun."

And in the act of the universe being all fucked up, I follow Ginger into the cab, avoiding Morgan's pointed stare.

For tonight, Ginger will erase the pain gutting my insides.

For tonight, she will be my *rebound.*

CHAPTER
30

NOAH

I'm lying in bed staring at the ceiling, thinking about last night—my actions and how everything in my life is completely messed up.

With Kate gone, leaving on a red-eye to New York City, I wallow in my own self-pity, trying to pinpoint exactly where it all got fucked up. This is why I need Kate in my life—her years of wisdom would've deciphered the mess going on in my head.

Our office is closed today for fumigation. Haden got a call early this morning of a rodent problem and notified everyone immediately. I welcome the break, and over the call, Haden senses exactly that. He happens to be great at giving advice, explaining how he and Presley came together after a rather complicated union. Then he tells me Ginger's quite a gal and to go back for seconds if possible.

I didn't even go for firsts. Bailing on her after she took me back to her place, which was an utter mess. Sorry, a dump would be more inappropriate. What a fucking waste of time.

A rebound is what I needed, and I failed at that as well.

I don't know how to gain control of my life. And there's nothing more frustrating than the loss of power—the inability to think straight and move on.

I know only one thing—it continues to hurt like hell.

And no matter how much I try, I can't stop picturing Morgan and her husband sleeping in the same bed, imagining his hands wandering over her body while she sleeps. Every time the vision pops into my head, I want to slam my fist through the wall and direct the pain elsewhere.

The door creaks open, and I expect to see one of the girls standing outside, but instead, I look up and see Morgan. Though my vision is tainted with only the color red, her beauty filters through and leaves me breathless. Fuck, I hate that she makes me feel this way, like some superpower that controls my emotions.

She's wearing a white dress with red heels, and her hair is tied up into a bun. I feel exposed lying here in only my boxers. *What the fuck is she doing here?*

"Charlie, let me in," she says, standing at the foot of the bed. "She just left with the girls."

"What are you doing here? Shouldn't you be with your husband and son?"

"Noah, please, don't you think after you ran off with some strange woman that I deserve at least to be able to explain myself? I'm hurting just as much as you are here."

335

I sit back, crossing my arms in the process. Not correcting her assumption on my actions last night, I continue to act cold toward her, allowing my anger to be seen. Morgan sits on the edge of the bed, keeping her distance. She may not feel it, but my urges are in overdrive because I fucking miss her, and she's way too close for me to be thinking straight.

"Wyatt and I met just out of college. It was a celebratory Vegas trip that went horribly wrong. A friend of mine had been drugged, and I was too busy getting drunk."

Her hands fidget with the edge of the blanket, carefully recounting her story. "Wyatt found her, and long story short, we started seeing each other. One night, completely out of the blue, we both decided to get married. I did love him."

It kills me to hear it. That fucking word does my head in. I bite my tongue, allowing her to finish.

"We'd only been seeing each other for six weeks before we tied the knot. My dad was livid," she reveals. "Two months after we got married, Wyatt's ex announced she was pregnant. I knew I couldn't go back to my old life of drinking and partying. My destructive behavior began the moment my mom died, and I didn't know how to cope. I wasn't like Scarlett. She knew how to deal with her emotions and move on. I bottled them up, then screwed guys like they were going out of style.

"Wyatt begged me to stay, and I did. Michael was born, and I fell in love with him. He wasn't mine, but he was at our house every second week. Over time, I treated him like my own."

I open my mouth without hesitation this time. "I don't get how you could love a kid who belongs to your husband's ex. And he fucking cheated on you."

"He did, sort of. They slept together a few days after he and I got together. I wasn't exactly invested in the relationship at that point. I was infatuated with the physical side."

Ouch. If that didn't stab me right in the fucking heart. You probably deserve that for being a heartless bastard.

"Right," I say with sarcasm. "So, you're allowed to fuck someone because he did?"

"Is that what you think this is, Noah? I didn't expect this to happen, especially with you."

"Well, I didn't expect this to happen, especially with you," I fire back. Both of us remain silent, only the sounds of the wind against the window echoes through the room. What now? How do I stop my growing need to touch her? The fact that she's here in this room is giving me a raging hard-on, and I hate her for that.

"Noah, when I first saw you, all I wanted to do was fuck you. That's it. You did something to me that I just couldn't understand. My body betrayed me on so many levels. I'd have happily just fucked you with no strings attached. And yes... you were a rebound. I was done with my marriage, and you were on my radar."

I don't know whether to be turned on or furious. Yet, I'm quick to judge her for wanting only that. A hypocrite for thinking it's okay for me to do that but not her, for men to sleep around but not women.

"I didn't mean to have feelings for you. I talked myself out of it the moment I sensed them creeping in. I haven't

337

even known you that long, but you've done something to me that I can't change even if I wanted to."

There are no more words left to be said. I need to be inside her because the feeling consumes me, and nothing in this world matters right now, all judgment aside. I lean forward and drag her body toward me, pinning her down.

"I'm going to fuck you," I whisper in her ear. "Because I don't know what else to do. Because I'm crazy around you, and you hurt me so bad."

Screw the foreplay.

I slide my boxers toward the middle of my thighs—enough to expose my cock—and shove her dress past her waist and over her head. Her panties, white and lacy thin, are pushed aside. The smell of her arousal teases me, and with no warning, I ram my cock into her pussy hard, watching as she arches backward while moaning into the empty room.

Her nails dig into my back. The slight pain only driving me harder into her, taking her possessively as if she's only ever belonged to me. The urge to blow teeters so close to the edge that I'm forced to close my eyes and gain control. When I open them up, her blue pools of lust are penetrating me.

I'm falling for her in ways I never thought possible.

And I don't know how to release myself from her spell.

I pull myself out quickly and flip her over, desperate not to stare into her eyes, voiding this moment of any emotion aside from lust.

She rubs her ass against my cock, teasing me

relentlessly. "You can turn me around, forget that I exist. But know this…" she pauses, catching a breath, "… I'm going to make it my mission to remind you that I'm selfish. I take what I want just like you."

With my mind already crazy and not thinking straight, I'm not quite sure I understand until she latches onto my cock and rubs it against her. The wet dripping off her pussy only makes for a perfect entry, and in one quick and sensual move, she guides me in until I'm sitting comfortably inside her again.

I'm coming undone.

I could easily fuck her hard until I come, but I want to savor this moment, using my knees to spread her legs wider. The view from above is breathtaking, her ass exposed as I watch my cock glide so effortlessly. My palm is twitching, rubbing her skin up and down until I've grabbed what I can and smack my palm against her cheek, creating a loud bang.

She begs me to hit her harder, and I do so, biting down on my bottom lip as the urge is almost impossible to ignore. I have to stop for a moment and brace myself for the finale.

Pulling out, her moan deepens at the loss of contact. Turning her over, I'm transfixed by the way her body reacts to me. Her skin is red raw from where I've been, and a dirty smile plays on her lips while she waits for me to enter her again.

I stand tall, kneeling above her as she lies innocently beneath me. My hand moves to my shaft, latching on as I stroke myself, refusing to break eye contact with her. The way her body reacts is such a beautiful sight, her nipples erect underneath her lacy bra and her chest rising and falling to the beat of my strokes. The moans escaping her sweet little mouth beg me to enter her again, but this time, I want it all.

With her thighs pushed down, I spread her legs wide open. She doesn't stop me—encouraging me to bury myself deep inside her. The tip of my cock settles at her entrance, the impatient side of me not slowing down, entering her relatively fast. She groans with her muscles visibly flexing. Her neck is exposed, ready for me to run my tongue along her skin.

She's at my complete mercy, my body thrusting deep in sync with her moans. I can smell her pussy—she's completely soaked. And every time my body makes contact against her clit, the sounds of her wet arousal echo between us.

Morgan warns me that she can't hold off. Reaching over the headboard, she latches on and raises her hips to allow me to enter her deeper. In and out, her eyes plead with me to fuck her is more profound.

"This is what your body does when I'm fucking you," I tell her, shoving my fingers further into her mouth and watching her wide eyes tear up in desperation.

I pull them out, her gasp following shortly after.

She moves her hand down and grazes her clit. "Ready when you are."

Spreading her again, I watch my cock slide in and out at a slow pace, savoring each thrust. The fire in my belly begins to rise, my legs wobbling in unison. I pick up the pace slightly, diverting my attention to her soaked fingers, rubbing her pussy in a wild frenzy.

Seconds later, she releases a loud moan, biting her lip as her face turns completely red. Around my cock, she twitches, and her orgasm has me undone. The fire has risen, and my body spirals out of control, every inch in a euphoric state as I hold my breath. Unwillingly, my entire body jerks forward, collapsing on top of hers.

Our chests beat against each other, our breathing uneven as we both gulp for air.

We remain silent, and I continue to stay inside her, never wanting to remove myself. And then, I demand what I should have all along. "I'm not going to share you despite what your circumstances are. I'm selfish, too. Leave him *now*," I demand, almost threatening her.

"It's not so black and white, Noah." She wiggles her body, but I lay my weight on her, refusing to allow her to break free.

"It's either them or me."

"You're giving me an ultimatum?"

"Yes," I voice, confidently.

"You don't understand, Noah. You don't have a child. I can't give up on him."

The fire in my eyes mirrors hers. The fury returning in just one breath that I can't reason with her. "He's *not* your kid."

"No, he's not. But I've been in his life since the day he was born. He's not like all the other kids. I tried to explain that to you, but you won't listen."

"Because it sounds like an excuse. Every kid is going to put on a guilt trip if their family is breaking up. You just don't want to move on," I tell her, the enmity driving me further and possibly to the point of no return. "And

341

why the fuck would you need to sleep in the same bed as your husband, huh? I bet you still fuck him or at least let him get you off."

"Fuck you," she almost spits. "You have no idea of the sacrifices I've made for Michael. And I'd do it all over again because he deserves no less. I didn't ask for a special needs stepson, but I got one and wouldn't change it for the world."

"Well, change it. As I said, it's them or me," I demand hastily.

"You fucking prick, get off me," she yells, pushing my chest forward. "Maybe I should ask you to end your ties with Kate? How does that feel, huh?"

Her jealousy over Kate still amuses me. There will never be anything between us, Kate has made that perfectly clear.

But Morgan should belong to *me.*

Like a possessed man in love, I'm rock-hard again, and without warning, I enter her pussy. Something I probably shouldn't do, but I don't give a goddamn fuck. I grab her arms, controlling her desperate need to push me away, using my hips to fuck her this time because the jealousy is driving me to the brink of insanity.

Underneath me, she swears at me to get off her, but I ignore her threats. Her body is telling a different story. Her nipples are erect under my touch, her teeth clenching each time my cock goes in deeper. Shaking her head back and forth, I want her to shut the fuck up because she belongs to me and no one else.

"You're a fucking asshole!" she screams in between her moans.

My hand moves toward her mouth, covering it while I take what's mine. And with just one surge, I've come undone again.

My heart beats erratically. My vision is slightly impaired as I try to gain control. My cock is so sensitive, the walls of her pussy clenching and making me jump slightly. I open my eyes and see her stare back at me full of rage. She pushes me again, and this time I pull myself off and collapse on the bed beside her. She's quick to move away, grabbing her dress and covering her chest.

"Fuck you," she shouts. "You don't just come inside me thinking you own me."

I'm too tired to fight her, continuing to lie there and stare at the ceiling. But something inside my exhausted brain tells me it's not over yet.

"Oh, that's right," I say. "Only your husband can do that."

The steam is shooting out of her ears as she races to get her clothes on, throwing her dress over her head in one swift motion. "And to think I was going to tell you that I love you," she sputters, momentarily beyond words. "I should save the words for someone who actually gives a fuck. Someone who loves me back."

And with her words said loud and clear, she leaves the room, abandoning me with only my thoughts.

Love.

The four-letter word that's ruined my life.

CHAPTER
31

NOAH

Misery really does love company.

It's been two weeks since the day Morgan walked out on me. I know I've been a prick toward her, but I refuse to conform to someone she wants me to be—a man who's willing to share her.

Haden and Presley offer to take over the account, sympathetic to my personal issues. I never want my personal life to screw with my work life, and so I continue doing what I need to do and communicate with Scarlett rather than Morgan.

Scarlett's great to talk to, and although she has an extremely hectic schedule, she finds time to chat without bringing up the subject of her sister. "You would totally love it out here," she tells me over the phone one afternoon. "Desert heat, and girls are dancing in teeny tiny bikinis."

"Another stripper movie?" I tease while typing an important email to a client.

"Of course, you'd say that." She laughs. "This is a romantic comedy, something different for me. My main lead is new to Hollywood, and they're really trying to push the chemistry between us."

"C'mon." I smile through my words. "You're telling me that's forced? You can charm anyone."

"He has a small dick," she blurts out.

I stop typing my email. "And you know that because…"

"Because he's wearing white trunks, and it's obvious. I keep telling his publicist that it'll really hinder his career if nude pictures leak out."

"Not to delve too much into the semantics, but perhaps it's cold. Unless you have him pinned to a bed and stand in front of him naked, you'll never really know."

"I guess it's best that we leave it a mystery, then. I'm not really a pin-a-guy-to-a-bed type of girl."

With my pen tapping against the glass desk, I fight the urge to continue this topic. I'm not in the mood, anyway. Or at least that's the lie I spin to myself.

"So, what are your plans this weekend aside from Haden and Presley overloading you with edits?" I ask, quickly changing the topic.

There's a moment of silence, followed by some voices in the background. She must be placing her hand on the receiver as I'm unable to translate the muffled sounds into words.

"I… uh… family stuff. A birthday," she follows in a hushed tone.

"Oh… who?" Immediately, I regret asking the

question, knowing all too well I won't like the answer.

"Michael."

I struggle to fight off the jealousy, gritting down and holding back my words because they aren't aimed at Scarlett. It looks like everyone will be playing happy families this weekend while I get drunk and drown my sorrows in some random pussy.

With my mood rapidly declining, I tell Scarlett that I need to go and finish some work. As soon as I hang up the call, I rest my head on the back of my chair and stare at the ceiling—my favorite pastime of late.

I honestly believe that as time goes on, I will forget all about her. That some other woman will pique my interest, and I would move on effortlessly. I didn't expect feeling sick every morning when I wake and don't anticipate the constant depressive state that comes with that feeling like my whole world revolves around her and nothing I do or say will make it go away.

And sometimes, I rejoice in a moment of feeling like my old self. Yet, it's always short-lived. Something or someone reminds me of her, and I'm brought back to reality faster than you can say the word 'broken.'

I've never felt so alone, walking through this like a nomad. Kate has been busy with work, according to Lex. I find myself distancing myself from her because frankly, I rely on her more than I care to admit. Equally so, she doesn't reach out to me. Something changed during her last visit. I have enough drama in my life and am not in the right frame of mind to add more.

I put on a brave face, never allowing anyone to see how much it affects me. Haden and Presley treat me like

I'm dying, forever fussing over me and inviting me over to forget about everything. When I tell them I'm fine, they don't believe me and give me a mountain of work to keep my mind busy. Long hours in the office help ease my troubled mind until the night sets in, and I'm all alone again.

Charlie's exactly the same, forcing me on numerous outings and adventures with the girls to clear my head. Lex never says much aside from understanding how I feel having been through a separation from Charlie for several years. He warns Charlie to take it easy on me and to stop treating me like a broken baby bird.

I can't agree more.

Late Friday afternoon, I decide I need to get away, and the only place I want to go is home, back to my old roots. I miss Mom *a lot*, and the second I walk into her house on Saturday morning after a tedious flight, she knows I'm ready to talk.

"Oh, kid." She places her arms around me and hugs me tight.

"I'm okay, Mom."

"You look like shit, Noah," she says without holding back.

"Geez, thanks." I throw my bag toward the corner of the room and head to the kitchen. Opening the refrigerator, I stand in front of it for minutes contemplating what to eat.

Somewhere in my self-absorbed bubble, I've failed to notice the moving boxes scattered around the room.

I grab an apple, taking a bite. "Am I missing something?"

"Sit down," she tells me. "I'm glad you're here, so we can talk in person."

Pulling out a stool, I sit with my elbows resting on the countertop while I wait for her to explain.

"I'm moving to California."

"Come again?" I ask, confused.

"Max and I—"

Quick to stand up, my eyes widen in shock as I almost choke on my apple. Pacing the room in confusion, my anger quickly erupts. "Max, as in Morgan's dad, Max?"

"Yes, we kind of started a relationship."

I stop just short of the counter, watching as Mom leans with her back against the countertop. In my entire life, she only ever brought home one man—Josh—a divorcée who owns a hardware store in town. I was nineteen at the time, and they dated for almost a year. I liked the guy, he had my approval, but they ended up parting ways because Mom said the spark was no longer there.

I had no idea what a spark meant, nor did I care to ask. It's difficult for me to remember that she's still young, and that most of her life was dedicated to raising me and not living her life like most teenagers or young adults should. And when you see her, you can tell she still looks youthful and nothing like me. She'd always tell me I look just like my dad. It was something she struggled with as I grew older. Her memories of him aren't fond, but like everything, she made sure I wasn't affected by his absence.

"But Max is old," I blurt out, not thinking clearly.

"I'm old." She laughs. "I know it's a change, Noah, but

you have your life, and I'm forty-four. I need this change."

"And Max is fifty-two. Isn't that illegal or something?"

She grins, walking over to where I stand and pats my hand softly. "He treats me well, Noah. We've really bonded."

I let out a sigh. "He's a good guy. But don't you think it's a big deal moving across the country for somebody you've known for like five minutes?"

"Yes, I'm scared but excited. Sometimes, when it comes to love, you take risks even if there's a chance your heart will get broken."

"Love?" I almost yell.

She never said anything about being in love with him. I thought they were just screwing around. Even then, that thought sends me into a blinding rage. *Argh, I can't win either way.* Karma really has her foot in my ass right now.

"I also got that job, so if things don't work out, I can still stand on my own."

I sit quietly and process her news. No matter which way I turn, Morgan will be in my life. Mom and Max's dating will no doubt make it difficult to avoid her. There's no escaping her.

"Mom." I keep my voice low. "What do you know about autism?"

She pulls a bottle of bourbon out of her kitchen cupboard, pouring us a glass. We clink our glasses together, then let out a rasp at the same time. It's something we occasionally do when life kicks our butts.

"My friend, Sandra, has an autistic son. I don't see her

that often anymore, but when he was younger, we used to meet for lunch. He was high-functioning. It meant that he could do what most kids could do but had challenges in certain areas."

"Like?" I ask, feeding off her knowledge.

"He was a whiz on the computer. Really smart and somewhat obsessed with being on it. When Sandra got a new job, he couldn't cope with the change… her being gone at night. It was difficult for them because she needed the money."

"I don't understand why she just wouldn't stick it out? A kid is a kid. Of course, they'll complain."

"It's not the same," Mom informs me. "He had difficulties communicating. It was a hard time for her family. Noah, maybe you should spend some time researching this. I may not be the best person to ask."

I don't answer her. It stresses me out even to think about it. Morgan doesn't come alone. She comes with a husband and a son who has special needs. It's too complicated. I want to go back to my old life when I didn't worry about anyone else but myself.

"Mom, there's something I need to do."

I stand and grab my wallet and keys. I move to where she's sitting and kiss the top of her head. I hate to admit it, but I'm glad she's moving to the West Coast.

***

The drive isn't long but gives me enough time to think carefully about my next move.

I park the car and walk toward the house. The lawn

350

is overgrown with garden beds requiring a good weeding. The porchlight is broken, but it doesn't matter since the Christmas lights are still up. I keep the smile to myself—the same lights have been up for the past five years. Tom had a Clark Griswold moment, and since then, he's left them up at his parents' house because he can't be bothered removing them.

The porch wraps around the house, and I can hear their voices while making my way around the back. Benny and Rose are sitting on a lounge chair, his arms casually wrapped around her. Tom is leaning against the pole, laughing along with them. They turn and watch me approach. Benny immediately looks straight into my eyes, keeping his expression rather still.

Rose offers me a warm smile—nothing sexual. Just a friendly welcome-back type of grin.

"Well, look what the cat dragged back," Tom says, folding his arms with a pensive gaze.

I keep my distance, just in case Benny's ready to take me out again. I probably shouldn't have worn my favorite t-shirt and shorts.

"Can I talk to you guys, please?"

Rose stands to leave. I place my palm forward, motioning for her to stay.

"I don't even know where to begin. I know I fucked up. There's no excuse behind that. Fuck! I can't even think straight," I babble incoherently.

Benny hasn't changed his expression, and Tom continues to watch me with curious eyes.

Rose is the first to speak up, "Who is she?"

"Excuse me?" I ask, narrowing my eyebrows.

"Who's the reason why you can't think straight?"

I don't say anything, and Tom interrupts, "Maybe I should fuck her, so you see what it feels like?"

The mouth on the fucker.

I want to punch his cocky grin but know full well he's egging me on to get some sort of reaction from me.

"A wise woman once asked me if I believed in karma. I do. Fuck me up, that's fine. But if you touch her, I'll pretty much rip your balls out and feed them to the coyotes."

"So then whip out your balls, and we'll call it even," Benny challenges, followed by a roaring laugh.

Tom joins in, and then it dawns on me that I can finally relax. These boys will always be my brothers. We had our rough patch, but we've gotten through it. I just need to chill the fuck out and let all of us be, have faith in our friendship, and make better decisions moving forward.

And stop screwing around with strange women because you never know what's around the corner.

"So, should we tell him the news?" Benny looks at Rose. She nods, and I wonder what the big surprise is.

"We're having a baby," she announces with a contented smile, happily holding onto Benny.

I'm happy for them yet sad at the same time. A baby means that Benny will be tied down with parental duties and zero time to hang out with Tom and me.

"Congratulations," I say with a smile. "Who would've thought... Benny, a dad?"

"Don't diss my dad skill. I can change a diaper like a boss."

"Dude, you've never changed a diaper," Tom chuckles.

"Nope, but I cleaned up your shit, Tom... when you sharted in my car." Benny howls, then walks over to hug me. "I miss you, man."

"I miss you, too, bro," I respond, patting his back.

"Geez, boys, don't get all *Brokeback Mountain* on me," Tom complains, scowling at our display of affection.

"Aww, someone's jealous. Come here," I tell him.

Tom runs over and throws himself on top of us, just like back in college. He has some weight on him—it's those damn steroids he takes all the time.

"So, Noah boy is in love, huh?" Tom pushes my chest, forcing me to use all my strength not to fall over.

"It sucks," I finally admit out loud.

"It ain't so bad." Benny smiles, making his way back to Rose. Argh, the two of them are too cute for my liking. It only makes me miss Morgan more. And I hate that I miss her. It's a sick carousel of emotions.

"Well, can't wait to meet her," Rose says.

"We're not together... it's complicated."

She chuckles softly, grazing Benny's arm as she speaks, "Someone once told me that love can do crazy things to a person. I'm sure you're acting pretty crazy right now. Take a moment to stop and think long and hard about what you want before it's too late."

I still remember the moment when I told her that. And now, the shoe is on the other foot.

I hang out with them for a little while longer before saying goodbye. We promise to catch up in the near future, but for now, I have only one thing on my mind.

CHAPTER
32

NOAH

It's my final destination before life as I know it will change forever.

New York City.

The last time I was here, it was a boys' weekend, which almost resulted in Tom being mugged for his shoes. One wrong turn, the three of us drunk, and our carefree attitude of thinking we owned the streets while running our mouths at random strangers.

We were lucky to come out alive.

Lex notified the receptionist of my attendance, keeping my visit between us for now.

With a friendly welcome, she offers me a refreshment before guiding me to Kate's office. I kindly decline, waiting for her to open the door.

After a polite knock, the door opens into a large office. The room is almost three times the size of Haden's office back in LA with sweeping views of the city and a large table positioned in the middle toward the back of the room.

The walls are bland, lacking a personal touch. Behind the table, Kate raises her eyes with an incredulous stare.

"Noah," she mouths, clearing her throat of a rasp. "Why are you here?"

"Can we talk, please?" I eye the receptionist, wondering how long she'll fucking stand beside me. "In private, perhaps?"

Finally, she gets the hint, but not before Kate nods for her to leave us alone. Kate motions for me to sit down across from her. The setting is rather formal, and although Kate looks incredibly sexy in her gray skirt and white blouse, there's a certain distance she keeps from me. No kiss hello or friendly hug to welcome me here. I narrowed down her stand-off behavior to being in work mode. She's told me several times that who she is in the office isn't the same person I know.

"How have you been?"

"Good," I lie, keeping my gaze fixated in her. "And you?"

"Busy."

The silence falls between us again, speaking a thousand words neither one of us can say.

This is it!

I have no other choice.

I've fallen in love with Morgan. For us to make it work, I need to let go of my past and admit that certain things will need to change.

"I came here because..." I search for the right words to verbalize how I feel without hurting her feelings. "I think I'm in love with Morgan."

Kate's expression remains fixed, her slow and steady gait gives nothing away. With her fingertips running against the edge of the table, her mouth curves upward into a small smile.

"Of course, you are," she tells me, "It was bound to happen."

"But I—" I stop mid-sentence, confused by her response. "How did you know?"

She purses her lips, tilting her head to the side. "Sometimes, you just know."

With a breath escaping my lips, I bow my head, ignoring the more pressing problem. We can carry on as friends, but we'd be burying the truth that our friendship will never be the same. Gone are the nights of texting with an occasional request for a nude picture just to drive each other crazy. Our impromptu visits to our laying in each other's arms to comfort our own heartbreak will all be a thing of the past.

This relationship stuff is hard, but I know Morgan has an issue with Kate, and there's no way I can balance the two women in my life.

And suddenly, I'm torn.

I don't want to say goodbye to Kate, but I can't ignore how I feel about Morgan any longer. Decisions need to be made, and for once, I have to make them responsible.

"Noah, it's time for you and Morgan. I'll always be here as your friend."

She says the words I need her to say. Almost as if she reads my mind and knows exactly what thoughts are jumbled inside of me, piecing it together to make some sort of sense.

"You'll be okay," I tell her, my voice low, unable to look her in the eye. "You always were going to be okay."

Rising from the chair, I stop myself from reaching out as I've always done, embracing her, smelling the scent of her strawberry shampoo while burying my face into her hair. Deep inside, I'm scared if I touch her, I won't be able to let her go. Desperately holding onto what we have because navigating through life without her by my side is a life not worth living.

She brings out the best in me.

I'm going to fucking miss her, but just like Charlie suggests, I follow my gut.

I say goodbye to Kate.

To us.

And to our friendship as we know it.

CHAPTER
33

NOAH

Just my luck, the flight is delayed—another reason why I hate flying. I'm taking the red-eye back to California to finally take charge of my life. I know I want her. I just don't know what I'm going to do or how to go about it. I thought that five hours on the plane might give me the answers I so desperately need, but between the screaming kids and the woman who excused herself a million times to use the restroom, I'm no closer to the desired outcome.

And five hours gives me too much time to think about Kate. I miss her, and I just left her. But I'm certain that all those feelings will disappear once Morgan is back in my arms.

I'm back to square one without a plan of attack on life in general.

What makes this non-plan more difficult is the fact that I have no idea where Morgan lives. The only person who can help me is Scarlett.

It's late at night, just after eight, when I drive to her place and pull up to the gate. The guard calls the house, and Scarlett's quick to let me in. As soon as I park the car, I step outside and walk with ease to her front door. Upon pressing the doorbell, she opens it within seconds, dressed only in a white negligee slightly covered in a matching white robe.

Fuck, she must have company.

My eyes narrowly avoid her ample tits, staring directly at her face instead.

"I'm glad you're here, Noah."

"I'm sorry," I say, looking around. "You obviously have company."

"No company, just you and me."

It clicks, finally. And I'm at a loss of what to do. If you had placed me in this exact situation two months ago, I'd have bent her over the expensive marble hall table and fucked her pretty little ass. *But she's Morgan's sister,* and I'm failing to understand her eagerness to please me knowing what happened between us.

She places her hands on my chest, caressing my shirt, and releases a soft moan. "Noah," she murmurs, her bright red lips teasing me. "I know you've fantasized about me. I know you pushed the book deal to get closer to me. Do you want me? I'm all yours."

Scarlett pulls me by the hand toward the kitchen. Only the light underneath the cupboards is switched on, leaving the room quite dim. Sliding her robe off, Scarlett jumps onto the countertop, spreading her legs open, giving me a widespread view of her pussy. I stare, in shock, then shift my eyes nervously to the fridge.

What the fuck is going on here?

I'm never one to be rendered speechless, priding myself on my excellent skills in situations just like this, but I'm completely stumped right now. No different than a sixteen-year-old boy losing his virginity for the first time. Awkward Jim in *American Pie* would sum this situation right up.

Her hands find their way around my backside, pulling me in closer to her while my body stiffens on cue.

"Fuck me, here, on this bench. Make me scream your name," she moans, tilting her head back.

Here, before me, is Scarlett Winters.

The most desired woman in the world.

Men want her, and women want to be her.

The same women who prompted this ridiculous bet with Charlie.

I grab Scarlett's wrist and pull it to the bench, restraining her. Just as I'm about to ask her how she could betray her sister and expect me to follow, I hear a gasp behind me. I turn around, dropping her wrist to be met with Morgan's hostile face.

"Morgan," I call out as she runs from the room.

I sprint through the house, chasing her outside until I'm within reach and pull her arm, stopping her.

She begins to fight me, thrashing her arms about while yelling profanities. "Let me fucking go, Noah," she cries as I try to restrain her

"Morgan, please. What you saw isn't what you think."

"You're fucking my sister! I know what I saw!"

"I wasn't fucking your sister. Please, Morgan. Look at

me," I beg, bending slightly, so our eyes are at the same level.

I can see the pain in her eyes, mixed with anger and hostility seeping through her veins as I clutch onto her hard. She's dressed rather casually in a pair of jeans and a white tank, yet still looks as beautiful as the first day I saw her. I've missed her so much and wish she'd understand that I didn't touch her sister and would rather be touching her.

I am making sweet love to her for the rest of my goddamn life.

She refuses to make eye contact but stills her body enough for me to be able to talk.

"I didn't fuck her. Would you just fucking listen to me?"

"Why, Noah?" She removes her arm from my grip. "You choose never to listen to me. Then you give me an ultimatum. Why should I even think about listening to you?"

"Because I love you."

There, I've said it.

The three special words I have never said to a woman before. And now that I've said them, I want to shout it out loud for everyone to hear. Relief washes over me, and I expect everything between us to be okay. After all, how can it not be since I've finally given her what she wants?

Her stare is wide and quizzical, her laugh that follows is strangely dark and disturbing. I'm confused by the way she's reacting. *Shouldn't she be in my arms telling me she loves me too?*

"You have a lot to learn about love, Noah." She silences herself while watching my confused expression. "It's quite easy to tell someone you love them. What's difficult is actually showing someone you love them. And until this very moment, I've yet to see anything which would make me believe that you love me."

I find myself pulling away, offended that she thinks my words mean nothing after I've finally confessed the truth. "And would the same not go for you, Morgan? What have you done to show me that you love me? You're still married. And I'm pretty certain you still sleep in the same bed with your husband even after I found out the truth," I say with distaste. "I should be asking *you* the same question."

"You're right. I've done absolutely nothing but carry the guilt inside for the last two months. I'm sorry you think that I've done nothing because, apparently, it's never about me but rather about everyone else and what they want."

Running my hands through my hair, it's my turn to laugh at her comment at how frustrating she can be. "You can't blame anyone else but yourself. You make the decisions. You dictate your own life. You can't keep using everyone else as an excuse, Morgan."

And as if I struck a chord, shaken her beliefs to the very core, she stares back at me with downcast eyes before the truth really does hurt.

"You know what, Noah? You're right," she says, confirming the truth. "I should live my life for me. Make my own decisions. And I'll start by making one right now." She moves closer, placing her hand on my chest to feel the beat of my heart. It's beating rather loud, thumping like mad. And with just one touch, it begins to slow because her touch alone is what it's been waiting for.

"I love you, but sometimes love isn't enough," she says faintly. "Walk away from me now. Figure out exactly what it is you want from me. Because I'll tell you this…" She stalls her words, keeping my curiosity piqued. "If you come back to me and tell me you love me, I'll take those words to heart and never let them go."

I resist raising my hand to caress her face because I do love her. But throughout all this, she's finally begun to understand me and knows that I need to do some soul searching because I can't give her all of me right at this very moment. There are too many unanswered questions, and I need answers before I take her into my arms and never let her go.

I choose to walk away, not because I'm weak but because I need to find strength.

And two weeks later, I find it.

CHAPTER
34

NOAH

I sit in the car watching the man who's the husband of the woman I love. The day is slightly overcast, or perhaps it's the LA smog I've grown accustomed to. Either way, it does nothing to help my already dejected mood.

There are many people around him from assistants helping with hair and makeup to the models themselves being photographed. With the camera in his hand, he switches angle and moves in closer while taking shots. He appears to be comfortable in his element, smiling happily, and directing the models into different poses.

He could also be smiling because he's married to the woman you love.

Tracking down Wyatt has been more difficult than I had anticipated. With Morgan and I apart and Scarlett refusing to talk to me after her sexual advances, it gives me no choice but to contact their dad, Max.

We have an exceedingly long chat about the situation.

Apparently, Morgan confided in him early on about her feelings for me, which is why he knew of us being together at the barbecue. The more he speaks about his relationship with Morgan, the more I realize he's just like my mom. And funny enough, it isn't just about me seeking his approval but equally him seeking my approval to date Mom.

You can only laugh at such a twisted outcome.

With bare feet, I walk awkwardly against the sand, my toes digging in as I make my way over to where they're shooting. An assistant asks me if I'm part of the shoot, attempting to usher me toward the makeshift wardrobe.

"I'm here to speak to Wyatt," I say flatly.

She walks over to where Wyatt's standing, and sure enough, he turns around to see me. He yells at the models to take five, removing his camera from around his neck and handing it to the assistant. With bare feet, he steps over to where I'm standing and extends his hand.

"Noah." He smiles politely.

I don't know why I shake it—it feels like a handshake with the devil. Or perhaps that's what I perceive in my head. I hate him because he has everything I want. Yet, hate is such a strong word for a man I know nothing about.

He motions for me to follow him to a quiet café that sits along the busy pavement. Venice Beach is bustling with many different walks of life, surprising me everywhere I turn.

We enter the building, and he orders a coffee, offering

365

me something to drink. I order a coffee too, but my insomnia is weighing heavily on my shoulder. The café is small, only a few scattered tables inside the air-conditioned area. Aside from the employees, there are only an elderly couple—possibly tourists—who sit quietly near the window, admiring the view outside.

"So," he says. "Let's talk."

I don't know where to begin. The conversation has replayed over and over in my head, yet here I sit without words. The only thing I do know is that I'm sitting here across from him because he's the key to Morgan and I being together.

"I need to understand your relationship with Morgan. This is complicated…" I trail off.

He takes a sip of his coffee, leaning back on his chair as he eyes me dubiously. He's roughly the same height as me, not as cut up but still quite muscular. His light blond hair is trimmed reasonably short, and I didn't notice before, but he has a tattoo on the side of his neck. I can't make out what it is, but I pray it's not her damn name.

"When I first met Mo, she was exactly like me, carefree and just wanting to have fun. We met on some wild weekend in Vegas, and despite your reluctance to hear this, it was purely sexual and nothing more."

I despise him calling her Mo. It makes me extremely jealous, more than the mention of their purely sexual relationship. His face, along with the rest of this room, is a friendly target to punch my fist into. But I have to hold back, curling my fists under the table and keeping my rage at bay.

"When her best friend was unresponsive from some date drug, we were forced to wait by her side at the hospital until she woke up. It was the worst forty-eight hours of our lives." He recalls the memory but not without reliving the pain that's etched all over his face, drinking more coffee to compose himself.

"I'd just broken up with my ex-girlfriend of two years, and when you start questioning life because you think someone is dying next to you... I acted cowardly and ran back to her. It was only one night, but that's all it took.

"But I moved on. Mo was fantastic, and we just fell in love with each other and life. We decided to get married on a whim. It was going great until we found out that Addy was pregnant."

The waiter comes over, offering us a refill, which we both kindly accept. After a quick break, he continues, "Morgan was upset, and I thought she'd walk away, but she didn't. Michael was born, and everyone fell in love with him, especially Morgan." His smile says it all. Morgan's a kind and generous-hearted woman despite her evil-queen persona when she's around me.

"Around two years ago, Morgan noticed that Michael had particular behaviors that appeared different from other children at his daycare. He communicated but not as quickly as the other children. Both of us narrowed it down to him developing slower, but then we began to notice other things. How when he played, he became fixated on certain things rather than pretend playing like the other kids.

"For the three of us, we were first-time parents, so we didn't really question it further, assuming his behavior

367

was simply different. It was his teacher who first raised a concern, telling us he had difficulty socializing with other children. From there, we decided to seek help while he was still young. He was diagnosed with high-functioning autism."

I had researched as much as I could in an attempt to understand exactly what it is. It was only after I'd read a number of parents' blogs and watched videos, it finally sank in.

Mom and I talked long and hard about it, and it helped that she also tried to give me the perspective of a mother in that situation because that's what Morgan is—a mother to Michael.

"Addy and I were devastated. We knew nothing about autism and blamed ourselves for him being that way. Morgan was the one who stepped up, learning as much as she could for the three of us to co-parent him and have him thrive despite the challenges he faced. Without her, I don't know what Addy and I would've done."

"Morgan loves him," I admit out loud. "She'll do anything for him. I'll never understand how she can be so selfless, considering he isn't her son."

Wyatt releases a light-hearted chuckle. "Because that's who she is, selfless Mo. That's why she's my best friend."

More words that hurt.

My mind drifts to Kate, but quickly, I push them away. Like a smoker addicted to nicotine, the thought alone can be deadly. I still miss her like crazy and everything about her.

But I need to focus on Morgan.

And as I take a deep breath, I realize that loving Morgan is more than just telling her—it's accepting her for who she is and accepting the people she loves—the *man across from me, his son, and me.*

"Our marriage didn't fall apart. We just didn't evolve together. We talked about separating and made the decision last year. We never, for once, thought it would be difficult for Michael. He didn't feel the emotions because that's something he struggles with but more so the change of routine. He struggled to sleep, and his tiredness affected his general behavior. Morgan was terrified he'd take a step back, and the behavior specialists suggested a slow but progressive change. I guess we just let it be and allowed it to drag on because it wasn't such an issue until you walked into Morgan's life," he tells me, and I detect slight bitterness in his tone.

I'm unsure whether there's resentment toward me for being the man who supposedly stole Morgan's heart. He's spoken about Michael, and it's plain to see that his son means everything to him. The love from a father has no bounds, something I have no concept of.

And it doesn't hit me until this very moment. I love my mom, and she does everything she can to make sure I have the best life possible. But no matter what she does, the absence of a father is something difficult to replace.

"Mo's my best friend. She always will be. I don't know what your intentions are with her, but she will always be in my life. I wouldn't have it any other way," he warns me.

"I love her." It's the only thing I can say.

369

"Then, if you love her, be with her."

I laugh, cocky perhaps but stumped by his willingness to just palm her off. "You make it sound so easy. It's not just about loving her. It's about accepting her choices. Her choice is to have Michael in her life despite the two of you being apart. This is why I need to know now if you're going to fight me for her," I tell him how it is. "I want this to work more than anything I've wanted in my life, but I'm not going to be second best nor pushed to the side. The moment I walk back to her, it's forever."

And I've finally made that decision. Being away from her only confirms one thing—I do love her. And that love consumes every part of me. The thought of not having her in my life tears me into a million pieces. I need to muster up my strength and patience to be a better man for her without compromising my own needs.

Wyatt stands, sweeping his keys into his hand. "Then let me take you to her."

***

There's chaos all around us, the sound of children's idle chit-chat combined with laughter everywhere you turn. The playground is busy with children running about, parents pushing the swings high into the air as the kids squeal with happiness. And just behind the area are the courts where I first saw Morgan play.

There's four of them—Morgan and three little boys. I recognize Michael immediately. He's standing distant from the other children but still listening to Morgan speak. I can't wipe the smile off my face—she looks cute in her little shorts and Chicago Bulls jersey. Damn. *How did I not know she went for the Bulls?* It should be a terrible sign of things to come, yet I brush it off because it's not important right now.

She sees us standing together behind the fence, somewhat shocked. Michael notices Wyatt and runs up to him, wrapping his arms around his legs. The other children just stare, their parents asking them to come over and have a drink of water while they take a break.

With the ball in her hand, Morgan slowly paces toward us, tilting her head, trying to hold back her smile.

"What are the two of you doing here?" she asks, looking at Wyatt, then to me.

"Hey, buddy." Wyatt kneels down to Michael's level. "Do you think you can count the number of lines on the court?"

Michael nods, running to the corner where the lines begin and evenly pacing himself while counting slowly.

Extending his hand, Wyatt hands Morgan an envelope, which he removed from his bag.

"What's this?" she stares, confused.

"Divorce papers," he says without hesitating. "You see, Noah and I kinda have an understanding now. I know he'll take care of you, and I know you'll still be in Michael's life."

Morgan's eyes refuse to leave the envelope, and slowly as she raises them to meet mine. She faintly whispers, "Michael can still be in my life?"

"He's a part of you, Morgan, and I want all of you," I tell her, smiling to ease the burden she's carrying. It's finally sunk in. The distance I need to go to show her how much I love her and what she means to me.

"We'll make it work, Mo. The three of us," Wyatt reassures her.

"Four," she corrects him.

He raises his eyebrows. "Four?"

"Please, Wyatt. You can come clean now about Jessica. I mean, gee, talk about a dirty mouth on that one."

I keep my laughter to myself as Wyatt nods his head, agreeing with a sly smile. "Well, I guess you know, then," he simply says.

"Timing isn't exactly her strength. Plus, I should've been a private detective with the skills I got," she jokes, then points her finger at me. "Just a heads up."

The three of us laugh as Michael finishes counting and returns with his statistics. *The kid is impressive.* Morgan informs us she'll finish their practice game as Wyatt and I stand on the side. He explains to me that sports are something Michael finds zero interest in. However, when it comes to watching on television, he's fascinated with the commentating, especially facts and stats of the game.

When they finish up, Wyatt offers to take Michael home. "We'll leave you two alone," he tells us.

Before he leaves, I kneel down to Michael's level but keep my handshake at bay not to overwhelm him. "Hi Michael, I'm Noah. A friend of Morgan's."

He listens, but stares at the sky, then gazes at me for just a split second before fixating on the ball. "Do you play basketball?"

"I do," I respond eagerly.

"Do you know that Michael Jordan won six NBA championships?"

I smile because I do know that. "Uh-huh, and do you know that he had six thousand, six hundred and seventy-two rebounds?"

Michael continues to stare at the sky as if he's thinking out loud. "That's a lot of rebounds."

Morgan and Wyatt smile back, keeping quiet as they watch Michael. He doesn't have anything else to say, so Wyatt decides to take him home, saying goodbye to both of us. When they're out of sight, Morgan's quick to jump into my arms and hold onto me as if her life depends on it.

"Thank you."

I bury my face in her hair, inhaling her scent and moving my head to plant a soft kiss on her neck. *I fucking miss her so much.* And with her in my arms, I want to be a better man—honest and faithful— and show her each day what she means to me.

"You know you're kind of stuck with me now?" I chastise.

"You know what?" She grins, her eyes sparkling inside my embrace. "You're worth all the heartache, Noah. Every single moment of it."

"I love you," I blurt out, perturbed by my sudden need to be so forthcoming with my emotions. "I'm not perfect."

"No, you're not," she agrees, letting out a sigh. "This will be hard."

"I know."

"You have to understand that it can't always be about you and me. Michael has certain needs and—"

I place my finger on her lips, cutting her off. "I believe you."

"Noah, I love you," she breathes, relaxing in my arms with a loving gaze. "But, are we crazy?"

"Crazy enough to make this work."

With a tilt of her head, her lips brush mine, a gentle tease making it passionate and demanding, leaving me wanting more. She slowly pulls away, out of breath.

"So where to now? You could come over. We can watch a movie?"

"Sounds good." I grin, dropping my hand to intertwine with hers. "What movie?"

"Have you ever seen *Pretty in Pink*? It's my favorite movie."

The corners of my mouth turn up into a smile as I fondly remember when Kate stopped me at Santa Monica pier, questioning me with such judgment in her eyes. I had no doubt the universe had its own plan, working in mysterious ways. Kate's and my friendship was all about timing. We were in each other's lives at the right time. I desperately want to text her that, at least— one more time. But quickly, I decide against it.

"I have, actually." Releasing a sigh with a carefree smile. "Someone important once told me it was a rite of passage into adulthood."

Morgan's laugh is soft and endearing. "You're the perfect man, Noah."

"Must be fate?" I tease, laying another kiss on her lips.

"Definitely fate."

CHAPTER
35

KATE

My eyes scan the room one more time.

Cardboard boxes are stacked neatly on top of each other, the contents scrawled on in broad black felt-tip marker. The furniture still remains, positioned the same as when I first moved in.

For years, this apartment has been home. Presley joined me as a roommate for a few months during her pregnancy before Haden swept her off her feet and placed a ring on her finger.

It has been a place of comfort, a place of solace when the world crept up on me, and I needed time to process my thoughts. New York may be the city that never sleeps, but thanks to this place, I slept comfortably each night.

Well, not *every* night.

Though as the tide turns, life evolves, people move, people change.

I check the time, noting the car service will be here any minute now. With my cell in hand and one more scan of the room, I complete a mental checklist making sure I have everything I need.

As my hand rests on the doorknob, I give myself one more moment to take it all in for the very last time.

Saying goodbye is never easy but shutting the door on my life here is long overdue.

The car service drives me to JFK, battling the peak-hour traffic as the driver listens to his music and thankfully doesn't engage in unnecessary conversation.

My gaze shifts outside the window, watching the city pass us by. There's a part of me that will miss the hustle and bustle, the lights and skyline, the action, and rushing around the streets. It has been my playground for the last four years, and being single in a city with over twenty-million people should, in theory, never make you feel lonely.

But the loneliness was palpable.

The driver asks which terminal I prefer, taking a turn with a sign indicating the airport a few miles ahead.

The decision to visit LA was an impromptu one yet with reason. Charlie officially went into labor this morning. Lex called me with a slight panic in his voice. Although he's done this twice already, when it comes to Charlie's well-being, his worry stems from a loving place.

According to Charlie, the baby is still breeched, and her C-section is scheduled for next week. However, it seems baby Edwards is incredibly impatient, wanting to make a grand entrance as soon as possible much to

Charlie's dismay.

All of this means a last-minute change to my itinerary, not bothering me at all because Charlie is my family. I want to say goodbye one more time because life has a funny way of passing and before you know it, years have gone by.

What does bother me is sitting next to a passenger in business class who has repeatedly tried to pick me up by bringing up his so-called wealthy lifestyle back in Texas. He owns a few cattle ranches and something about chickens. The man is a lot older with a slick ponytail holding his gray hair back. Okay, so when I said a *lot* older, I mean he could pass for my grandfather.

Why can't I attract the younger men? For fuck's sake.

Somewhere during the talk of a rooster mating with a hen, I excuse myself to finish some work on my laptop. That has been my plan for this entire plane ride if Mr. Chatty didn't corner me from the second the seat belt sign went on.

When we land in LAX, I couldn't have exited the plane faster, weaving in and out of the crowd toward the driver holding up the sign *Kate Hamilton.* Relieved to get out of here, I follow him to the black SUV and request he head to the hospital.

On the drive over, I check my cell, which is flooded with texts, missed calls, and several other notifications. My eyes gravitate towards Lex's text.

Lex: *The baby is here. See you soon.*

I smile, though annoyed he didn't mention the sex of

the baby given that they chose not to find out, and everyone has been waiting. Eric started what he called a 'baby pool,' and bets were on as to what sex the baby would be and when it would arrive. The C-section was a game-changer, but both Adriana and Rocky were adamant the baby would come earlier.

The driver pulls into the curved entrance, just shy of the main doors. We agree on a time for him to return, and with a quick exit, he drives off down the driveway and back onto oncoming traffic.

I reach the gray double-doors, and detecting my presence, they automatically open into the foyer. My eyes dart around the open space until I see the information board. With a polite smile to a group of young doctors walking past me, I step toward the maternity ward, pulling my eyes from the polished linoleum floor and catching a glimpse of the hallway that stretches beyond.

Taking a quick elevator ride up to level three, I check my cell one more time and notice the poor coverage. There's another set of double doors marked 'Maternity Ward.' I push them with ease as they swing open so effortlessly.

A draft of air hits my face, warm with the familiar disinfectant smell hospitals are known for. As I stroll down the hallway, I pass a different set of doors with a hand-sanitizer dispenser, stopping momentarily to sanitize my hands, then continue to the main desk to ask for directions to Charlie's room.

A few rooms away, toward the end of the hallway, I knock on the door gently, not to startle anyone, especially the baby. The door is wide open, and I see Lex first. Still dressed in his suit, unshaven, he appears tired though coupled with an elated expression.

"Come in." He grins, motioning me with his hands.

With small steps, almost tiptoeing, I move past the entrance and see Charlie in bed—the baby resting against her bare skin. Her tired eyes still radiate joy, her skin color slightly pale, no doubt from the sheer exhaustion of the last twenty-four hours.

"You came."

"I wouldn't have missed meeting..." I trail off, noting the blanket is white and not forthcoming with any hints as to the sex of the baby.

"Her," Lex announces, pushing Charlie's hair away from her face with admiration. "It's another girl."

"She's beautiful," I gush, unable to hide my elation. "Do we have a name yet?"

"Addison Elisabeth Edwards."

"Perfect." Smiling at both of them, I remember the gift I brought from the city. "Oh, I have something for little Addison."

I reach into my large purse and pull out the gift bag, handing it to Lex. He pulls the contents out— tiny onesies with 'I Heart NY' printed on the front, and the other is Yankee's themed as it's both their favorite baseball team.

"They're so cute," Charlie simpers, gazing at Lex as he holds up the tiny apparel. "Where Mommy and Daddy chased fate."

Lex removes baby Addison from Charlie, holding her to his shoulder. He's in his element, a doting father and loving husband. It's strange to think only four years ago, Lex was not the man he is today.

As I bring myself closer, I open my arms as Lex carefully places her in them. From the second she lays in my arms, a feeling of loving warmth washes over me as I stare into her little face. Bringing my lips to her forehead, I place a gentle kiss and inhale the familiar baby scent. Tiny toes peek from her blanket, dangling so I can admire just how cute they are, like little buttons. Her head, covered in brown hair just like her older sister's, is so fragile, terrifying me that I may break her.

"Are you ready for Paris?" Charlie asks while trying to sit up. Lex gently scolds her as she winces in pain.

I nod quietly. "Yes, all packed and ready to take Paris by storm."

"Meet a Frenchman and have beautiful French babies." Charlie smiles, wistfully.

"Hey, don't think because I'm in a maternity ward, I'm getting all clucky," I scold her, playfully. "There's plenty of nieces to keep me occupied. You stick to your role of procreating, and I'll still do mine of spoiling them with gifts."

There's a commotion as Eric enters the room, tangled in a mass of balloons. They're a neutral color— a palette of greens and white—and more noticeably, one large balloon which says 'Yay, Baby! Boo, Sore Vagina.'

Letting out a loose chuckle, I shake my head at his in-your-face congratulatory words.

"Well," he sneers, eyeing me from head to toe. "Look what the cat dragged back to LA."

"Did you reshape your brows?" I question, ignoring his dramatic entrance.

Eric clasps his hand against his chest. "OMG, can you tell? I told Jorge not to make me look like an aging Asian grandma."

Charlie and I burst out laughing simultaneously. Eric is vane at the best of times, and no doubt, my questioning will give him a complex which I'll never hear the end of.

Handing the balloons to Lex and kissing Charlie on both cheeks, he peeks into my arms to admire baby Addison.

"Oh Charlie," he cries with his hand pressed against his mouth. "Mazel tov."

"We're not Jewish, Eric."

"Yes, but my new neighbor is, and he's trying to make something of himself in the business we call show. I thought I'd expand my religious beliefs, you know, just in case."

"Um... hello?" My judgmental eyes wander back to Eric. "Are you forgetting about someone called Tristan?"

"He's doing great." Eric is unable to meet my gaze, fidgeting with his stiff collar.

"And?"

"He's coming back in a month, so we'll see what happens."

Charlie glances at me, rolling her eyes at the same time I cross my arms, exasperated.

"You can't fight love, Eric." I sigh heavily, trying to convince him. "It's like a force to be reckoned with. It's all about timing. Tristan's coming back, and now is your time."

"Do you really have to go?" Eric pleads, resting his head on my shoulder. "Who else will talk me off the ledge when it comes to making bad decisions?"

"Um… are you forgetting about me?" Charlie huffs, giving off an annoyed stare. "Honestly, Eric. You're not thinking about the bigger picture here. Kate, in Paris, means connections to French men."

Eric's eyes widen with curiosity as Lex lectures Charlie on encouraging Eric's behavior.

And in a moment when I can have easily talked myself out of going, staying in a place where everything is familiar and comfortable, another reason for my impending departure stands at the door.

Noah.

It's been almost four months since he stepped foot in my office and basically ended our friendship then and there. I saw it coming, and I sensed Morgan questioning our friendship, hence his distance. So, I did the only thing I could do—I made it easy for him and falsified my happiness.

There kind of was no other choice.

My feelings blurred the friendship line between us, and what hope did I have falling for someone who was in love with someone else? Just like a good business decision, I cut ties and wished him on his merry way with no hard feelings.

But now, he's standing in the same room. Still tall, muscular, and with a lingering stare consuming me in a way I had purposely forgotten. Assuming he came straight from work, he's still dressed in a navy business shirt and gray tailored pants. The sleeves are rolled up to his elbows, and in his hand, he's carrying a bouquet of pink lilies.

Why does he have to look so…

Don't say it.

Don't think it.

"Hey," he greets, his eyes searching mine while I try to compose myself.

"Hey," is all I manage to say.

Eric, Charlie, and Lex watch in silence, their eyes darting back and forth, making it all the more uncomfortable. The only thing missing is a tub of popcorn in their hands.

Adriana strolls into the room, making an even larger commotion. With her own daughter in her arms, Lex takes her from Adriana so she can hold Addison.

There's a constant chatter in the room, along with laughter and anecdotes while Addison continues to be passed around. A doctor and his intern walk in, prompting Eric to sharpen his attire and ask questions based on his knowledge of *Grey's Anatomy*. It's comical, to say the least.

With a quick check of my cell, I note the time, having to leave for my flight to Paris. The change in itinerary meant I'd still be able to make an important meeting but don't have the luxury to spend more time here in LA.

Still keeping my distance from Noah, I say goodbye to everyone, swallowing my emotions as Charlie and Eric both break out into tears. Charlie has a valid reason—her hormones are all over the place. Eric, on the other hand, is the queen of emotional outbursts.

Eric embraces me tightly, his arms around me not willing to let go. "What will I do without you?"

"The same thing you've done for years, call me several times a day. We're only an ocean apart."

"Please, Kate, my geography isn't the best. Remember when I thought Ecuador was part of Africa?"

"We all remember that." Lex snickers.

"I'm jealous," Eric pouts. "You know that, right?"

"Always." I smile before I kiss his lips, hugging him one last time.

Not wanting to hurt Charlie, I lean in and hug her as best as I can, warning her to take it easy. Wiping a tear that falls down her cheek, I promise to text her the second I land. As for Lex, we hug goodbye, but unlike the rest of them, I will see him in a few short months for a summit in London.

"Can we talk?" Noah asks, rubbing the back of his neck after Adriana lets go of me.

We walk into the corridor, moving aside to allow people to use the walkway.

"So, you're going to France?"

I nod, keeping my distance to maintain my rational frame of mind. "Yes, tonight."

"How long?"

"Indefinitely," I state with finality.

With a downturned mouth, his eyebrows gather in with a pained expression.

"Kate, I... I'm sorry. I know things are weird between us, and I miss you."

Three simple words that shoot to my core, disrupting the peaceful surroundings I'd created over the last few months. I swallow the lump forming in my throat, keeping my responses factual.

"You have your life, and I have mine."

His stare widens as he nods while pressing his lips together. Perhaps I'd hurt him by not returning the sentiment, but what would be the point?

"There's something I have to tell you." He begins fidgeting with his cuff, lowering his eyes, unable to meet mine as they did moments ago. "Morgan and I are... we're expecting a baby. It wasn't planned. I mean, an accident but still..."

The smile on my face remains the exact same. My stomach has its own agenda, a wave of nausea crashing around like a vicious storm. If silence is to fall around us, maybe, just maybe, you might hear the slight crack of something inside me breaking.

But I'd learned, over the years, to be the person everyone else has wanted me to be.

Right now, Noah needs me to be his friend, who understands his life is moving on. He's about to start a family. That's as committed as you can get.

Yet inside, I know whatever chance there would have been between us has come to a crashing halt.

A dead end.

The final nail in the so-called coffin of what my over-imaginative brain occasionally conjures up.

I shouldn't need a man to love me. I try to tell myself that almost every day. I need *me* to love me.

And Paris is the perfect place to rediscover who I am at this stage of my life. Trust the timing of life. Noah was the perfect storm, taking me with him on this journey and making me see life with different colored glasses.

"Congratulations, Noah. I'm happy for you. For both of you. Accident or not, it's a blessing." I smile, quickly checking my cell. There's a message from the driver, a traffic jam which will extend our travel time back to the airport. "Listen, my car service is waiting to take me to the airport. All the best, Noah."

Raising my head, I take a deep breath, telling myself to be the bigger person and not allow my emotions to ruin this moment.

"Kate... hold on."

With reluctance, I allow my eyes to meet his, gazing at his handsome face if not for the last time.

"I love you."

I take it back—these are the three words to break me.

Noah's bright-eyed stare begins to imprison me. But I tell myself over and over again that his love for me remains purely of a friendship which blossomed from two strangers who needed each other at that time.

And so, as I think of the time we spent together, I can't help but smile back at him.

"I know, Noah. I'll always love you," I profess, allowing whatever it is between us to finally run free. "Go live your happily ever after. It's long overdue."

"You'll be okay," he's quick to remind me. "You know that, right?"

"You've always promised me that, and you've yet to

prove me wrong."

And with our final words, I say goodbye and walk away.

Noah Mason will always be a part of my life, someone who came when I needed him the most, a purpose in his timing.

Life is all about timing.

Now my new journey begins, and as the doors close behind me, and I leave my friends behind, I take a deep breath and welcome the endless possibilities.

Paris.

Inside my jacket, my cell vibrates. I chuckle softly, guessing it's Eric reporting something gross he saw which has freaked him out. And just when I prepare myself to talk him off the ledge, my footsteps stop as my eyes freeze on the screen.

Dominic: *We need to talk.*

The words are like dynamite, the aggressive nature of the explosion restricting my breathing. Out of all days and all the moments, how is it that his timing could be so inconvenient. Then, when I didn't think it could get any worse, my cell begins to ring with words *Private Caller* flashing on the screen.

"Hello," I swallow, trying to compose myself.

"It's me," he murmurs over the receiver, his voice low with a slow beat. "I made a mistake, Kate... it should have been you."

And just like that, my past collides with my future in a fleeting moment.

in
Chasing Heartbreak
An Enemies to Lovers Romance
The Dark Love Series Book 6

OTHER BOOKS
BY KAT T. MASEN

#JERK
#B!TCH
Bad Boy Player
Bad Boy Rich
Mister Rebound
Arrogant Aussie: A Hero Club Novel

Roomie Wars
Wedding Wars
Baby Wars
Roomie Wars Box Set (Books 1 to 3)

The Dark Love Series
Chasing Love: A Billionaire Love Triangle
Chasing Us: A Second Chance Love Triangle
Chasing Her: A Stalker Romance
Chasing Him: A Forbidden Second Chance Romance
Chasing Fate: An Enemies-to-Lovers Romance
Chasing Heartbreak: A Friends-to-Lovers Romance

Kat. T. Masen

CONNECT
WITH ME ONLINE

Check these links for more books from
Author Kat T. Masen.

READER GROUP

Want access to fun, prizes and sneak peeks?
Join my Facebook Reader Group.
https://www.facebook.com/groups/ifyoulikepinacoladas/

NEWSLETTER

Want to see what's next?
Sign up for my Newsletter.
https://www.kattmasen.com/subscribe

BOOKBUB

Connect with me on Bookbub.
https://www.bookbub.com/authors/kat-t-masen

GOODREADS

Add my books to your TBR list on my Goodreads
profile.
https://bit.ly/2AuHnMT

AMAZON

Click to buy my books from my Amazon profile.
https://amzn.to/2DOsUif

WEBSITE

http://www.kattmasen.com/

TWITTER

@authorkattmasen

INSTAGRAM

@authorkattmasen

EMAIL

kat@kattmasen.com

FACEBOOK

http://www.facebook.com/authorkattmasen

ABOUT
THE AUTHOR

Born and bred in Sydney, Australia, **Kat T. Masen** is a mother to four crazy boys and wife to one sane husband. Growing up in a generation where social media and fancy gadgets didn't exist, she enjoyed reading from an early age and found herself immersed in these stories. After meeting friends on Twitter who loved to read as much as she did, her passion for writing began, and the friendships continued on despite the distance.

"I'm known to be crazy and humorous. Show me the most random picture of a dog in a wig, and I'll be laughing for days."

Made in the USA
Middletown, DE
20 October 2023

41168083R00236